NICODEMIA STATION BLUES

All Things Found

Book 3

ANTHONY W. EICHENLAUB

To my dog Bear. He may not always point me in the right direction, but he always leads enthusiastically.

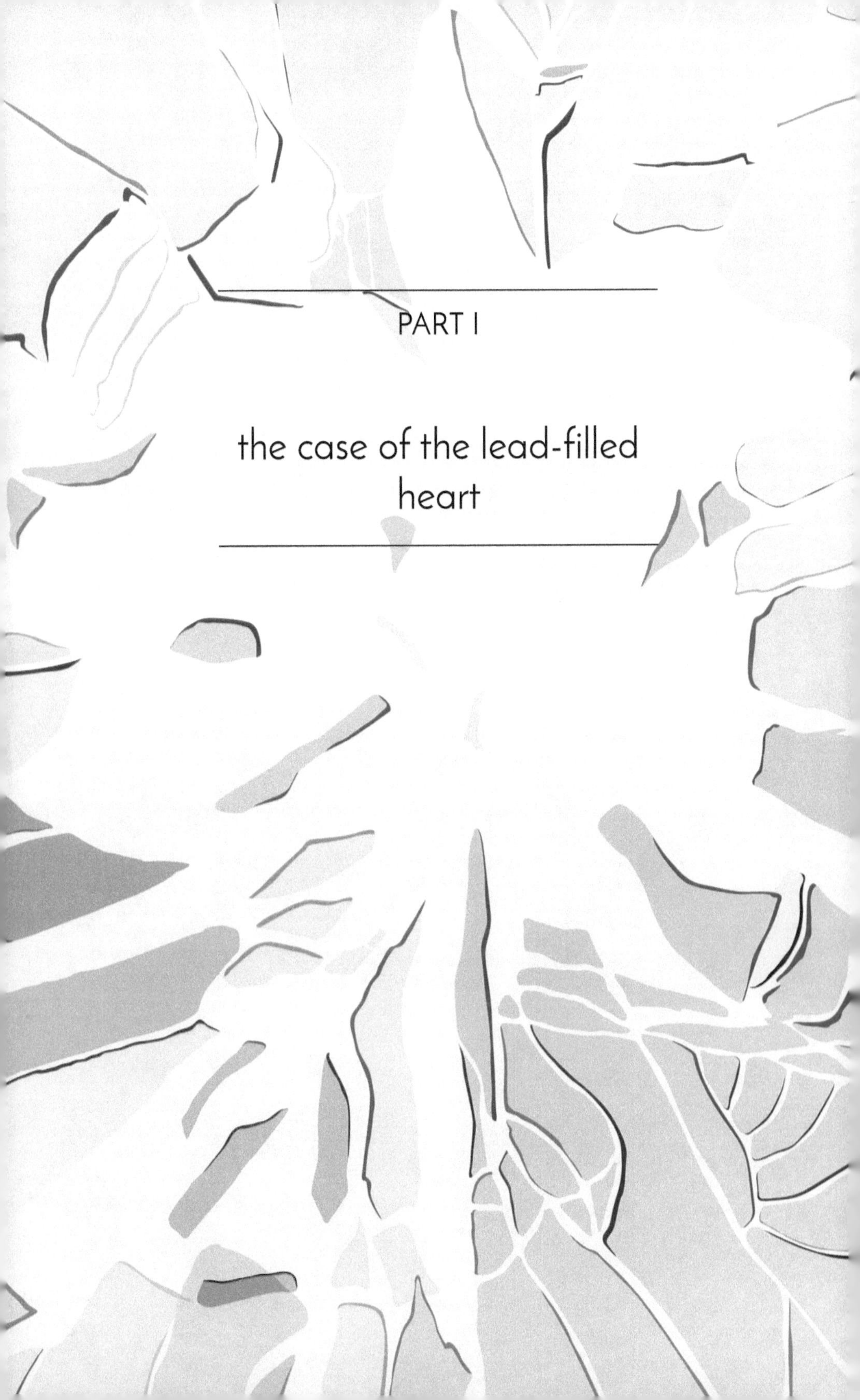

PART I

the case of the lead-filled
heart

AT FIRST, there was no reason to think that a bullet fired from a gun was anything other than what it was: one murder in a city steeped in pain. One mercy in a world of malice. I should have avoided the case at all costs. It should have been obvious from the get-go that the job was bad news.

Then again, maybe a job that reeked of lousy consequences didn't seem so bad after a long string of jobs that just plain reeked.

"Demarco," I said by way of introduction outside the dingy door of the small apartment, "Jude Demarco. All things found, all things fixed."

Gregory Wells peered up at me from the open door of his Lower Fish District home. He was oldest man in the whole of Heavy Nicodemia and looked the part. His thick, blue-framed glasses made his eyes look like they might pop out of his head. "You're not my regular plumber."

"Folks are complaining about the smell." A vegetative rot wafted out of the man's tiny apartment, competing even with the sour, slick smell of the Lower Fish District. "I work for dimes."

He stepped aside to let me in. "You can fix anything?"

"Only if it's broken."

"You're not my regular plumber," he repeated.

He was right. I wasn't.

"Quite an accomplishment, being the oldest guy in the Heavies," I said, picking my way through his cluttered apartment.

I was a big guy and there was hardly a space where both my elbows could swing without knocking over a relic of Wells's long life. His age was especially impressive considering he had even outlived almost everyone from the other beads of the station. Nicodemia's Heavy bead had the lowest average lifespan. Both Haven, whose spin-simulated gravity was closest to that of Earth, and the Hallows, which featured luxurious lightness, boasted longer average lifespans by at least a decade.

"All's I had to do was wait," Wells said.

"You're a patient guy?"

"Not very."

"Well, it's a good thing I'm here."

The creases in the old man's jawline deepened.

It only took a few minutes to disconnect the trap under his sink. "What did you flush down here?" Black gunk slopped onto the floor as I pulled the plumbing apart.

The raisin of a man peered at me over a handheld tablet computer. "I can wait for my regular guy."

"Regular guy's going to take weeks."

"Not for me."

I dredged another clot of black sludge out of the fiber-steel tube. The vegetable reek rolled out of the pipe. "Are these pistachio shells?"

Wells peered over his tablet as another lump of shells clattered onto the floor. Plumbing wasn't exactly my area of expertise, but it hardly ever got anyone killed. Investigator, medic, handyman. I'd take any job the residents of Nicodemia had to offer. Sometimes it even paid.

I rapped the pipe on the floor one last time to verify that it was clear of debris. How long had he been stuffing shells down the sink? "Are pistachios the secret to longevity?" I asked.

Wells said, "Burt always asks that, too."

"Burt?"

"My regular guy."

"What do you tell him?"

"I go on a long walk every day, and I avoid the bad districts."

"That's a lot of districts."

"Depends on your definition of bad."

There was a knock on the door and Wells left me as I mucked out the rest of the pipes. I took a long, flexible wire and snaked it as deep as I could down into the black tube. Gray water opened pretty quickly into a larger pipe, so I knew from experience that there wasn't far to go. As the final clump of shells came dislodged, I heard another voice at the door, too low for me to hear.

"You're not Burt," Wells said.

The voice mumbled. I started fitting the pipes back in place.

"Demarco?" Wells spat my name like it was a curse. "Who the hell is Demarco?"

This time, I heard the voice a little clearer. "He's trouble in a trench coat."

I shoved the trap back in place and sat up. "Anders?"

Wells blinked at me from the door. "Who the hell is Anders?"

"He's the guy you're talking to," I said.

Behind him, Patrol Officer Second Rank Paul Anders stood in his blues, hat clutched to his chest in performative respect for the elderly. His face brightened when he saw me. "Demarco! Thank God."

"Wouldn't be my first choice."

"Someone said you were in this building. I've been knocking on ever door."

I hauled myself to my feet and looked him right in the eyes. "Why is it never a friendly visit?"

"Because you're not that friendly." Anders glanced back down the hall. "You know what I needed to go through to track you down today?"

"All the bad districts?"

"Heavy Nicodemia isn't so bad," Anders said. He was a beat cop and should have known better. A while ago, the crime lords had run into some trouble, and the bead had been scrambling to solidify its criminal identity. Was it a crime family town or a place of pure anarchy? Maybe it was somewhere in between. All I knew was that I dealt with the worst of it every day.

I turned to Wells. "Five dimes is the usual for a job like this."

He narrowed his glassy eyes at me. "You aren't the regular guy."

"I'm aware."

He looked down at the floor. "You've left a mess," he said, finally.

"I usually do," I said.

"That's the truth," said Anders with a crooked smile. Anders was the only cop I genuinely got along with in Heavy

Nicodemia. He was also a decent man and almost what I might call a friend.

I washed my hands in the sink. Wells's towels all looked like they hadn't been washed in the last decade, and maybe not the one before that, so I dried my hands by running them through my somewhat shaggy hair. "Dimes," I said to Wells, feeling a little bad for charging the old man. "I gotta eat."

Wells disappeared into the apartment's clutter.

"If I'm so bad, why are you coming to me?" I asked Anders.

"It's a unique case," Anders said. "Figured we'd get a unique perspective."

"We?"

"I'm working under a fella named Smalley. Detective."

"That so?" He had my interest. Anders had wanted to be a detective since he joined the force. "Is this an official mentorship?"

"More like an assistant position with no expectation of advancement."

"Sorry to hear it."

"You and me both."

Wells dropped three dimes—not five—into my open palm, without anything resembling an apology. Rather than protest, I let the old man shuffle me outside.

"Level with me, Anders," I said once we were on the street. "This Smalley guy know what he's doing?"

"Usually? Yes. This time? Not a clue."

"What's so special about this case?"

"I'd rather let him show you." Something about this Smalley guy made Anders nervous, and I didn't like it. "He said not to reveal too much. We'd like your take, and he doesn't want to taint it with too much prejudice." He said that last bit like it was a direct quote.

I said, "You gotta give me something."

Anders sighed. He stood in the doorway looking up at me for a long time. He was tall for a native of the Heavies. They tended to grow short and burly from a combination of gravity and nutrition. He was clean-shaven and square-jawed, though, and if I had to take the measure of it, I might call him handsome. He didn't deserve the hard time I gave him, but fair was fair and probably none of us deserved the hard times we got.

Meanwhile, I was a monster towering over the residents on the street. It was a miracle I'd managed to maneuver around the tiny apartment to get old Wells's plumbing under control. Times had been rough for handymen excommunicated from the Trinity AI.

A gray haze had fallen over the bleak afternoon. The three beads of Nicodemia all had the same general layout. They were a spiral, wider in the center and pointed at the top and bottom. The beads spun around a great false star, absorbing heat and energy from a constant flow of power. Heavy Nicodemia was at the very end of a big chain, making its centrifugal gravity the most intense of the lot. Wells's apartment was in the lower third of the spiral, and therefore one of the heaviest of the Heavies.

"What's the story?" I pulled a pack of cigarettes from the pocket of my tan trench coat and offered one to Anders. When he refused, I lit one with a slender lighter and watched the smoke drift upward into the yellow cone of light. "I need to know what I'm walking into."

"You really happy doing jobs like that?" Anders said, sticking his thumb out at Wells's apartment building. The red fiberbrick rose into the gloomy night. The building might have been one of the originals from back when Nicodemia was a generation ship destined to distant stars.

Now that we were here at the distant stars, the ship became a station. The poor and derelict Heavies became poorer. More derelict. Meanwhile, the wealth of the Hallows only grew.

"There are dimes in plumbing," I said.

"The blue would take you," he said. "You have the skills. All you need to do is reconcile with Trinity and you'd be a proper detective."

My laugh sounded more bitter than I intended. "If being a detective is so great, why does Smalley want my help?"

Anders fixed me with that inscrutable gaze cops get when they know you're up to no good, but they can't prove it.

"Yeah, yeah, I get it. I can go places you can't and find things hidden from regular folks." Being excommunicated had its advantages. Sure, Trinity wouldn't open doors for me or turn on lights if I was the only one in the room, but it also wouldn't hide uncomfortable truths from me. That, and people never expected to find someone walking in the dark. "But part of being the upstanding, loyal arm of the law means *not* hiring people like me."

"Unless it's absolutely necessary," said Anders.

"Which is why I'm curious."

Nicodemia's central spiral featured a trolley track, which rumbled with activity all hours of the day. Now, as gloom settled over the expanse above, a trolley rolled to a stop not far from where we stood. Anders motioned me to follow and waved it down. It waited for us, something it never would have done for an excommunicated fellow like myself.

Once aboard, he said, "You remember a while back when that guy from Earth showed up with an Earth-style revolver and a handful of lead bullets? Remember how everybody freaked out?"

"Lead bullets can cause real harm to the station."

"Which is why they're not allowed, and when they show up, they disappear fast. That guy's gun was confiscated and destroyed. Trinity absolutely freaked out until we verified that it was destroyed."

"So what's the problem?"

Anders fixed me with a gaze more serious than I'd ever seen on his young face. "We've got a victim with a heart full of lead, Demarco."

"And Trinity's freaking out?"

"Not a single blip." He held my gaze. Finally, after a few slow breaths, he blinked. "Trinity's not tracking the weapon, not identifying the shooter, and not pushing the police to mobilize. Nothing."

I watched the bustle of Heavy Nicodemia's gray afternoon as it hurtled through the emptiness of another day nestled among all the nothings it failed to fill. Hearts were broken. Livelihoods lost. The bent wailings of a sad guitar pierced the damp atmosphere, rising above the tops of buildings and falling deep beneath the fiberstone streets. Heavy Nicodemia didn't sing the blues—it *was* the blues. Something about this bead resonated with the deep misery of the soul and refused to say that everything would be fine. It wouldn't be fine.

But life would move on anyway.

That's how we played the blues in Nicodemia.

"I'll help," I said. "Can't say it'll do any good, but I'll help."

———————————

Chapter 2

———————————

ANDERS LED me straight to the center of Heavy Nicodemia's great spiral, where the Cathedral of Saint Francis of Assisi towered above a bleak and abandoned yard. By the time we arrived, the light gray of the foggy afternoon had transitioned into the dark gray of the Nicodemia night. Lights like pinpricks dotted the exterior spires of the neogothic cathedral, and the entrance lay open like a tomb. Inside, a police-blue glow deepened the tone of the fiberoak pews.

"A church job?" I said, hardly believing where he was taking me.

"The victim was a technician," said Anders as we stepped into the blue glow of the sanctuary. "He was called in to work on the church's recycler."

"The one that's used for funerals?"

Before Anders could answer, a man in a cheap three-piece suit pushed his way through the double doors to the right of the sanctuary.

"It's about time," the man proclaimed. His voice boomed

in the resonant space. His thick mustache twitched under his narrow nose. He stuck out a huge hand with stubby fingers. "Smalley."

I shook the hand, more than a little taken aback by the man's iron grip and three-pump power shake. "Demarco," I said when he released me.

"The kid says you know a thing or two about disappearing." His eyes raked over me, then dismissed me as if I were as insignificant as a grain of sand on a trolley track. "I sent him out hours ago."

"Pretty impressive that he found me at all, if you think about it," I said.

He crinkled his nose at me. "Guy your size? Hard to believe anyone ever loses you."

"Sometimes I wonder if I've ever *not* been lost."

Smalley peered at me and his bushy eyebrows furrowed. "All he did is ask your sister."

"Clever." My sister, Angel, didn't always know where I was, but she had an uncanny ability to send trouble my way.

Smalley grunted and motioned for me to follow. We left the sanctuary and moved into a room drowning in blue police lighting. There were a couple of uniforms standing around like they were tired of trying to look busy. In the far end of the room, the wall was dominated by a round bronze door. The recycler. It was closed at the moment, but during a funeral it would open to allow the casket and body to return to the station's ecosystem.

"The last good deed," I muttered. A person's final donation to the station was the one good deed they couldn't avoid, like the opposite of original sin.

"And the man who works on it." With a sweep of his hand, Smalley gestured at the corpse in the center of the room. "Don't mess up my crime scene."

The man lay in a dark pool of blood made black by the blue lights. He was a slender man with blond hair and round glasses. A flickering reflection from the bronze recycler door played across his angular features, transforming his gaunt features into something demonic. Without stepping any closer, I could see, just under the breast pocket of his coveralls, the bloody wound that was probably the killing blow. Another wound had pierced his shoulder. The name embroidered into the other side read, *Rawls*.

I took a light from my pocket and shone a pure white across the scene. It didn't reveal anything I wanted to see. Blood shone like a dark mirror in moonlight, and the man's face showed the thin lines of scratches across the cheeks. I stepped a little closer.

"There was a fight," I said, "but not recent. Maybe a day old."

Smalley grunted. He held up a clear plastic envelope with a gray lump in it.

I didn't take the envelope but shone my light on the pitted surface. It looked like a tiny asteroid suspended in a sheen of its own ice. "Lead?" I said it as if it were a guess, even though Anders had spoiled the secret.

"Found it there." Smalley nodded to the bronze door.

On closer inspection, I saw the bullet hole. The door wasn't solid bronze. There may have been a sheen of real bronze over the molded fiber of the door. The texture of the imitation metal was cracked. Splinters spread across the floor several paces away from the door's surface, plainly visible in my white light. The bullet had done some damage to the door, even after winging the victim.

"Could have been worse," Smalley said.

"A man's dead."

"Techs tell me that the big recyclers like this use a reinforced bladder of recycling fluid." He knocked on one of the walls next to the chamber door. "Bullet hits anywhere from here to the end of the first pew, and we've got a fluid leak."

"Sounds wet."

"It's the kind of wet that eats the floor, walls, and anyone made of organic material."

"Even as it is, it'll need some serious repairs in here before the next funeral," I said.

Smalley said, "We tried the door. It's not going to budge."

I drew the obvious conclusion. "So, you know the gun wasn't recycled here."

"No way they could get in. No records of it happening. No evidence that the broken door was rammed shut after the murder."

"That's a lot of damage for one bullet."

"Small caliber," said Smalley. "Probably just a twenty-two. Clipped his shoulder."

A spray of blood peppered the floor, wall, and door. Far more spray than expected from the plastic or ceramic bullets common in Nicodemia. Those lighter bullets killed well enough, shredding organs and exploding flesh, but they didn't punch like a lead bullet, even a small-caliber one. The big bronze door had been closed when a single shot was fired. That shot made its mark across the room like an abstract artist splattering a canvas.

"Messy," I said, still peering at the pattern of blood. Something about it drew me. It was a graphic display of the man's soul violently leaving his body. "Any idea who Rawls was, other than a recycler technician?"

"Just a cog in a machine. A nobody doing his nobody job." There was a hint of irritation in Smalley's voice.

"Nobody is nobody, Smalley," I said. "Your job ought to have taught you that."

"We're all nobody, Demarco," growled the detective.

I took a step back. "Rawls arrived to run diagnostics on the recycler. Something was broken, and the church called in a maintenance request." I looked to Smalley.

He nodded a confirmation at my assumptions.

I pointed at the open toolbox next to the body. "He started setting up his tools before opening the recycling chamber. Tools like these are specific to the trade, and when a guy like this works on a big job, he wants the whole array of tools spread out before him. It's like he's a surgeon and he doesn't want to have to go digging around once he's elbow-deep."

Anders poked his head in the room. "Dispatch says they have something."

Smalley kept his gaze focused on me. "Keep going."

"He wasn't here very long," I said. "His box is still mostly packed. You'll want to check his time of death against the church's Mass schedule. A gun like that's going to make some noise, and even the most oblivious Catholic won't be able to ignore that."

"Is that your professional opinion?"

"Is there a problem?"

"The gun's not showing up on any records. Not through Customs, not through crime records, not on any video surveillance. It's a ghost."

"Trinity will track it."

"Not this time."

"That's why you think I can help?"

The detective scoffed. "It was Anders' idea. He thought you were good at this kind of thing."

"Am I?"

"Passable." Smalley's mustache twitched. "Surveillance puts Rawls entering the church through the back door at the same time as the seven o'clock mass let out in the front. His timing is perfect, so he must have known the schedule."

"And his killer must have known *his* schedule."

"How do you figure?"

"You still think this is random?"

"It's not been ruled out." Smalley's gruff voice was small.

He couldn't have truly believed that it was a random killing. More likely, he was clinging to the hope. The alternative was too ugly.

Ugly and difficult. The blue had a reputation for laziness. I wondered if Smalley bucked the trend. It didn't seem like it. The question was: why was I there?

"The way I see it, the killer had to have been shooting from here." I stepped into position and crouched down a little to indicate the correct angle. "Rawls was working on unpacking his toolbox. Heard a noise and stood up. Bang." I pulled the trigger of a finger gun. "Rawls dies immediately. He collapses backward because the punch on a bullet like this is a kick to the chest. One of the bullets continues into the door, and the killer turns tail."

"How does that make it not random?" asked Smalley.

"Because right here"—I stomped my foot—"is about a mile away from that door. If someone had stumbled in on Rawls, they could have easily left before he saw them. If he had something they wanted, why not just sneak up behind him, pop him on the head, and take it." I reconsidered. "Or better yet, steal it from his toolbox as soon as he moved into the other room."

Smalley blinked. "It's a stretch."

"It's a fact."

He waved me away from the spot where the killer had been standing. "It's a theory. We'll consider it." When he saw that I wasn't to be mollified, he said, "Random violence is a lot more common than you think."

"No violence is random," I said. "Not a murder, not a theft. Nothing."

"Not even the wreck of a shuttle?"

The words hung in the air like rotten meat. My parents had been killed in the wreck of a ship called the *Benevolent*, and I'd been the one to cause it. At my command, the ship had spun off into the void, disconnected from Haven Nicodemia, where it was attempting to dock. It had been—and still was—the most shameful thing I'd ever done. Trinity had rewarded me for it—for prioritizing the safety of the station over the safety of my own family—by granting me the mixed blessing of excommunication. That wreck was the sin that ate away at my soul every hour of every day.

Smalley's dark eyes bored into the side of my head. "I guess we'll find out more when the *Benevolent*'s orbit brings it back around."

My palms felt like cold fish. "Back around?"

"Lot of secrets on that ship," he said, coming closer. "That going to be a problem?"

"You don't need my help," I said. "Anders says dispatch has a lead."

His mustache twitched. "You and I both know that won't play out."

I swallowed the acid taste of my tongue. "It's not a random killing."

"Then prove it."

I didn't know what his game was or why he wanted me close. I didn't know what dirt he thought he could pull up about the *Benevolent*. All I knew was that he was going to learn something about the wreck that I thought had been flung out into the farthest depths of space and lost forever. He knew I needed that the way a junkie needs to take one more hit before it all goes black.

I took one last look at the crime scene and breathed in the reek of its consequence. This case could change everything. It could *ruin* everything.

"I'll find your killer," I said. "And you'll tell me what you learn about the wreck of the *Benevolent*."

Chapter 3

I STARED at my own haunted eyes in the hazy mirror on one wall of the tiny storage space above my sister's diner. Behind me, my giant dog Cain snored, taking up half of the tiny bed in my tiny room. I shrugged my coat onto my shoulders, and it hung from my bones like a tarp thrown over a bag of sticks. I wondered at how much mass I'd lost recently. Sleep had danced out of reach for most of the night.

"Come on, Cain," I growled. The dog's eyes moved to watch me, but he didn't move. "You want breakfast or what?"

He moved. The dog wasn't built for the Heavies. He'd been bred and trained in much lighter gravity, and while he'd adjusted just fine, he still struggled with motivation. Then again, didn't we all?

My stomach rumbled. Of the three dimes old man Wells had given me, I'd turned one into booze and paid the other two in tribute to the gods of gambling and fortune. Despite the distractions, Smalley's words still echoed in the back of my skull, no matter how much I tried to drown them out.

The wreck of the *Benevolent* was no accident. It was murder. It was the one case that broke me.

Investigations over the years had turned up a few truths. First was that the ship had been tampered with. No ship in normal operation would have all its blast doors open. It just didn't happen. The mode the ship needed to be in to make that happen was one that it entered only during manufacture and maintenance. If a proper lockdown had been functioning, the people in the ship wouldn't have all been killed when I pulled that trigger.

But I *did* pull that trigger. It was my hand that released the ship from dock and killed everyone aboard. Whether or not someone else had tampered with safety mechanisms, I told the ship to disconnect when the docking became dangerous for Nicodemia. Every technician and every pilot I spoke with swore that the call I made was correct. It potentially saved the city. All it cost me was my parents. It cost my sister the use of her legs.

"Bright and early today," said Angel as I pushed past her in the narrow door between the diner and the kitchen. She rolled in her wheelchair and dominated the whole diner with her presence.

It took me a moment before I realized it was nearly noon. "The *Benevolent*'s orbit is bringing it close."

She fixed me with a stony gaze. "Leave it, Jude."

"Close enough that they're planning an expedition."

My sister was the kind of woman who bent her will against the world, and more often than not the world blinked first. She owned a small diner in the lower quarter of Heavy Nicodemia, forgoing our heritage as descendants of the Hallows—a life that would be much easier with her disability —for a life in which she controlled her fate. Angel's wife, Helen, was the only one who could keep her in check.

"She's right, Jude," said Hellen, placing a hand on my shoulder. "You should leave this one."

"I'm planning on it." A lie, but was it really a lie if there was no expectation of belief?

Hellen handed me a breakfast sandwich. Wheat toast with a fried egg and some cheese. She kissed Angel on the cheek. "Good luck at the meeting today." With that, she disappeared into the back room.

"Meeting?" I said.

She shrank a little. "I'm leading a neighborhood improvement group."

"Leading?"

"It's not my fault I'm outspoken." She gripped the handles of her wheelchair. "I spoke up too much at the meetings and now they've elected me onto the board."

"That's why I stay in the shadows."

She looked me straight in the eyes. "Just stay away from the *Benevolent*, okay, bro?"

When I didn't respond, Angel rolled back to refill coffee for her customers. When she was finished, she grudgingly plucked a cup from the rack and poured me a cup.

"Thanks, sis," I said and proceeded to devour my sandwich. It was heaven between two pieces of toast, and my stomach rumbled when it was finished. It would have to be enough, though. I felt bad enough taking even this from my sister.

Anders entered the diner on the tail end of the lunch rush. "Good, you're here."

"Is this another blue ambush?"

"That wasn't an ambush." Anders had the decency to look like he didn't believe his own words. "I still need your help."

"How's the pay?"

"I'll buy you lunch."

I tipped my empty coffee cup to him. "I've got everything a monk could possibly want."

"Then help me out as a friend."

"Friends don't ambush each other."

"That's not true," he said. "Hi, Angel."

"He's scaring away my customers, officer," my sister said. "You're finally coming to clear him out of here?"

"Only if he'll come without a fight," said Anders.

"There's always a first," said Angel.

I stretched my back, placed my fedora on my head, and followed Anders out into the streets.

"Smalley said you were inclined to help," Anders said.

"That doesn't sound like something I would say."

"We're canvassing," Anders said once we'd made our way upspiral a few blocks. "And I don't know if you've heard this, but this uniform isn't always welcome in some of these lower neighborhoods."

Anders used his exceptional Karma to acquire a cheese sandwich and a bag of chips. He offered them up to me and my mood improved with every bite. I washed them down with a bottle of lemon-flavored water.

"Who's our target?" I said.

He handed me a list. It wasn't a long one.

"Liz Rawls," the woman said in the doorway on the seventh floor of a dingy tenement. She wore a frumpy gray robe over a moth-eaten T-shirt, and her hair was wrapped up in a bandanna. She carried a curly-haired toddler on her hip. When she spoke, she spoke to me rather than to Anders. "Sure, I called it in when he didn't come home. It worried me."

"When was that?" I asked.

"About noon yesterday."

"How long had he been gone?" A door opened down the hall and an elderly woman peeked out at us.

"Come on in, I guess," Rawls said. She picked her way across the cluttered disaster of the apartment floor. "Can I get you anything?"

"No, thank you," Anders said. "We won't take much of your time."

I shot him an annoyed look. In my line of work, it was never good to turn down an offer, even if the woman offering didn't look like she had a lot to spare.

"He was gone a lot," she said. "Recyclers are busy work, you know? All the metals in them make it hard for the automated robots to do the necessary repairs."

"Is that so?" I asked.

It was Anders who explained. "I looked this up. The heat required to work with the tempered alloys tends to degrade the fiber materials used to make the robots."

"Why not just make robots tougher?" I asked.

"Then Grant would have been out a job." Rawls waved a hand at the squalor of her apartment. "We wouldn't be able to afford all this luxury."

"Were they short-staffed?" I asked, trying to get the conversation back on topic. "Is that why he had to work so much?"

She said, "He was ambitious."

"I see."

"Look." Rawls sat on the ratty sofa. "Grant didn't have any enemies. He didn't get involved in all the stuff going around. Nobody had it in for him, and I might have had some words with him, but there wasn't anything that should have got him killed."

"And yet," I said.

"Yeah." She drew a long breath. The toddler pushed

away from her and wobbled a short distance over to a teetering stack of blocks. "I just…" Her voice cracked, but she pieced it back together again. "I just don't think there's anything I can say to help you guys find his killer. His whole life is within one floor of this tenement. Friends. Cousins. Coworkers. We're all right here. The only time he left was to go to work. The recycler repair business might not be glamorous, but it didn't exactly make you a lot of enemies." Her shoulders shook. "I don't know what I'm going to do."

I placed a hand on hers, unsure how much a ragged man like myself could ever manage to comfort someone like her. "I'm sorry for your loss," I said. "Really. We don't deserve what we get sometimes."

It must have been the wrong thing to say because she wept on my shoulder for a good five minutes. When she finally finished, Anders plied her with a dozen standard interview questions, and we took our leave.

"You think she's holding back?" Anders asked as we moved to the next door in the long hall.

"Not intentionally."

"What do you mean?"

I knocked on the next door, which was promptly answered by a man in a stained button-down shirt and threadbare slippers. We spent the afternoon interviewing neighbors and forming the complete picture of the Rawls's home life. Liz Rawls had been right. There were words exchanged. Some were harsh.

Nothing that would get a man murdered.

With every interview and with every question, we formed a picture-perfect image of a man who did what any man would. He raised his kid. He argued with his wife. He spent time with friends and too much time at work. In his spare time, he contributed to the sluggish community of the borderline impoverished people of his apartment building.

"Maybe Smalley was right," said Anders as we finished our last interview. "The guy is a nobody."

"Nobody's a nobody," I said. "And if it looks that way, then we need to dig deeper."

"There's nothing there," said Anders. "We've dug deeper. He's a paint-by-numbers husband and father. What else is there to it?"

"My father was paint-by-numbers too," I said. "Then I learned that he was the linchpin in an art smuggling operation. We're going to need help."

———

"IS this some kind of police ambush?" Retch asked as I dragged Anders into his well-guarded alley.

"You know Anders," I said. "He's decent."

"In my experience, decent people are the ones who have the biggest problem with me." Retch had grown in the past few months. He wasn't only taller – from spending time in the lighter gravity of the Hallows – but his hormone treatments had helped him put on muscle and even a hint of facial hair. The Church, which I had to admit was packed with decent people, had a problem with trans boys like Retch, even when it pretended at ambivalence.

"Decent's not the same as good," I said.

"Ain't that the truth." Retch leaned against the fiberbrick wall. The angle of the alley against the false sun in the center of the station cast the whole area into permanent shadow, but a single streetlight lit him with its amber cone. He'd hacked off his hair recently, and the lazy spikes cast shadows over his face, making his quirky smile look crooked and strange. "You never visit anymore, Demarco."

"Your neighborhood scares me."

"Well, living in your sister's diner was causing some problems with logistics."

When I first met Retch, he lived in a warehouse. Angel had sheltered him for a while until he got back on his feet, but he never much liked being tied down. He said he found it stifling.

"This is a business visit," I said.

"Of course it is."

"Anders?" I motioned to the cop.

Anders showed Retch a picture of Grant Rawls. "We're wondering if you've seen this man around anywhere. Gambling. Sex. Drugs."

"The usual." Retch took the photograph and peered at it in the amber light. The muscles of his neck twitched. "Not a bad-looking guy."

"Not a living one either," I said. "And we'd very much like to know why."

"Check Trinity." He offered the photo to me.

I didn't take it. "This was a church job."

"Most dangerous place in town." Retch wasn't wrong. Trinity respected the sanctity of the Church, which translated to minimal surveillance in any of the many churches, synagogues, and mosques throughout Nicodemia. Seeing that I wasn't going to take the picture back, he stuffed it in his pocket. "Maybe I'll ask around."

"It'd be a huge help," I said.

"We should talk about payment."

A muscle in my jaw twitched. I was usually able to lean on Retch's kindness for minor help from his gang, but lately he was starting to charge me something closer to the usual rate. "I'm all out of dimes," I said. "And Anders doesn't deal in under-the-table currency."

Retch turned his dark gaze on Anders. "Maybe I'll have to take payment in the form of a favor." He stared at the cop through hooded eyes and took a lazy step forward. "Things are getting rough around the Heavies these days, Mr. Officer. Lot of bad people out there who might need a little attention."

"I'm not going to be your legal hitman," said Anders.

Retch took another step forward. For someone from the Heavies, he was lanky. The boy had turned into a tall and wiry teen, and he stood even taller than Anders. "I'm not saying I want to be the new crime boss," he said. "But some-one's going to be. There's a whole lot of favors you could do people by nudging things in the right direction."

I moved between Retch and Anders, palms out to keep Retch back. "Find out what you can, kid. I'll make sure it's worth your while."

He gave a hint of a shrug and leaned back against the wall. "I'll see what I can do."

As we left, we passed the kids who made up the Screaming Jesus gang. They weren't overt about the threat they posed, but these kids were the ones lost through the cracks of society. They were the shadows under the boot of an oppressive government, and they knew exactly what they could get away with.

"Hey, Demarco," Retch called before we had the chance to turn the corner.

"Yeah?" I called back.

"It was good seeing you again."

"You too, kid." I tipped my hat at him. It *was* good seeing him. He might be a low-grade criminal and a top-notch troublemaker, but he was one of the few people I could trust in this big, busy city. To Anders, I said, "Where to now, boss?"

"We eat," said Anders.

"Twice in one day?"

"It's a special occasion." When he saw I wasn't going to respond, he continued, "That tip we took yesterday? It's a sensitive one." He gazed up at the hazy sky, which was starting to hint at the warm tones of a setting sun. "I need you to do this one on your own."

"And where am I going?"

"Haven," he said. "I need you to talk to a guy."

"The criminal sort?"

"Worse," Anders said. "Antique dealer."

Chapter 4

EVEN A LOUSY LEAD like the one Anders gave me was enough to justify a trip up the chain. Haven Nicodemia had a different smell to it. Better coffee, thriving green spaces, and well-regulated eateries dominated the gentle wind circulating through the vast open spaces. My steps practically bounced in the lower gravity. If it weren't for the rigid social structure and the scowls of the locals, I might have even considered Haven to be pleasant. It hardly even bothered me that I was wasting my time.

The lead was the kind of tip that probably popped up every time anyone ever sniffed the powder-scorched scent of a lead bullet in any of the three beads of Nicodemia. The bullets were rare enough that one of the only legitimate places to find one was in the stock of the most eclectic and impressive antique shop in all of Nicodemia. Fortner Heirlooms was big enough to have its own gravity well—big enough to run by its own rules.

"A bullet?" the woman behind the counter said with deadpan irritation. "Who's asking?"

"A concerned friend."

She barked a bitter laugh. "Kaegan Forner doesn't have friends."

"Is he the boss?" I asked.

"He's not available at the moment." The woman was a few years younger than me and as soft in the middle as she was hard in the eyes. Her brown hair was highlighted with the kind of ashy gray that nobody would ever describe as silver. "There's no guns missing from our storage facility."

"You sure about that?"

She flipped a switch and peered at the readout on a desk-mounted screen. "Yep."

"Mind if I take a look around?" My bones ached from the reduction in gravity, and my spine was still decompressing.

She spread her arms wide to indicate the antique shop. "Be my guest, officer."

"Just a private contractor," I muttered.

Fortner Heirlooms was an antique shop nestled into the lower reaches of Haven Nicodemia. Like almost everything in Haven, the shop closed when the sun set, so I arrived as it opened with the day and the streets filled with the denizens of the busiest shopping district. Outside, clean air filled with yellow simulated sunlight, and people bustled to their busy jobs in the industry of the middle bead. Inside the shop, the space was eerily quiet, as if a forced and oppressive calm had descended over this little corner of existence. It was as if time had forgotten this little place.

The impression might have been intentional. The antique shop featured artifacts from across the ages, from before mankind had left Earth to the more recent ages of humanity's efforts to establish itself in a new solar system. A silver belt buckle from the American Civil War sat next to a box carved from actual wood containing a brass nozzle of some sort.

"It was part of the first fire suppression system aboard a Trinity ship," said the woman, now lingering at my elbow. "Later discarded in favor of the fibersteel equivalents." She picked up the nozzle and tossed it to me. It was as big as her fist and heavy as a brick. "Fibersteel's a tenth of the weight, but don't you think there's something impressive about this thing?"

I hefted the piece and frowned. "This was for water?"

"They never use water to put out fires in a station. Not even the original engineers were that dumb. The newer fire-retardant chemicals are extremely corrosive on brass, though. More foam than liquid. Fibersteel can handle the stuff, but the weight of the brass makes it easier to aim." She took the nozzle from me and rapped it on the fiber resin case hard enough that I flinched. Then she held it up and showed me that it wasn't scratched at all.

"I'd be more worried about you breaking the case," I said.

"Fiber resin cures harder than fibersteel." She put the nozzle down and picked up a long sword with a line of resin along the length of its blade. "Bonds permanently with steel, too, so it's a good way to make display pieces out of dangerous objects."

"People collect this stuff?"

She pursed her lips. "No so much as they used to."

"Tough times?"

"Lots of good investments to prop up Dad's business."

"Dad's?" I asked.

One wall of the antique shop was filled with weapons, but none of them were the projectile variety. I peered at the shining surface of a sword the length of my forearm. It looked like a sharp edge, but I didn't bother trying to take it off the wall. It was tethered in place with a strap of fibersteel.

Again, the shopkeeper hovered. "All the weapons are peace-locked."

"Even the guns?"

"You see any guns here?" She plucked a butterfly knife from the rack and flicked it open. The sharp edge of the blade was blunted with a sheaf of resin.

"There are kids in the Heavies with more dangerous weapons than that," I said.

With a snap of her wrist, she closed the knife. "My father has a deal with Trinity, and that deal requires that everything we sell stays safe." She gestured at the door with the closed knife. "Which means we don't really need a visit from people like you every time someone fires a weapon down in that squalor."

I bristled at her tone. "What did you say your name was?"

She looked at me with a gaze so cold it hurt my lungs. "Anya."

"Anya, I'm not here to shake down your father's legitimate business. I'm not even here to imply that your guns were used in some crime down the chain. All I want to do is learn a little about the weapons we're dealing with. Maybe get a history lesson or something."

The bell over the door chimed and a man pushed his way in.

"Blaize," Anya sighed.

Blaize bore a striking resemblance to his older sister, minus the gray in his brown hair and the fact that his body didn't contain a single ounce of excess fat. He wore a tight red blazer that showed off his biceps. A pair of sunglasses that shone like spilled oil rested in the tousled nest of his hair.

Blaize blinked at her for several seconds before tilting his head at me. "You'll have to forgive my sister. She's usually just in charge of paperwork and she's mad because she's not very good at it."

Anya scowled. "What my brother means to say is that I run this place, and he's tired of being my little flunky."

"We're all *Dad's* little flunkies," said another voice from the door. Behind Blaize, another Fortner sibling entered the small shop. The slender girl couldn't have been a day over twenty, and she wore black like it was her own funeral. She was the waif of the group, practically disappearing when she leaned against the door frame.

"Mia," said Blaize without looking at her. "Be a good little flunky and go tell Pop I've got the shop under control."

Mia shot Blaize a look that I couldn't quite interpret. It was something between fear and intense dislike. Respect, maybe. "Who's the goon?"

Blaize said, "Some cop from down the spiral."

Mia looked to her sister, but Anya didn't respond.

"Now," said Blaize, shooting me a sickly salesman smile, "how can I help you, sir."

I towered over the man. He might have perfectly sculpted musculature, but I had mass and a whole lot of grit. "I've been helped," I said. "The lady was just answering some questions for me."

Anya said, "I do need to get going."

"Maybe I should just talk to Kaegan," I said.

"Pop's busy," said Blaize.

"Murder doesn't clear his schedule?"

Blaize's jaw clenched. "If you have questions about something, I can help you." He gestured at Anya. "She was just keeping the place open for me while I ran an errand."

"She doesn't usually work here?"

"Maybe she does."

The whole interaction was flicking the red flags in the back of my skull. "Problem is, I hear that this place has the biggest antique gun collection in all of Nicodemia, but I don't see a single one on display."

Blaize guffawed. "You think we'd keep something like that out front?"

"How many pieces do you have?"

"Enough," he said.

"You ever fire them?"

He didn't blink. "There's a maintenance routine."

"These guns work?" I said.

"Functional antiques are worth more."

"So, you *do* sell them."

"Do you see any guns on display?"

"Tell me about this maintenance routine?"

"Once a year. Clean, shoot, clean. Keeps everything in good condition."

"Where?"

"We have a vault."

Mia turned up her nose, "That place smells like grandpa."

Anya agreed with a nod and a wry expression.

"It smells like history," said Blaize. "Like freedom."

"Locked in a vault," I said.

Blaize narrowed his eyes at me. "It's more like a display case inside a vault."

I was liking this family less and less with each passing second. "How about a tour?"

"No," said Anya and Mia simultaneously.

"The contract says we have to let the police inspect everything whenever they ask."

"He's not police," Anya said. "Or so he claims."

Blaize strolled around the outer wall of the cluttered

shop, running a hand on the shelves as if to check them for dust. "You're not the blue. You're not the inspector. You're not Trinity."

I said, "I'm the man who watches the blue when they get out of line. It's me who throws a wrench in the corrupt machines of politics. When nothing works in the wide broken world, I'm the guy who shows up and fixes it. Something's broken in Nicodemia, and I don't care if I have to tear the whole thing down to bare metal to figure out what. I'm ready with my wrench, kid, and you're looking a whole lot like a bent gear."

His saccharine smile turned genuine for a split-second. "Maybe you and I ought to head over to the firing range."

Chapter 5

I HADN'T LIKED Blaize very much at first, but as I grew to know him on our walk across town, my dislike blossomed into genuine hate. We moved through the bustling streets of Haven Nicodemia, and the overconfident, blustering weightlifter fumbled every interaction with everyone he met.

"Hey, honey!" Blaize called to a girl who couldn't have been more than twenty.

The girl crossed to the other side of the street. Somewhere, a busker played J. J. Cale's "Call Me the Breeze," and the piercing morning sunlight reminded me of a desperate need for caffeine.

"Hurry up, old man." Blaize bounced on his heels with impatience as I waited for the corner coffee shop owner to hand me a fresh brew.

"You don't drink coffee?" I asked.

"I don't put anything in my body that won't make me better."

"It's on him," I said to the barista as she handed me the fiberboard cup.

The barista frowned, but waved me away with the brew. My first sip burned my tongue, but coffee in Haven Nicodemia was a pleasure no matter what temperature. Something about the single G gravity made everything about brewing the perfect beverage that much better. It was one of the few things Haven had over the Hallows and one of the many that it had over the Heavies.

Blaize bounced on the balls of his feet.

"Fine, let's go," I said, unable to endure Blaize's impatience. "Where's this range of yours?"

He winced. "We don't talk about it out here."

"Then let's not be out here."

He led me through the dark outer alleys of a lower Haven district. Tall office buildings stretched high above and suits outnumbered the casually dressed, two to one. This was a financial district if I had my guess, and the looks Blaize got as we passed told me he was recognized by the people here. Disliked but tolerated. A necessary evil.

"Hey up top!" Blaize lifted an open palm to an awkward middle-aged man in a cerulean suit and matching tie.

The man met the awkward high-five. Blaize followed the slap forward, stepped into the man's personal space, and grasped his shoulder, dragging him along with us, even though it was the opposite direction from the way the man was hurrying.

The man sputtered, "I'll have your—"

"Don't worry about it, Oliver. Take a break sometimes, yeah?" Blaize jostled the man so hard I could hear his teeth clack. "I mean, get your payment in, but that's not why I'm here today, okay, bud?"

"Y-Yeah."

Blaize shoved the man away and laughed at how he stumbled. "Later!"

"L-Later." The man grasped his briefcase like it was a flotation device and scurried away.

"Antiques must be big business around here," I drolled.

Blaize draped an arm around my shoulders. "Big business indeed."

I didn't crumple like the man in the suit had, but I could feel Blaize's strength. He wasn't just showy muscle. The man was built like a pitbull, and he knew it. I took a sip of coffee, shrugged him off, and kept walking.

The farther from the central spiral we went, the darker the streets became. The towers closed in around us and the sky loomed close as the flickering bright of the ceiling high above. Here in the outer reaches of the spiral city, the illusion of big open spaces gave way to the harsh practicality of the station we lived in. The crowds thinned until our footsteps echoed in a lonely drumbeat across the fiberstone cobblestones.

Then, we reached the vault.

It sat behind a gray fiberstone façade nestled between two drab office buildings. The place had an abandoned look. The door was a plain black slab. When Blaize approached, it didn't open automatically. He opened a panel with a manual crank and gave it a twist. The door slid open, revealing a dimly lit room with white marble floors and four thick black columns. The far wall was dominated by a shining metal door. Next to that stood a man of medium height in a gray suit that almost acted as camouflage against the drab wall.

"Huff!" cried Blaize. "What's up, my man?"

Huff was a pasty-white lump of a human being. His sausage fingers fiddled uncomfortably at his sides, and he peered at me through thin round glasses. "Your father wanted me to remind you—"

"It's all right, Huff!" Blaize slapped Huff on the back so

hard the man nearly collapsed. "I totally got this. I'm going to give the big guy the whole lesson."

"But—"

"Dad can deal with it." He kicked the door gently with his toe. "Open her up."

Huff drew a rattling keychain from his pocket and held it up to the light. "I'm Harley Huff," he said to me as he worked. "Second in charge under Kaegan Fortner."

"Jude Demarco," I said. "Handyman, medic, and occasional freelance detective."

The key clicked into place and Huff pulled the heavy door open. "Sounds like you keep pretty busy."

"If I'm not careful."

Blaize pushed past Huff to enter the building. As he did, he punched a control panel on the wall and the lights flared to life in a wave through what at first appeared to be a long empty warehouse. He rushed across the room to where a small side room branched from the main space.

"I'm sorry," said Huff. "He can be a bit much."

"He likes to give everything a hundred percent, doesn't he?"

A weak smile brightened Huff's pale face. "More if he can manage it."

The room wasn't a warehouse, and it wasn't connected to Trinity's main surveillance. That much I could tell by the absence of automated systems. No automated lights. No automated locks. Even the air-handling had to be manually activated, which, it turned out, was what Blaize had run to do before anything else. It made sense. The air smelled stale and dry, but there was an oily aroma that dissipated as soon as the filters were activated.

"Come here much?" I asked Huff.

"Only when someone needs the lesson."

"Is this going to be the kind of lesson that leaves bruises?"

Huff nodded at Blaize, who was crossing the long room back to us. "When the young Mr. Fortner is involved, almost every lesson leaves bruises."

Blaize spread his arms wide. "Welcome to the range!"

The final lights flared to life in the far end of the room, and I saw the heavy stone wall and a row of human-shaped paper targets. To one side, an enormous safe stood next to a counter, atop which sat another stack of targets and a pair of ear protectors. Blaize manipulated a dial on the safe, careful to keep his body between the numbers and my prying eyes. I listened to the ten-digit tone of the safe's code as he punched in the rhythm.

The safe unfolded into a flat display case filled with the meanest-looking guns I'd ever seen.

"Smith & Wesson, Glock, Walther, Colt. Micro-compact, compact, fully automatic." Blaize practically bounced as he spoke. "We got the biggest gun collection in all of Nicodemia, Mr. Demarco."

"How?"

Blaize grinned. "They've been in the family since the beginning."

Huff said, "If it's rare, then the Fortners *must* have it, and functioning guns are the rarest thing in Nicodemia."

"And you all take care of them?" I asked.

"Well, Lorrel hated guns," said Blaize. "Thought they were too dangerous."

"They're all functioning weapons, though?" I said.

Blaize hefted a large handgun. "Every single one of them."

The first thing that struck me was that every gun was black or dark gray. Modern guns in Nicodemia were flashy colors. What was the point in having a gun if it wasn't obvious? These guns were made for something other than bravado and peacock showmanship. They were killing machines, meant to accompany a man in the dark. The guns were arranged in sets, with each company's products making a proud display of sidearms. The dull black Glocks were on pegs near the top, each gun only a very slight variation on an overall theme. They were small weapons—probably too small to comfortably fit a hand like mine, but perfectly comfortable for Blaize.

The Colt row only had three labeled slots. The first held an ancient-looking single-action army revolver. Its black was shinier than the Glocks, but the gun had significant heft. This was a weapon for war in an age long since lost to history. The second was labeled as a government series 70 model. It was also big and foreboding, but the design was utilitarian—a killing machine almost boring in its banality. The third Colt slot was empty. The label said it was meant for a Blued Python with a six-inch barrel, and the outline dwarfed the single-action army revolver. It had a longer barrel than the series 70 model—and the series 70 was already too big a gun.

The only other empty slot was cut out for a Walther PPK, a tiny weapon by comparison.

Smith & Wesson was by far the largest collection. It ranged from the micro-compacts to fully automatic, as Blaize claimed, and there was even something labeled as an M&P 15 Pistol Braced weapon—an efficient implement of murder if I've ever seen one. Blaize plucked a weapon out of the Smith & Wesson row and held it up for me to see. The label said it was a Model 41. He lovingly, gently placed it back in its place.

"Favorite of yours?" I said.

"That's my baby," he said, aiming down the sights at

some invisible spec on the wall. He set the gun back in its place. "Sometimes you find a gun that just fits, you know?"

I didn't know.

Huff cleared his throat. "Trinity doesn't allow these weapons to exist outside of this room. The whole vault is shielded from penetration and completely devoid of Trinity's sensors. These weapons are powerful here, but step outside that door and you'll find yourself in a room with no oxygen."

I had never heard of Trinity having such a severe reaction.

"Let's shoot!" Blaize picked up one of the heftiest guns on the rack—the Colt revolver—and opened a cabinet below to reveal ancient boxes of ammunition.

"Is that lead?" I asked.

"We have copper too," said Blaize with a serious frown. "It's not the same."

Huff rolled his eyes.

"You keep a tight inventory on that, right?" I asked as Blaize loaded bullets into his revolver.

He blew out a puff of air. "Nothing's missing. Not guns. Not bullets." He held the revolver up next to his shit-eating grin. "Nothin'."

"What about the empty slots?"

Blaize's brow furrowed.

"The collection isn't complete," said Huff. "Never has been."

With a whoop, Blaize stepped up to the range and fired six of the loudest shots I'd ever heard. The last echoed in the cavernous space and rang in my ears.

Huff held out the ear protection to me. "You may want this."

"What?"

Blaize pointed the gun at me. "Your turn, buddy." Then, with a grin, he turned the gun around and handed it to me grip-first. "Let's see what you got."

While I loaded the revolver—a clumsy process that made my fingers feel like swollen slugs—he replaced the paper target. The human-shaped target featured highlighted points for shots that would give a quick kill, which seemed a bit morbid. His paper target had three shots in the head and two in the heart. Only one shot had gone wide, nicking the imaginary enemy in the upper arm.

"Nice shooting," I said.

His grin somehow widened even further. "It's not like ceramic bullets," he said. "Those plastic guns just don't have the heft."

"They kill well enough." I had seen plenty of tough men and women shredded by plasti-ceramic bullets.

"Yeah, and they're stopped by a thick shirt." Blaize pointed at the target, which now seemed impossibly far away. "Shoot."

With a sigh, I stepped up to the range. My heart whooshed in my ears. I drew a long breath. Then another. I waited until my nerves mellowed and my heart slowed. The gun fit well in my hand. It was a large piece, but Blaize was right that it felt a million times more substantial than the plastic printed weapons. The whole piece was a brick in my hands, drawn by a tremendous force.

Boom!

The first shot didn't even hit the paper. A spot on the solid wall lit up in a puff of dust, and the kick sent a shockwave up into the muscles of my shoulders.

Blaize guffawed. His laugh went high like a hyena and echoed through the whole range. When I glanced at Huff, I saw a fraction of the annoyance that I felt deep down in my gut. I felt sorry for the pasty little guy. He had to deal with the Fortner kids every day.

"Damn," I said.

"I know, right?" said Blaize. "Thing has some kick!"

My second shot hit the paper, but not the broad-shouldered human outline. The third popped against the target's hip. My final shots hit meat, and the last one even touched the edge of the target zone around the figure's heart. I set the gun down on the counter. My hand was numb.

Blaize didn't waste a moment. He darted down the range, gesturing for me to follow, which I did. He grinned at the paper target, which dangled there like a limp flag flying in no wind. It was a testament to my lack of skill with a firearm, and both of us knew it.

"I shoot a plastic gun well enough," I said.

That made Blaize laugh.

Beyond the target, Blaize approached the wall. Up close, I could see that the wall wasn't a fiber derivative, since it had managed to stop the bullets. Several smashed lead plugs lay on the floor in front of the wall. One had penetrated enough to stick, but it came out when I pried it with a thumbnail.

"Is that what it looked like?" Blaize asked.

"Pretty much," I said, trying to remember the lead bullet in the little baggie that Anders had shown me. "This is bigger."

Blaize grinned like a kid in a candy shop. "Then we got more shootin' to do."

After a day of shooting with Blaize Fortner under the eye of Harley Huff, we concluded that the bullet used in the murder was likely a .22. Using debris from around the warehouse, we were able to simulate the impact of a bullet hitting a person, as well as observe how the bullet deformed as it smashed into a fiberoak panel. The palm of my hand was numb, and the air smelled pungent like a mix of sulfur and pepper. After firing guns all day, my whole arm felt strange, and an ache in my bones felt like it was settling in for the long haul.

"Small- to medium-sized pistol," said Blaize. "Small bullet. The .22 long probably wouldn't have been able to pass through the vic's torso, but the shot that winged him slammed into the fiber and got all smashed up like this." He held up the bullet. It was almost a perfect replica of the one from the crime scene.

I picked up the gun that had produced the matching bullet. It was like a toy in my big hand, and it was far from the flashiest of weapons. It showed some wear, and I wondered if the almost-invisible crescent indent on the grip affected its value as an antique. "Smith & Wesson Compact. So, one of these was the murder weapon?"

He shrugged. "Lot of guns shoot this ammo, but that bad boy's got the right punch."

Huff said, "It's a small gun. Easy to hide."

"Customs is pretty thorough." I peered at the gun case again. There were several empty spots. "How would someone get their hands on a weapon like this?"

Blaize said, "Steel like this can't be fabricated. It would need to come through Customs."

"Which is impossible," said Huff.

"So there can't be many around, right?" I said. "A few dozen, maybe?"

"Find a weapon like this walking around the station," Blaize said, "and you've found your killer."

Huff took my arm and led me away toward the door.

"Well, now you know what you're looking for. If you don't have any other questions, then I really do have more work to do this afternoon."

"How common are Smith & Wesson Compacts really?"

A smug smile touched Huff's lips. "Extremely rare."

"How about on Earth?"

"Extremely common," said Blaize, imitating Huff's nasally tone. "They made these things or something similar for a hundred years."

"More," Huff admitted. "Even after printed guns became common, political factions on Earth kept these small firearms in style."

"I'm not really interested in politics," I said.

"Some of them are *very* collectable," said Huff. "Which is why the Fortner family has maintained this collection for so many generations."

I didn't pretend that I would ever understand the antique collector mentality, but then again, I lived a life so impoverished it would give most monks pause. "How common are these in Nicodemia?"

"Most collectors don't show off their possessions."

"They also wouldn't move them through Customs, would they?"

"They wouldn't move them at all," said Huff. "The regulations around these require them to be locked away in special containment facilities."

"Like this one," I said.

Huff's jaw clenched. "Look, Mr. Demarco, this has gone on long enough. We've taught you all about firearms, just like we always do when law enforcement comes around. These weapons aren't common, but they aren't unheard of either. I don't know what you might find in the Heavies, but I do know that the killer couldn't have gone far, and they wouldn't have given up a gun worth a fortune like this."

I tipped my hat to Huff and made my way to the heavy door. "If I have more questions, I know where to find you."

"Call ahead next time," Huff said. "I'll put you on the schedule."

Chapter 6

AFTER A ROUGH RIDE in a too-cold cargo compartment, I stepped off the chain back into the Heavy Nicodemia night.

The difference between the two beads was shocking. Haven was a city of the middle class. People worked their day jobs and slept at night. Heavy Nicodemia worked and played in equal measures at all times. It was filled with the constant noise of a living city from tip to tip, always.

A dropbox near the exit from Customs contained a slender slip of paper with an address written in Retch's scrawling handwriting. No hint about what I'd find there. I set out down the spiral. About halfway, I walked along the spoke road toward the darker outer edge of the district. It felt good to stretch my legs after a day at the firing range with Blaize and Huff.

As the district grew darker, I set my attention to my surroundings. The streetlights didn't illuminate me, but that didn't put me at much of an advantage here. The dim red lights barely outlined the shapes moving through the shadowy streets. Men in long coats walked beside scantily clad women.

Women in form-fitted bodysuits blended with the textures of the dark gray bricks. My size made me a focus for the attention of a group of teenage boys, but I suspect it also kept me safe from them. I could hear them muttering under the crimson glow of a nearby lamp. They knew I didn't belong.

Retch's address led me to a building with an unlabeled set into a red brick façade. A pair of burly fishermen outside kissed so passionately it might have been their last day in Nicodemia. They didn't even pause when I brushed past them and pushed open the door.

If the streets outside had been a playground of light debauchery and sin, then the inside was something else entirely – a twisted orgy of pulsing lights and thrumming music. The electronic bass throbbed so deep I could feel it in my groin. It hit my chest so hard it made breathing difficult. All around, flesh writhed, and slick sweat filled the unfiltered air.

"Hey stranger," said a voice near my ear.

I turned to see Retch wearing a pair of slender jeans and a mesh shirt. "Aren't you a little young for a place like this?"

"Aren't you a little dour?"

"I prefer to think of myself as serious."

Retch grinned. His pupils were dilated, and he had the kind of slick disconnect that I tended to associate with hard liquor or cheap drugs. "Cut loose a little, Demarco. You could use a break."

I opened my mouth to protest—I was there for work, not pleasure—but all that came out was, "I could use a drink."

He led me through a maze of flesh and sin to a side room where the penetrating beat of the low-fi music was slightly abated by heavy walls and thick curtains. A woman in a top hat and green-tinted glasses served drinks from a rack of a dozen unlabeled bottles.

"Whiskey," Retch said.

"The kid'll have a soda," I said.

The woman eyed me through her tinted glasses. I wondered briefly what she thought of me—a giant among these Heavies—but she shrugged and poured our drinks. Retch didn't complain about the soda, making me wonder if it really was a non-alcoholic drink.

"What have you got for me?" I asked.

He frowned. "Work, work, work."

"I spent the day shooting guns at a wall," I said. "I think a little progress in this investigation would do me some good."

"Did you kill it?"

"What?"

"The wall." He flashed that loose smile again. "Did you kill the wall by shooting at it?"

"No."

He punched me on the shoulder. "That's what I mean, Demarco. You're always too serious. Let's just have some fun for a while. Like old times."

"I remember old times. It involved you pointing guns at me."

"And that didn't get us anywhere either, did it?" He leaned close. I could smell the sweet of his soda on his breath. "And what's the common denominator there, huh?"

"Kid, if I could take guns out of the equation, I'd do it."

"Maybe you'd better have a chat with Trinity about that."

I would. I wasn't looking forward to it, but interfacing with Trinity needed to happen sooner or later. The key was I'd want to have as much information as I could before going to see what the computer knew. That would make it more likely that I could come away with something useful.

The music changed, morphing into a high buzz of thrash metal. The lights changed with the tune, but the other patrons in the room didn't seem to notice. They leaned closer to each other to whisper nothings. It felt profoundly uncomfortable to witness the intimacy in a way that not even the raw flesh from the other room could compete with.

"You need to unwind a little, Demarco," said Retch.

I closed my eyes. The kid was right, of course. He was always right about this kind of thing. "You shouldn't be here," I said.

"I'm used to people telling me where I shouldn't be," he said. He raised his hands over his head, showing off his gloriously masculine body. It had taken a lot of work and some serious hormone replacement to get him comfortable in his body. I had helped him get what he needed, but the Church and Trinity weren't so supportive. "Yet. Here. I. Am."

I tipped my glass to him, because I couldn't think of anything better to do. "I should have brought you today," I said. "The antiques dealer had some pretty interesting goods."

"I think we both know I'd probably have stolen something."

"If you had, you'd be in the kind of trouble that doesn't even bounce off someone like you. Those folks have clout. Makes me nervous." The last of my whiskey burned on its way down. "You know, I think I could go for another one of those."

This time, Retch returned with two bitter beers, keeping one for himself. I decided it was best not to protest. Best not to look down the neck of a free beer.

Hours passed in the club, and the clientele grew milder. A release of tension rolled through the sex-crazed crowd. A trio of singers made their way up to a small makeshift stage, and the thundering music gave way to live performance. It wasn't much better than the canned stuff, but it was quieter. Retch laughed at the outfits people wore, as if it was all there for his amusement. Maybe it was.

Then, when I couldn't stand it anymore and the whiskey threatened to roil my empty stomach, I asked, "Why are we here, Retch?"

A wide smile split his face. "I *knew* I'd get you to cave."

When I blinked, my eyes almost didn't have it in them to open again. "You were right," I said. "I needed to relax a little."

Retch leaned close and whispered conspiratorially, "Rawls wasn't a workaholic. He was a"—he made rude gesture—"aholic."

It made sense. Rawls had a dull home life and a stressful job. The guy needed to unwind from time to time, and night-clubs like this unnamed rave provided an outlet for the darker side of the recycler technician. It was a whole branch of his life that the blue had failed to explore. I leaned forward and said, "Who?"

Retch didn't twitch. "Doesn't much matter in a place like this, does it?"

"Someone like Rawls doesn't come to places like this for transient hookups. He's a connection former."

"Like you?"

"Basically the opposite of me."

The corners of Retch's lips flicked up for a fraction of a second.

"A man like Rawls falls in love. I saw it in his history, and I saw it in the pain it caused his wife. He forms connections to people, and when his relationship with his wife faltered, he decided to connect to someone else." I waited as a particu-larly loud wail of music rang through the room. "So, who is it I need to talk to?"

"It's the hot bartender."

"You're lying."

He pressed his fingertips to his chest. "Me? Lie? You'd better go strike up a conversation with her just in case."

"Retch." I hoped he could hear the warning underneath the drunken slur of my voice. It was getting harder to concentrate on the facts of the conversation.

"It's not her," he admitted, "but you should probably still talk to her. She's a looker."

I did my best to resist the temptation to glance at the bartender. She was a tall woman with sleek black hair pulled back in a pair of braids. Her smile had the kind of radiant charm that made men fall and dimes roll. Our eyes met and I looked away.

Retch grabbed my chin and scratched my week-old stubble. "You'd better visit a decent barber before you talk to the ladies, old man."

"I've been busy."

"You wanna know who's a good barber?" His tone hinted at amusement. He pointed behind me to where a man in a silk vest and tight shorts chatted with a tall woman. "That guy."

I bit back a retort when my slow brain picked up on what he was telling me. "He's the guy?"

Retch grinned. "He's the guy, Demarco."

Chapter 7

CLIVE WHALEN sized me up with a raised eyebrow. He was hardly recognizable as the man Retch had pointed out the night before. He wore a shapeless gray smock and sensible shoes, and his hair was swept to one side and plastered in place. "How about a wash, a trim, and a shave."

"Whatever you got for a couple of dimes," I said.

"Trust me," he said, "the wash is for my benefit."

He took my coat and hung it on a rack in the corner. The place was empty that early in the morning, and I was a little surprised that I didn't detect a hint of exhaustion in the man's movements. He couldn't be operating on more than a few hours of sleep. I sure wasn't. He sat me in a chair, which he immediately spun around and leaned back into a sink. He whistled a tune as he scrubbed the filth from my hair.

I said, "Listen—"

"Shh."

He didn't speak again until he'd cleaned and dried my hair. As he made the first cut, he said, "I don't usually get folks like you in this early."

Folks like me? "It's a special occasion."

"Got a date?"

"Two dimes to rub together isn't special enough?"

"I suppose it might be." He pinched a hank of hair between two fingers and drew it out from my skull. "Few inches?"

"Make it respectable."

"Well, you're no fun."

"Fun's a matter of perspective, I guess." The first locks of hair fell to the ground. I debated whether it was a good idea to talk while he was still working. "Grant Rawls knew fun, if I understand correctly."

The barber froze for several heavy seconds. "Knew?"

He didn't know? "Killed at work two days ago."

Whalen grunted, then continued to work in silence. It struck me that he didn't seem surprised about the technician dying at work. The job shouldn't have been *that* dangerous.

"What can you tell me about him?" I prompted. "He have any enemies? How's his relationship with the wife?"

Snip. His hands were warm against my scalp. "You'd have to ask her."

"People lie."

Snip. "What makes you think I won't?"

"You have an honest face."

That got half of a laugh out of him. He worked in silence for several minutes, trimming more than a little from my mangy mane and buzzing the sides until they looked as neat as they ever had. I almost didn't recognize myself in the mirror.

"You do good work," I said.

"Now who's the one with the honest face?"

I rubbed my scruff.

"Yeah." Whalen placed a heated towel on my face. It

smelled like lavender. "We'd better get this cleaned up for you."

As he sharpened his straight edge razor, I caught a glimpse of him looking at me through the mirror on his wall. I said, "He died alone."

"Is that supposed to make me feel better?"

"We all die alone. It's the heartless end punctuation to the sentence of our lives. Some of us end with an exclamation mark. Others with a full stop. Rawls ended with a question mark."

Whalen worked up a lather, pulled the towel from my face, and started painting my chin. "You're looking for a *who*?"

"Right now I'd settle for a *why*."

The razor shone in the man's hand. His movements were swift and smooth, without a second's hesitation to give my coarse beard anything resembling a chance. Then, he paused the blade on my jugular. "She was a nightmare," he said. The blade moved and the tension drained out of the moment. "An absolute nightmare."

"The wife?"

"This is told in confidence, mind you," said Whalen. "There's a secrecy to a barber's shop that's as sacred as the Church."

"I understand."

"We didn't always sneak around," he said. "A few years ago, Grant and I would spend our days off together like any other best friends. We went to school together. Got in trouble." He paused. "Not the kind of trouble that interests you, though. Most Grant ever did was nick the documents from a recycler so we could laugh at the latest gossip. No, we never did anything that would make anyone angry enough to kill. Not back then and not recently."

"Then the wife came along?"

He ran a blade up my Adam's apple. "She was fine at first. She and I got along just great. Once they were married, though, Grant had fewer and fewer days that he could come around." He let out a sigh. "It happens, though, right? Friends drift apart. He coupled with someone and I was left here without a partner. Maybe it would have been different if I had someone. Then, later, when they had a kid, it got even worse. Liz didn't want me coming around at all then, not even just to check in."

"She forced you out, then. What did he do about it?"

"Nothing. We went years without seeing each other. Never even sent any messages." He touched my upper lip with his razor, scraping away the scraggly beginnings of a mustache. "Then I hear this rumor."

It was the kind of statement that begged for a question, but I let him supply his own prompts. Once a man like Whalen got talking, it was best to just let him continue. Any extra interruptions would just get in the way of a good story.

"I get a lot of rumors here. It's part of the job. Well, I hear this rumor about a rave downspiral. Wild parties— usually a lot wilder than my usual entertainment. It sounds good, but I never really got up the courage to go out on my own. I've got a good thing going on here. No need to do something that might mess with my Karma." He ran the blade along my cheekbones and perfected my sideburns. "But there's a rumor that Grant is going to these things, and *that* gets me curious. If straight-laced Grant is going, they can't be so bad, right? And I miss the guy. We always had so much fun together."

He took a step back and peered at me with one eyebrow raised. Returning to the sculpted corners of my face, he said, "So, I started going. I knew the moment I stepped into my first rave that I'd be back. It was wild. I could feel the pulse of it for days. Then I ran into Grant."

He set his razor down on the counter and didn't speak for a long time. His eyes got a far-off look, and he stared out into the warm tones of morning street.

"We weren't intimate before, but when we came together at the rave, everything just clicked. It was like it was always meant to be." He gave a slight laugh and met my gaze. "Maybe Liz knew something all those years ago, after all."

"Intuition, I suppose."

"Yeah." He toweled off my face and showed me my handsome mug in the mirror. "He wasn't going to leave her. We were fine as we were, Karma notwithstanding."

"Trinity can be a tad on the prudish side."

"When it comes right down to it, I'm glad we did what we did. It showed me that there should be more to life than work and sleep."

I plucked my coat from the rack and shrugged it on. "You'll keep going to the raves?"

He chewed his bottom lip. "I'll probably find a more socially acceptable way to meet guys, but it's going to take me a while to get that courage up. He was—" Whalen choked on his words.

"He was something special," I filled in for him. "Sorry for your loss."

I left Clive Whalen a blubbering mess on the floor of his small studio barbershop. I hoped for his sake he didn't have any customers soon, because he was in worse shape than I'd ever left an interviewee. He would have been better off if I'd busted into his home at night and bludgeoned him with a rubber hose.

And I still didn't have answers. All I had were more questions.

Chapter 8

LIZ RAWLS WORE a sky blue uniform complete with an apron with a donut logo emblazoned on the front. She bore her toddler on her hip and hurried toward her apartment building's main daycare facility, which was already bustling with activity.

"New job?" I asked, falling in step next to her.

"Grant's gone. Bills aren't."

The Karma system was built with the specific goal of valuing things like raising children and caring for family members. The original creators of the system designed it to provide everything a couple might need to raise their children properly without needing to resort to excess work. It was pleasant sometimes, remembering the lofty ideals of those who designed a system so poorly. Rawls was a single mother —not an unheard-of circumstance—and even with that slight variation, she would need to make compromises to her ethics that would erode her Karma over the next months.

Either she needed a way to contribute to society in some

other way or she would find herself living at the gritty bottom of subsistence.

She chose work. That meant leaving her kid in daycare.

"I have a few more questions," I said.

"I figured."

"What's that supposed to mean?"

"It means you look like the kind of guy who asks too many questions and doesn't like the answers."

Accurate. "I won't take much of your time."

Rawls shouldered her way into the daycare.

I followed. Children of all ages shouted and ran. The place stank of vomit. It wasn't any worse than an average daycare or school facility, which meant it was a horror like few I'd seen in the grand city of Nicodemia. A line of parents looking to drop off their children formed in front of a cluttered desk.

"You got till the end of this line," Rawls said. "Then I gotta go to work."

"What can you tell me about Clive Whalen?"

She blinked. "Trouble."

"Dangerous?" I knew he wasn't.

"Yeah," she said. Interesting. "Yeah, he was dangerous. He had Grant mixed up in a whole lot of trouble before they finally broke it off."

"When did that happen?" A parent checked in, and we shuffled forward another space. There was a shout, and a ball zoomed past my face fast enough to break the sound barrier.

"Years ago." She shifted the toddler on her hip. The kid struggled, having finally decided that he wanted to be part of the chaos. "Little bit after we married."

"And Grant hasn't seen him since?"

Again, she shifted the toddler on her hip. She turned to watch a pair of kids as they ran past, but I could see that she was only pretending at distraction to give her more time to answer. Finally, she said, "No."

I watched her twitch. She knew that I knew she was lying.

Another parent finished checking in, and Rawls stepped up another space. There were only two more families before us, and the line was moving fast. "I wasn't my husband's keeper." She hefted her kid on her hip. "I have enough trouble with this one, and Grant had his own life."

"I thought that life existed only in the confines of your building."

"And work. He always spent a lot of time at work."

"Was he stepping out?" He was, but did she know it?

"He was ambitious." Her jaw clenched like she was trying to bite the words in half.

"But he never seemed to get ahead." I sidestepped as a kid brushed past, running from a couple of boys in sports jerseys. The line moved forward. "He was stuck."

She fixed me with a half-lidded gaze. Somewhere, a baby cried. "People don't always get what they deserve, officer."

"I'm not the blue," I said reflexively. "You can talk to me, and I won't tell them anything they don't need to know."

She hit the front of the line and worked with the daycare worker to hand over her toddler. With surprisingly little drama, the kid separated from his mother and ran to the shiny fiberplastic toys across the room. When Rawls exited the chaos of the daycare, she deflated visibly. The vital life force that had made her a proud warrior-mother now left her a tired, empty soul. True to her word, she turned to leave without further discussion. She'd given me my chance, and now she was going to leave.

"Liz." If I was going to get anything from her, I needed to shake her down, but a niggling little scrap of my soul told me not to reveal her husband's darkest secrets. She had enough pain as it was.

She stopped, and the morning foot traffic flowed past her like a stream around a boulder. "I knew," she said. "I knew they were back together. The sex. The raves. All of it. But he always came back to me. To his *family*. That's what was important." The only hint of emotion on her face was the slight softening of mascara around her eyes. "They used to run a documents scam a long time ago. Did you know that? Before we were married, those two got into some dark stuff. Could have cost Grant his job, but that ended when he married me and I made him give it up. They never went back to it after that."

"Are you sure?" The words were dry on my lips.

She stared at me from across the street. The cold light of late afternoon cast her features in stony contrast, like the statues of some long-dead civilization. She might have stared at me for a millennium without ever giving an inch.

"He loved you," I said. "Didn't he?"

She left without another word, disappearing into the crowd as I stood in stunned silence. Liz Rawls had known about her husband's dalliances. She'd known about the raves, and she hadn't told us a single thing in our first interview. Why had she hidden that information from the police? It hadn't escaped me that she'd only spoken once I'd promised not to alert the blue. There must have been something more that she was hiding—a big lie hidden beneath all the little lies.

My brain could only work as fast as my feet hit the cobblestones, so I walked. I moved upspiral at first, traveling along the middle streets of the long arc upward through Heavy Nicodemia. Even my short visit to Haven left my knees aware of the contrast in the pull of gravity. Every step made my muscles ache, and every pause made my knees creak. But I moved forward and sorted through the scant evidence I'd collected.

Grant Rawls's relationship with Whalen didn't seem to matter. This wasn't a jealous rage killing. Her behavior didn't fit that. It also wasn't his lover ending their relationship in the most violent way. Both of them came across like they were dripping with guilt—neither of them felt right for the murder.

Plus, how would either of them have come across the weapon? Not only would they need access to a gun, but they would need to be dumb enough to fire the thing where it could be traced. *Should* be traced. Even in the church, it should have been possible to trace the weapon. Trinity would keep close track of such a dangerous weapon. My visit with the Fortners told me that the weapon used was rare. Exceedingly rare. Only the wealthiest of the wealthy would have access to that gun, and firing it would be like pointing a big blinking arrow right back at the owner.

Something was still missing.

My feet took me to the outer rim of the station, where the shopfronts were all cloaked in the gloom of poor artificial lighting. The cobblestones were covered in soft lichen at the edges of the streets and the air smelled cool and damp. I scratched my chin, surprised to feel smooth skin there. The barber had done good work, I thought. It was going to take some getting used to.

If not the wife or the lover, then who? My mind kept coming back to the alleged document scam the men had once toyed with. Were they starting to go back to their old ways? Liz didn't catch me as a jealous killer, but what would she have done if she'd learned that they were risking her family— her son—by continuing an old, dangerous scam?

Still, it came back to access to that weapon. She didn't have it. Not without connections that I still wasn't able to establish.

But what if their scam had angered someone else? I walked faster. The street passed by as I spiraled upward along the long perimeter road. I passed through the warehouse district behind the Cathedral of Saint Francis of Assisi, and saw the members of Retch's young gang lingering at the edges of shadows. They all knew I wouldn't bother them, but they still watched me like I was a shark moving through dangerous waters.

Across the road in front of me darted a pair of cats: predators playing with prey. Still, I walked, and the mystery grew.

It was time. I needed to speak with Trinity.

The ship's AI wasn't a person. It didn't go through all the muddled-up mess of establishing a true identity, even though some people preferred to anthropomorphize it like that. It was more like a complicated maintenance routine. Hundreds of them, really, all tangled up together in a weighted program meant to support the bead until the end of time. Its focused goals were body, soul, and community, and each bead took its own angle at supporting those three competing ideals.

There weren't many places I could speak directly to Trinity's full interface, but the one that felt most appropriate was the site of the murder. It was a liminal space—a space between worlds. In this case, the worlds were that of the living and the dead.

The warehouse district spat me out near the utility entrance at the back of the massive cathedral. A large hauler sat in the wide alley behind the church, and several men and women worked to unload a long fiberoak bench—a new pew for one of the side chapels. They didn't bother to look at me as I passed them on my way into the church.

Priest Cano, however, caught me immediately. "Looking rather handsome, Jude."

I ran my fingers through my short hair. Maybe the haircut had been a mistake. "It'll grow out," I said. I didn't slow down in my walk.

She sidled up next to me and took my elbow in her gentle grip. "We need to talk."

"Did you tell the blue everything?" There was no chance she'd withhold information, but I had to ask.

"They're back," she said. "Scanning for the weapon."

"Good." If Trinity didn't pick it up coming out of the cathedral, then there was only one obvious place it could be. I stopped walking and turned to the priest. "Is there a problem with that?"

"Besides an invasion of our sanctuary? No, not really." She drew a deep breath. "Jude, I can't stop thinking about how dangerous this is."

"Murder has a tendency to be that."

"This is a *church*. Religion is sacred. You know that. We're not supposed to be monitored in here. This is outside the view of Trinity, but only as long as we can keep this space safe on our own."

"You don't want people to get the idea that this is where they can get away with crime."

"They *already* have that idea," she hissed. "And it's been happening for a while now. The new gangs in town don't have the respect for the church that the old gang bosses used to show."

"Reminiscing for Saint Jerome?"

That got a wry grin out of her. "You never would have thought it, would you?"

"Do you think this killing has to do with the new gangs?"

"I told the blue that I thought so. They were going to follow up on it."

They would. I trusted Anders to get that much done, and Smalley didn't seem like the type to overtly ignore a decent tip. "I'll ask Anders about it."

"I'm worried about you too," she said.

I rubbed my smooth chin. "Worried I'm too dangerously handsome?"

She stepped back. "I'm afraid that you've been in over your head so long you've forgotten what breathing feels like."

I fixed her with a hard look that I hoped was more warning than fury. She knew not to push me into returning to the Catholic faith, but here she was jostling right up against the line. Next step was to ask me to attend Mass. Pretty soon she'd have me singing in the choir.

But I wasn't ready for that. I wasn't ready for any of it, not even the very first step toward reconciliation with the Church. She saw that in me. She *had* to have. Something in her pushed her to push me, and it was fine as long as she didn't cross that line. Not now.

"I'm in over my head, Priest," I said, "but there's work down here below the surface. Work that needs to get done, and I'm the only one to do it."

Cano fixed me with those bright priest eyes, which dug right down into my soul. "Are you, Jude? Are you really?"

I left her and entered the funeral chapel.

Chapter 9

THE CHAPEL WAS in worse shape than last I'd seen it. Evidence tags dotted every surface, fingerprint dust anointed the pristine fiberoak pews, and half a dozen cops crawled all over the place looking for more evidence. When I entered, Anders flagged me down.

"Trying to squeeze a little more blood from this stone?" I asked.

"Other leads dried up, and the info you sent about the weapons gave Smalley some ideas."

"The Inspector thinks you'll find more here?"

"It's about the gun," Anders said. "Small-caliber, lead-bullet handgun. It should be easy to track, right?"

"Sure."

"I mean, it is. No doubt about that. Any standard scan would tag the thing as soon as it left the cathedral. Evidence shows that it never left the chapel."

"What evidence?"

"Evidence." Anders rapped his knuckles on the pew. "It's *here*, Demarco. We're *positive* that it didn't leave the chapel."

"You would have found it."

Anders shrugged. "These churches have dozens of hidden compartments and little nooks."

"Sure."

"It *could* be here. If we can find the murder weapon, we'll be making progress on the case."

"If you find the murder weapon here, you're not making any progress at all. You need to tie it to a killer."

He rapped the pew again, this time hard enough that I worried he would bruise his knuckles. "I need to tell you something."

"Demarco!" boomed a voice from the entrance. Smalley strolled in, a scowl on his red face. "Where have you been, young man?"

"I'm working on my follow-up report," I said.

"This is an *investigation*, son. We will be thorough or we might as well do nothing at all."

"I'm trying—"

"This better be good," he snapped. "I'm missing my niece's fifth grade graduation for this.

A glance at Anders gave me nothing. "You were right about the Fortner family. They were experts on lead-bullet weapons."

Smalley bustled past me to look at the officers scouring every inch of the chapel. "We need a break in this case, Demarco."

"You're not going to find it with all your coppers locked in this room."

"None of the gangs have the resources for something like this," Smalley said. "Swordfish. Crimson Hawks. Screaming Jesus. Penultimate. They're all small time. No real threats."

Screaming Jesus was Retch's gang. They weren't exactly harmless, but it bothered me lumping in his ragged group of kids with some of the truly dangerous rising organizations. And he was calling them *all* harmless.

"We'll find that gun," said Smalley. "Anders, show him the breakdown."

"Uh, yes sir." Anders drew his tablet from a pocket and showed me a series of images. "Every one of these dangerous weapons has been tagged, peace-locked, and categorized. The information is shared between beads, and the owners and locations are all being verified."

The images that flashed by were crisp and well lit, but they weren't the kind of sales images purveyors of weaponry tended to use to sell their wares. I would bet my last dime they came straight from Customs, and every single weapon had been thoroughly tagged and registered.

"Peace-locked?" I said as I peered at the images.

"They drill a hole through the barrel," said Anders. "Then they damage the firing pin and weld the trigger. Customs does this on every gun they discover, and there is not a single registered lead-capable weapon in Heavy Nicodemia that isn't peace-locked in this way."

Sure enough, the guns in the images all had a bright weld at the base of the trigger. A small hole in the barrel near where a person's fingers would guarantee a painful experience for anyone trying to fire the weapon. I took it on faith that the pins were broken. That much wasn't visible in the images.

"It's impossible to repair damage like that," said Smalley. "Any attempt leaves the metal weak and encourages the kind of failure that'll take off fingers." His mustache twitched with something like a cruel smile. "There are records of criminals trying it."

The guns scrolled past. Some were the matte black of the Fortner collection; others were silver or even gold. A few looked like they were more for show than function, but most had the simple, efficient weight of machines meant only to kill.

"Fortner's weapons weren't peace-locked like this," I said. "I fired them myself."

"Fortner has a unique exception," Smalley said.

One of the guns on the screen looked familiar. It was a Smith & Wesson Compact like the one I'd fired at the range. I remembered how the weapon didn't quite sit right in my hands when I shot. It was too small and simply not built for hands as big as mine. Anders flipped to the next image.

"Hold on," I said. "Go back." When he scrolled back, I peered at the image. It had clearly been peace-locked. The hole in the barrel was a cold dot in the matte-black steel. I closed my eyes and tried to remember the weapon I'd fired. I'd held it in my right hand, and the weapon had been exquisitely maintained. There was a small indent on the grip shaped like a crescent moon. "This is one of the weapons I fired."

"Can't be." Smalley pointed to the hole in the barrel. "If you fired this weapon, you'd lose a finger."

I wiggled all my intact fingers.

"This gun is registered to an Agatha Hilde," Anders said. "She collects antiques and owns several old weapons."

"Have you checked in on it?" I asked.

Anders replied, "I dropped in yesterday for a quick inventory. She wasn't exactly cooperative, but she showed us everything that was registered."

"I'm telling you"—I shook the screen in front of Smalley's face—"this is the weapon I fired. The one you found must be a forgery."

Smalley snatched the screen from my hand and frowned at the image of the weapon. "Trinity checked the provenance. We know exactly where it's been for the whole hundred years since it boarded the station. We even weighed it. Exact match."

"That's something I'm going to need to clear up with the big machine." I stepped up to the front of the chapel where a track led from a platform to an ornate fiberoak altar. "Anders?"

"You got it." Anders sent some commands to his tablet, and in a moment, the wall behind the altar opened. Normally, this would be when the casket and corpse entered the recycler, never to be seen again. That wouldn't happen this time. I stepped through the gaping maw to the edge of the afterlife and waited as the wall quietly slid closed behind me.

"Trinity," I said.

The walls exploded into blue brilliance. A word across the surface read, *Reconcile?*

"Not today, Trinity." I strolled around the central processing slab where casket and body would be broken down to their constituent molecules. "I have a few questions."

"Proceed." The voice was digitized and deep. Its low vowels rumbled in my chest. On the screen across from me, the blue figure of a faceless human appeared. Trinity always made these figures for me to interface with when we spoke, but they were always different. I wondered if this was indicative of anything.

"A weapon was fired in that room right next door. Lead bullets. Where did that weapon go?"

Trinity might block the information from the blue, but speaking directly to the AI in a liminal space like this gave me the authority to override such edicts. It also gave me the ability to understand *why* those edicts were in place, and after a few days of searching, I was starting to get pretty curious.

The wall's blue lights swirled for several long breaths, and then, in a smaller voice, Trinity said, "No guns have been fired."

"What do you mean?" I stepped closer to the wall. "There were bullets. There was a body. This was a murder, Trinity, and the gun is one that fires bullets that could endanger the station."

"No guns have been fired in this vicinity."

"Then where?"

"No guns have been fired."

I swore. This was harder than I'd expected. There had to be another angle. I tried to sort what I had learned through the investigation. "Show me where Liz Rawls was at the time of the killing." When Trinity didn't respond, I rattled off the window Smalley had given me for the murder. "And give me an hour on either side."

I despised the idea of prying into her life like this. The expectation of privacy on a space station was almost nonexistent, but people believed that only the AI could pry into their private lives. When I learned that Trinity would show me whatever I wanted, I had decided not to abuse the power, even if it meant doing all the legwork for an investigation with my own lousy legs. If I was going to look into someone's feed, then I needed a damn good reason.

A wireframe diagram of the Heavy Nicodemia bead appeared on the wide screen. It was shaped like a child's top —wide in the middle, narrow at the top and bottom. The inner spiral ran all the way up and down, except for spaces at the very tips designated to either Customs at the top or the maintenance tunnels below. Then, two-thirds of the way down, a blue dot appeared.

"I meant the whole time period," I said.

The dot didn't move. With a wave of my hand, I zoomed in closer.

"She wasn't kidding, was she?" I mused. "She really didn't get out much."

Liz Rawls's dot wasn't moving because during the entire window she didn't leave the apartment. That eliminated her as the person who pulled the trigger, but that didn't help much. I *knew* in my gut that she hadn't done it. I ran the same search for Clive Whalen. Jealous lovers did make the best murderers, but Whalen didn't strike me as jealous. No, those leads were both dead-ends.

That left the inkling of an idea about the documents. If Rawls had stolen documents, he might have drawn the ire of someone with the kind of power it took to own a truly dangerous weapon.

"Trinity," I said. "Before he worked on the cathedral recycler, Grant Rawls fixed a bunch of other recyclers through town. It's what he did. Show me the list of locations that he worked on in the past week." It would have been between the time that he last saw Whalen and the time of his death.

The list was almost entirely small-scale residential areas, restaurants, and public spaces. Only one stood out.

"What's the story on this government records office?"

"Document destruction facility twelve," said Trinity. "Expired employment contracts, flight records, legal briefs, and confidential task outcomes."

Not sure what any of that meant, I said, "Did Rawls remove any documents while he worked on the recycler?"

"Affirmative."

I blinked. He might have taken something important. Dangerously important. "What did he take?"

"Grant Rawls left the facility with a confidential task outcome assigned by Kaegan Fortner."

"Fortner? You're kidding me."

Trinity was not kidding me. The guy with all the guns suddenly looked a whole lot like the guy with the motive. Pieces clicked together in my head, but there were still a lot of holes.

"What was the task?" I asked.

"Data has been purged." This was standard. Trinity's working memory was only so big, so sometimes data was archived on paper. After a decade, if it wasn't needed, those records were destroyed. Fortner's task, whatever it was, had been deemed low enough priority that the records were scheduled to be destroyed. Unfortunately, the recycler broke —something that happened fairly frequently in the poorly maintained facilities of the Heavies. Rawls had arrived to fix the machines, and maybe on his lunch break he'd picked up a little light reading from the backlog.

Then he'd kept it. Blackmail leverage on one of the wealthiest people from Haven. The blackmail had led to a backlash, and Kaegan had sent someone with a gun to kill Rawls.

Only, why had he used a signature weapon like that? Nothing in what I knew about Kaegan Fortner pegged him as sloppy. He hadn't even made the mistake of meeting with me.

His kids, on the other hand, might make the mistake. Blaize was just the kind of guy to send a message with a lead bullet. At the very least, it meant the blue had another lead in their case, and it meant I was going to need to track the family down for another conversation.

"Kaegan was assigned a confidential task?" I asked, wanting to be completely certain.

"Negative."

"Then what did it have to do with him?"

"Kaegan Fortner assigned the task and approved its outcome."

"Assigned it?" I furrowed my brow. Kaegan wasn't in a position to be assigning tasks, was he? Usually, these confidential tasks were a function of the Trinity requiring human intervention outside of its scope. If Kaegan was assigning tasks, did that mean he was an agent? "Who did he assign it to?" I asked, unsure if even that basic information would be saved. "Where did this task take place?"

Trinity's screen blurred, and a single recovered image appeared. It was a picture of Rawls in a cafe late in the afternoon. He had a cup of black coffee next to him, and the document on the table clearly showed the name "Kaegan Fortner" and two other pieces of relevant information.

The first thing I noticed was the location. Whatever the task was, it took place on the *Benevolent*—the same ship that had killed my parents. My heart hammered in my chest. The bitter acid of anxiety bubbled in the back of my throat. It all then turned ice cold. There on the bottom of the document, I saw the partially obscured blur of a single word.

It read: *Demarco*.

The machinery of the recycler—the liminal space where I currently spoke with Trinity—clunked. Something boiled through the pipes, a hole in the center of the floor opened, and the air started filling with caustic gas.

Chapter 10

"TRINITY," I growled, "open the recycler door."

"Recycling in progress," toned the voice. "Please stand by."

I pounded on the sturdy exit. It was the shining steel of a recycling encasement—the same steel that made recyclers difficult to work on in the first place. I cast around for anything that might help me escape, but there was nothing. The blue had already scoured the area for clues, so anything left behind from Rawls's work was gone.

"I'm still in here, Trinity," I said. "Shut down the cycle."

"Reconcile?"

"Dammit, Trinity, I'm not ready to reconcile." Reconciling might convince it that I was something worth not recycling, but it would mean stepping back into the world. "I'm not ready," I repeated.

Trinity made no response. A coffin-sized rectangle in the center of the floor opened. This was where the dead went when they were done hanging around for their grieving families. It was the first step for anyone not destined to feed the fish. Get broken down into constituent parts. Become part of the great chain of life aboard Nicodemia. It was the last good deed.

A flicker of blue drew my eye. Trinity's display glitched on one rectangle of the wall. The image was juttering and strange.

I got a thumbnail under the panel and pried. Acid ate at my esophagus with every breath. The air filled with ragged fear and my eyes blurred. My thumbnail broke painfully. I swore. Blood smeared across the flickering blue image on the wall—the genderless form that Trinity had taken for our conversation.

"Stop the recycler, Trinity."

The hissing changed. Another smell roiled through the chamber, this time sickeningly sweet, like a dive into the confectioner's oven. And it *was* an oven. The heat was unbearable. When had that happened? My head grew foggy. I grasped at the panel again.

"So help me God, if you don't stop this sequence I'm going to tear the guts out of this whole wall."

The panel shifted. My knee hit the floor before I realized I was dropping. I pried the metal plate free—it pivoted on one attached bolt. Behind it, an array of wires and lights swam like soup in my blurred vision. I coughed. In the center of the room, the enzyme fluid bubbled up into the pit. That was where it wanted me. This would return me to the great cycle.

"I won't reconcile," I said. My arms were so heavy. The big lump of fat I called a head wobbled on my neck. With my back pressed against the broken wall, I slumped. "It's not going to work, computer."

It had never done this before. I avoided liminal spaces when I could, but only because they were uncomfortable—not because they were particularly dangerous. At every breath, death dragged into my lungs. The sickening sweet now drowned out the acidic bitter, and all I felt was the aching numbness of the approaching end. The panel was too high to reach. My body wasn't working right.

"It's not going to end like this." I reached into my pocket and pulled out a pack of cigarettes. Fumbling them half a dozen times, I finally managed to light one and stick it between my lips. The dry rasp of smoke mingled with the enzyme gas and twisted my lungs into a knot. Next, I stuck the earpieces of my music rig on and set the music to random. A voicey guitar riff split the tectonic plates of my skull. "Better," I muttered. "Better."

It took me a moment to realize that it was playing Eric Clapton's version of "Knockin' On Heaven's Door." Appropriate.

"Reconcile?" Trinity's voice was a dull echo in the back of my head. This was as threatening as I had ever seen the strange AI. It had been designed specifically to avoid such threats, but then again, I always insisted on living outside the rules.

Dull fury burned in the space behind my chest. I pushed myself up, cigarette still burning in my mouth, and slammed a fist into the space behind the wall. If it was going to kill me, then I was going to cause it some trouble on my way out. "I'm not going to reconcile," I said. "Not now. Not ever." The components gave way under my blows. Fibersteel bent and plastic shattered. A piece must have cut me, because there was blood everywhere.

A hum like a thousand locusts sounded somewhere. At

first, I thought it was coming from my music rig, but it wasn't. I pressed my head to the wall and listened. It was faint, but the wall panels shook with it. The damp clung to my cheek where I touched the surface.

Then it burned. The flesh was slick where the damp enzyme ate my skin.

"And I was just starting to feel handsome," I said.

I wiped it off as best I could, but it hurt in a blinding, catastrophic kind of way. I swore and stared down at my bloody hand. It was doubled in my vision. Whatever Trinity was poisoning me with was more powerful than that final surge of adrenaline.

The wall panel. It swayed in front of me. Holding it in my short-term memory was like wrestling an eel, but some small corner of my brain understood that it was important. If Rawls had been working there, then maybe it was a critical system. It was my way out.

Darkness. All at once, the walls went black and the dull glow from below faded to nothing. Grasping, I found the hole in the wall. I probed with bloody fingers for something— anything—that might give me control over the recycler. The locust hum increased.

Then I saw them. At the corners of the panels around the room, insect-like creatures skittered free, lighting their way with an ominous blue that pierced right into my brain. One appeared at first. Then another. Then hundreds. They skittered along the floor toward me, then flew through the air. Shimmering wings made that locust sound, and their mandibles gnashed in anticipation of breaking this big old hunk of meat down to its constituent parts.

A spark snapped and burned my fingers. I pulled back and sucked my filthy hands. Below the pit in the center of the recycler, the glow returned. It was red, and the tiny blue lights swarming around me stood in stark contrast to its unsettling promise of hellish afterlife.

"Not today, Trinity," I growled, surprised at how rough my voice sounded. The mist in the air stung my eyes and clawed at my lungs.

I swiped at the bugs, catching one with the sleeve of my coat. It sputtered and fell, but ten more took its place.

"Not! Today! Trinity!" Taking the corner of my long coat, I netted more of the bugs, forced them to the ground, and crushed them under my heel.

Then, they stung. One landed on my neck and sank its sharp mandibles into my flesh. When I swatted that one away, another crawled into the soft flesh of my armpit and bit. Another took a notch out of my ear. I roared, but even I could hear that my roar was weak. Whatever the gas was, it wore at me.

I was on my knees, but I didn't remember dropping. I was on my stomach, but I didn't remember falling. Silence swallowed everything.

"Demarco!" The voice was so far away it might have been in another bead. The locust buzz was gone. Warm orange light washed over me.

Hands hooked under my armpits, one digging right into the stinging wound. I didn't have the energy to protest. I was dragged across the slick floor, and a vague noise in the back of my head warned me of the enzyme there that would eat my flesh. Destroy everything I had ever owned. Someone sprayed a pine-scented foam over my whole body. Neutralizing agent?

And Eric Clapton still sang about knocking on heaven's door. I had a pretty good feeling that I wouldn't be let in if I knocked on that door. Not tonight. Not ever.

"Reconcile." Trinity's voice boomed. Not a question, as it always had been. It wasn't even a request.

It was a demand.

And even in my addled, damaged state, the threat was clear.

Chapter 11

"HE'S UP," said a voice. It took me a moment to place it as Anders.

Against my better judgment, I peeled my eyes open. I was on a short cot in a drab room. The walls were fibersteel and a single door stood open to a well-lit hall. Anders sat in a chair by the cot, and a glass of water stood on a tiny nightstand.

"I'm in jail?" I asked. My voice made my head throb.

"No," said Anders. "I mean yes, but no, you're not under arrest."

I winced at his words, not because I didn't like what he was saying, but because they were physically painful. The memory of my time in the recycler was a smudge across a broken window pane. "What happened?"

"You stepped into a recycler," Anders said. He helped me prop up my head so that I could properly look at him. "It tried to recycle you."

I waved him off. "Trinity…"

But how much did I want to tell Anders? How much could I say? And *what* would I say? Trinity, the benevolent

AI responsible for all our survival, wants me dead? Trinity, the perfect machine that has kept the station safe for hundreds of years, has made a mistake? *Was* it a mistake? At the time, it sure felt like malice, but there could have been something else going on. The liminal spaces of the station were the only places that I could interface directly with the machine, but they were never *safe* places. Maybe I was just there at the wrong time when a cleaning sequence was initiated. It could have been a glitch in the programming.

"You know, a lot of cultures have used near-death experiences to speak with their gods," Anders said, "but I gotta say, I don't think it's a good idea."

"Trinity's not a god."

"And you're not a prophet."

I forced myself up into a sitting position and took stock of my wounds. My coat was gone, along with my music rig. Skin that was exposed to the enzyme was pink and sensitive, but it wasn't as bad as it had felt. My eyes were sandpaper. The nicks where the tiny robot insects had started to break me down were bandaged neatly. By the feel of it, there wasn't anything I needed to worry about, but I worried anyway.

"Your coat's ruined," said Anders. "We got that stuff off you right away, but the coat was already on its last threads."

"My music rig?"

"Salvageable." He pulled it from a uniform pocket and handed it to me. Rust paint flaked off the colored earpieces, and the labels were gone from the buttons, but some quick experimentation proved that the device still worked. That was something, anyway.

I let out a rasping sigh. Music was the only comfort in a big world of pain and ruin. If I didn't have the blues, I don't know what I'd do.

"You need to arrest Kaegan Fortner for Rawls's murder," I said.

"Don't worry about that," said Anders. He stood and leaned out the door to peer down the hall. "Smalley's on his way here. He'll explain everything to you and then you can be on your way."

What was there to explain? "This has to do with the *Benevolent*, Anders. It's all tied up together. Fortner. My family. Rawls saw a document—"

Anders put a hand on my shoulder, keeping me from standing. It was for the best, because the whole room started to spin.

"I get it," I said. "But you gotta listen."

"We got the killer," Anders hissed. "And your contract is up."

"You're brushing me off?" I said, forcing myself to my feet. "All this and you're not even going to listen to what I learned in there?"

"Smalley is ready to close the case." Anders stood between me and the door. "We're done."

"Am I under arrest or not?"

His jaw set hard and I could see the priorities battling in his head. He knew he couldn't physically stop me—not if I really wanted to walk away. That wasn't the only way he could detain me, though. "I'm asking you as a friend." His voice was a measured calm meant to placate an agitated beast.

It didn't work. "And I'm asking you to step aside," I growled. "As a friend."

He stepped aside and waved me toward the exit. There was a crease of hurt and betrayal between his brows and a hint of stress in the set of his shoulders.

The lights flickered when I stepped into the hall. Darkness rolled down the long white hall in a wave, pausing for a brief stutter of a heartbeat over my head before rolling away to nothing. I touched the wall as I walked, unsure of my own balance as I made my way down the hall. Everything was changing, and I didn't like it.

Doors lined the hallway, and each had a small window. I looked in each as I passed, but they were empty.

"Demarco," said Smalley from the far end of the hall. Anders watched from the open door of the cell I had just left. "You're going the wrong way."

I blinked. He was right. The direction I had picked took me deeper into the jail. It wouldn't lead to my escape. Instead of admitting my mistake, I continued down the hall, looking in each of the tiny windows.

"Demarco!" Smalley strode forward. "You listening to me?"

"I hear I'm not on your payroll anymore," I said. Another empty room.

"You're trouble, you know that, Demarco? I never should have hired you in the first place."

"You need to arrest Kaegan Fortner," I said.

"I'll do the arrests that I need," said Smalley.

Anders said, "Sir, more evidence—"

"Can it, Anders." Just before I reached the final door, Smalley grabbed my wrist and spun me around. His iron grip sent spikes of pain up the length of my arm. "Come on," he said. "We'll show you the door."

Anders said, "Demarco deserves to know the whole story."

"He doesn't deserve anything," said Smalley. He fixed me with a piercing glare. "If he so much as sneezes, I want him back in one of these cells. We don't want anyone else getting hurt on his watch."

"Did you find the gun?" I said.

"It's none of your—"

"There was another gun missing." That stopped him in his tracks.

"I never said—"

"If you didn't have the gun, then we wouldn't be having this conversation." I twisted free of his grip. He was either trying to keep me from moving farther down the hall or he was trying to establish some kind of physical dominance. Either way, I wasn't about to let him do it.

When he desperately made another grab for me, I knew which it was. I sidestepped him and looked in the final window.

"You were right about arresting Fortner," said Anders. "Only not about which one."

Anya Fortner wore gray coveralls and her hair was pulled back in a tight ponytail. She wasn't wearing any makeup, and her hands were folded in her lap. Behind Smalley, two more cops entered the long hallway.

"Demarco," said Anders in his most placating tone. "I really need you to leave."

I raised my hands, palms out.

Smalley jabbed me in the gut with one of his stubby fingers. "She came back down here, put the murder weapon on our desk, and made a full confession. You want to tell me someone else is guilty when that's the evidence you're up against?"

They led me through the building, past open floors filled with desks and a reception area decorated in drab blue. On the steps of the police station, I could see the bustle of activity as the blue rallied for another foray into the dark night—another battle in the war against crime.

The gangs were rising in Heavy Nicodemia. Smalley

didn't have time to deal with one little murder in one corner of one church. His whole team was consumed by the fight for the soul of the entire bead.

"Just one more gang," I said as they released me in the street.

"What's that?" asked Smalley.

"You're just one more gang. One gang in the never-ending battle for the streets." I waved towards the gathering troops. "The blue might be the oldest gang in the Heavies. That's all I'm saying."

Smalley's face went red, and his mustache twitched. "Listen here, Demarco. The force is all that sits between civilization and chaos. We did a good thing today. We caught a person responsible for a murder in the city's most sacred space. The priest is happy. The wife feels she's getting justice. The people know that there's order in the world and that nobody's going to get away with something as bad as this. They'll sleep tonight."

Smalley turned to leave, but I wasn't done. "You got into this job because you believe in the truth."

He stopped at the top of the stairs. Anders stood with the door open, watching me carefully.

Finally, Smalley said, "Sometimes the truth isn't enough."

"That's what I'm here for." I took a step back up toward him. "You could have let me die in there, Smalley. You and Anders pulled me out because you believed it was the right thing to do. People should be allowed to live. The truth should always be pursued."

He turned back to me. "What are you saying?"

"I'm saying, let me talk to her. Let me see if there's something else we can do to get to the bottom of this." I knew in my gut that Kaegan Fortner was behind this somehow, but I needed evidence. "Even a career man like yourself can see that there's more to the story."

He fixed me with a hard inquisitive gaze. "Off the books."

"Off the books," I agreed.

"You said there was a missing gun?"

"Far as I could tell."

"Come back tomorrow." His mustache twitched. "We'll have a conversation with her. No promises after that."

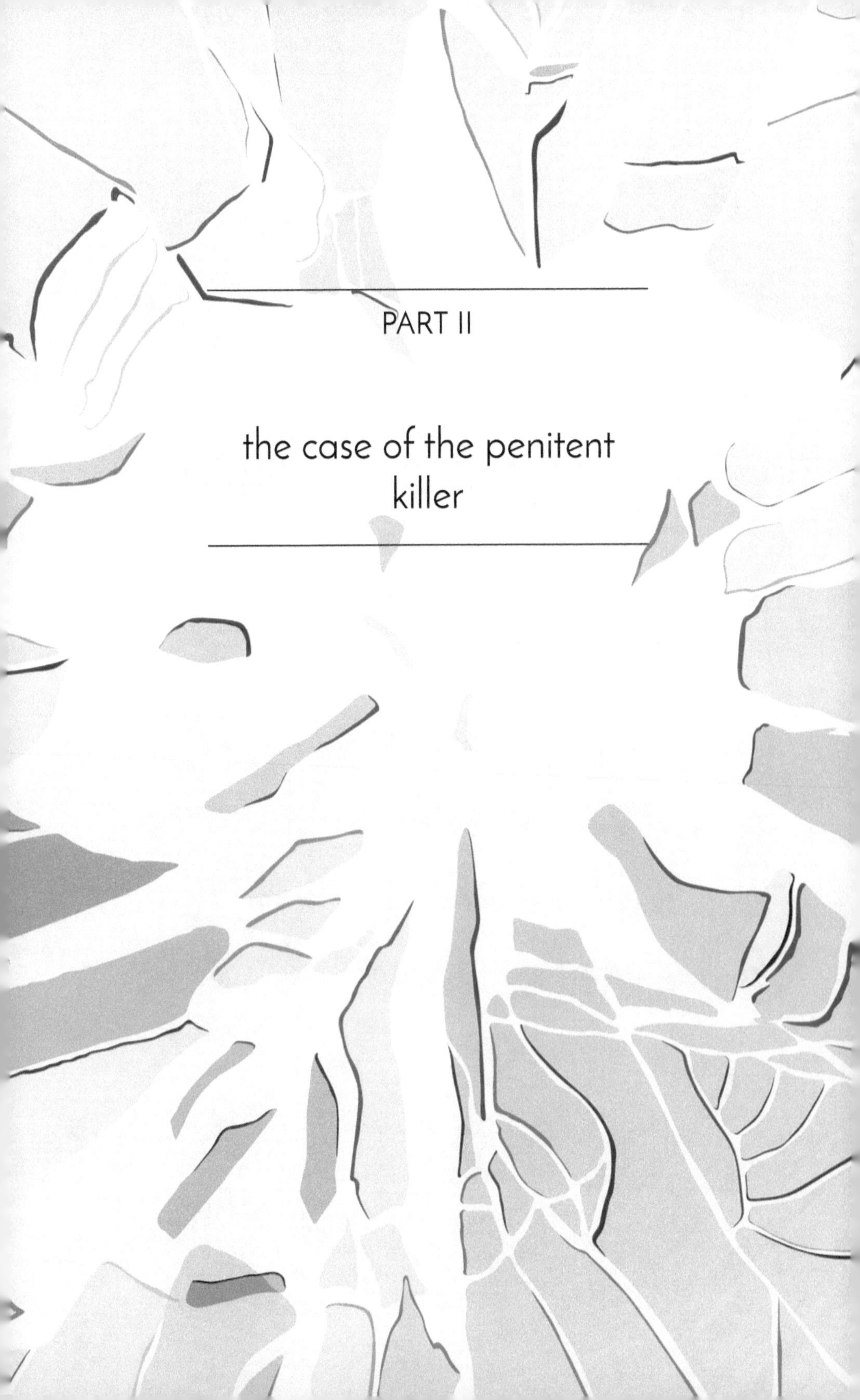

PART II

the case of the penitent
killer

Chapter 12

HALLOW NICODEMIA FLOATED UNBOTHERED by the weight of the world. Haven Nicodemia toiled against the ever-present draw of the depths below. And Heavy Nicodemia writhed under a grinding bootheel. Gravity was a hell of a metaphor in the city of Nicodemia.

The only gravity I gave a damn about was the ever-present pull of my only remaining family. Again and again, I returned to my sister, a steady elliptical orbit pulling me closer then flinging me away. We had been close for a while, it seemed to me, but I knew how elliptical orbits went. It was only a matter of time.

Cain, a dog big enough to have his own gravity well, pulled harder than anything Heavy Nicodemia had to offer. He'd been genetically modified and raised on the low gravity Magdalene Moon, got himself involved in some mild dogfighting, and then was rescued by my sister in the Heavies.

"He's *your* dog, Jude," Angel said as the monster nearly pulled my arm out of its socket. "Show him who's boss."

"*He's* boss."

She wheeled her chair after me as I left the diner. "Don't give him the treats until he heels."

Cain pulled.

"He's already eaten all the treats," I said.

"I gave you a whole handful of raw liver," Angel said, exasperated.

"I kept the hand," I said.

Cain pulled harder, and I stumbled after him.

"You're the boss," my sister called after me. "Act like it."

"I'm not the one giving orders." But she was already gone.

Cain had adapted exceptionally well in the Heavy gravity. Angel had hypothesized at first that he wouldn't take to the tougher environment, but he'd adapted with the help of some mild anti-inflammatory pills and a whole lot of treats.

"Good boy," I said.

He cocked his head, so I scratched behind his ear. His generous jowls wobbled appropriately.

"I'm better with people," I said to the dog.

"Is that so?" My sister's wife Helen rolled an empty cart around the corner and joined me on the path. She was a mousy woman with a bob of dark hair.

"You can *punch* people," I said. "Changes the dynamic."

The false sun was about to warm the sky, but the streets were still mostly empty. I'd slept in my room above the diner, and despite the chaos of the last few days, I almost felt well rested. The cool air that blew damp mist down the Heavy Nicodemia spiral drove straight through my thin button-down shirt, but nobody in this part of the city sold coats in my size. I'd need to tough it up for a few days until I could visit Haven.

"Cold?" Hellen asked.

"It's brisk."

"You need a coat."

"It'll warm up."

She elbowed me. "You're very optimistic, aren't you?"

"Not as a rule." Money was going to be a problem. Angel always sent me on my way with a full stomach, but agreeing to be off books with Smalley meant no pay and no support. I'd be scrounging what I could for the foreseeable future.

"Ask your sister for help," Helen said as she veered off toward the morning market, which was starting to form in the pre-dawn glow. Vendors sold vegetables and fish and warm coffee that smelled a thousand times better than it probably tasted. "She can afford it."

Cain pulled. I walked. We wove our way through the narrow alleys across the lower districts as the sky brightened and pedestrians started to spill from their towering tenements.

Something was very off with the Fortners, and Anya's easy confession didn't help. Even more important, something was off with Trinity. I didn't have any evidence that Trinity's attempt to recycle me was connected to the case, but it was the only place I knew to start.

Following Cain's lead—I *wasn't* the boss—I veered outward into the narrow streets, where there would be fewer eyes to silently judge me. The only people were those lingering after raucous nights as their recreational drugs slowly oozed out of their systems. Their haunted eyes followed me as I walked, and as I passed them, a few turned to follow.

Cain ignored them, so I ignored them.

Light bled from the central spiral into the outer reaches, but where we went it was more shadow than light. The cold buildings sprawled over gray streets where the lamps did their failing best to fight back the encroaching dark. As I progressed, I caught fleeting sight of the men following me.

I stopped around a blind corner, holding Cain as hard as I could to keep him from pulling away. When the two men rounded the corner and landed right on my trail, I said, "I've got one dime, fellas, and I guarantee it's not worth the fight."

"Who says it'll be a fight?" said the shorter one.

The taller one had a mop of tangled black hair, and the other had buzzed his male-pattern baldness down to stubble.

"We got no beef with you, Mr. Demarco," said the tall man.

"None at all," said the other guy.

Behind them, another half dozen men and women slimed their way into the alley. They all wore some variation on the same filthy rags—clothes ruined by the oil and dirt of some menial job or other. These were people who worked, as far as I could tell. Or, at least, they were people who had worked up until recently.

"Fleck said we all needed to know what you looked like," said the tall guy. "Now we do."

"Who the hell is Fleck?" I asked.

The men and women dispersed into the alleys as quickly as they had come. I tried to follow the tall man, who seemed to be the leader, but Cain wouldn't budge. When he finally moved, I decided to stick to more populated areas, as if that might help. Looping upspiral into the main drag, I angled past shopfronts opening for the long day ahead. Once I was back near the inner spiral, I angled down again.

"Angel appreciates all the work you put in with Cain," said Helen, rejoining me with her cart now of fresh produce for the diner. "Even if you're not good at it."

"I don't understand how she gets Runt so well trained." Runt was my sister's pitbull, and the most obedient dog to ever set foot on a space station.

"Respect," said Helen.

I threw an arm around Cain's neck. "You respect me, don't you, buddy?"

Cain growled. I retracted my arm before I lost it.

"It's a work in progress," I said.

"Hey help me unload this," she said when we got back to the diner.

With a fair amount of coaxing and the promise of more treats, I got Cain back into his pen in the yard behind the diner. Back in the kitchen, I unloaded the cart and put away the produce.

"Hey, Helen," I said, an idea coming to me. "What would you do if you needed ingredients that weren't strictly legal in Nicodemia."

"I would change my menu so that I didn't need that thing."

"But what if it was, I don't know, important to you. What if you had someone important coming by and they wanted something exactly as they had it back on Earth."

"What are you getting at, Jude?"

I almost fumbled a couple of heads of lettuce as I loaded them into the refrigerator. "Nothing much. I'm just wondering how a regular person would pick up illegal goods without raising flags."

"I wouldn't know," she said dryly.

"Oh, come on," I said, thinking of Anya Fortner and the weapon she had supposedly smuggled through Customs. "What would you try first?"

"Keep pushing, bro," said Angel from the doorway.

Crap. "Sorry, sis," I said. "Just trying to bounce a case around in my head."

"We're not your coworkers," said Angel. "We're not your criminal accomplices. We're not your flunkies."

"I've always thought of you as more of a goon than a

flunky, sis." The joke fell about as flat as a drunk on a Heavy Nicodemia night. "I think Trinity is trying to kill me."

Angel didn't even blink. "You've been gambling again."

"Is that what your neighborhood improvement group tells you?"

She fixed me with the kind of judgement a person only gets from family.

"A little," I admitted.

A raised eyebrow.

"Yesterday, in the recycler, it was like Trinity activated specifically so that I would get killed."

"Trinity doesn't even know you exist," said Angel. "You've explained this a dozen times. You're nothing. A blank space. So, why *wouldn't* it start the recycler with you in it?"

"It felt personal," I said, loading the carrots into the crisper drawer. Root vegetables grew well in Heavy Nicodemia, and carrots were one of the few crops Angel and Helen could get cheaply and consistently. "And it knew I was there. We were having a conversation."

"Promise me you'll stop gambling, Jude."

"This wasn't because of the gambling."

Helen stopped working. "From what I hear, Trinity's not just one big guy, though. It's a lot of little systems and they don't always talk to each other."

"Maybe one of those little systems has it in for me," I said.

"Sure, bro," said Angel. "It's going to have to wait in line, though, isn't it?"

Somehow that didn't make me feel better. The cart was empty, so I steered it to the door.

"Promise you won't go out gambling again," Angel said.

"I promise," I said, hoping she couldn't tell that I only half meant it.

"Not even if it's part of a case," she said.

Crap. "I promise."

Helen shot a warning look at her wife. "We really do appreciate your help, Jude." She held the door for me as I pushed the cart out. When I was almost gone, she took my elbow and pulled me close. "It's not about knowing how to sneak anything anywhere. It's about knowing someone who knows."

As I walked upspiral, the trolley carted the fishermen of the lower docks to their daily jobs. The flow of pedestrian traffic moved mostly downspiral, providing a constant stream of groggy, dark faces – people who didn't bother to raise their eyes to look at me. Heavy Nicodemia never slept, but in the early morning, before the awful coffee could totally take effect, it seemed like maybe it wanted to.

Knowing who to know. It made sense, of course. If Anya Fortner *wasn't* connected to a genuine criminal organization through her family, then she would at least need to know someone in Customs who could sneak the gun through.

Assuming she even needed to do that. The gun might have been in the Heavy bead already, being stored by the collector Anders and Smalley had located. If that were true, then it might have been easier to document that the gun hadn't moved.

I pushed the cart up to the marketplace and deposited it in the rack on the side of the street. A dime was ejected from the console, and I caught it before it could roll away. It was kind of Helen to let me collect on her deposit. I'd at least have enough to afford a meal later in the day.

By the time I left, the marketplace was crowded. Far away, the blue chased some poor soul through the crowded streets. I stepped from the cluster of stalls that made up the market back into the flow of traffic, narrowly avoiding a collision with an automated cab.

My sister was right. I was excommunicated. Trinity didn't know I existed, so it didn't steer away for my safety. It didn't turn the lights on for me or engage ventilation so that I didn't suffocate. There was no reason it wouldn't engage the recycler with me in it. Staying there had been a bad idea.

But it sure had felt personal.

Another cab blasted down the spiral toward the docks, narrowly missing me. I stepped closer to the wall. I needed to pay better attention. It almost felt like *that* near miss had been an attack. The rider shouted at me as he was swallowed by the amorphous crowd.

Unsettled, I continued on my long walk upspiral. The whole way, right up until I reached the drab brick building of the police station, I felt the eyes of the people watching me.

There was no more time to worry about the dangers all around me.

It was time to poke some holes in a confession.

Chapter 13

"I SHOT HIM," said Anya Fortner.

"Seems solid," I said.

"He had it coming." She wore a gray jumpsuit and her brown hair had dulled since I last saw her in the antique shop. Her sunken eyes watched Smalley closely. "Six shots. One of them winged him and struck the wall."

We sat in a stark white room in the middle of Heavy Nicodemia's police station. To my immediate right sat Smalley, and next to him Anders scribbled in a small notebook. The conversation was being recorded, but my presence alone was proof that recordings wouldn't always show the whole truth. Trinity would have me edited out before the data even touched permanent storage. Behind us, the mirror hid another couple of cops.

For an open-and-shut case, this interview sure was drawing a lot of attention.

"Explain to Mr. Demarco how it all went down," said Smalley.

Anya glanced at the table, where a gun sat in a plastic

evidence bag. It was the Smith & Wesson Compact, the same weapon I'd fired at the range.

"I already told you," she said, "Rawls had some kind of vendetta against my family. He sent me a message threatening my kids. When I went to confront him about it, he wouldn't back down. It was him or my family. Easiest decision any mother could make."

"Very plausible," I said.

Smalley shot me a dark look. "Even if that means you won't see your kids for a very long time?"

"Even if." Her eyes were dry and bloodshot. Maybe she didn't have any tears left to shed. Maybe there wasn't anything worth shedding tears. "Look, I did what I did," she said. "Can we just get on with the sentencing?"

Smalley consulted a tablet. "Your Karma isn't going to save you, Ms. Fortner. Even the best Karma doesn't let you get away with murder, and our records cast some doubt on your standing in the community." Nobody knew a person's exact Karma, not even the blue.

"I'm not expecting to get away with this." Anya raised her hands, palms out. The chains attaching her to the table clattered. "That's why I turned myself in."

I said, "Fair enough."

Smalley glanced at me. "Is that all you have to add, Demarco?" He said it in a tone that clearly indicated that he wasn't expecting me to have anything else.

And I didn't. Not really. But I *did* have a little conversational fishing to do. "Ms. Fortner, you were married, correct?"

"My kids have a father," she said.

"Two kids? Do they have names?"

"Most kids do."

"How old?"

"Six and eight."

"Boys?"

"One boy."

"A girl?"

"My eight-year-old prefers a certain amount of fluidity in gender. I don't see how this is—"

"Who killed the father of your children?"

She blinked. "I never said anyone killed him."

"Who?"

"I—I don't know."

I leaned forward over the table. I towered over the residents of the Heavies, but Anya Fortner was from Haven. She didn't wilt under my looming presence. "Was it the same person who helped you get that gun through Customs?"

"I just carried it through." She said it without a second's hesitation, which meant either it was a heavily rehearsed response or it was the truth.

"You carried it through." I picked up the gun. It felt light in my hand, and it had the same crescent indent on the grip that I had seen at the range. This was either that exact gun or a very similar twin. So close a forgery that it even replicated superficial damage. "One of the most dangerous and forbidden contrabands in all of Nicodemia, and you just walked through a Customs checkpoint with it." I slammed the gun down on the fibersteel table, shocking Anya so she pulled back. "No scans picked you up. No pat-downs. No detectors flagged anything suspicious. Trinity didn't even make a note that you were nervous on your way through. You did that while carrying this gun?"

"Yes." Her voice was small. "I carried it through."

"And back again."

"There are advantages to wealth, Mr. Demarco."

"And then, because it was so easy the previous two times,

you brought it through a third time just so that you could turn it into the blue along with your confession."

"I was afraid!" she shouted. "My family was in danger. What would you expect me to do? Confront this horrible man without a weapon?"

I stared at her.

"I wasn't—I wasn't planning on using it. It was for protection." All her rage and energy left her in a single long sigh. "I didn't mean to kill him."

"Tell me about Blaize," I said. In the corner of my eye, I saw Smalley's sour expression. He didn't know the direction I was taking this interview. Neither did I. "What's the history between you two?"

Anya's expression remained carefully blank. "He's my little brother. I practically raised him."

"You did a lot of the work around the house, didn't you?"

"You could say that."

"Would *you* say that?"

"Yes."

"And when something went wrong, you were always the one to clean it up. Not your father. Was your mother in the picture at that point?"

"Our mothers never stuck around long," said Anya. "And we never had much trouble."

"I find that hard to believe."

Smalley cleared his throat. "Do you have what you need, Demarco?"

"It's the curse of wealth, isn't it?"

Anya said, "I don't know what you're talking about."

"There's always something," I said. "The richer you get, the bigger the something."

"What are you getting at, Demarco?" asked Smalley.

"I need to speak with her alone," I said.

Smalley glanced at the woman. "I'm going to take a break, but Anders here will keep everyone in line." On his way past, he put a hand on my shoulder. "Keep it civil."

"Always."

Once he was gone, we sat in silence for a long time. My gut told me that Anya was hiding something, but I still didn't know what. If I kept fishing, I might figure it out, but Anya was a smart player in this game. She'd lead me by the nose if I wasn't careful.

Finally, she said, "Was that it?"

"I'm waiting for the truth," I said. "Sometimes it takes a while."

Her gesture rattled the chains on her wrists. "All I'm doing is telling the truth."

"It's not the right truth."

"The right truth? What the hell is that?"

"When I came by the shop yesterday, Blaize and Mia didn't think you were supposed to be there. Why were you there?"

"The blue warned me that they were sending someone around." She glanced at Anders, who was still taking notes furiously. "I figured it would be best if I was there."

"To prove you had an alibi."

"I wanted to show that I wasn't hiding."

"No," I said. "Someone like you—someone who gets the job done the way you do—wouldn't be rattled by something so trivial as a murder."

She fixed me again with her blank expression. "I'm good at masking."

"I bet."

"All I had to do was chat you up a little and send you on your way. It shouldn't have been a big deal."

"But Blaize wanted to take me to the range."

Her jaw hardened.

"No," I said, putting the pieces together in my memory. "That wasn't Blaize's decision, was it? It was your father. He didn't trust you to handle it, so he sent Blaize to clean things up."

"You're making things up now," Anya said.

"It's a habit I have when things don't make sense."

"I'm giving you sense."

I tapped the evidence bag with the gun in it. "Why isn't this peace-locked?"

"You'd have to ask the collector who brought it from Earth."

"And that would be?"

"Ancient history." She leaned forward and looked me straight in the eyes. "We deal in antiques, Mr. Demarco."

"You killed an innocent man, Ms. Fortner."

"That so?"

"Grant Rawls was a technician."

"People can be a lot of things all at once."

"Like how a mother can be a murderer?"

"Something like that."

"I'm not buying it," I said. "You say Rawls was a threat. What kind of threat could have affected you so badly. He didn't even live in the same bead."

"He was a threat to my kids."

"And Rawls, with a lousy job and no ability to travel to Haven, was going to be a threat to the kids of a wealthy family like yours?"

"Not all threats are physical."

"Not all mothers are murderers."

"I don't see your point, Mr. Demarco. Why are you here?"

I glanced at Anders. "Aren't I supposed to be the one asking the questions?"

"That was my understanding," Anders said.

To Anya, I said, "What did your father have to do with the wreck of the *Benevolent*?"

This time, she blinked. "Nothing."

"That was one," I said to Anders.

"One what?" asked Anya. "What do you mean?"

"A lie," I said. "I don't always catch lies, but sometimes it's so obvious it's like it's been stamped with a big red *X*."

"He had interests on the ship when it went down," Anya said. "A lot of businessmen lost something when the *Benevolent* went down."

"I lost my parents," I said.

"If only we could all be so lucky." Her furrowed expression hinted that she regretted the words as soon as they were free. "He's not the easiest man to be around."

"No, I suppose not, but you're not here to talk about him, are you?"

"I'm here to confess my crime and come clean under the law."

"A noble goal."

She scratched at the raw skin under her handcuffs. "Are we about done here?"

I tapped a cadence on the fibersteel table. I still didn't know everything I wanted to know, but to learn more I was going to have to tip my hand. Instinct told me it was worth it, but it was still unsettling. My words would make it back to Kaegan Fortner. I had no doubt of that.

"One more question," I said. "An easy one."

She motioned for me to continue.

With a glance at Anders, I said, "What did the documents prove?"

"Nothing," she said.

"Are you sure about that?"

"Positive."

I glanced at Anders. "That smelled like a lie. Did you think that smelled like a lie?"

"I don't even know what documents you're talking about," he replied.

"If the papers don't prove anything, then you really did kill an innocent man," I said to Anya. "No proof means no blackmail."

"Who said anything about blackmail?"

Rising, I said, "You have options here, Ms. Fortner. I'm no lawyer, but if you were pressured into what you did—"

"I did what I did," she snapped, her eyes locked on the gun in its evidence bag on the table. "If you're so caught up on finding the truth, maybe you should figure out why my kids were being targeted in the first place. Look into why my father was a target."

Leaving the room, I pushed through the door to where Smalley and two officers watched through a screen. In the room, Anders finished with some technicalities, taking down Anya's details with minute precision.

"Documents, huh?" grunted Smalley.

"It was a hunch," I lied.

"Lot of those going around."

I watched Anya interact with Anders for several minutes, unable to think of anything else I needed to know from her. Or, rather, anything else I thought I could reasonably expect her to tell me the truth about.

"She's guilty," said Smalley. "We have the weapon. Case closed. Anything else is a waste of department resources."

His words played over in my head several times before I picked up on the problem.

"Do you have the recording of that interview?" I asked.

"Sure." Smalley handed me a tablet from a rack on the wall. "Help yourself."

I took the device. The screen stayed blank, refusing to acknowledge my existence. I handed it to one of the officers. "Run this for me."

He gave me a skeptical look, but when he touched the screen, it flared to life. With a few movements he found the video.

"Rewind to her big lie," I said. I wanted another look at her face so that I could compare it to her earlier claims. Her poker face was good, but everyone had a tell.

The officer scrubbed the video back to the point where Anya said, "Nothing." Her left cheek twitched, and her blink was a fraction of a second too long. Then she glanced at the gun on the table, still in its evidence bag.

I let myself back into the interview room. I picked up the gun in its clear plastic envelope and hefted it. It was the Smith & Wesson Compact, and it exactly matched the one I'd fired at the range. Except it didn't feel right. Like the other guns I'd handled, this one felt oddly heavy, as if an item's weight were somehow proportional to its danger, but the balance was off.

Anya's eyes did not move from the weapon as I paced.

Anders said, "Demarco—"

I slammed the weapon down on the fibersteel table. Both Anders and Anya jumped, but Anders recovered quickly. Then he was shouting and trying to stop me as I slammed the weapon again and again, first on the table and then against the wall.

"Stop!" roared Smalley.

I stopped.

"What is the meaning of this?" He snatched the envelope

from my hand. Inside, the gun was a twisted pulp, with metallic fibers jutting from the ruined edges of its broken frame.

"It's a fake," I said. "Fibersteel construction with a lump of lead to get the weight right. It can't be the murder weapon."

"How did you know?" Smalley said.

I didn't. I had trusted my gut, and now I had to justify my risk. "The real weapon is excommunicated. It *has* to be." I knew from the sudden tension in Anya's shoulders that I was right.

"Like you," said Smalley.

"Like me."

Smalley stared at me for a long time, like he was trying to decide if he should arrest me or throw me out an airlock. Finally, he landed on a third option. "This doesn't change the confession," Smalley said.

"She's lying."

"I can't *do* anything about that." Smalley ran his fingers through his thin hair. "See, Demarco, that's the difference between the blue and some common gang. We have rules we must follow, and a solid confession like this isn't something I can push back on."

"She's *lying*."

"There's no proof of that."

"The real gun is still out there."

Smalley opened his mouth to respond, but I was right, and he knew it. "If it's Fortner's gun, then there's still legally nothing I can do."

"If it's Fortner's and we can show that it's not being properly controlled, then you need to confiscate all of his weapons."

"Anyone ever tell you you're too optimistic?"

"Every single day," I deadpanned.

"Find the real weapon for me, then," he said.

"Are you listening to me? It's probably excommunicated. Impossible to find."

"Find that damn ghost gun, and I'll bring you with me to the *Benevolent*."

I stared at him, my heart pounding in my throat. He was asking the impossible, but this was it. This was the deal that would get me the answers I needed—the answers I feared the most. All I had to do was find something invisible in a city full of lies. And Trinity wasn't going to help.

"Save me a spot," I said. "And I promise, if I find that weapon, you won't need to worry about it again."

Chapter 14

SOME DETECTIVES ENJOYED SIFTING through mountains of documentation. It beat chasing down suspects or wrangling answers from unwilling witnesses. The odds of an afternoon of research getting a person killed were very low.

Still, research could be a real pain in the ass.

Anya was right about one thing: if I wanted to know why the murder weapon wasn't peace-locked, I was going to need to do a little research regarding its origin on the station. I didn't want some ancient antiques collector, though. The weapon collector would be a worthless scofflaw too wealthy to be touched by the likes of me. I needed a different kind of scofflaw.

The person I wanted was that collector's contact in Customs. The weak link. The stain in an otherwise grubby line of security. If I could locate that Customs agent, then I could start finding some answers.

I was knee deep in the government center's paper division before I was caught.

"Excuse me!" said a woman in a blue blouse and horn-rimmed glasses. She held a document binder like a cudgel. "You aren't supposed to be here!"

I looked up from the fiberoak table, deep in the lower reaches of long-term document storage, surrounded by cardboard boxes. The dim lights had only come on when the woman arrived, so I had my lighter out to help scour the ancient archives. "I'm not supposed to be a lot of places, ma'am."

"Leave this instant," she said. "And is that fire?"

When I moved, the flame flickered dangerously close to a stack of loose flimsies. "What do you know about Customs employment records?"

She snatched my narrow lighter from me, flicked it off, and dropped it on the table. "This is not safe."

"These papers read like the who's who of drab nobodies," I said.

With her lower lip pressed hard against her teeth, the woman stalked from the room. I flicked my lighter back on and attempted to find my place as the lights faded behind her. On any other day I might have stuffed the papers in my coat and run off, but I was feeling charitable.

Instead, I read as fast as I could. Employment records had survived the first round of recycling due to their sensitive nature. Customs was a heavily monitored position, since discrepancies in the movement between beads—or from outside, for that matter—could have long-term consequences for the city. Even small additions of mass moving from the lower bead to the upper could destabilize the station's spin.

That's not even considering the socially destabilizing effect from importing weapons or other contraband. Trinity was a closed system—or as close to one as could be managed. A single corrupt Customs officer could cause problems a hundred years down the line.

Or sixty-two in this case.

The light bloomed in my little room. "There he is," said the woman, pointing at me.

A woman nearly as tall as me—and twice as hard—stepped into the room. Her meaty arms pressed at the brown security uniform, and her glare was so intense it seared my already-sensitive skin.

The paper I'd found was a table of employee attendance records. It showed absentee records for each employee, and it listed the most recent days that those employees had excused absences. I needed to cross reference it with the shipment arrival record for antiques from Earth.

The goon pressed a thumb to my lighter, putting it out.

"Look," I said, hoping to buy more time.

She grasped my forearm and neck and slammed me into the wall. Papers flew from the table, and one of the boxes at my feet tipped.

"I was trying to keep this neat," I said.

"This is a restricted area," said the woman in the blue blouse.

Grasping at the security officer's thumb, I managed to give myself enough air to say, "I'm only going to ask once."

"Ask what?" said the giant. "To live?"

"All I want is two documents."

"The answer's no," she said. She slugged me in the gut and dropped me to my knees.

"Throw him out," said the woman in blue. "Don't let him back in." She left the way she'd come, apparently done with my reasonable request.

Which was fine because I was about done being reasonable.

The security officer snarled.

"I need those papers." I drew in a deep breath, cracked my neck, and squared off.

The fight was fast. All the best fights are. Even afterward, thinking through the details of the whip crack of battle, I could never quite settle on the exact sequence of events. All I knew was that I swung for the fences. There was a quick feint involved somewhere. She jabbed my ribs at least once, because when we finished, I couldn't breathe for a full minute.

My haymaker landed on her temple. She slammed against the filing cabinet, spun, and hit the floor like a pallet of fiberbricks.

The lights faded to darkness, because why have lights on if there were no conscious people in the room?

"Thanks a lot, Trinity," I muttered. I groped in the dark and found the woman, checking her pulse. Strong. She'd be fine.

Probably.

I found my lighter on the floor and flicked a spark. Papers were scattered everywhere, and I could hear movement in the halls outside.

"Two documents," I said. But which two?

In a panic, I swept up the stack of papers. Navigating by the too-dim light of my flame, I shuffled through the stack, discarding papers as I ruled them out. Shouts rang up from behind me. Either they'd found the goon or she'd recovered already.

Papers flew behind me as I ran. Research was a real pain in the ass.

A pair of swinging doors opened out into a broad warehouse. Stacks of paper documentation lined the aisles while tall forklift robots retrieved and stored narrow boxes. The filing system was archaic and expensive. Whose idea was it to have paper storage on a space station? It was one of the more ridiculous things about Nicodemia and the other rotating cities. Then again, in a city this size, fraud was rampant. The only thing that could keep it in check was the existence of physical documentation. I flipped through another dozen papers.

"Aha!" I cried as I found one of the two that I needed. I stuffed it down my pants, having no better place to store an important ancient document.

Movement behind me prompted me to run farther into the warehouse. I dodged a forklift robot. As I did, the machine moved, slamming into my hip and sending my papers scattering again. The lighter flew from my hand and landed with a crack. Its tiny reservoir of fuel darkened the floor.

There was a dim glow in the warehouse. Somewhere close by, a search party followed my trail of discarded papers. I scooped the papers back up—wasting precious time.

Light flared all around. I ducked behind the robot, which continued to work. My eyes adjusted to the light, and I shuffled through the remaining papers. I'd *seen* the one I needed. I *knew* it was there.

But I couldn't find it. Paper after paper fluttered to the floor as I discarded those that were useless to me. I had planned to put everything back where I found it, but research was such an incredible pain in the ass, and I was done with it.

There! I found the document and filed it with the other one. I'd have to read them closely later, because—

What was that smell?

"Smoke!" someone shouted from one aisle away.

Then I saw it. A thin white tendril of smoke curled up to lick the bottom row of cardboard boxes. I stared in horror at the thing. This was a paper archive—presumably the worst place for a fire in all the city. A fire in here could rage through the whole archive in mere minutes, overwhelming the station's filters and choking people in their homes. The whole bead might need to be evacuated.

But it wouldn't come to that. Every shelf on every aisle was equipped with fire suppression. The one by my leg burst with a caustic flow of foam. I dodged—too slow. The slick foam coated the floor and my foot slipped. I landed face-first in the mess of discarded papers.

"There he is!" I looked back to see a couple of brown-shirted security officers pointing fire extinguishers at me.

Feet skidding, I scrambled forward. Another goon stepped in front of me. I shouldered him hard, slipped – foam still on my shoes – and barreled past. My arms windmilled. A robot veered in front of me. There was a clang as an extinguisher dented the shelf near my head.

Then I was up and running. I hit the exit at full speed and didn't slow down until I was swallowed in the government district's afternoon crowd.

I pulled the documents out of my pants and uncrumpled them. Where the spray foam had touched them, the ink dissolved and smeared. The paper was wet and weak, like sugar in hot water. Holes spread through the printed sheets, but I managed to flatten them and stop the damage from progressing.

They weren't ruined. Not completely, anyway. I breathed a sigh of relief when I read the faded text on both charts and cross-referenced the employees with their living situations. Only one name popped out as suspicious. A guy by the name of Pan Whistles. I had my Customs officer.

Research could be a real pain in the ass.

Chapter 15

RORY'S RAMSHACKLE was situated on the border between two lousy neighborhoods. It smelled of cheap whiskey, greasy food, and the damp sour sweat of the working class. When I got there a few hours after sunset, it was half full of dock workers.

I stepped inside and the place went quiet.

Rory looked up from the bar, where he was polishing a foggy beer glass with a clean towel. He was a wrinkled old bastard—more scowl than man at this point in his long life. "We don't need trouble, Demarco."

After a heavy pause, the crowd returned to the somber task of consuming whiskey. I bellied up to the bar and folded my arms on the table. It felt odd wandering around without a coat. It had been one of my only possessions, and now that it was gone, I was naked without that thin synthetic armor against the world.

"All I need is a bite, Rory," I said. "It's been a rough few days."

Rory didn't stop polishing his glass. "Used to be a fella would get some work done around here."

"Where's Jason, anyway?" I asked. It probably wasn't wise to remind the old man of his lazy son, but I didn't have many other options.

"Got a job," Rory spat. "Says he doesn't want to do this anymore."

"Working the docks?"

"Soccer," spat Rory.

"Good for him."

Rory slammed the glass into its rack and plucked another from the dishwasher. "I was going to leave this whole place to him."

I looked around the dive bar. A patina of smoke clung to the fiberwood walls. In the corner, a couple of drunks were on the verge of either fighting or kissing. "He's always wanted to play soccer."

"Oh, he's not playing," said Rory. "He's coaching. Got a bunch of kids together to form a team."

"Good for his Karma."

"How do you suppose abandoning his father weighs in?"

"I could use a meal," I said.

Rory served whiskey to a couple of men in filthy coveralls. I sat in awkward silence for a long time while he pointedly ignored me. After a while, he whistled to someone in the back kitchen and a while later returned with a burger.

"Much appreciated, Rory." I took a bite. It was low quality imitation meat and the bun was stale, but I was pretty sure it was top notch on his menu. "Do you want me to talk to Jason?"

The old man placed his hands palm down on the bar. "Listen, Demarco. I told you we had enough trouble without you coming here. Some folks are looking for you, and they're not nice folks. You'd better finish your meal and get moving."

"Trouble will find me whatever I do."

"Sure," Rory said, "but don't let it find you here."

I said, "Tell me where I can locate a guy named Pan Whistles and I'll be on my way."

Rory narrowed his eyes at me for a dozen heartbeats. Finally, he said, "Name's familiar." He punched a few commands into a nearby screen. The screen showed the image of a man with skin like a leather punching bag. Rory's eyes sparkled. "Sure, this guy used to come in back in the day. Old piece of shit."

"Where is he?"

"You're not going to like it."

In Heavy Nicodemia, there were a number of places a person could go after retirement. When they could no longer participate in the vast, complex world around them, most people moved in with family. Taking care of family was a great source of Karma, and elderly people with great Karma were actually a significant boon to the household. Services were easier to come by. Food was better. In theory, it benefited everyone to have Grandpa hang around until the day he died.

Not everyone *liked* Grandpa. Many families sought places for their loved ones—or not-so-loved ones—to live out the twilight of their lives. Farther up the spiral, there were homes like the Terrace, with an open view of the bustle of traffic. There was the Amber Garden, with its courtyard full of statuary, accented with a variety of plants. Some, if their Karma wasn't up to the nicer places, would stay at one of the tiny nursing facilities throughout the city.

Then there was the Pit. Nobody was left out in Nicodemia, but an elderly person with low Karma had no resources to gain placement in the nicer places. They'd get on waiting lists to forever find their names bumped down by more deserving members. They would plead with family to intervene, but it would never work. There was never quite enough. They would end up in the Pit.

I found the place down in the bottom arc of the long spiral, just before the entrance to the docks. The two-story building had a single long balcony, currently lit only by the dim amber of cheap bulbs. Even though it was late at night, several old men and women sat lined up on the balcony, sitting in cheap folding chairs or flimsy wheelchairs. They looked out on a narrow view of the docks where many of them had once toiled their long days in hopes of deserving a better retirement.

"Pan?" I called up to them. "Pan Whistles?"

The people ignored me and I didn't blame them. To them, my voice must have come from the darkest patch on a gloomy street. I might as well have been a ghost.

I stepped forward into the dim light.

A lady as ancient as Earth itself glanced at her partner, who remained perfectly still. "He's not interested," she said.

"I'm not selling." I knew the nursing home wouldn't let me visit so late at night. Not with low staffing in a suspect neighborhood. I found a corner of the balcony and jumped as high as I could, grasping the railing with my bruised hands. Heaving with all my strength against the heaviest of heavy gravity, I pulled myself gracelessly onto the balcony.

The lady watched me with bright eyes. She sat in a wheel-chair, but the man next to her was situated in a folding chair that leaned hard to one side. He stared forward and didn't react to my presence. From their vantage point, they could see a narrow view of the central hollow of the city. Far away, through the haze of the glowing night, the slanted arc of the spiral city bustled with light and noise and life.

I knelt on one knee to bring my massive form closer to the tiny old lady. "Not a bad view."

She licked her dry lips. "Could be worse. Down the row they only have a view of the docks."

"I've always liked watching the dockworkers do their thing," I said. "Salt of the Earth and all that."

"Bunch of lugs who don't know what's good for them."

"Were you a dockworker?"

"Farming fish ain't what it used to be," she said. "It's all side hustle and smuggling these days."

"And you didn't side hustle?"

Her eyes twinkled. "You either make a fortune in dimes or you dedicate your life to gaming the Karma system."

"Sounds like you got the worst of both."

She tapped her nose.

"Mind if I speak to this Pan Whistles fella?" I asked, sticking a thumb out at the guy next to her. He was even older—and even leatherier—than in the picture, but I was sure it was the same guy.

"Funny kind of name," she said.

"It ain't!" the man next to her exclaimed.

"He talks," said the woman. "Glory be, Pan talks!"

Pan Whistles grumbled like he was chewing cud. When he spoke, his rotten teeth showed behind cracked lips. "I talk plenty, woman. Wasn't going to talk to this fella."

"Well, you're talking now," she said.

"I won't take much of your time," I said.

"We got all night," said Pan.

I glanced at the door behind them. There was a window in it, but there was no light coming from inside the building. "They leave you out here?"

"Until the nurses come around for end-of-day routine," said the woman. "It might be a few hours."

It made me sick to see the level of care the elderly got in an area like this. Maybe it met their basic needs, but certainly nothing more. I looked down the row of balconies at the others. They all looked bored or asleep. At the very end, a nurse helped an old woman rise from her chair and shuffle indoors. Pan was right. We had a while.

"I need to know about your time in Customs," I said.

Pan's lips turned up in a sneer, but he didn't respond.

"I know that you had a deal on the side." I showed him the crumpled, half-dissolved papers. "The numbers show it pretty clearly, Pan. Your accommodations were far above standard Customs official, and look." I pointed at a barely legible row of the spreadsheet. "There are two entries for your storage facilities. Official and unofficial. You used that second facility to smuggle goods to someone."

The woman pressed her fingertips to her chest. "Oh, Pan, how could you?"

He shot her a dirty look. "We were all dirty back then," he said. "Including Midge here."

Midge's eyes twinkled with mischief.

Pan continued, "Not much I can remember anymore. I'm old."

"Anything you got could help."

He scratched his long fingernails on his knee, then held his palm out. "I could say the same thing."

Midge elbowed him. "Pan, the man just wants help."

"He's excommunicated," Pan said, not taking his eyes off me. "You saw him walk past the lights, didn't you? This here's a man in the dark. Even if I answer out of the goodness of my heart, it's not going to help improve my situation one bit. This man's a black hole gobbling up Karma."

He was right, of course. Trinity didn't acknowledge me, and therefore any good deeds sent my way wouldn't be paid back in kind. The man wanted dimes. Hard currency could help in ways Karma couldn't. Unfortunately, I was out of dimes.

"There's a woman in jail for a crime that I don't think she committed," I said. "You'd be doing her a big favor if you helped track down the origin of the murder weapon."

"Jail," Pan said. "That sounds like three square meals and an unlimited supply of reading material."

"Pan," Midge gently chided her partner.

"Yeah, yeah. The company's better here." The old man slumped.

"Word has it you were in charge of peace-locking guns at the Earth port." I leaned in close. "Seems some of those weapons got in without being disabled."

Pan's lips clammed shut so tight he might as well have glued them.

"Here's the thing, Pan," I said. "One of those guns shot someone, but murder's not so much my concern as is danger to the station posed by lead bullets."

"Lead?" asked Midge. "Like from the movies?"

"I saw the damage of those bullets as they punched into the fibersteel walls. There was a lot of kinetic energy there, Pan. Lot of risk if that kind of thing made it into the wrong part of the ship."

Midge said, "Trinity would stop it."

Pan sunk deeper into his chair.

"Who got those weapons, Whistles?"

He was silent for a long time. In the distance, the police blue flashed across the dark buildings. Pan's eyes glistened in the light.

Finally, he said, "It was only the once."

"Who was the client?"

His lips twisted like he was chewing on a lemon.

"I need to know who it was," I growled. I hoped the implied threat would be enough to shake his amnesia.

It wasn't.

Sometimes the end justifies the means, but people who figure that the end justifies the means are usually the kind of people who eventually get steamrolled by someone else's means. I didn't want that to be me. A tiny spark of conscience, deep down in the hidden part of my soul, told me there must be other ways. The tangled weave could be untangled in another way.

But the ends justified the means.

I took hold of Whistles's loose robe and heaved him out of his chair. As I shoved the tiny man toward the railing, Midge's tiny fists slammed into my back. It was only a one-story drop, but in this heavy gravity it would be a bone-crunching landing for the little guy. The people all along the row of balconies started to notice.

"Who was it, Whistles?" I hissed, my face inches from his.

"I don't know!" he cried. "Please!"

Midge changed strategies and took hold of my foot. It was a good move, but I simply had too much mass for the little lady. I pushed Whistles out a little farther over the edge. "You're getting real heavy, Whistles."

Tears streamed down his face. "Excommunicated guy," he said. "A real mook! I never got his name."

It made sense. "Where is he now?"

"Dead. Died a long time ago." Whistles glanced behind him at the short drop. "I swear it! The deal went south and he bled out in the gutter." His gaze flicked to something behind me. "Just like you're going to, you fucker."

I moved just in time to prevent my left kidney from taking the worst of it. Midge plunged the scissors into my side, and the dull blade scraped across my ribs. It was all I could do to shove Whistles back onto the balcony. The wound stung. Blood matted my loose shirt.

Midge was a porcelain doll facing down a bull. I could have taken the blade from her. I could have crushed both of them. Down the row, the residents were starting to shout for help, but help wouldn't come soon enough.

But I had what I needed—or at least I had everything I was going to get. I grasped the railing and lowered myself to the ground. It was far enough that I didn't want to jump, but as I eased myself down, Midge stabbed at my fingers, scissors clacking against the fibersteel railing.

"Asshole," she said as I dropped away and disappeared into the darkness.

Chapter 16

THE PROBLEM with tracking down a long-dead
excommunicated man was that there were no records. Not in
the digital file. Not in the paper file. The only shadow of the
person's existence was rumor faded over the long years.

People like me tended to not leave legacies.

Midnight had come and gone in the city that didn't sleep,
and the banter of traveling packs of Heavy Nicodemia's
disreputable population turned from pleasant revelry to
grumblings of discontent. The mood didn't only match my
own; it amplified it.

I slumped on a bench near Angel's Diner, which was
closed for the night. It's possible I drifted off, as the sky was
already starting to glow with hints of the morning's light.

Retch sat next to me on the bench. A dull ache throbbed
deep inside my wound, and when I touched the bandages, my
fingers came away wet.

"You need stitches again, don't you?" Retch finally said.

"I'll be fine."

"You know that's not true."

"It's impossible to give yourself stitches on your own back," I said.

"That's the closest you're going to get to admitting that you need help, isn't it?" He handed me a bottle of foul-smelling liquor covered in a paper bag. "Come on."

Retch wasn't exactly a trained medic, but he knew the basics well enough. I had taught him how to treat injuries and minor afflictions—better to have him taking care of his people than to let them manage on their own. The skills had made him popular among the Screaming Jesus gang, which was a little bit of a mixed blessing.

The medical center was empty that time of night. I took a swig of the liquor and lay face-down on the table in the small, sterile room. Medical consoles were one of the few pieces of technology that still worked for me, so I ordered up the wound kit and closed my eyes as it printed one.

Retch slashed through my shirt.

"Hey," I protested weakly.

"The shirt was already ruined, Demarco." He continued to cut all the way up to the armpit. "Your pants are ruined too, but I'll let you keep them for now."

"Thanks." It came out more like, "Shanksh." Maybe the liquor was even stronger than I thought.

It wasn't strong enough, though. Retch tore the taped bandage from my side, stoking the ember of a dull ache into a raging fire.

"Oh, tough it up, Demarco," said Retch. "Did Fleck's goons finally track you down or something?"

"I tussled with a pair of nonagenarians," I said.

"What the hell is that?" He jabbed the needle into my flesh and drew the long thread through.

When I could speak again, I said, "Nonagenarian is a

word they use to describe people who have survived long enough that they shouldn't be messed with."

"Huh." Another poke. "I assume you didn't learn your lesson."

"Probably not." I furrowed my brow. Thoughts were slippery and I didn't like it. "What's with this Fleck guy?"

"Willie Fleck," Retch said, as he pulled another thread through. "How out of touch are you?"

I tried to twist around to look at Retch, but he smacked me and made me lie flat. It was probably for the best. "I've heard the name," I said. "He's had his people watching me."

"He's an information broker. Kind of a self-styled kingpin."

The next several stitches didn't hurt at all. "Whash in this shtuff?" I asked, sloshing the booze around in its bottle.

"It's just vodka, Demarco." He pulled another long thread through. "I'm almost finished."

"Fleck," I said.

"Kind of an asshole. He's been gaining influence for a while now. There are a lot of idiots getting sucked up into Saint Jerome's power vacuum, though." He tied off the thread. "Anyway, Fleck's the kind of guy who likes to know everything about everyone. The asshole's been around since the beginning of time and he's always just kind of lurked around in the shadows. I think he's making his big play now, but who knows how long he's been setting things up."

The room swam around me, swaying back and forth until I was afraid I might fall off the table. I held up the bottle and stared at the paper bag containing it.

Retch took the bottle from me. "I swear it's just alcohol, Demarco." He set it down across the room. "I think you might have lost a lot of blood."

I motioned at the medical console. "Synth," I said.

Retch punched through the commands to order up some synthetic blood. He expertly inserted the IV and started to hang the bag.

"Wait," I said, blinking slowly. The edges of my vision grew gray and I struggled to form my words. "Test it."

"What?"

"Test the synth."

"Why?"

I couldn't think enough to understand, let alone articulate, why. Something didn't feel right. A hot coal of distrust burned in the back of my chest. I eased myself around so that I could lie on my side while Retch worked.

"Extract a drop," I said.

"I've never had to do this before." Using a needle, he drew a single drop from the synth blood.

"Mix it with my blood," I told him, gesturing at the plentiful supply I'd left for him.

He gave me a strange look but located a still-wet smear of blood to use in his test. The red synth blood formed a bead on the moist surface and shone in the white lights.

Then, it curdled like old milk, first stiffening on the surface, then warping as if it were twisting from inside. The whole effect took less than a minute.

Retch squinted at it. "What the hell?"

"Bad print," I said. "It happens sometimes." It didn't. Never in all my years as a trained medic had I ever seen a bad print of synth blood. It always worked, and it *always* was typed correctly for the patient. My head was a dark fog, thick with the desire to solve the mystery that threatened my life at every turn. The robots that got in my way in the warehouse, the transports on the streets, and now the medical terminal itself were all part of a plot to take me out.

And Trinity was at the center of it.

I blinked hard to clear my head, but when I opened my eyes again, Retch was finishing work on my wound. I must have lost time, because the dull ache had returned.

"I've packed it with med gel," he said. "Just like you showed me." Then, because he must have on some level understood what was happening with the synth blood, said, "I used supplies from the general stash. Generic stuff, so that we didn't need to use the printer."

"Good." My voice was a dull rasp. "Thanks, Retch."

"And I got rid of that vodka," he said. "I don't think it's good for you. Low blood count and all."

"Tell me again about Fleck?"

"Information broker," he said. "A real asshole, but the kind of guy you can trust to be an asshole, so it's not so bad."

"I don't think I know anyone like that."

He dabbed the flesh around the bandages, cleaning the dried blood from my pasty skin. "Turns out I may have a soft spot for reliable assholes."

My shirt was ruined, and Retch was right about my pants. They had enough blood that no amount of hoping or praying was going to hide it. If I wanted to swim with the sharks, I'd need a change of clothes. That old lady might not have hit any organs, but she'd done quite a number on me.

Outside, the cruel bright of morning shone through the haze of a false sky.

"You sure you don't want me to just go grab something for you?" Retch asked, eyeing my tattered clothes.

"I don't think our fashion aesthetics are anywhere close to adjacent, kid." The stitches felt tight when I walked.

Retch didn't try to hurry me. He just kept pace and helped me avoid areas with heavy traffic. "I know a place," he said.

We made our way through the waking streets of Heavy

Nicodemia. A dull throb in my side slowly blossomed into the full scrape of raw, exposed nerves. When we passed people in the streets, I got the sympathetic stares of someone recovering from a particularly exciting night of revelry. Maybe that's what it was. Me and the nonagenarians had a hell of a party. It was great.

It wasn't long before we reached Retch's destination. Grenadine Tie didn't look like the kind of place that would have clothes in my size. It had a neon pink façade, and the door was flat black. It looked like a nightclub or a particularly upscale brothel.

Brothel. It was definitely a brothel. Inside, scantily clad men and women lingered in the smoky haze of another night savored by the languid vampires of the lower districts. The eyes that wandered my direction took in my countenance as if I were no more interesting than a delivery boy on a Monday afternoon. Low murmurs of sultry voices danced at the edge of my hearing.

"Nance," Retch said, suddenly suffused with charm. "How about giving us access to the lost and found?"

A person of indistinct gender waved a chartreuse boa limply in the direction of a plain door near the polished bar. "Be my guest," they said.

"They're a disreputable bunch," said Retch on our way back to the door, "but I'd take disreputable over dishonest any day."

"You and me both, kid. Maybe that's where we went wrong."

The Grenadine Tie's lost and found closet was larger than it had any right to be. Several racks were stuffed to exploding with the musty leavings of a whole generation of customers. Retch crossed to a shelf on the far side of the room and removed a bin.

"No," he said as he pulled shirts out one by one. "It's not just a lost and found. This also serves as kind of a costume shop."

"You're going to dress me in costume clothes?"

"All clothes are costumes, Demarco." He tossed a shirt to me. It was a dark-blue button-down shirt with collars wide enough that even I didn't recognize the era in which it might have been fashionable. "It's an expression of who we want people to think we are."

"I want people to think I'm me." I tossed the shirt back.

"Same," Retch said, distracted. "Hey, do you ever wonder if there's going to be an end to this excommunicated gig of yours?" He tossed me another shirt.

White, this time. Reasonably modern. "There's a hole in this one," I said, poking my finger through a burn mark around the left nipple.

"Oh, that should go in that bin," Retch said, indicating the shelf next to me.

I folded the shirt and stuffed it into the bin. Next to that, a row of long coats hung on a rack, so I started flipping through them.

Retch considered a bright orange shirt but wisely tossed it aside. "I mean, I get it. Being outside the system gives you a certain perspective. It's useful. But you could help people from inside the system too. Just be a regular guy." He tossed me another white shirt. "Is there any way out for you?"

I held the shirt up to the light. It was entirely too transparent for my modest sensibilities. "I can reconcile," I said. "But that means forgiving myself for everything I've done, and I don't know if I can do that."

"Correction," he said. "It means *saying* that you forgive yourself."

My hand fell on a black coat. Full length and with

numerous pockets. The material was a heavy synthetic wool, and it came with a hood. I plucked the coat from the rack and shrugged it on. It was a perfect fit. "Reconciliation always comes with penance."

He eyed me in my coat for a good long time, then nodded his approval. Elbow deep in the bin, he was silent for a long time before he came up with a black loose-fitting shirt and a pair of slacks. Holding them up to me, he said, "Get dressed."

"All black?"

"You don't need to be the man who walks in the dark," he said. "From now on, you *are* the dark."

"Ominous." His words had a certain appeal.

"Plus," he said, "there's someone you need to meet, and you might as well look good for it."

I furrowed my brow, trying to figure out who he was talking about. Then it occurred to me—there was only one person looking to meet with me. "You're taking me to Fleck, aren't you? You lied to me."

He flashed me a crooked grin. "Disreputable *and* dishonest. *That's* why you love me so much."

Chapter 17

AND THAT'S how I found myself clean-shaven with a fresh haircut, dressed in black, and meeting with the seediest information broker of all Heavy Nicodemia.

Willie Fleck had the mustachioed face of a jovial grandfather and the hands of a man who worked for a living. His dark-blue shirt was fitted perfectly to his heavy frame, and his white hair parted down the left side of his smooth skull with immaculate precision. When he stepped into the rooftop cafe, his eyes twinkled at me with malicious delight.

It was mid-morning and Retch had long since left. He told me that the meeting had been arranged and that I didn't much have a choice in the matter. The bitter coffee did wonders to clear my exhausted brain, but the damp air atop the roof in the outer section of the Heavies made me regret all my life choices that had led up to that particular point. It was almost enough to make me swear I'd do better.

The place was empty except for Fleck, a couple of bodyguards, and the sullen barista sitting behind a fiberoak countertop. Across the rooftops, a flock of pigeons cooed their way through a world unfriendly to anything with wings.

"It's a miracle they've survived so long," said Fleck as he sat across from me. "What with them being made from food."

"Pigeon's a bit gamey," I said, "even for the residents of the Heavies."

"I'm sure you're right," Fleck said, "Some Earth cultures kept pigeon instead of chicken because they could range for food and always return to the coop. It made them useful in sieges."

"I hear you've been looking for me."

Fleck sipped his black coffee. His eyes twinkled. "You're not an easy man to find."

"You know where I hang my hat."

He raised an eyebrow. "A man like you could accomplish a lot in this city, Mr. Demarco."

"Because I'm excommunicated?"

"You're willing to stand up to the Catholics. That Church is a heavy blanket over the furnace of this city. It stifles us, Demarco. From what I hear, you understand that."

"I'm not against the Church, Fleck."

"You're not *for* it either. You're a free thinker. You ever notice how free thinkers are always the ones responsible for progress?"

"Depends on the kind of progress you're looking for."

"Management." Fleck took another sip of his steaming coffee. "I'm looking for a change in management."

My coffee had long since stopped steaming, and I scowled at it like it had betrayed me. "I don't think I'm management material."

He barked out a sharp laugh. "That's good to hear, young man. I'd hate to have too much competition."

I looked at him through narrowed eyes. I didn't like the

impression I was getting off this guy. It was the kind of saccharine grandfather vibe I expected when I saw the curls at the tips of his mustache, but he'd done something to it. He'd weaponized the grandfatherly joviality into something perverted. Dark.

"It's a dangerous position being on top of it all," I said.

He chuckled. "That's why I'd like to get on your good side," he said.

It wasn't common knowledge that I was involved in the killing of Saint Jerome, the previous crime lord of Heavy Nicodemia. Retch knew, of course. A few others, maybe. Anything outside of that was nothing but rumors, and rumors in Heavy Nicodemia weren't worth last week's catch-of-the-day.

"If you want to get on my good side," I said, "tell me about the gun that killed Grant Rawls."

"You're a historian now?"

"Provenance matters," I said. "In this station, there's no way that gun should be untracked. I want to know how many others there are and why this went unnoticed."

The curls of Fleck's mustache twitched. "It seems to me, the person you want to talk to is Anya Fortner."

"Then what good are you?"

He bristled at that. "Mr. Demarco, I don't know if you've noticed, but the bead is in chaos. The blue is on full alert every night. Robberies and gang violence plague the streets even during the day. Without proper self-governance and strong leadership, this city will not last."

I stared at him over the still surface of my cold coffee. "Body, soul, community."

"Trinity can only go so far. There have been other cities. Bethsaida didn't break all at once, you know. It rotted from the inside, just like Nicodemia's doing now."

Bethsaida as the bogeyman for the idealists of Nicodemia. It had fallen over a hundred years ago, victim to some catastrophic failure of its internal systems. The lingering fear that Nicodemia could go the same way was motivation on all levels of society. From the scientists who ran the asteroid-detecting systems to the janitors who kept the maintenance robots clean. "I thought you weren't a historian?"

Fleck said, "The signs are there for anyone looking."

"And the solution is to put you in charge?" It was the same argument Saint Jerome had once used. The basis of community didn't require perfection from its leadership—in fact, the argument was that it required a certain level of corruption. "I don't buy it, Fleck."

"No reason you should," said the older man. "I can only speak the truth. Can't guarantee anyone will listen."

I didn't like Fleck. Something lingered under the pleasant conversational tone in his voice. There was a threat there. An almost aggressive wave of likability that had the negative side-effect of triggering all the red flags in the back of my head. He was up to something, and whatever he wanted was something only I could provide.

"I'm listening," I said.

"The blue took one of my people. Guy by the name of Wen Cheng."

"The blue takes a lot of people."

"Word is you have friends in the force."

"I haven't had a friend since I was in grade school."

This got a chuckle out of him. "All I want is to talk with him."

"Call the station."

"Trick is, he doesn't want to talk to me." Fleck leaned back. The bodyguard near the door shifted his weight. There was something uncomfortable in the air and I didn't like it. "I want you to get him out for me."

I stared into the deep dark of my coffee. This was the problem with information brokers. Nothing came without a cost. And when it did, it was always a meager selection of the whole truth. I figured I could trust Fleck to tell the truth, but no way could I trust him to tell the *whole* truth. If I wanted that, I'd need to do the research myself. "What's Cheng in for?"

"Wrong place, wrong time," said Fleck. "The blue wrapped him up with a group of petty thieves."

"Then he'll go free soon enough. A Trinity review should set things straight."

Fleck looked at me with a flat gaze until my palms itched. "Things aren't straight, Demarco. They're not going to be straight."

"And Cheng's got something you need right away."

"Something like that."

In the distance, the blue lit up their sirens and mobilized. The wail of their vehicles paired with the red and blue flash of lights to illuminate the hazy interior of the city station. All around, the people of Heavy Nicodemia went about their business, and I had to wonder: was the city really failing the way Fleck claimed? Were things *actually* worse than they ever had been before?

The people of the Heavies had always clashed with the blue. That was a constant. Even back when Saint Jerome's criminal empire ruled the streets, there had always been a low level of chaos. Retch's Screaming Jesus gang had run a steady pickpocketing operation. Other gangs had fought and stolen. Any city across the vast empire of humanity suffered the same problems. Disquiet. Discontent. The very best humanity had ever done was hold a civilization three days from disaster. Cut off food supply, and any city across the history of time would collapse. Many had.

But Fleck was claiming something different. He was claiming a discontent that stemmed from the community that was growing organically following the rule of an oppressive crime lord. Were these growing pains or was society itself dissolving into the acidic slurry of the waste pit of time?

"To me," I said, "it all comes down to the gun." When he didn't respond, I continued. "It doesn't matter to me if there's discontent. People have a right to protest the sour taste of their daily lives. That's the soul of this place, Fleck. It's finally thriving after years of oppression."

"People are dying."

"People are *living*."

Fleck sipped his coffee.

"The gun bothers me, and you're right. I need to talk to Anya Fortner without the presence of the blue. If you think I can help you free your guy, then you can get me into that jail."

He considered my words carefully, then gave a slight nod.

"Here's what's going to happen," I said. "You get me in there, and I'll deliver your man. I get to talk to Fortner while I'm there, and you get to see your man walk free."

"How do I know you'll follow through?"

That's how it was with brokers. They needed fair exchange, and as far as he could tell, if I got into the jail with his help, there was no more reason for me to help him free Cheng. "You're going to do a little research for me."

His mustache twitched. "What do you need to know?"

"Pan Whistles didn't know who he gave the guns to. I need to know where they were between Whistles and Fortner. Somewhere along the way, someone made a decoy copy, and I want to know the history of that too."

Fleck sucked on his teeth. "I'm not a historian."

"But I bet you know one."

He swallowed the last of his coffee. "You have a deal, Mr. Demarco."

"You really think you can get me inside the jail?"

"The blue is always changing their security system," Fleck said. "And I happen to be good friends with one of the installers." Fleck strolled to the edge of the roof. Overlooking the city, he said, "I'm not just talking about discontent in the criminal population, you know. It goes deeper than that."

Standing next to him, I watched the city traffic ooze through the crowded streets. "Did you ever think that you might be the source of this discontent?"

"I pay my informants well, Mr. Demarco. You can't fault me for that."

"Iron can't fault oxygen for the rust."

Fleck held up a key. "The new system has only one physical door, and this will open it. The rest is fully automated, and I've been led to believe you'll have no trouble with that."

"It depends," I said, taking the key. "Automated defenses, I'm fine with. They ignore me. Automated doors, on the other hand, also ignore me."

"You shouldn't have a problem," he said. "And Demarco?"

"Yeah?"

The blue patrol sped past on the streets below, chasing someone on a scooter. Pedestrians scattered to avoid the dangerous pursuit.

"Midnight," Fleck said. "We'll have a distraction."

Before leaving, I pounded back the rest of my bitter, cold coffee. It was bad enough to curl my nose hairs, but in my line of work, caffeine is never wasted.

"Midnight," I said as I pushed past the bodyguard. "You'll have your guy."

Chapter 18

EVERY TURN around every corner gave me a prickle at the back of my neck. Fleck's people watched. It wasn't the same people every turn, but they were definitely there. A noodle vendor's eyes tracked me through the crowd. A man in a shabby suit walked half a block behind me for three blocks. A blues guitarist slowed his song as I approached and stopped playing as I rounded the corner. I wound my way upspiral all the way to the government district, then all the way down to the docks. They tracked me the whole way.

Midnight was an eternity away, so I found a broken piece of fiberoak and wrote, "Jude Demarco: All Things Found, All Things Fixed" in block letters. Then, I settled myself onto a bench downspiral from Saint Francis of Assisi, put in the earpieces of my music rig, and closed my eyes.

I was three-quarters of the way through a Muddy Waters album when a voice said, "Do you fix electrical junctions?"

Without opening my eyes, I tapped the sign.

"Yeah, I see that," said the voice. It was a young girl, and she carried a tremor of trepidation. "But can you do it without getting yourself killed?"

I opened one eye and peered at her. Older than I had guessed. Maybe a teen. Her long blonde hair was messily braided, and her clothes bore the frayed mark of hand-me-downs.

"Nothing I've done has ever gotten me killed so far," I said.

"Our apartment's been out of power for a week."

A week was a long time, even in Heavy Nicodemia. I didn't want to think about what they might have done to earn the bad Karma that would put them so far down on the repair priority list. "I take dimes or food."

"We have food."

I followed the girl down through the narrow alleys. As the afternoon sun beat down through the hazy sky, the crowds of the Heavies thinned, and the streets took a warm, almost friendly glow.

"Where do you live exactly?" I asked as we passed through the back end of another district.

"Not much farther," she said.

The streets grew dark, shrouded in the heavy grays of twilight, even in the middle of the day. I had walked every street in Heavy Nicodemia more times than I could count. My feet knew every cobble and every curb. There were no surprises for me in the slums of the lower quarter or the shine of the upper expanse.

This girl's neighborhood, however, was a surprise.

"This used to be called the Aspens," I said.

"That was a long time ago." The girl peered back at me. "You're still going to help, aren't you?"

The Aspens were one of the nicer neighborhoods in the lower quarter. Close enough to the docks for a short commute; not so close that it caught much of the smell. The neighborhood was named for the white-barked trees of old Earth, none of which grew well in the heavy gravity, but the theme was apparent in the styles of the benches and the shape of the buildings.

But the whole place was dark.

The girl pointed to a central square where all the streets of the district converged. A statue of an aspen tree stood in the middle of a dry fountain, and a panel in its side was torn wide open, its guts spilling out onto the fiberstone floor.

"Aster," snapped a man in dockworker's coveralls. He had a scruffy beard and big, meaty hands. "What are you doing?"

"Papa," Aster said, clearly taken aback. "Aren't you supposed to be at work?"

"Get out of here," the man said to me. "We don't need people like you."

Aster's fists clenched at her sides. "He can fix it."

"We don't need the trouble that comes with people like him," the man said. "Now get out of here."

Aster said, "There's no trouble, Papa. He just needs food, and he'll leave."

The man stared at me, his jaw clenched.

The girl was right. The district needed power. They couldn't cook or clean or live without it, and eventually the lack of air circulators would cause sickness. Already, the district lingered in the stench of garbage piling up in recyclers and filth failing to be cleaned up in the streets.

More eyes blinked at me from the shadows. The drab forms of a dozen people shuffled forward, attracted to the noise in the center of their little neighborhood. The Aspens used to be a nice place full of nice people. Not long ago, I'd wandered through the district, amazed at how well put together the community was. It had been pleasantly welcoming.

No more. I saw in the dark glower that these people didn't want me there. They wanted to be left to their own devices.

"Trinity might not come," I said. I didn't want to remind them that they were low priority, but it was the crux of the matter. The meat in the meal. "You're in a starvation cycle."

"We got food," one lady said from the back of the crowd. "We got what we need."

"That's the problem," I said, hands raised in supplication. "For some reason your community's Karma has dropped. Trinity sees that you have your needs met. Body, soul, community, right? Body is taken care of because you have enough food stored up. Stress like this actually binds your community together."

"And that makes this a test of faith," said Aster's papa. "We need to believe that Trinity will take care of us."

"No." I tried to speak over the rumble of the crowd. "It's not that. As long as you aren't in a true emergency, you'll stay low priority. It would be better if you were starving or threatened. As it is, there will always be a repair job of higher priority."

"Until our faith in the system brings our Karma up," the man said.

"Your faith isn't in question here."

The crowd's murmur rose to a dangerous level.

"Look," I said, "I'm sorry. There's a lot going on and it's possible you won't see any help for quite some time."

The crowd closed between me and the statue. They weren't going to let me near the junction to even assess the needed repairs.

"Please," I said. "You won't be judged negatively for letting me help. You're *never* judged poorly for letting others help. That's a core tenet of the system." People never understood how Karma wasn't a constrained resource. There could always be more good in the world, and letting others help was almost as good as helping others. When it was clear the community wasn't going to let me near the junction, I found Aster in the crowd and gave her an apologetic look. "Sorry, kid."

Then I left, feeling guilty for abandoning a community in need. Eventually, their situation would reach a crisis and Trinity would repair their systems. By then, they would be fully impoverished, with no resources to help them survive the next challenge. More of them might turn to crime, and the cycle would continue to drag down the community's Karma. It was a cycle that would feed itself until somebody figured out a way to break it.

And in all my years in Heavy Nicodemia, I had never seen anyone solve that.

Maybe *All Things Fixed* was more of a claim than I should be making.

Having failed to make it on my own, I did what any good detective would do. I went home to mooch off of family. The diner was dismal and empty in the late afternoon. The clanks of pots and pans came from the kitchen as Helen prepared for a modest supper rush. My sister rolled her wheelchair up to me and peered right down into my soul.

"All black, huh?" she said. "You supposed to be the angel of death?"

"How's Cain?"

"Lonely."

"I've been busy." Nothing like a visit home to make a person feel inadequate. "You know anything about Willie Fleck?"

"Different name. Same, same."

"Yeah, well, this guy's got his claws in a lot of cakes. Best if you steer clear."

She leaned forward. "Is this one of those things like with Saint Jerome where you told me to stay away while you were actually working for him?"

"That's not how I remember it."

"Yeah, well, for a self-proclaimed detective, you sure do have a lot of holes in your memory."

I said, "He wants me to break someone out of jail."

She laughed. It was a sharp, mean laugh, and I couldn't help but think it was directed at me. "That should be an easy one to turn down."

"I said I'd do it."

"You picked a funny time to start lying."

We sat in silence for a long time. She'd always been tough on me, but after the crash of the *Benevolent* over almost a decade and a half ago, she'd really soured.

But she was right. Going into the jail was a bad idea. There wasn't much of a prison system in Heavy Nicodemia. The truly unrepentant were sometimes shipped to the colonies to live out their lives, but everyone else was given a path to reform. They lived in the jail only so long as they couldn't safely be reintegrated with the community.

The jail was a death trap for me. One locked door, one failed escape, and I'd be trapped for good. As I had told Fleck, automated defenses ignored me, but so did automated doors. If I got locked somewhere, it might be weeks before anyone found me.

"Tell Anders if I don't come back," I said. "At least that way someone will come looking for me."

"And you'll be in a pile of trouble. You think we need that kind of stress, Jude? Things are bad enough around here."

"You have your diner," I said. "You have Runt and Cain."

"*You* have Cain," she snapped, "and you aren't training him very well. He needs attention, and that means you need to be around more."

I bit back a series of retorts that I knew wouldn't help my situation. "Please," I said through gritted teeth, "I just need you to convey the message if things go bad."

She fixed me with a cold stare. It was a stare only disapproving sisters could pull off properly. It cut right down to bone and turned me into a quivering pile of garbage.

But she relented with a slight nod.

"Clear out before the supper rush," she said. "I can't afford the tables."

Chapter 19

I SPENT an evening wandering the lowest streets of Heavy Nicodemia. My excuse was walking Cain, but I was the one who really needed to move. The big mutt found interesting smells on every surface, snuffling with his big floppy jowls until I finally pulled him along. He may have looked like a monster, but down to his core he was a hound, driven by his nose no matter what the cost.

Maybe we had more in common than I thought.

Then, after dropping Cain off in the yard behind the diner, I wandered the streets alone. I passed a thousand souls living a thousand lives with a thousand problems that I couldn't fix. Night fell like a damp blanket across the dockyard streets. Light from dim lamps followed the lonely travelers of the lower districts, shedding a mockery of the light of salvation over all who were lost.

All but me. I walked in the dark, stepping away from the light as best I could.

When midnight struck, I was a half block from the back

entrance to the jail. Blue patrolled the area with abandon, but the shadows swallowed me whole. They wouldn't find me unless I wanted to be found, and I wasn't that desperate. Not yet.

The distraction wasn't anything fancy. The crash of a cycle. A well-timed robbery. A fight broken out close to the jail. The patrols reacted predictably, and I had a straight shot to the jail. This was my chance.

I took it.

Cameras that wouldn't record me swiveled across a street shining with the damp of a recent rainfall. Alarms that would warn the blue of anyone else's presence ignored me as I approached the rear utility dock.

Using the key that Fleck had given me, I unlocked the big loading door. It slid open easily, and I ducked under, rolling it closed after me.

I was in.

The next door wasn't locked to keep people out. It was locked to keep people in. When I passed through it, I broke a match in half and jammed it into the latch, holding the door open. My heart skipped a beat as the door closed, but I verified that it would still open. I wasn't trapped. Not yet.

The jail was a single long spiral—an of imitation of the greater Nicodemia design. The cells ran up along the entire outside length, and the inner empty space was open so that a few guards could monitor the entire population with ease. Keeping to the shadows, I entered the spiral. Across the spiral, a guard worked his way upward. If he spotted me, he'd trigger the alarms. I'd be done.

Above, another guard made his way downward. If I wasn't spotted from across the open expanse, I'd be trapped in a pincher as the guards made their patrol.

An open cell would come in handy, but the first few I passed were occupied. Worn, sullen faces stared out from a distance more like a thousand miles than the few paces that they really were. My heart pounded. My back ached.

Then I saw it. An open cell. I made my way for it, skirting the edges of a pool of light cast by a dimmed lamp. My heel scuffed against the hard concrete floor, and I ducked through the light and into the cell. I forced my breaths to come long and slow as the patrol passed.

I needed a way to find Anya Fortner and Fleck's guy, Cheng. Fortner was a new prisoner. She'd be closer to the top, where the short-term cells were located. Cheng was recent too. The dock I had used came in at the middle of the spiral, making it easier for food and supplies to be delivered to the residents of the tall prison.

The second guard passed my cell on his way up, so I waited a long count and followed. It was my best chance to move upward without being spotted. I moved quickly through the dark spaces between lights, checking each cell as I passed for the prisoners that I wanted. At that midnight hour, most occupants were dead to the world. A few were awake but in what appeared to be a fugue state. I didn't know what had been done to them. They must have been drugged. The implications solidified into one more brick in the wall between Trinity and the teachings of the Church.

Then, only one turn from the top, the guard hit the end of his patrol and turned to walk his long distance back down. There weren't any open cells nearby.

But I saw Cheng sitting in his cell. Taking the key Fleck had given me, I unlocked his cell and stepped inside. Still paranoid about getting locked in, even though I had the key, I didn't close the door completely.

He sat there stock still in the shadows of the cell. The

lights were off, and the bars of his cage cast lines across his ragged face. Long strands of greasy hair fell across his face, and his eyes showed whites around a glistening core of amber brown.

I put my finger to my lips to indicate silence. I found a shadow in the corner to stand in, and stayed there as the guard approached. I sent up an empty prayer that the guard wouldn't notice the gap between the sliding cell door and the wall. That tiny sliver of dim light cut a line right across the cell and ran over Cheng's haunted face. One glance, and the guard couldn't help but notice.

His footsteps approached—a slow drumbeat of impending doom. Closer, closer.

He stopped close to the cell and cleared his throat. Through the bars of the cage, I could see the man's shadow of a beard in the dim hallway lights. His hat shadowed his eyes, and I couldn't see if they drifted our direction. A thousand rapid heartbeats passed before he started walking again.

Cheng said, "Fleck send you to finish the job?"

"The job's to set you free."

"Dead's a kind of free, I suppose. Better than most of this lot expects anytime soon." His voice came out flat and unaffected.

"What do they have you on?"

His only indication of emotion was a slightly rapid breath and an almost imperceptible furrow of his brow. "Had a cousin who went to jail once. Came out a changed man." He let loose a long sigh. "They always say reform is the focus of incarceration."

I touched his shoulder. "I'm here to get you out of here."

"Reform's not a real thing," he said. "Escape's not a thing. It's just compliance."

"Some would say that learning compliance is a kind of reform."

He finally met my gaze with his haunted eyes. "They've got me here for a long time, then."

"I'm here to get you out, but I need to find someone else, first."

He stared at me. "There's no escape."

"Sure there is. We go out the way I came in. Fleck will help you disappear."

"You don't understand." His hands shook where they rested on his knees. "Fleck's worse than this place. They let us out, you know. Down below, there are learning centers. Rec centers. We gotta earn it—"

"You shouldn't need to earn anything, Cheng. I looked at your record. You don't deserve this place."

"I'm a criminal."

"Wrong place, wrong time."

His chest rattled in something like a laugh. "They say Trinity's always watching, but Fleck is the one people worry about. I should know. I was his eyes not so long ago."

I leaned close to the man. "What did you see, Cheng?"

He clenched his fists. "I'm smart enough not to talk. He sent you to test me. Well, I'm passing that test. I'm not talking, no matter what." He met my gaze again, defiant this time. "Happy? Is that good enough?" His voice boomed in the tiny space.

"Keep it down," I hissed.

Cheng stepped up to his door. He gripped it in his fists and for a second I was afraid that he would slam it shut. Instead, he did something much worse. "Hey!" he called. "Hey guards!" He rattled the cage and banged as loud as his dull fists could manage.

"Dammit," I said. I gripped him by the shoulders and tore him away. "What are you doing?"

"I'm not leaving," he said. "I can't go anywhere. There's nowhere to go. Nowhere outside Nicodemia. Nowhere inside." He gripped my coat in his two hands and gave me a shake. "Don't you get it, mister? I got myself arrested on purpose. This is my last chance at escape." All traces of stupor vanished from his expression.

A spotlight shone from across the open space into Cheng's cell. By chance, I stood in a narrow shadow provided by the narrow cell wall. Cheng's face was cast in a sharp black-and-white by the intense light, the narrow crags of his features widening into chasms. I dropped him, pulling my paws out of the hazardous light.

"Send them away," I said. "I'll let you stay."

He stared at me with a dull expression. His eyes shone in the too-bright light. He placed his hands on the cage and flashed something like a half-drunk smile. "It's all right, guys," he said. "Bad dream."

"Not going to work your way down like that, Cheng."

"Aw, come on, fellas," Cheng said. "We all have our rough patches, right?"

The spotlight didn't disappear. It shifted slightly, so that I had to hunker back against the wall to avoid detection. For a long time, Cheng squinted out into the hallway, unable to adjust to such a searing explosion of light. Then, finally, with a thunderous clack of a large switch, the light disappeared, dropping us into pitch black.

Only then did I start to breathe. "You're right," I said. "There's nowhere to go that Fleck can't find you." It was then that I realized Fleck's real goal in sending me. He didn't want me to break his guy out of jail. All he wanted was for me to show up when the guy thought he was safe. After all, if Fleck could get one guy into the man's jail cell, then he could get another. I was there to put the fear of God in Cheng, and I didn't even need to rough him up. "He can't send anyone else," I said.

The whites of Cheng's eyes flashed in the darkness. He leaned against the far wall of his cell and sagged like the air had gone right out of him. "That bed right there was the first good sleep I'd had in a decade."

I stepped across the room, conscious of how I loomed over the shorter man, but unable to do anything about it. "I'm not here to threaten you, Cheng, and Fleck can't send anyone else. Not like he sent me."

He shook his head. "You don't get it, do you? He's every-where." His legs gave out slowly, and he sat on the cold floor.

"Then let me take you to the Hallows. His influence is less up there."

"There's no such thing as sanctuary," he whispered. He turned his head to look past the bars of his cage.

His words shook me. I'd heard them before, but from the priest. "Did Fleck have something to do with the murder in the church?"

Cheng's eyes went even wider.

"Tell me." Now I was really looming over him. My fists clenched. "If Fleck had something to do with that—"

"Nowhere," Cheng said. "Nowhere."

Then, he did something I didn't expect. Not in a million summers on a million planets. Cheng kicked the sliding door open. I lunged to catch it before it slammed, and when I did, Cheng scrambled through.

And by then I knew my mistake. There wasn't an escape for Cheng.

Except for one.

He vaulted up onto the railing and stood atop it, staring at me. Guards shouted from above and below.

The spotlight blazed against Cheng from behind, and he spread his arms wide. He was an image of the cross, burned into darkness by the ferocity of the spotlight. I had to raise an arm to shield my eyes.

"I'm sorry," he said.

And he jumped.

Chapter 20

THE GUARD RAN past Cheng's cell at full speed as if he thought he might reach the bottom in time to save the suicidal prisoner. The spotlight pointed down into the depths of the spiral prison, plunging me once again into darkness. I was gutted. Horrified. The man had thrown himself over the railing, but it was as bad as if I'd pushed him myself.

Fleck, I reminded myself. This was Fleck's doing.

It didn't make me feel any less guilty.

Tragic as Cheng's suicide was, I'd need to process it later. At that moment, it was a distraction. Tragic as Cheng's suicide was, I'd need to process it later. At that moment, it was distracting me. Fortunately, though, it was also distracting the prison. It was just the distraction needed for me to find Anya Fortner. I could only hope this conversation would go a little better.

Turns out it didn't happen at all.

I located her cell near the top of the long spiral. The tiny screen outside listed her name and prisoner rating. She was a model prisoner, it turned out. Destined for great things among the captive population.

A note below her name said, *Transferred to Haven.*

Transferred. When? Why would she have been transferred already?

Below, Cheng's death rousted the guards like a kicked hornet's nest. I needed to leave soon before they decided to do a sweep of the whole place. Making my way down the spiral, I located the shipping dock where I'd entered. The alarm systems blared and flashing lights filled the rooms with a pulsing blue. The loading door opened, and an emergency vehicle flashed its blues.

I sidestepped into a shadow as a crew of ambulance workers flooded past. It was too late, of course, but there were procedures to follow. People didn't survive falls in the Heavies. Jump off a table, break a knee. Jump a few stories onto a fiberstone floor, and they'd scrape you up with a spatula.

Once the medics were past, I strolled through the open door as if freedom were my right. A few seconds later, the oppressive night swallowed me whole. I was out.

It took Fleck's people almost an entire half-hour to locate me. At first, I kept to the shadowed streets, using darkness for cover until I reached a more populated area. I thought if I could get enough witnesses, Fleck might be hesitant to cause much of a stir. This was probably a bad assumption, but it turned out to not matter. They found me before I made it to the inner spiral. Someone must have seen me in the shadows and reported my presence, because before I knew it, I was surrounded by four goons.

"Boss wants a chat," said a man in a tight-fitting T-shirt and a blue baseball cap.

"Tell your boss his man's dead."

The guy blinked. "I got a feeling things will go better for me if you tell him yourself."

They led me through the streets to a rooftop high up the spiral that overlooked a series of drab government archive buildings. The glass fronts of the brutalist structures shone in the simulated moonlight of the Heavy Nicodemia night. Fleck perched alone on the rooftop's only chair, and a bottle and glass of bourbon sat on a small table next to him.

Two of the goons stayed on the roof with us, including the guy in the baseball cap. I couldn't help but notice that two was the exact number that it would take to lift me up and throw me off the roof. One might have gotten the job done. Two of these musclebound goons was overkill. Cheng's face as he stepped off the edge was burned into the back of my skull. His features were dark, and the spotlight formed a halo around his head.

Fleck plucked the glass of bourbon from the table and gave it a swirl. "Wen Cheng was my only friend growing up," he said. His voice slurred a little, which didn't make me like my odds. "Thick as thieves, we were."

I bit back a comment about his current profession. He didn't need another reason to dislike me.

"Do you ever wonder where things went wrong, Demarco?" he asked.

"Knowing won't make it any better."

He took a swallow of bourbon and tipped the glass toward me. "Oh, I'd wager you're wrong about that. You're thinking big tragedy, but you don't know what led up to it, do you? You don't know the"—he searched for the right word— "machinations."

"There were no machinations, Fleck. We were aboard the *Benevolent* and it crashed. The only conspiracy was the coverup, and that ship's long since sailed."

"I loved him, you know." He poured another two fingers of bourbon into his glass and set the bottle down too hard. "It was never going to work out, but I did everything I could for him. I involved him in everything."

"You crushed him," I said.

Anger flashed like lightning behind his eyes. "It was his own damn fault!"

I stepped forward, and the bodyguards tensed. "He feared you at the end, and you knew it. That's why you sent me. I was one last message to a man who had done everything he could imagine to get away from you. Turned out there was one place he could go you couldn't follow." I plucked the bottle of bourbon from his table and took a swig. "Or are you planning to find him there too?"

Fleck twitched a finger and one of the bodyguards put a hand on my chest, taking the bourbon from my grasp.

I raised my hands in supplication and stepped away. "I'm more interested in whether or not you're planning on sending *me* after him."

He fixed me with a hard gaze. "Haven't decided."

"Fair enough."

"We were teens," he said, staring off into the distance of time. "There was this teacher. Real hard-ass. Liked to give pop quizzes at random intervals. This was math. Calculus." He met my gaze. "Wen and I both tested good at math."

"Sure," I said, unimpressed.

"There we were, back of the classroom, not a damn clue what we were doing, getting ready to fail the first class we'd ever failed." He emptied his glass and refilled it. "Then we got to figuring: it's all about patterns, right?"

"Calculus?"

"Teaching. This asshole of a teacher—Mr. Burnheart—

didn't make everything up every year. He ran basically the same pattern. Probably even ran the same tests."

"So you found someone who had taken his class before? Sounds a lot harder than just learning calc."

"Calc is hard, you piece of shit."

"Fair."

"We were going to fail out, so we needed something. Burnheart wasn't just a hard-ass. He also wasn't a very good teacher. Half the class was going to fail out." He swirled bourbon, but didn't drink. "Wen and I asked around. Nobody was talking. Upperclassmen thought that it only made sense if the younger generation had to suffer, same as they did." A mirthless grin touched the corners of his mouth. "Now that I'm old, I think I see their point. Fuck 'em, right?"

"Sure."

"Wen had the idea that people just needed a little leverage. It was *his* idea, this whole information thing. Did you know that? Nobody fuckin' knows that."

"I didn't know it."

"Yeah, well. They're going to know it now." This time, when he drank the bourbon, he refilled the glass halfway. There were only a few swallows of bourbon left in the bottle. "At first when he brought her to me, I thought they were dating. I was *so* mad, I almost wrecked the whole setup. He had charmed her, sure, but she was there for me. She was there so that I could ask the hard questions, and when I did, she had the answers I wanted.

"See, Burnheart had a thing for girls like her. There were lines he wouldn't cross, of course. He was a married man, and he needed to keep his Karma up or he'd be reassigned from his teaching job. But girls could tell he was creeping on them. This girl—I don't even remember her name—told the story of how uncomfortable she felt around Burnheart. It wasn't incriminating. Nothing like that.

"It was a story, and a story well told is more powerful than any blackmail ever will be. We started finding more of them. Girls willing to tell their pieces in the private corners of campus. In cafes and restaurants. In their homes. Words are powerful, Mr. Demarco. Trinity heard these voiced concerns, and suddenly, Burnheart's Karma took a nosedive."

"You got him fired?"

Fleck swatted at the idea like it was a buzzing fly. "We were kids. More severe stuff happened later. This was just enough pressure. After we were sure Burnheart noticed his changed situation—when he really knew his job was at risk— I stayed after class and asked him a few questions."

"So, it *was* blackmail."

"Not at all." Fleck downed his glass of bourbon in one great swallow, then dripped the last dregs of his bottle into the glass. "It was really more of an insinuation. I hinted that I could change the rumor mill in his favor, but I needed a more stable position from which to work—the position of having better grades. *Everyone* needed better grades."

I looked out over the city. All it would take to murder me was one good shove, but the view of Heavy Nicodemia was fantastic. "Still sounds like blackmail to me."

"It was a manipulation," Fleck said. "Leering at teenage girls might be creepy. It might cost Karma, but Trinity weighs things differently if it's bad enough for people to talk about later. *That's* what makes information powerful."

"You deal in rumors."

"I deal in *truth*. It *has* to be rooted in truth or it doesn't work."

"You avoided incriminating Cheng all these years."

"Wen Cheng never got one spec of dirt on his hands,

even these last few months, when things got really dark. I took over a lot of the business. He was always the best at what he did, but my kind of network has its advantages too."

"Enough that he was afraid of you."

Fleck slumped back in his chair and stared at the amber liquid in his glass. "He didn't want to go big, but an organization like this tends to grow or die."

Maybe he wanted me to debate, but it wasn't somewhere I was willing to go. Was he right? Maybe. A business like his would dead end in disaster, but nobody knew if it would happen next week or in a hundred years. That thought led me back to Fortner and his children. "How many generations have the Fortners run Haven?"

"More than they deserve," Fleck said.

"Tell me the truth, then, Fleck," I said, turning back to him. His glass was empty, but he still held it in his big hand. "What happened to that gun?"

"I think you already know."

"Suspecting isn't knowing," I said. "You of all people ought to understand that."

"But sometimes it's enough." All the rage was gone from his eyes and he took my measure. He wasn't going to have me killed. I could see it in the lazy way he sagged in his chair. "There was someone like you. Someone excommunicated. They did something to Trinity that erased the guns from the register. Kept them hidden, even when they moved around the streets. The idea was that these guns would go up in value, because the new owner was going to be one of the greatest antique collectors in all of Nicodemia."

"Kaegan Fortner?"

"Geraldine." His oily gaze took in my reaction. "Kaegan's mother. She ordered the shipment, had her man in Customs process it, and fixed the guns so they'd be invisible. She even had phony guns manufactured so that it would look like the transaction was legit."

"No middle man." I wondered if I could manage the same trick. Could I make something invisible as well? Probably not, now that Trinity was turned against me. "That was when the Fortner business really took over Haven, wasn't it?"

Fleck fixed me with his hard gaze, his voice sharp, not a hint of alcoholic slur. "Businesses like these, Demarco. They grow or they die."

"There's no more room for Fortner to grow," I said. "Not in Haven."

"A man like him isn't going to let a few borders get in his way," said Fleck.

"Grow or die," I said. "You ever think it's better not to be in this business at all?"

"Wen asked that same question."

"And the answer?"

"You tell me," he said. "You're the one who delivered it to him."

____

Chapter 21

____

INSPECTOR TOBIN SMALLEY stared at me over the vast expanse of his cluttered desk. It was midmorning, and the disagreeably bitter coffee that the police precinct brewed had cooled to a disagreeably bitter sludge.

"It was a legitimate transfer," he said, his mustache twitching as he spoke. "Nothing we can do."

"Anya Fortner committed a crime in the Heavies and she should serve time here."

"Her father's in the Hallows. He made a request to have her transferred, and it was granted."

"*You* granted it."

Smalley leaned forward. "A judge granted it. There was trouble at the jail last night. You know anything about that?"

"There's trouble everywhere."

"It must seem like that."

"What's that supposed to mean?"

Smalley took a sip of coffee. Anders appeared at Smalley's open door, but Smalley waved him away. Anders disappeared back into the understaffed precinct. Another morning, another crisis. The place was barely holding together, and I could see the stress in the bags under Smalley's eyes.

"They're laundering Karma," I said.

"Prove it."

"You know I can't. That's why we have the blue."

His mustache twitched again. "We're too busy putting out fires to look into white collar crime."

"Murder's not white-collar crime."

"It is when they do it right." It was the smartest thing he'd said since I met him.

"I still haven't found the real murder weapon," I said, "but we know the one she brought in was a fake."

"I know you don't have any respect for the police, Demarco. Yeah, that's right. I did a little asking around. You've been trouble more than a few times for this precinct, whether or not Anders seems to think you're a good resource. It's nice to hear that your disdain for the blue includes our friends up the chain and not just us here in the Heavies."

"You're really screwing this up, Smalley."

He showed his palms. "Outta my hands."

"A judge?"

"Yeah. A judge."

"You blue are a bunch of thugs."

Smalley stood, kicking his chair back so it slammed against his bookshelf. "Get the hell out of my face, Demarco." He jabbed a finger at me, and his elbow brushed the rim of the coffee cup. "It's people like you we worry about around here. People ghosting around, causing trouble that Trinity can't help us fix. How about you tell me where you were last night? Got any witnesses around midnight?"

"Some people sleep at night."

"Not you."

Fair. "Anya Fortner's hiding something."

"Not our problem," said Smalley. "Not anymore."

"Justice is your responsibility, Smalley," I roared. "Push papers all you want, but you let her go when you had a choice to fight it."

Smalley fumed. He leaned forward with his palms flat on his desk next to the tepid cup of coffee. "I've got violence in the streets, Demarco. *Real* violence. Ongoing. Right now." He stared at me straight in the eyes. "It's breaking down, Demarco. This is how it happens. We're getting ready for a big shift in power around here, and the only thing keeping it from pure chaos is the blue bodies you see right outside that door."

I whispered, "Then do better."

He stared at me for what seemed like a dozen hours. His mustache covered the thin, bloodless line of his lips until finally he broke and said, "Maybe we should." He picked his chair up from the floor, righted it, and settled down into it. "Why do you care so much?"

"Somebody has to."

Smalley scanned the papers strewn across his desk. "Then there's this shit," he said.

I read the papers upside down as best I could. One word struck me as particularly significant. "The *Benevolent*."

"Things were slow when I agreed to do the *Benevolent* investigation. Everything going on—and now this murder investigation."

"Don't back out of this deal, Smalley."

"I want that gun destroyed," he said. "I want all of them destroyed."

"Finally, something we can agree on."

Smalley straightened the stack of papers.

"I'll need to talk to Anya Fortner," I said. "I know where her father keeps his guns. Trinity ought to be flagging that whole set as dangerous contraband, but they have an exemption. I'm the only one here who can track down why and get the exemption removed." Plus, leaving the Heavies meant getting away from the instance of Trinity that was apparently trying to do me in. "It all fits, Smalley. We can work together on this."

The detective still hadn't located whatever paper he was looking for. "You'll consult?"

"Make it official if you need to."

"I'll need you to sign some papers out in the office."

"Fine."

He finally found what he was looking for and yanked it from the bottom of the pile. His coffee cup, sitting precariously already, did a header and spilled its lukewarm muck across a dozen cases. "Crap," grumbled Smalley. He shoved the paper at me. "Get out of here, Demarco. Anders! Bring a towel!" He scrambled to rescue as many papers as he could. Brown stains spread across half his documents. "Anders!"

I took the proffered documents and left Smalley's chaotic office, passing a rather panicked looking Anders on my way. After signing some papers with the receptionist in an otherwise empty precinct, I collected a small stipend of a roll of dimes and made my way out.

"How did it go in there?" asked Anders, catching up to me on the inner upspiral street. A trolley rumbled past on its way to the government district and Customs.

I flashed him the dimes. "Landed a paying gig. Could have been worse."

"Going to gamble it away?"

"I thought I might eat first."

We walked for a while. He wore his blues, which drew more attention from passing pedestrians than I particularly wanted. When we reached the government district, the buildings turned gray and drab, and the population matched. Customs would be next, but I wanted to consider my options before leaving, so I stopped at a balcony overlooking the open space. Far away and below, the Cathedral of Saint Francis of Assisi dominated under the hazy morning light.

"He's under a lot of pressure," Anders said, "but he does care about doing the right thing."

"I had to poke him a little to get the bees buzzing. Otherwise, he wouldn't have given me this." I held up the documents he'd handed me. One corner was stained with dark coffee.

"The Rawls report? I thought he closed that one."

"Smalley knows as well as I do that Anya's hiding something. He's out of his league fighting it, but he knows something stinks." I bought a pack of cigarettes and a new lighter from a nearby vendor and offered Anders a smoke, which he refused. I lit one for myself and watched the movements of a thousand citizens far across the empty space. "He's right about one thing."

"What's that?"

"Heavy Nicodemia is on the road to a new normal. It's not going to be easy. It's not going to be nice." I drew a lungful of death and slowly exhaled. "But we're walking through the dark right now. We don't know what path we're taking, and we don't know how far we need to go, but when we step back into the light, everything's going to be different." I closed my eyes and imagined the whole bead spinning around me.

A trolley stopped at a nearby station, and my sister rolled off in her chair. Behind her, attached by the loosest lead, was my giant dog Cain. I'd asked her to meet me with him, and she'd agreed. Anything to get me to take the dog to the upper beads, where he could relax his gravity-worn joints.

"Thanks," I said, stubbing out my cigarette on the low railing.

"You owe me one, bro," she said, but there was the hint of a smile on her face. As much as she loved the diner, she enjoyed getting free of it from time to time.

"I owe you more than that, sis." As soon as I had Cain's leash, he pulled as hard as his corded muscles could pull. It was all I could do to keep him under control. To Anders, I said, "Send word if you learn anything."

"I always do."

With that, I took my leave and approached Customs. In the middle of the day, the lines weren't too busy. I normally skipped lines, taking the freight elevators instead of the more crowded passenger transports. Not this time. I no longer trusted Trinity not to void the elevators into space or fill them with inert gas. Hell, maybe it would sanitize them with fire. There was just no way to know, and presenting such an easy opportunity wasn't really in my best interest.

The Hallows instance of Trinity was a whole separate configuration. It would have its own take on me and my priorities. It would ignore me in different ways and adjust its world accordingly. It made sense for me to plan for anything, whether it was another attempt on my life or a shift in how the city's systems behaved in my presence.

But all I could think of was the *Benevolent*. There were only a few days before Smalley's mission, and if I was going to convince him that I could be part of it, then I needed to solve this problem with the guns. I needed to figure out why Anya Fortner was lying. I needed the truth.

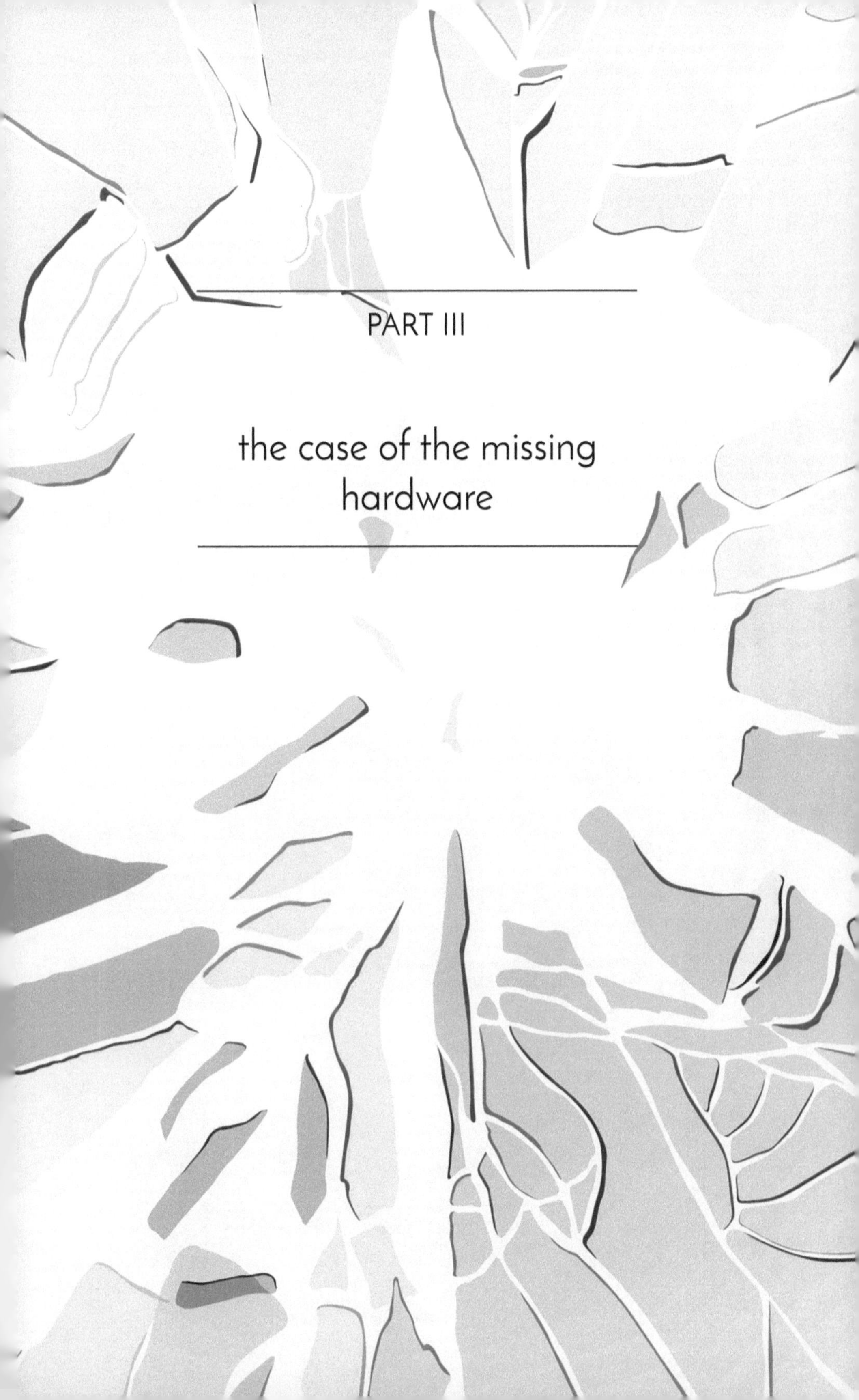

the case of the missing hardware

Chapter 22

THE MOST NOTABLE difference between Hallow Nicodemia and Heavy Nicodemia wasn't the gravity, though that was significant. My joints unfurled in the reduced pressure. It was a profound relief, and Cain's bouncing exuberance showed that he felt it too.

The biggest difference was not the light, though that certainly made an impact. The simulated sky of Hallow Nicodemia was a soul-scouring deluge of sunlight. I picked up a pair of cheap dark sunglasses at a local vendor and still squinted against the too-bright glare. The Heavies were the constant gloom of twilight punctuated by the sharp bright hangover glow of day. The Hallows sky shone so bright a person had to worry about it sunburning their bones.

It wasn't even the population. The residents of the Heavies were a stocky bunch, crushed during development by the smothering hand of all that extra gravity. In the Hallows, even the genetically average grew straight and tall. They strolled through wide, well-lit streets with confidence and safety. They looked down on their lessers with disdain. The

Heavies wore corruption on its sleeve, with district lines drawn by the ebb and flow of powerful gangs. The Hallows swayed to the tunes of corrupt art dealers and powerful magnates. It was a world of legal corruption and fortunes built upon the backs of the unfortunate.

The biggest difference between the two beads was none of these things.

It was the smell.

After spending so long in the fish rot stench of the lower Heavies, it was almost possible to forget how the weight of it crushed the soul more than any gravity ever could. It lingered in the clothes and in the skin of its residents, despite the very best in air filtration technology. It clung to the very fiberbrick of the buildings and sloshed in the drinking water. The fishy aftertaste tainted everything from wine to vegetables to bread to coffee. In the Heavies, every sense was suffused by the taint of industry.

The same was true of the Hallows, but to a significantly different effect. The Hallows smelled of the growth of vegetation. Crops grew strong and huge in the Hallows. Fruit was always ripe. Corn grew in dense rows, configured in hydroponic factories to produce the most of the given tiny space. The Hallows produced the bulk of edible plant material, but also the majority of flowers, perfumes, and sweets. Their world was a pleasant mix of lilac and rose. Sunlight suffused with pine and cedar.

That, above all else, marked the Hallows as the pinnacle of paradise.

Therefore, it was no surprise that a powerful man like Kaegan Fortner had chosen it as his home away from home.

"Well, well, well," said a police officer named Echo as soon as I'd taken three steps into the Sinless district. As soon as I had entered the bead, I had contacted the police, who had agreed to meet up, but on their terms. The man's double chins danced with disapproval. His badge glinted in the morning light. He glanced at his partner.

His tall partner, Halders, folded his arms. The scruff of his goatee twitched as he spoke. "Thought you liked it better down the chain, Demarco."

"Sometimes what we like isn't what matters," I said, nudging Cain with my boot. The big dog gave a messy snort.

"Here for a walk?" said Echo.

"I need to talk to someone."

"Don't we all."

"Someone in blue custody."

"Take it up with a judge." Echo leered at a pair of women leaving the Sinless District. They were scantily clad and laughing a hyena laugh.

"Thought I might owe you one if you did me a solid," I said. "Fair exchange and all that."

"Nothin's fair in the Hallows," said Halders. "You've been around the block enough to know that."

"Who's the customer?" asked Echo.

"Anya Fortner."

Halders gave out a long whistle.

"What?" Echo asked.

"Fortner?" said Halders. "Up in the Gardens."

Echo nodded, as if understanding.

"The Gardens?" I asked, wondering what I was missing.

"Follow along," said Echo. "Maybe you'll learn something."

Echo and Halders descended into the relative dim of the Sinless, a section of town known for being exempt from the effects of Trinity's Karma. The heavy scent of drugs and sex lingered over the dusty cobbled streets, and eyes watched from behind every shade.

When I gave Cain a tug, he let out a bubbling sigh. "Come on, dog. They're getting away."

The dog rolled his eyes to look at me, but didn't bother moving his massive head.

"What's it going to be, Cain?" I tapped the pocket of my coat where I kept my treats. "A bribe?"

He watched my fingers. I moved them into the pocket and his body tensed. I took them out, and he slumped back down.

"This is ridiculous." I tugged his leash, but the collar around his neck just sunk deeper into the folds of his ample flesh. "Come on, Cain."

He closed his eyes.

"You really only care about treats?"

At that last word, his eyes opened and his head whipped around. I pulled out a stick of cured meat and tossed it in front of him. He pounced and it was gone.

"Come on, then."

Finally, properly motivated, Cain followed me into the Sinless.

Men and women lingered on the streets watching as the blue strolled past. There wasn't anything particularly illegal in what was happening, but the looks of contempt were enough to raise my hackles. We wove through the district until we caught up with Echo and Halders near a small massage parlor at the base of a spiraling tower. Somewhere, a call to prayer marked the time of day.

"I thought you fellas were too high rank to walk a beat," I said.

Echo put his back against the parlor's door. "Never too high a rank to help with public relations." He unclipped the loop around the stunstick at his belt. To his partner, he said, "Ready?"

Halders nodded, gripping his own stunstick.

"Now hold on," I said.

But it was too late. Echo pushed through the door. His stunstick crackled menacingly, and he shouted, "Now listen up. We're here for answers and we want them *right now*."

What happened next could only be described as a shitshow. Through the open door, I saw a woman in a golden sari react to Echo's entrance. With a tremendous heave, she upturned her desk. Paper and little metal balls crashed to the floor, scattering across the smooth marble of the entryway. She turned and smashed a button on the wall. All the lights went dark.

Echo shouted from the gloom, blinded. Halders stepped back, not quite inside the building yet.

But I was born in the dark. My eyes adjusted quickly enough to spot the movement as the woman ducked back into one of the doorways.

She was headed out the back, but I said nothing.

It didn't matter, since Echo and Halders weren't listening. The other door inside burst open, and all I could see was the tremendous eclipse of a human being lumbering through the dark. A stunstick crackled, the lightning snap briefly illuminating the crowded room. It found flesh with a sickening thump, but the big man didn't slow. He slammed Echo into the wall.

Cain growled. He'd been a fighting dog for a time, and the violence agitated him. He pulled hard enough that my arm nearly popped from its socket, but I held tight. Backed up.

The room went dark again. Complete black. There was violent movement.

Then, the biggest man I'd ever seen came barreling through the door. His dark skin was stretched over great rolls of fat. He was completely naked, his perfectly smooth skin marred only by several welts, presumably from the stunsticks. He slammed into me hard.

Cain snarled and snapped. Teeth biting air. The man yelped. Fell. Scrambled up. Ran.

I watched his ample naked ass disappear down the street.

"Go, go!" yelled Echo. Inside the building, the blue was still moving forward. They had lights now, shining like stars from their shoulder harnesses.

Cain hadn't stopped pulling. He wanted to chase the naked man. He was the strongest damn dog I knew, but he wasn't able to get traction on the cobblestone road due to the low gravity of the Hallows. His long nails scraped and scrabbled as he struggled to pull free.

"C'mon, Cain," I said. When he didn't listen, I braced myself and pulled him into the parlor and closed the door. As soon as the path closed off, he relaxed.

I didn't.

The sounds of a struggle came from the door to the right. A reddish flash of moving lights. A grunt and a thud. I didn't know what Echo and Halders thought they were accomplishing, but I couldn't think of any situation in which this would be considered success.

Cain's hackles prickled across his back, and his stubby teeth shone when the light flashed our way. He wanted action about as much as I wanted a clean pair of socks.

"Sorry, bud. Sometimes we don't get what we want." I wrestled him away from the door.

Halders cursed and there was a crack like a gunshot. It wasn't the thundering boom of one of Fortner's lead slinging pistols. This was the more common ceramic bullets and printed gun found in the criminal underclass of the Heavies. The flashy guns could do just as much damage to human flesh as a lead bullet, but they wouldn't punch through most structural material.

Another scream rose from the other room. Finally, unable to resist anymore, I entered the room.

Echo had his stunstick planted at the base of a man's neck. A red fibersteel pistol lay across the room, and Halders sat with his back to the far wall. When I entered, he looked up at me with a sweaty, weak rictus of a grin. He held a hand to his ribs.

We were in a storeroom of some sort. One wall was lined with shelves. White jugs printed with chemical symbols filled half the space. The other wall was dominated by a fibersteel countertop, which was covered in lab equipment. The tang of acetic acid seared my nostrils.

I knelt at Halders' side and peeled his hand away from his ribs. There was no blood. No wound. His uniform was covered in the powdered remains of a ceramic bullet.

"Armor?" I asked him.

He winced. "It seemed like there might be trouble."

"You were lucky," I said. "Some of these ceramic bullets can get through thin armor like this." Lead bullets would have torn through it like paper.

"It still hurts," he said.

I gave him as good a test as a field medic could, checking for concussion and broken ribs. "Bruised, probably," I said after checking him out. "Nothing to worry about." I helped him to his feet.

By then, Echo had cuffed the man and hauled him up.

"Public relations?" I asked.

"Violence is a kind of relation," said Echo.

"And that's why I'll never be a cop," I muttered.

"We wouldn't take you anyway," said Echo, shoving his

prisoner into the street. "Too much of a history of malfeasance."

"What exactly did you expect me to learn here?"

"Respect," said Halders. He was struggling to keep up as we ascended from the Sinless District.

"So you caught a guy," I said.

Halders shook his head. "Echo wanted you to see what we do here. He thought maybe if you saw how we broke up labs like this, you might respect what we do for all of Nicodemia."

"What does it matter if one lab in one district gets shut down?" I asked.

Echo gave his prisoner a shove. "We've been working on this lab for months. They've been supplying the whole city— all three beads—for the last decade, and they're responsible for half the custom pharmaceuticals in Haven and the Heavies. Maybe you've lost sight of what the blue does for the people, but we haven't, Demarco. We're the ones always here fighting to keep this place under control. We're the ones on the side of justice, no matter what."

"It's the *no matter what* that bothers me."

"It should," said Halders.

"Fine." I pulled Cain to a stop. "Tell me I can visit Anya Fortner."

Echo stopped and stared at me with hard eyes. There was something like sadness that both softened his expression and made it icier. "That's the other lesson," he said. He glanced at his partner. "Even Halders and I can't get you in to see someone like her."

"Do I need to talk to your boss?"

"No," said Halders. "Nobody on the force is going to give one inch on this one."

Echo said, "You need Kaegan Fortner's permission if you want to talk to her."

"He outranks you?"

Something broke in Echo. He sagged in his uniform like he'd suddenly stepped into higher gravity. "That's the other half of the lesson, Demarco." He glanced over his shoulder where the city rose above us in the long spiral. "In this city, the rich always outrank the good."

Chapter 23

IF THE RICH outranked the good, then Kaegan Fortner might have been the boss of God himself. I found him in a sprawling green estate upspiral from the Cathedral of Saint Lucy of the Light in a district dominated by generational wealth. I arrived in his study late in the afternoon as the golden glow of the Hallows sun shone low in the domed sky. Beethoven's Moonlight Sonata played somewhere in the indistinct distance.

"I expected you sooner," said the man in the high-backed chair. He didn't swivel around to see me, but the hairs on the back of my neck told me I'd been watched the whole way in.

Cain settled his massive form into a ball at my feet. I knelt and scratched him behind the ears. "The antiques business is treating you well."

His chair spun slowly and the man faced me. He was of medium height with white hair and a well-trimmed beard. His steepled fingers were long and narrow, and the wrinkles at the corners of his eyes were softened by the extra flesh on his bones. When he pierced me with his sharp blue eyes, I felt the crushing sense of being measured—my value compared to that of a wooden desk brought from a time when kings ruled the Earth. Behind him, centered between two video windows, was a portrait of a beautiful woman with gray streaks in her brown hair. She could have been Anya Fortner's sister. A better bet was that she was her mother, Carrie Fortner.

"My father had an eye for the business," Kaegan Fortner finally said with an apologetic twinkle in his eyes. "And at a certain point, wealth begets wealth."

"I wouldn't know anything about that."

"Your parents would."

"They don't talk much these days."

"I was sorry to see what happened to them."

"So were they."

"They were always a boon to our social circles."

"My father was the center of an art smuggling ring."

"We all have our vices."

"Not everyone he dealt with was reputable."

"Reputation is an entirely distinct property from virtue, don't you find? Your father brought beauty to the Hallows, and his work was appreciated. If only we had known how he struggled, maybe we could have helped him." Fortner's desk was clean, and the reflection of him in its polished glass surface danced as he spoke. "Speaking of reputations, I'm glad you found your way up here, Mr. Demarco."

"That's a first."

"You are here because you want to speak with my daughter."

I said, "That's the rumor."

"Rumors are the heart of your business, aren't they?" Fortner said. "They're mine too. Like my father used to always say, nobody knows a community quite like an antiques dealer. You never know when an estate is going to shift hands or when a previously thriving bead is going to descend into the kind of chaos that results in the trade of great wealth."

"I'd hardly call the Heavies *previously thriving*."

"Let's call it productive, then." Fortner's smile showed exactly the right number of teeth. "Saint Jerome ran a rather efficient operation, I hear."

Saint Jerome had been the crime boss for decades. His role in shipping stolen artwork had made a lot of people wealthy in both dimes and Karma. "The new guy won't last."

Fortner raised an eyebrow. "Is that so?"

I thought back to Fleck's expression when he learned that Cheng was dead. "Doesn't have the fortitude for it." I don't know why I told him that. Kaegan's disarming smile was chipping away at my usual reticence.

"Well." Fortner's index finger tapped on his desk. A nervous twitch? "Thank you for the tip."

"You were right," I said. "I want to speak with your daughter. I'm told you're the man preventing it."

"I need her case handled discretely."

"She confessed to shooting a man. I think your family's reputation has already taken the hit."

"That isn't what I mean."

This time I waited without saying a word. Men like Kaegan Fortner were allergic to the vibrations of their lessers' voices, so I figured the best way to hang him was to let him spin his own rope.

"Blaize told me you visited the vault. You've seen the guns and fired them." Fortner stood from the high-back chair and strolled to one of the nearby windows. The frosted glass cleared, revealing the manicured, lush landscape of an unin-habited courtyard. "Before my father passed, he told me that there were only three things of true value. The first was our reputation. Nothing we could ever buy or sell would be as important as that. As antiques dealers, we are purveyors of trust. Every transaction we make must be built on a trustworthy foundation, no matter how much our buyers depend on verifying their purchases. It is always on *us* to give them a deal built from the truth.

"The second thing is family. Family can be trusted above all else. Even if we hate our siblings or despise our parents—and believe me, I did have words with my father from time to time—we can always depend on each other. My father believed that family was more valuable than almost everything in all of Nicodemia.

"But the guns." Fortner's lips twisted into a sneer. "They were more important than anything to him. He always told me that the guns were more valuable than God himself. They were the finger of death, and there was nothing in the entire city that could hold up to them. A Fortner's only true purpose in this life is to keep those guns safe. When I had Anya transferred here, I assumed she had been falsely accused. Some kind of setup by those barbarians in the Heavies." He flashed a look back at me. "No offense."

"None taken."

"Turns out I was wrong. She betrayed her family. That's all there is to it. She stole a gun from the secure vault." The glass of the window hazed again, then cleared to reveal a crystal-clear image of the shooting range where I had tested each of Fortner's firearms. In the view, Blaize Fortner had one of the guns disassembled on the counter. He cleaned the piece with a meticulous attention that I would have thought the bouncing, energetic man could never manage. "There are some things that are sacred to this family," continued Fortner. "These guns are more than just our legacy. My father worked tirelessly his whole life to collect them from all over

Nicodemia so that they could be placed in our protective custody."

A lie. Not only a lie—a blatant one. That or Whistles, the Customs agent, had lied. I wondered how much of what Fortner told me was also untrue.

"You're isolating her," I said.

He looked up at me. "I can't afford to have her talking. She's betrayed us once. How much has she already given them?"

"Them?"

"That's the worst part." Fortner pounded his desk. "I don't know who. She won't tell me. Won't even drop a hint to me. It's infuriating. I've been nothing like my cruel father, but she's always despised me. Ever since her mother died, she's had nothing but venom for me."

"Let me speak with her."

"I want what's mine, Demarco." Fortner watched his son work on the screen for a long time. "I want what belongs to this family. When Anya took that weapon—when she stole from me—she did more than take something valuable from my vault. She put her whole family in danger. She put the *guns* in danger."

She put everyone else in danger too, but that didn't seem to bother Fortner. "Must be rough."

"I have been told that you can be hired to find things."

"For the right price."

He said, "Find me the gun that she took."

"Get it from her."

He placed a hand on the gilded frame of his wife's portrait and gazed up into her image. "I want the Walther PPK back. The police have it and that is not acceptable."

"Walther PPK?" He was confirming that the weapon

used was one of the two missing from his vault. "Is this a Trinity feed?" I nodded at the screen.

"Trinity has nothing to do with these guns."

So, the theory that at least some of the guns were excommunicated still held. "Your goons shouldn't have trouble picking it up if Trinity's not going to stop them."

"We could if we knew where it was," Fortner said.

"Are you telling me there are limits to the influence of wealth?"

"I'm offering to buy your services. I think the limits are yours to impose."

"Fair."

He stared at me, apparently still expecting an answer.

I thought back to the display. There had been two guns missing. "What about the Colt Python?"

Surprise registered in the widening of his eyes, then disappeared under his mask. "You won't need to worry about that."

"All the same, I'd like to know where it went," I said.

"It's a fine gun."

"It's a *missing* gun."

"I'm afraid the Python's been gone long enough that picking up its trail is going to be problematic."

"I live in problematic."

"All I want is the PPK, and I want it as quickly as possible." Fortner waved at the screen and a view of the gun safe appeared. The Colt Python and two other slots were empty. One was the Model 41, the weapon that Blaize had worked on.

"Send your loyal son," I said. "I'm already on a job."

"Blaize is the kind of hammer that thinks every thumb is a nail."

Fortner had to know that I would never bring him the gun

if I found it. He was playing at something, and I didn't like it. "What's the catch?"

"Take him with you," he said. "Show him how a real detective handles a problem like this."

"I've been called a lot of things," I said, "but a real detective is pretty far down that list."

"Nobody likes false modesty." He gnawed on the words like they were meat clinging to a bone. "We both know what your unique position gives you. You can take what you want, edit core Trinity processes, and search archives hidden to the rest of us. Hell, you could kill if you needed to, and it wouldn't cost you a shred of Karma."

"Because I don't have any to start with."

He eyed me. "Your father was a good man. He provided for his *family*. Don't you wish you could do the same?"

"I could reconcile," I said, "but that would mean giving up my luxurious lifestyle."

"Even if it would mean a better life for your sister? Better supply stock for that diner of hers. A better life for her *wife*." It wasn't lost on me that the little display of knowledge about the only people who gave a damn about me was a not-so-subtle power play.

And it rankled. The guy was really starting to itch until he burned. "Listen, Fortner," I growled, "you have a funny way of hiring a guy to do a job. Usually, there's an offer of payment and a discussion of terms somewhere in the mix."

"Your father—"

"Quit bringing up my father," I growled. "He's dead. He's been dead for over a decade, and he was a piece of shit when he was around. Sure, he provided for us. He did it by poisoning the well and tearing a hole in our futures." I breathed hard. "Then he died."

Fortner stared at me, completely unmoved by my

emotional outburst, as if he had expected the whole thing. On the screen behind him, Blaize continued to clean his weapon. The screen faded to black.

"The *Benevolent*," Fortner said, sounding genuinely resigned. "I know."

"It was pretty hard to forget."

"I lost my eldest son on that ship." He glanced up at the portrait. "You're not the only one who's lived with tragedy, Jude."

I desperately wanted to ask him about the confidential task he'd ordered, but I couldn't find the right words. I knew he would never tell me the truth, especially if it involved Lorrel. "I'm sorry for your loss." I somehow meant it.

"Get me back the gun that Anya stole from me," he said. "You know it's dangerous to have out there."

I thought of the gun rack in the shooting range. I could still feel each of the deadly weapons—weapons that could really *only* be used to kill—and I could remember how they felt as I fired them on the range. Fortner was right. They *were* dangerous. "I need to talk to Anya before I agree to anything."

"And I told you," Fortner said, his voice laced with warning, "I want that gun."

"So, you're telling me if I bring you the gun I can speak with your daughter?" The deal was sour all the way through. "That's your offer?"

"That's the offer."

"I'll think about it." I wouldn't. I left the way I came, more determined than ever. Fortner's weapons were a hazard in the city of Nicodemia, not only to its citizens but to the station itself.

Chapter 24

"IF A RICH MAN wants you to do something," I told Cain, "you probably shouldn't do it."

He looked at me as if I'd just imparted the most valuable nugget of wisdom he'd ever heard. Then he sniffed the gigantic turd he'd just left in the shrubs outside Saint Lucy of the Light. Can't say which he enjoyed more.

The bright reflections off the modern cathedral threatened to bake the skin right off my bones. I led the dog away from his sinful act of vandalism and made my way farther downspiral. The central space in the Hallows was wider than the other two beads, leaving for a vast open space for flying taxis and other floating transports. The too-bright brilliance of the bead made my head thump and my eyes ache, but it *was* beautiful.

"Fortner wants that gun," I said to Cain. "Makes sense. He owns it, after all." He'd had those guns in his vault for decades. He could legitimately point out that there were no records of any of them ever leaving.

Then again, there weren't any records of them being used

this time either. Cain sniffed at a trellis full of trumpet-shaped flowers. Bumblebees drifted lazily from flower to flower. It smelled heavy and sweet, like the lilacs but denser. Cain marked the spot. It was his.

"Maybe sending me to find the gun isn't about finding the gun." This was ridiculous. The dog couldn't understand me. Why was I talking to him?

It *did* help me sort through my thoughts. I had always tried to have someone I could confide in. In the Heavies, I could always talk to Retch. Maybe he wasn't exactly trustworthy, but ideas bounced off him just fine. Here in the Hallows I was alone.

In the Hallows, *everyone* was alone.

I needed to figure out how and why that gun was invisible to Trinity. It was a major flaw in the record-keeping, and it needed to be resolved. The fact that more weapons were missing made it even more urgent.

Fortner wanted me to meet Blaize in Haven, but I wasn't in much of a hurry. Instead, I decided to pursue questioning Anya on my own. If anyone was going to tell me how the gun's interactions with Trinity worked, it would be the woman who had exploited it.

I thought of Fortner's guiding principles. Family. That's why he'd had Anya transferred. The guns were important, of course. My gut told me that he was exaggerating how important they really were. What use could a few powerful guns be in a ship run by an AI. It's not like there was a government to overthrow. Nothing with central power anyway.

No, Fortner's guiding principle had to be his family. They meant everything to him. That made Anya's betrayal so much more powerful, and to me that meant Anya was where I needed to focus.

The courthouse in the Hallows sat nestled between a

community garden and a library the size of a small mountain. It had a red fiberbrick façade and the whole building was designed around a lush courtyard garden. I let Cain run unleashed in the confined space and followed the signs until I found the courtroom where Anya's case would be processed. If there was going to be a chance for me to speak with her, it would be here. I settled into a bench directly behind the defendant's fiberoak table and watched as cases rolled by.

Judge Pinker was a man with pale, mottled skin under a mop of silver hair. He wore a black robe and narrow eyeglasses that seemed to pinch his severe face. His eyes had the kind of wrinkles a person gets from living an entire life without once smiling. I took an instant dislike to the man based on his looks alone, but as far as I could tell, he was fair in all his rulings.

A woman who admitted that she had stolen from an employer was given time in reform. A man who had allegedly murdered a prostitute in the Sinless was sent to a full jury trial. By coincidence, the chemist Echo and Halders had dragged in sat before Judge Pinker. The list of crimes he was accused of took fifteen minutes to name, but in the end, he was only sent to full trial for three of them. The other crimes were noted and attached to the case.

Then, Anya Fortner sat in front of the judge. She wore the orange jumper of the Heavies judicial system, and her hair was pulled back in a functional ponytail. Her frown creased the corners of her mouth, and her otherwise olive skin was pasty and pale.

After a vaguely ceremonial sequence, Judge Pinker peered down his long nose through his glasses. "And what charges do we have here?"

A woman on the other side of the court stood and read from a single sheet of yellow paper. "The charges all come from a court in Heavy Nicodemia, your honor. Two counts smuggling of a weapon, one count resisting arrest, one count second degree manslaughter."

"Manslaughter?" I muttered to myself. Anya must have heard me, because her jaw hardened. She pointedly did not look my direction, so I leaned forward. "We need to talk, Fortner."

The judge checked his watch. The metal on the wristband glinted in the warm overhead lights, showing off an elaborate crescent in a cluster of stars on the band. It looked old. "What does the defendant plead?"

All eyes turned to Anya. She glanced at the man next to her—her lawyer, presumably—who he nodded. She stood, careful not to rattle the chains on her wrists. "Not guilty, your honor," she said.

I didn't mutter anything this time, but the plea didn't make sense to me. She had confessed, hadn't she? With a full confession on record, her best bet at an easy reform was to continue confession before law and God. If she denied guilt now, she needed to defend herself, and that defense would be severely undercut by the confession.

Anya stared straight ahead as the procedure continued.

"What evidence will the prosecution be entering into record?" the judge droned. I wondered how many times he'd said that exact phrase that day.

The prosecution stood. "There is a full confession, your honor. Written and signed while in custody in Heavy Nicodemia. Her recorded movements put her near the cathedral where the crime took place, and records indicate communication between the defendant and the victim prior to that meeting."

Judge Pinker checked his watch again. Anya's frown deepened. The prosecutor continued his list of evidence, including detailed tracking documents regarding Anya's exact location at the time of the murder.

"Lies," Anya whispered.

"Then prove it," I said.

This time, she glanced back at me. Even the split-second distraction was noticed by the judge. He cleared his throat pointedly, and Anya returned to staring straight ahead.

Her expression, even in that tiny split second, had burned itself into my mind. There was something there I wasn't expecting.

No, that wasn't it. I *was* expecting it. The straightening of her lips. The pinch of her brow. She was afraid, and my words had triggered that fear.

I watched the judge for a while. He checked his watch again, clearly bored with the long-winded prosecutor. The courtroom was warm. Too warm. The air inside was heavy like a weighted blanket pressing down on my lungs. The minutes rolled by. This was taking longer than any of the judge's previous cases, and every piece of evidence the prosecutor entered into record seemed to bore the judge even further.

"Stop," said Judge Pinker. He gestured with one hand. "Approach the bench and bring that list."

The prosecutor blinked. This was apparently contrary to their norms, because Anya's lawyer whispered in Anya's ear before approaching the bench. The three spoke in hushed tones as the judge read the prosecutor's paperwork.

"Trinity couldn't track your gun," I whispered. "I want to know how."

The prosecutor and Anya's lawyer returned to their tables. The prosecutor's jaw clenched with barely contained rage. A vein in her neck bulged and her cheeks flushed deep red.

"Anything else, prosecutor?" Judge Pinker asked.

"Not at this time, your honor."

"Would the defendant care to add anything?"

Anya and her lawyer hissed a quick exchange, but I couldn't quite pick it up. The lawyer approached the bench. "My client would like to add that her Karma record is perfect. She had justification for everything she did, and none of the evidence that the prosecutor has presented rises above circumstantial."

The judge cleared his throat. "The confession?"

"Coerced, your honor."

In his seat, the prosecutor seethed.

"What is happening?" I asked.

Anya gave a little shake of her head. Her skin had gone pale and her hands trembled in her lap.

The judge drew a long breath. "This is an interesting case," he started. "The prosecution has done a fine job collecting evidence on short order. The communication records and movement transcripts are very compelling on their own. Of course, the case depends upon a confession that this court simply cannot admit. We have seen coerced confessions in the past, of course, but this one is particularly egregious."

"It's not," whispered Anya. Her lawyer placed a hand on her arm to quiet her.

Judge Pinker continued, "It has come to the attention of this court that the defendant, Anya Fortner, was not present during the events that led to the death of Mr. Rawls." He nodded to Anya's lawyer. "The Haven Trinity has noted Anya's presence around the thirtieth block of the warehouse district during the time of the murder. Given that Ms. Fortner is, as far as this court knows, incapable of being in two places at once, we must draw the conclusion that she was not present at the murder scene. Since no direct observations are available showing her present, we must conclude that this case cannot go forward."

Across the room, the prosecutor stood up. "Case is withdrawn, your honor." The words came out like a curse.

She was going to walk.

The smattering of viewers in the benches murmured behind me.

"What's happening," I said to Anya.

She shook her head, as if she could deny her own freedom.

"What's happening," I repeated. When she didn't reply, I said, "You confessed, Anya. I was there. *Why* did you confess if you didn't do it? Who was coercing you?"

The bailiff led Anya through a door in the front of the courtroom, no doubt for processing and then release. That was it. Justice was finished with her.

The judge checked his watch again, cleared his throat, and called the next case.

Chapter 25

ANYA WAS ALONE. She was dressed in the plain grays of cheap printed garments. Her hair was pulled back in a simple bun, and her nervous eyes scanned the nearby crowds. It was twilight in the Hallows, and the light from the false starlight kept the streets well lit. She didn't see me. Even Anya Fortner had been trained to avoid looking into the darkest shadows.

Following her proved difficult. Immediately after stepping from the courthouse steps, she summoned a ride. It came in the form of a single-seat rickshaw pulled by a single motorized wheel. Once she settled in, it zipped forward, and I had to hurry to keep up. Cain was on my leash, and as soon as I started, he loped along beside me like it was nothing.

Trinity hadn't done anything to attack me since I left the Heavies. Different bead, different Trinity. Still, I was nervous as I stepped out into traffic. Vehicles might not swerve toward me, but they wouldn't avoid me either. The Hallows didn't run a central trolley like the Heavies, which meant there were no tracks to make traffic predictable.

One glance back and the woman would spot me. One swerve into the side streets and she'd easily lose me.

But she didn't even make the attempt. She rolled straight down the spiral, zipping through traffic directly toward the upper Customs structures. She was making a run for the chain.

Tongue dragging, slobber flying, Cain hunted. He seemed to sense something about this walk that was different from the others. He moved with purpose, barreling his way down the long spiral. His big nose snuffled at the hard road every few minutes, and his jowls wobbled. As we moved, he pulled harder and harder until it was all I could do to keep him under control.

Anya finally glanced back. Her haunted eyes danced over the rumbling crowd. I didn't know what she saw, but her sunken expression darkened and she hurried away.

I slowed in case she looked back again. Cain pulled, but I muscled him under control. His claws dug into the hard ground, but I still had mass in my favor. We moved to the other side of a cluster of nuns, who walked so slowly it was all I could do to restrain Cain.

"A bit of discipline would do him well," said the nun closest to me, eyeing Cain. She was tall and her skin had a gray pall to it that I often identified with corpses and fish.

"That's what they said about me too, Sister, and look how I turned out."

There was an art to following anyone through a closed system like Nicodemia. It didn't matter how close I could get without being seen. It didn't matter how well I could see her from afar. There were places in the city where a single person couldn't properly follow someone. These choke-points led into narrow passages with long sightlines. They were places with lots of exits or exits that went places a person couldn't follow. Without extensive backup, it was impossible to track someone if they really didn't want to be followed.

One such chokepoint was Customs.

I left the nuns as Anya entered the Customs building. Unlike a lot of chokepoints, Customs only had one entrance and one exit. Unfortunately, the exit was all the way down in Haven. I could risk the cargo route, bypassing Customs, but if she decided to double back, I'd wait all day before figuring it out. She'd be long gone.

And I didn't have any backup. Not even a single person to put at the Hallow-side Customs exit. I cursed myself for not dragging Retch along. The kid might be abrasive, but he was reliable in a pinch.

No, I had to make this call on my own. Would Anya try to ditch me by doubling back, or was she headed for something in Haven?

She was clever. My first encounter with her told me she was smart, and she was hiding something. I had yet to figure out what that something was, but I knew that Anya was the kind of person who could lose a follower if she wanted. All it would take was a short flight through town or a jaunt through one of the Hallows' many hedge mazes. Instead, despite being afraid of a tail, she'd come straight to Customs.

The determination behind the haunted look in her eyes told me everything I needed to know. She was running toward something as much as she was running from. If she was in Customs, she was there for a reason.

And that reason *had* to be in Haven.

I didn't like the prospect of riding cargo down the chain, but the alternative involved moving through the long lines in Customs. Not only would it be obvious to Anya that I was still following her, but it would take far too long. At best, she would have a ten-minute head start on me when I stepped foot in Haven.

The elevators that ran constantly along the chain between beads carried mass between beads. They moved down the chain, looped around, and then made their way up. It was a constant exchange of goods, balanced perfectly to avoid destabilizing the spin of the station. The downward elevators were loaded in a busy warehouse next to the Customs office, and was managed by the same. Every parcel was checked and every food shipment was evaluated carefully for contraband.

The automated systems ignored me, of course, but they didn't ignore Cain.

"He's with me," I told the Customs official.

The man scrunched his wrinkled face and stared at the tablet in his scarred hand.

"I'm excommunicated," I said. "Exempt from Customs."

"We'll have to account for mass," he said.

"They didn't on my way up."

This rankled the man. His wrinkles deepened. "They're supposed to."

"Well, maybe you can account for my dog's mass, and that'll be enough."

This didn't placate him at all, but a bundle of silage slipped from a nearby forklift, and he was distracted enough that I managed to slip into the next container. With a boom and the click of the lift, we were on our way.

Cain whined. I scratched behind his ears and pulled him close. He licked my face. Was his whine a reaction to my own anxiety? My heart pounded and my mouth ran dry. Trinity could easily kill me. The air in the container grew cold at first, and then warm. I'd never know if the oxygen mixture went too high or too low. I would have no warning if the container's air were voided into space.

It made me consider the few close calls I'd had in the Heavies. They hadn't been overt murder attempts. Not really. They had been warnings. The recycler could have finished me. Any fast-moving vehicle on the spiral road could have swerved and taken me out.

But they hadn't. Instead, they brushed close enough that I felt the fear of God. Maybe that's all it was. Trinity was warning me of something, and even in direct communication it wasn't able to fully articulate its message.

I only wish I knew what that message was.

The air smelled of acid, like the scouring bots that cleaned in the dark corners of the night. The searing sour tickled my nose and set my hackles on edge. Cain whined again, and I knelt to comfort him with a rub behind his ears.

"You and me, old boy. We've got this covered."

The container was dim already, but it plunged into darkness. I held the dog close, less to comfort him than to comfort myself. After all, Cain was the one living creature in the container that Trinity might consider saving. Anything else was likely vermin. Or me.

An electric pulse ran the length of my body. It tingled deep in my spine, and made my fingers burn like overused muscles. Minutes passed like hours, and time lost itself in the long dark blackness of space. A queasy churn roiled deep in my guts, and a feeling like being disconnected from the whole world washed over me. There was a special weightlessness there in the emptiness of the long ride on the chain. As the container accelerated down, what little gravity the lower end of the Hallows gave me disappeared to nearly nothing. All around, the cargo shifted under its tight cords.

Then, with a thump, the container docked with the Haven bead. For a long time, it sat in a holding pattern. Every few minutes, it rumbled forward, shifting under my unsteady body as it moved into position for unloading. I'd been through the process before.

But this was taking forever. Even in the timeless black, I could tell that the minutes were stretching into hours. The whole plan required me to get to Customs before Anya. If I didn't, I'd never be able to pick up her trail. If I couldn't follow her trail, I'd never learn where she hid the guns or how they became invisible.

Finally, the lights returned to all their dim glory. With a hiss, the door on one end of the container opened into the Haven Customs warehouse.

Cain did not need any encouragement. We stepped from the container. We were one in a long array of docked containers. Aisles stretched out before us, choked with machinery meant to unload and process containers as they arrive.

A voice from one side stopped us before we could go anywhere. "Hold on." It was the Haven end of Customs, here to inspect an anomalous container.

"It's me." I had been through this Customs office a hundred times.

The man stepped forward. He had a crown of ginger hair and his Customs uniform had certainly seen better days. I didn't recognize him. "This is a cargo-only area," he said.

"And I'm cargo." I made to push past him, but he blocked my way. The crackle of a stunstick behind me twigged me to the fact that he'd brought backup.

"Your dog set off all the alarms."

I glanced down at Cain. It made sense. If Cain hadn't tripped the alarms, I would have been able to sneak out through the automated security. That's what I had done before, and it was what I'd do again. With Cain along, I couldn't get through anything. They had probably been watching a video feed and trying to figure out where the dog came from my whole ride down.

"I'm running late," I said, taking a few dimes from my pocket. "What do you say we leave this alone."

The Customs agent stared at me. "I don't know what kind of—"

"Look," I interrupted, realizing the meager bribe wasn't going to work. "Check your systems. You won't find me. Check your records. I've never been here. Check your gut. Nothing good can come from stopping me." I stepped forward, and Cain moved with me. "You got a flag in the system because this dog isn't on the proper registry. He's not properly crated, but no crate will contain this dog. He's not properly sedated, but good luck putting this dog to sleep." I tilted my head back, indicating the guy behind me. "Do you think a stunstick is going to slow this dog? He'll bury the stick and the hand that held it before you can have the decency to start bleeding. Cain walks where he wants, when he wants, and right now he's only interested in leaving with me. You want him to be interested in something else? I guarantee you won't like it."

Cain punctuated this speech by lying down and snoring gently. I muttered a curse under my breath.

"Look," said the Customs agent. "It was fifty-fifty whether or not we gas that container before opening the door. Next time we see that dog on our scans, we're not going to mess around." He stepped aside. "But for now? Get out of here."

"Fair enough," I said, pushing past him. It took a tug to get Cain to come with, but he moved, protesting the heavier gravity.

Cain wasn't the fastest guy in town, but we needed to hurry. We barreled through the automated warehouse and through the cargo doors to where a dozen trucks were being loaded so that they could disperse goods throughout the station. Men and women toiled in the late afternoon light, facing the exhaustion of the end of the day with the vigor of anticipated freedom.

I led Cain around the complex, through narrow streets, until we reached the opening that led from the Customs office where even then travelers poured from the exit gates.

"Where is she?" I asked nobody in particular. Was I too late?

Cain's ears pricked up. He sniffed the air and pulled on his leash.

Then, she was there. She hurried through the dense crowd, elbowing her way forward, heedless of the annoyed looks left in her wake.

The crowd sat between Anya and me, but nothing splits a crowd like a giant dog. We made our way to the other end of the square just as Anya broke away and disappeared into one of the smaller side streets.

But by then, I knew exactly where she was going.

Chapter 26

I HEARD her scream before I saw the residence. It wasn't a scream of pain, but it contained some of the most tortured anguish I'd ever heard. As I approached the door, another throat-ripping, soul-rending scream tore through the narrow alley.

Anya Fortner's home was an angular two-story building with windows looking up at a wide view of the central spiral. Short strips of greenery flanked the sidewalk leading up to the wide-open red door. A tricycle sat askew in the grass next to a dark-eyed doll.

Kids. I should have known from the tenor of her scream. I should have known by her hurried step.

She screamed again, "You asshole! I'm going to kill you!" A crash came from the open door that made me think she might have thrown a sofa across the room.

I stepped into the building. "Ms. Fortner?" The rec room held an entertainment screen, and children's toys were scattered across the floor. A distinctly un-thrown sofa sat along the far wall and a single open doorway led to the kitchen. "Ms. Fortner, I'm here to help."

Another crash. Smaller this time. Anya Fortner stepped into the doorway and leveled a gun at my chest. This wasn't one of the lead-slinging pistols taken from her father's vault. This was a neon green holdout pistol. Single shot. Tiny. It didn't pack the punch of a full-sized weapon of war, but it was enough to kill me exactly once – no more, no less.

I raised my hands with the kind of deliberate caution a person used when handling radioactive waste or a rising soufflé. "We need to talk."

"Talk!" She stepped forward, gun pointed at my heart. "Talk? You want to talk? Did *he* send you to *talk?*"

"I'm here to help," I said. Was I? It seemed like the best thing to say at the time. I was there to grill her for information. It stretched the definition of *help*. "Your kids are missing."

Her face was flushed with rage. "You better talk, mister. I've had about enough of you following me around, and I've got one bullet here that says you're not going to do that anymore."

"I can help you find your kids."

"What the hell do you know about my kids?"

I glanced around the room. A single tablet sat askew on the floor near a coffee table. Two dolls were crumpled into the corner: one blonde, one dark-haired. A stack of building bricks had been scattered across the soft green carpet, but I didn't know if this had happened before or after Anya's furious rampage through the house.

"Two kids," I said. "The younger one is into building. Maybe six years old. Destined to be an engineer of some sort. The older one I'd guess is around eight. She has an interest in social things like caring for kids or gathering for pretend parties. There's a red-headed doll missing from that set, and my guess is she took it with when she was taken. They both like video games. Neither of them is much for the big screen."

The whole time I spoke, Anya didn't move. It was nice; it meant she didn't shoot. It was also not nice; it also meant she was still pointing that gun at my pounding heart. "How do you know about the big screen?"

I glanced meaningfully at the coffee table. "No controller. Kids that young aren't great at voice controls, so if they're using the big screen, they'll have a remote. It's not on the coffee table. It's not on the floor. That means it's put away. Based on the status of everything else in this room, I suspect things that get used don't always get put away. With you gone, these kids would have been with your wife, and she's not one to impose too many controls."

She took another step forward. Half the distance between us was gone, which only meant that shooting me was going to be like shooting the broad side of a church. "Wife?"

I settled my attention on the white gold ring on the finger of the hand wielding the gun. It had a scrolling design and a diamond that glinted in the warm light. "Wife. Significant other. Very close friend. I'm not here to discuss your love life, Anya. Someone lives here with you and your two kids. A nanny, maybe?"

"Wife," spat Anya. "For now."

Exploring that tension didn't feel like my best path to leaving without any perforated organs. "Who took your kids, Anya?"

She jabbed the air with her pistol. "Tell me who sent you."

"I can help—"

"Tell me!"

She said it with such force that I rocked back on my heels. "Trinity sent me."

Anya blinked. When she spoke again, it was barely a whisper. "Not my father?"

"I don't work for him. The blue from down in the Heavies sent me too, but I'm pursuing something more important than anything they want."

"You're here about the murder." She finally lowered the gun.

I lowered my hands. "Why did Rawls need to die?"

A bitter laugh twisted her lips. "You think I'm going to trust you?"

"Trust is a dangerous word."

"You're excommunicated."

"I work for Nicodemia, and the gun—the one used to kill Grant Rawls—is more important than you know."

"It was one of my father's guns," said Anya. She paced through the room, artfully dodging the scattered bricks. "He always told us Trinity would flag those damn things outside the range."

"How long have you known about his guns?"

She stopped pacing and looked at me through half-lidded eyes. "I remember the day he showed them to me. He always wanted me to take over the business. Sent me to school for it. Every choice I ever made had to get me closer to being the businessperson he wanted me to be. By the time I graduated from college, I hated him so much.

"Then he took me to the range. He showed me what Blaize showed you. Power. Real power. And wealth like nothing I've ever seen. Those guns are the kind of blatant Karma-destroying extravagance only the highest tier of new money can achieve. And there they were, with a stock full of ammunition and a blank spot in Trinity's omniscience.

"He told me they were insurance. There are stories of AI systems going off the rails, you see." She said it with a hint of sarcasm. "My father believes that the guns would let him pierce the processing core of the ship if that ever happened. How Nicodemia would function without Trinity, I don't know. Probably a slow descent into chaos, if you ask me. As if that's not already our trajectory."

"Velocity matters."

"Feels like we're moving pretty quick these days."

"How did he make them invisible?"

She stared at me. A glimmer of recognition burned behind her eyes. "He took my kids." She looked down at the single-shot holdout pistol in her hand.

"Who?"

"They were supposed to stay safe as long as I took the fall for Rawls' death. That was the deal. I didn't ask to be set free." She started pacing again. "It doesn't make any *sense*."

"Who, Anya?" I stepped forward, but the gun came back up to ward me off.

"That's enough, copper."

"I'm not with the blue." Not entirely true, but if I was being honest with myself, my loyalty was up in the air.

"You want to help?" She gestured wildly with her pistol. "I'll tell you how you can help. Tell Trinity to excommunicate me. I'll sneak up on the bastards and snap all their necks."

"Now settle down," I said, palms forward again to show that I came in peace. I didn't like the look of that neon pistol. "Do you know where the kids are?"

She stepped forward and jabbed at me with her gun. "If you get me excommunicated, I can ask Trinity. Isn't that how it works?"

"Most folks think excommunication is a Church thing. A moral failing."

Anya stared at me. I got the distinct impression she was trying to decide if I was worth it. I wasn't, but she maybe didn't realize it. "He told me about the guns right after I lost my brother."

Fortner had told me that his eldest son died on the *Benevolent.* "You were a second choice."

"Blaize and Mia were too young. Lorrel was too dead." She waved the gun like it was a magic wand. "There I was, ready to be free to the world with a bright future, only to find my father had me slated to run his antique empire."

"A lot of folks would consider that a blessing."

She pointed the gun at my heart. "Are you going to help or not?"

"I won't ask Trinity to excommunicate you."

"Then what good are you?" Her shoulders tensed. This woman wasn't a killer. Her shoulders tensed and her jaw hardened, but she still didn't pull the trigger.

Pushing my luck, I stepped forward. "Nobody's ever lost in Nicodemia, Anya. Not you, not me, and not your kids." Another step. I didn't break eye contact. "Now, I don't know what drama you have going on, and maybe that's none of my business. What *is* my business is the way the murder weapon is rattling around in the glass cage that's keeping all of us alive. Your father says those guns can pierce Trinity's processing center? I'd bet they could go a lot deeper. A stray bullet could punch through generators and protective shielding. It could flood us all with a slow trickle of radiation. A little lead in the wrong place could change the world."

I took her gun.

It was a risk. She might have shot me. For once, I didn't screw things up—my meaty fist closed over her whole hand and held it still before she could even pull the trigger. She cried in pain and spat curses at me. Nothing I hadn't heard before. With a twist, the gun was mine. I dropped it in the breast pocket of my new wool coat.

As the action settled, Cain appeared at the door. His leash trailed the mangled remains of the fibersteel fencing I'd tied him to. He snuffled at the air and let out a low growl. It gave me an idea.

"Let's start again," I said. "My name's Jude Demarco—handyman, medic, and detective. I hear you've lost your kids. Do you have anything around here that smells like them?"

Anya glared at me with a burning hate so fierce I had to check my hair didn't start on fire. "Yeah," she finally said. "Pretty much everything."

Chapter 27

"CAIN!" I growled.

Cain ignored me. Trailing Anya through the Hallow streets had been a brisk walk through corners and shadows. Following Cain through Haven was a flat-out sprint through crowded, startled masses.

It was as if he were bred for the exact purpose of tracking by smell. Anya had brought out some dirty laundry. Cain had snuffled it and cast around as if he knew what he was doing. Then we led him in a wide circle around the block. Far enough that he didn't get confused by the house. Not so far that the circle would take too long to manage.

Cain always pulled when he was on a leash. It was one of the habits Angel always wanted me to train out of him. When she walked him, he was a gentle giant, leaving just the right amount of slack on the lead. When I walked him, it was a constant contest of strength and mass—a contest in which we were surprisingly well matched.

But this—this was *really* pulling. My shoulder socket

ached. His claws dug into the hard fiberstone streets, and he forced his way forward.

When the leash finally snapped, it was all I could do to keep up.

"Slow down!" shouted Anya from a block upslope.

My legs ached and my lungs burned. Cain stopped at a corner and cast about. His floppy jowls smeared slobber over the gray streets.

"Hey, watch it!" A hot dog vendor caught his cart as I barreled past, narrowly avoiding a catastrophic toppling of his livelihood.

I muttered an inadequate apology.

An automated rickshaw blindsided me. It slammed hard into my hip, sending shockwaves of bone-wrenching pain through my side. I sprawled across the ground, making the least artful roll possible. The leash slipped from my grasp.

Gasping in pain as much as from lack of oxygen, I stumbled to the corner where I'd last seen Cain. The crowd flowed back in, forgetting the trauma of Cain's passing.

There! I ran left where the cries of alarm hinted at Cain's passage far ahead. After another block, I caught up to the dog and saw him duck into a dark alley. An automated drone buzzed too close to my head, but I ducked in time to avoid its dangerous blades.

Only when the drone curved around for another swipe did it occur to me that Trinity was hindering me. The drone accelerated with a whine and steered straight for my head.

Hindering? Yes. Trying to kill? Maybe.

But this wasn't Heavy Nicodemia. Had the machine's murderous intent spread upward?

If it was trying to kill me, it wasn't doing a very good job. I ducked left and grabbed air. The drone swept high up toward the false sky above. There were a dozen ways it could come at me. I had no choice but to continue.

Anya caught up to me at the alley entrance. She grabbed my elbow. "What are you doing?" she gasped.

"The dog has the scent."

"So, get your dog under control." When she saw my expression, she said, "You have a dog that big and it's not under control?"

"Training is a priority."

"It should be your *top* priority."

"Finding your kids is higher on the list right now."

Cain barked from somewhere in the darkness. I stalked into the black, lights illuminating only as Anya followed. The dog's barks echoed down the shadowed walls of the alley, making an eerie double bark that muddled his location. As I reached the end of the alley, I saw Cain a short distance away, sitting on his haunches and looking back at me.

As soon as I appeared, he smashed his nose to the ground and started again.

"He's waiting for us," I said as Anya appeared by my side.

"Quit standing around, then." She pushed past and followed the dog.

Now that we knew the dog would wait—and he did at every corner—we no longer had to run. Cain led us down-spiral through the outer reaches of the upper Haven districts. There was the glitzy Diamond District, with its extravagant housing and wide streets. We passed an area known as the Greens, where all the walls had been painted an awful shade of deep olive. A bot district just below the halfway point of the bead was filled with drones and robots. Men and women worked on the devices to keep them maintained so that the bots in turn could maintain Nicodemia.

All the while, I watched the skies. The drone that had

swiped at me drifted high above near the false sky of a ceiling. I could see it as a dark spec against the gray-blue backdrop. There was no way to know it was the same one, but whenever I looked up, there it was.

"We're being tracked," I said.

"I don't know your story," said Anya, "but that's pretty normal around here."

"Not for me."

"I want my gun back."

"That pea-shooter?"

"What are you going to do when we find my kids? *If* we find my kids."

"I'll negotiate."

"Really?" Her voice dripped with sarcasm. "What do *you* have to negotiate with?"

"I'm very persuasive."

A worker shouted in alarm. The bot that he was working on spun out of control. It was a street sweeper the size of a buffalo, and its spindly arms flailed about. It twisted and thrashed, and the man scrambled backward.

The sweeper toppled, and I had to sidestep out of the way. Its limbs kicked and thrashed. Its sweepers whirred and grasped for the street. It was like a helpless infant, squalling on the floor.

"I don't like this," I said.

"What, the kidnapping of my kids?"

"I was thinking more about the danger to my own hide, but yeah, the kidnapping thing, too."

Cain barked far ahead. We picked up our pace and quickly exited the bot district. The place we entered was a managed warehouse, packed with machinery and loading equipment. After the noise and bustle of the bots, it was like walking into a ghost town. There was old dust on the windows, and the storage buildings stretched high into the sky. Under our feet, the cobbles were cracked and broken.

"I didn't think Trinity abandoned districts," Anya said.

"Trinity doesn't abandon anything. This is part of the body, soul, community mandate."

She kicked a stray chunk of broken fiberstone. "This kind of thing shouldn't happen in a functioning system."

"The abandoned district is like a release valve."

"I'm talking about the kidnapping."

"Who took your kids, Anya?"

For a whole block she said nothing. Dimly lit gray buildings stretched high above us. "It's the same people who wanted me to take the fall for that murder."

"And you didn't fall."

"I tried," she snarled. "My damn father had to ruin it."

"And now your kids are gone."

"I tried to tell him not to interfere. He had to have known there was something going on. He could have interfered but…"

"But what?" When she didn't respond to the prompt, I tried again, "Who are we going to find there, Anya."

"I don't know."

"You spoke with them."

"I don't know!" Her voice echoed in the empty district. "My family has a lot of enemies, Demarco. You should know, since you're one of them. It could be one of a dozen families up there in the Hallows. All pieces of shit, if you ask me. They're why I wanted out of the Fortner fortune. Not because my siblings are morons."

She wanted out. She said it as if I already knew all about it. I filed the information for later. "That's why you want to be excommunicated," I said, the pieces finally clicking together. "So that your family can't track you down."

"Jail would have been just as good," Anya said.

"Reform's no walk in the park."

"From what I hear, there *is* a park, and walking through it is part of the path toward reintegration into society."

"That's true in the Hallows," I said. "Reform in the Heavies isn't quite so nice."

"Figures."

We were at the base of a long hill. The broken cobbles stretched for several blocks ahead of us, lit only by the dim sky beyond. At the top of the hill sat Cain, a solid block of muscle and bone backlit by the gray light beyond. He watched us walk up the long slope, waiting for us to get halfway up before turning to look at the building on the left side of the street.

It was the only lit building for three blocks. A warm yellow glow shone through the cracks of closed drapes on a two-story rambler of a house. It sat at the edge of the towering warehouses, the fence in its small yard making the line between the warehouse and residential halves of the abandoned district. Its fiberwood porch sat shrouded in dust and gloom. The neighboring houses formed a perfect matching street of little houses, all the same, but only this one emitted any kind of light.

"We go slow," I said. "Assume they're armed."

She spun on me. "You could still make me excommunicated."

"Lady, I don't even know how I'd do that."

"Trinity will do what you ask." She gestured at the empty houses around us. "You have the ability to make places like this better. All you have to do is talk to Trinity."

How did she know about that? "Trinity and I aren't exactly on speaking terms at the moment."

"Because you're not doing it right."

"No," I said.

"What?"

"No. I won't ask Trinity to excommunicate you. It's more curse than blessing, Anya. You don't deserve that life any more than you deserve the family God dumped you with. But with family, you can make things better." I looked at my own hands. "There's no making this better."

"Maybe you're not doing it right," she deadpanned.

"We take it slow. Case the house from all sides. Make sure they aren't going to sneak out the back while we're crashing in the front. This needs to be done right if it's going to be safe for your kids."

"You really won't do it?"

"Really."

She slugged me in the chest. "Asshole."

Her punches hurt, but I did my best not to show it. "I'm the guy going out of his way to track down your kids."

Her jaw was so hard it could crack diamonds. "Let's go then."

"Slow and quiet," I repeated. If we were lucky, we could get the kids out without ever alerting the kidnappers.

I turned to finish the long walk up the slope just in time to see Cain charge into the house, snarling, barking, frothing at the mouth.

"So much for slow," said Anya.

And then we ran.

———————————

Chapter 28

———————————

"COVER THE BACK," I said without bothering to see if Anya had heard. I needed to get to Cain before he killed someone. For all I knew, he thought we were hunting children instead of just tracking them. The thought sent a shudder down my spine.

The front door hung on broken hinges. Cain's snarling barks echoed in the empty house, reverberating on fiberoak walls and rattling empty glass display cases. The air smelled of dust and stale sweat and—

Blood.

A scream punched through the night. Not a child. My heart hammered.

I turned right and went through into a dining room. In one corner, a young girl—maybe six or seven—pressed herself hard against the wall. In another corner, a man ineffectually fought off my giant dog with the torn, bloody flesh of his left arm.

"Cain!" I yelled.

The dog didn't listen. Shit. He clamped back onto the arm and shook like he might tear it off.

"Down! Back! Drop it!" I shouted each command, doing my best to imitate my sister's commanding voice. It didn't work.

A crash shook the house. It came from the back door. Anya? I had to keep my cool. If I plunged in now, I'd be fish food. I took in the scene, forcing myself still.

Cain wrenched at the man's arm. A blood-spattered gun sat on the floor a short distance away. Large caliber. Plastic. Cain might have spotted it and attacked. That or—

I saw it. A fresh gouge marred Cain's shoulder. When he dragged the man back and shook him, fresh dark globs of blood spattered onto the floor.

"You shot my dog," I growled. My cool was melting fast. "Cain. Drop it."

This time, Cain spat the man into the corner. The guy clutched his shredded arm and backed as far away as he could. The dog didn't have him anymore, but the guy wasn't out of the water yet. If he so much as twitched, Cain would be all over him. Another crash came from the back of the house.

Gunshots.

"Stay," I said.

Cain stayed put. The medic in me wanted to check the guy's wounds, but there were more urgent matters.

I stepped into the other room and ran smack into a murder scene. A man in a button-down shirt and tie fired at a middle-aged woman. Not Anya. Her wife? The bullets took her in the chest, and she staggered back.

Screams.

This time it was children.

They hid behind a battered old sofa. Stuffing flew everywhere. Ceramic bullets shattered on impact, sending the fluff up so the room looked like a snow globe.

All the man had to do was aim his gun at me and I'd be done, but he wasn't looking at me. I slammed a fist down on his outstretched arm. The gun skittered away.

He ducked my next clumsy swing—frustration flared—then landed a jolting rabbit punch in my ribs. I grunted, breath knocked sideways. He followed up with a blinding cross to the jaw, his ring cutting a burning gash in my chin. Blood spilled hot down my neck. I was reeling.

"A boxer," I said, bringing up my guard. "I hate boxers."

"Nobody says you need to be here." His eyes darted to the spot near the door where his gun landed. It was too far. If he went for it, I'd have him before he was halfway there.

"Who do you work for?"

He feinted with a lead hook, which I copped to, then with a left jab, which I didn't. The follow-up cross caught me solid in the bruised ribs. I gasped, pain like lancing electricity through my side. The guy was fast, his punches like slugs of iron.

But I was big. Big still mattered for something, didn't it?

No. No, it did not.

He pounded me twice more in the ribs—each shot a white-hot spike—before I forced him to dance back. "I'd like to see you fight sometime," I gasped.

"You could still walk outta here."

"I have a few questions first."

I didn't feint. I didn't dance or dodge. I swung hard and straight, aiming a fist through to the back of his skull. As my swing cut air, though, he was long gone. Ducked to the right. I came back at him with an elbow, followed with a left hook.

Connected. A glancing blow. I tried to tangle him up, but the bugger rolled with the punch and came back swinging. A fist clubbed the muscle of my right arm, and my hand went numb. He jabbed me in the stomach, and I tasted acid.

He danced away. His eyes went wide, but he wasn't looking at me.

The sound Anya made could have come from a dying animal. She pushed past me and fell to her knees in front of the woman dying on the floor.

The man went for the gun. I dove. Hands grasped his arm as he latched onto the gun. I pressed him down. Leaned into him. Maybe extra mass *was* an advantage.

"Get the kids out of here," I growled at Anya.

Her only response was a wail of grief.

The man twisted. His gun swung toward me, but I wrestled it down and battered his hands against the floor. The weapon skittered free.

Now I had him. Up close and wrestling, the advantage was mine. I twisted his arm and forced his elbow into a lock that was clearly painful. He swore at me. Squirmed.

"I said I want to ask a few questions," I said.

"Get judged, asshole."

"Who do you work for?" A little more pressure on the elbow.

His face went red.

"Anya," I said without taking my eyes from the man. "You need to get your kids out of here." In the corner of my eye, I saw her move. Good. If she got them out of danger I'd have some semblance of control over the situation.

Assuming Cain didn't try to eat the other guy again.

The click of a cocked pistol told me she wasn't leaving. Not yet.

She stood with the gun in two hands, aiming it straight at the man's head. "Move, Demarco." Her voice was an icy avalanche.

"He's down," I said, shifting slightly to keep myself between the man and the gun. "He's helpless. Leave him to me and I guarantee he'll do a stint in reform."

"Reform," she spat. "He doesn't deserve reform."

"And your kids don't deserve to watch a man die."

The kids were still behind the sofa, the older one's mop of hair visible around the corner. He was watching everything. Anya saw this too. Anything to break the tunnel vision she must have been experiencing was a good thing, as far as I was concerned. Her wife was dead at her feet. Every emotion she was feeling was valid, but I couldn't let her kill this man. He was my only lead to the real killer.

Anya was a real killer. The way she held the weapon. The dead look in her eyes. In that moment, I believed she could kill the man. I knew it in my heart. Everything I had seen in her before was gone. This woman had a cold heart.

Then she relaxed. Her shoulders dropped almost imperceptibly. Her finger loosened on the trigger. She breathed.

"That's right, Anya," I said. "I know you want more, but it's up to people like us to do the right thing. There's enough death in Nicodemia without us helping it along."

"Yeah," she said, as if speaking to me from a great distance. "Yeah, I guess you're right."

The front door slammed. I twisted to look through to the other room where I'd left the other man.

He was gone.

With my movement, Anya had a clear shot.

She took it. A single gunshot rattled the walls. The man went slack in my grip. I stared at Anya, and my wide eyes must have scared her, because she turned the gun at me.

"You can question the other guy," she snarled.

But the other guy was gone. In the other room, I saw why. Cain lay panting where I'd left him. He had licked his wounds, but he was clearly in a lot of pain—every time he drew a shallow breath, the blood from his gunshot wounds welled up. He looked up at me and whined.

The man's trail of blood ran all the way to the door, and then disappeared. I could follow him. He couldn't be moving very fast.

But Cain was injured worse than I had thought. I placed a hand on the dog's muzzle. At my touch, a long sigh shook the loose skin of his jowls.

There was movement behind me. Anya was finally leaving with her children. I wasn't going to follow her, and I wasn't going to follow the man with the injured arm. He'd bleed his way all the way to a hospital, probably. Maybe he'd connect with members of his gang for medical treatment. If I let him go now, I might never track him down. He was in the wind.

I propped Cain up and took a good look at his wounds. One in particular looked bad. It was in the muscle of his chest and the folds of his flesh concealed it. When I moved the skin around, I could feel pieces of the shattered bullet deep inside the muscle. It wasn't a fatal injury. Probably.

But I couldn't risk it.

I cared about the dog more than the case.

And God be damned if I was going to lose him now.

Chapter 29

ANIMALS AREN'T TERRIBLY different from humans, and my medical training gave me the basics. I knew how to extract the shards of ceramic. I knew how to stitch the wound. There were nuances for how to prevent the dog from reopening that wound, but Trinity's medical instructions helped me navigate them. Getting the right amount of anesthetic into his big dog veins had been a challenge, but I figured it out. When I was finished and all of his wounds were bandaged, I loaded him into a cart and rolled him down to Customs.

"Rough day?" asked my sister as she wheeled up to meet me. It was morning already, and I knew by her expression that she had better places to be. I was only glad that the message I'd paid a kid to send had made it to her.

I touched the bandage on my chin. I'd cleaned myself up a little but taking that beating hadn't made me any prettier. The ache of exhaustion sank deep into my bones. "I should wear black more often," I said. "It hides the blood."

"Doesn't hide the stink." She looked past me to Cain,

who slept in my stolen cart. She cupped his big head in her hands. "How's this guy doing?"

My mouth went dry. "Sis, I'm sorry—"

"I shouldn't have expected so much from you."

The words couldn't have hurt more, not even if she'd rubbed them into my eyes with a bucket of sand. "Once the drugs wear off, he'll need a cone."

"Should we get going, then?"

I took a step back. "I can't come with, sis."

"He's hurt."

"There's been another murder."

Her expression went flat. "Then go."

"He'll be better off with you."

"I said, go."

By the time I made it upslope to the abandoned district, the bustle of the Haven morning was in full swing. Even in the warm glow of morning, the district stayed shrouded in the gray of twilight. The ceiling high above wasn't the false sky found most places in the spiral, but instead was the dull black of a dead screen. Light poured in from the sides of the district—now that I had a good view of it, it wasn't more than a dozen blocks—but shadows persevered all the way to the edge.

I was afraid that by the time I got back, the house would have been picked over. In any other district, the bodies would have been discovered and reported. Trinity would have sent cleaning bots to scrub the building, and a crew of workers would have hauled the body away. Police. Cleaners. Everything back to normal. Just like down in the Heavies when Rawls was killed.

The man's death played on repeat in my skull. Anya's grip on the gun. Her shot right between the man's eyes. Her grief at the death of her partner.

Everything felt wrong about the whole thing, and I couldn't put a finger on it.

At least the evidence was still there. Before I left, I'd have to get someone to report it. Trinity could handle it from there. For the moment, however, I needed one good long look at the murder scene.

It was worse than I remembered. Either the haze of adrenaline masked the horror of the scene or the dull light of morning revealed it. There was blood everywhere. The room where Cain had attacked the man was in ruins. Cain's bloody claw marks were gouged into the dark fiberoak floor. The heavy dining table was overturned, and one of its smashed legs was half-wedged into the wall. Nothing gets in the way of my dog. I drew a deep breath. There was something I needed to know.

I went back to the front door. It was broken on its hinges and a bright smear of blood crossed it at an angle at knee level. Cain's blood. He had been wounded before he attacked. If Cain's blood was on the door, did that mean he'd been hit before he attacked? I tracked the blood all the way out into the street, where he had waited for Anya and me to catch up.

I whispered a prayer that he would recover and swore that I would work on his training in earnest as soon as he was able.

There was another streak of blood on the door, this time higher up and on the inside. This was the shooter's blood. He'd pushed the door open with his ruined arm, meaning—

The gun was missing. I distinctly remember it landing in the corner. Had it been there when I'd left? I didn't know. It didn't make sense to me that the shooter would pick up the gun and leave, but he must have. I stepped from the house and followed the trail of searing red droplets. He had taken a hard left outside the house, then made his way through the low architecture of abandoned district. If I had followed him, I might have caught him as he tried his best to move away without using the roads. He was headed downslope. I found a place where he stopped to bandage himself. After that, there was no obvious trail of blood.

Back in the house, I finally built up the courage to step into the other room. It was far worse and smelled of the sour sweet of death. Brains and blood and bone decorated the walls, covered in the snow-white fluff of sofa innards. I did my best to ignore it all, and instead knelt beside the man on the floor.

He looked younger in death than he had in life. The back half of his skull was gone, but his eyes were empty of the hard disdain he'd shown in life. Gone, too, were the wrinkles that came with a constant scowl. All that remained was the smooth skin of a boy trying desperately to make his way in a hard world.

A quick check showed no identifying papers and no jewelry. His identity wouldn't be hard to establish with the help of Trinity, but I didn't have that luxury. He wore a cheap suit, athletic shoes, and a blood-smeared hat on a stand near the door might have been his. Not much to go on, but together it was almost a uniform for organized crime in Haven. The blue would probably find that he had loose associations with underground gambling or some local loan shark. Not the kind I'd expect to be pegged for kidnapping.

I was missing something, and it lingered at the undiscovered edge of my mind.

The woman's death hadn't been so clean. He'd shot her in the chest before I entered the room, and I didn't know why. She had taken three bullets and fallen straight back. Based on the angle of the sofa, she would have been in full view of the children as she passed away. My mouth tasted like acid, and for a fraction of a second I didn't mind the shooter's fate. He had murdered a woman in cold blood in front of children who had loved her.

One of the hardest things we can do is realize that we don't deserve to judge anyone, not even the guilty. Of all my failings, this was one I visited most often.

Her dark skin was pale now in death. She had broad shoulders and a double chin. A beauty still lingered in the depths of her full cheeks, even in death. She was average height for a native of Haven, but her features bore a resemblance to the Travelers of the Hallows. If I had seen her in life, I might have been able to pick which family line she came from. As it was, all I could see in her features was a life cut too short. She wore a thick overcoat atop flannel pajamas. They had been taken in the middle of the night, after all. The kidnappers would have forced her to wear the overcoat, since moving through town in a flannel nightie would have been suspicious. The pockets of the coat were empty.

Why had he shot her?

I knelt beside her, careful to avoid the worst of the blood, and touched her cheek. She was cold already, and an unnatural stiffness resisted my touch.

"What happened last night?" I whispered, as if she might speak the truth.

But in Nicodemia, sometimes the truth was hidden in the dark hearts of the dead. Maybe all things could be found, but not everything could be known.

Then I saw it. Under the sofa, a glint of color caught my eye. Using my lighter to illuminate the space, I saw a crimson grip and blue barrel. I tried to reach it, but my fingertips only pushed it deeper into the dark.

A woman's booming voice rattled the front door. "Halders, mark that blood trail. Echo, come with me."

The blue. I stayed low and moved back through the building as the cops entered through the bloody front door. I found the place Anya where had entered the building—where she had stood to shoot the boxer. I saw the tiny, bloody footprints where the children fled with their mother. Following the hall to the right, I found the exit. Its lock was broken. She must have forced her way through when she heard gunshots.

Quietly, I pushed the door open and made my way onto the cramped back patio. I climbed the fence straight back, and as the flashing blue converged on the ruinous crime scene, I escaped into the abandoned district.

Chapter 30

I WANDERED the streets and napped on a bench in the distant reaches of a garden district. Exhaustion pulled at me like the dark void of space. I had half a mind to let it take me. My jaw ached. My ribs clicked every time I stretched too far. There was something happening in my left knee that defied proper medical explanation. A wise man would have given up, but I was like Cain on a scent. There was no stopping me, even when stopping was a good idea. Even if stopping meant survival.

A real investigator would have spent more time analyzing the crime scene, but the blue wouldn't look kindly on my presence, so all I could do was recreate the scene in my mind. It helped that I had been there when it happened, but there were pieces I was missing.

For instance, the guy who had shot Cain. When had he retrieved his gun? It had been across the room in the corner. He would have had to pass closer to a dog who had just mangled him in order to reach a weapon that had already failed to stop said dog.

People did things that didn't make sense all the time.

Maybe Cain had passed out and the shooter had the confidence to get the gun. Then why not fire into the other room? He could have at least had a shot me. He probably would have been able to take Anya out. It would have been messy, but he would have saved his buddy and shown his boss a little initiative.

I flexed my jaw. Of all the hits I'd taken from the boxer, that was the blow that had really stung. Lying back on the bench, I stared at the shimmering blue sky above. The day had stretched long, even though I couldn't remember sleeping.

Why had he shot Anya's partner? They'd gone through the trouble of dragging her and the kids all the way out to the abandoned district just to have everything devolve into chaos?

Drawing Anya's single-shot holdout pistol from my pocket, I held it up in the shimmering light. Red grip. Blue barrel. Compact. Efficient. The gun under the sofa had been similar. *Very* similar. If only I had been able to get it out in time so that I could compare the two weapons, then I would know if they were from the same manufacturing set.

But it made sense. Anya had a holdout pistol. It made sense that her wife—girlfriend, lover, close friend—had a matching weapon.

The question, then, was *why* did she have it. She had just been kidnapped. They would have taken her weapon. Had they left it somewhere she could get it? That seemed sloppy, but some of these thugs were pretty dumb.

Only I didn't get that impression from the boxer. He was at least moderately competent.

She might not have been kidnapped. Maybe she had followed the kidnappers same as we had, and she happened to break into the house as we approached. The coincidence in timing seemed too much, but Cain's arrival might have caused the distraction she had needed. If she had moved on the boxer, he might have reacted violently. The children would have hidden behind the sofa, and when I stepped into the room, the boxer was distracted, giving me the jump.

It was the best I could do to make the pieces fit, and the tragedy of it all was a sour taste in the back of my mouth.

Later in the afternoon, I returned again to the scene of the crime. From the top of a neighboring duplex, I watched the swarm of uniformed officers move through the perimeter and slowly process the scene. It would be hours before they vacated the premises. Possibly days. They would post a watch. If I needed to get back in, it would have to wait.

Not that I would find much else on the scene. The blue of the Hallows might be corrupt and incompetent, but they knew how to process a crime scene. After some time passed, they carted the bodies away for processing. Forensics, funerals, recycling.

"Are we going to find you had something to do with this?" said a voice behind me.

I didn't turn around. "I sure hope not."

Halders sat next to me on the balcony's only other rickety folding chair.

I glanced back and saw Echo's big form scowling at me from the top of the ladder.

"You ought to answer the question properly," Halders said. "Or Echo's going to be the one asking."

"Tough business down there," I said, nodding to the blue loading one of the bodies onto a cart. "Any idea who the victims are, or who they work for?"

Halders touched his chin. "Looks like you've had a rough day."

"Ran into a door," I said.

"A sharp one?"

I frowned and touched two fingers to the bandage on my jaw. They came back bloody. The cut might have been worse than I thought. "Maybe I talk too much."

"Maybe you don't talk enough."

"Maybe."

We sat in silence for a long time. Finally, Halders said, "Am I going to find anything down there linking you to the murders?"

His wording struck me as peculiar and more than a little generous. He wasn't forcing me to lie, which was more of a kindness than I expected from the man. "I don't think so," I said. "But the door I ran into might have looked a whole lot like the dead guy's fist."

Echo scoffed behind me.

"Like you said, I've had a rough day."

"Here's what I don't get," Halders said, leaning close. "A guy drops in a bloody mess in the middle of a busy neighborhood. He's got marks on his arm like he's half-digested by the local wildlife, only there *isn't* any local wildlife. Never has been." He drew a long deep breath. "But there's a trail. Echo and I get the call. We've got a reputation for dealing with crap like this, so they summon us down from our cushy jobs in the Hallows. Suspicious activity, the message says."

"Who's the guy?" I asked.

"Doesn't matter."

"Seems important."

"He's just a guy."

"If you say so."

Halders continued, "We follow the trail, being the excellent sleuths that we are. It leads us around a bit. There's a point where he stopped to do some bandaging." He nods to my bandaged chin. "Nothing quite as expert as that, but I suppose he's doing it one-handed, and he's got to be in a hell of a lot of pain."

"He could have gone to a medic station or a proper hospital," I said.

"Lot of folks stay away from places like that," said Halders.

Echo chimed in with, "Hospital's a great place to die."

"They're also a great place to get reported," said Halders. "Whatever the case, this guy didn't go to one. He wasn't even headed toward one, as far as we could tell."

"Where is he now?"

"We spent some time poking around his hidey hole." Halders leaned back and the chair creaked dangerously under him. "Didn't find anything."

"No gun," said Echo.

"No knife. No weapon at all. No identifying papers. Nothing on the body either."

Mildly annoyed, I said, "Is that what's confusing you?"

"The trail got stronger then. Up till that point, it was a drop or two every dozen steps. This was a line of blood leading straight to this district." Halders made a grand gesture at the dim housing around them. "Echo says they should have blockaded this area when it went dark. I say it wouldn't have made a difference."

"It's about legal culpability," said Echo. "Ethically speaking."

"Sure," I said. "You make an effort to keep people out, knowing that they'll get in anyway. That way at least it's not your fault when they get hurt."

"Ethics," said Echo.

"I must not be great at ethics."

"We found a gun down there," said Halders.

"But it's not the murder weapon," I said, understanding where he was going.

"It's a single-shot holdout pistol," said Echo. "Good for a little cosmic revenge before the bad guys get you. Not good for much else."

"More like cosmetic," I said.

Halders curled his lips in disgust. "That gun has the stopping power of a stiff breeze. And odds are decent it'll shatter and blow a few fingers off."

"Seems like a person ought to be careful with their guns, then." I thought of the gun in my pocket.

Halders said, "The one we found hadn't been fired. There must be another gun, and since the guy didn't have it, we think there might be at least one other person present at the scene."

"Good deductive reasoning."

Echo said, "Then we spotted you."

"I like the quiet."

Echo took the lapels of my coat in his meaty fists. "Listen here, Demarco. We've had enough of your crap. It's time to come clean. What's the story down there? Or do I need to drag you down to the station and forget you in a cell?"

"Echo," said Halders, a warning in his voice.

"It's fine," I choked. "I'll talk."

Echo's grip eased, but he didn't let go.

"Word was these goons had a couple of kids that didn't belong to them."

Echo's death grip eased. "Where are the kids now?"

"No idea."

"Did you shoot anyone?" Halders had both hands on the rail and was looking down at the crime scene below. A damp breeze ran down the length of the long street. "We're tired of cleaning up your messes."

"If I thought you could clean up this mess, I wouldn't be here."

Echo cinched my collar tight until my airway was the size of a pin. "Listen here, Demarco. My partner here thinks you're not responsible for all this, but I'm not convinced. Trouble sure does follow you." When my knees went weak, he shoved me to the floor, where I collapsed in a heap. The bandage tore from my face, and I could feel the trickle of blood down my neck.

I knew better than to fight back with these guys. I might have been able to escape, but they'd make my life hell if I did. "This time it was me following the trouble."

"Why?" asked Halders.

"I need to find their boss." I pressed the bandage back onto my wound, but it was soaked through and wouldn't do much good. Something Halders had said stirred the sluggish flow of my memory. "Let me see the guy's ring."

"What ring?" Halders said.

"The dead guy. He had a ring."

"There was no ring," Halders said, earning a sour look from his partner. "No harm if he knows that."

"My chin says there was a ring." I touched the wound.

"There was no ring," said Echo, but I had his interest.

"Someone must have cleaned the crime scene. If they had taken the man's ring, then that ring must have been important." I tried to picture the thing in my mind, but I'd never gotten a great look at it. "Did the other guy have a ring?"

"No identifying marks on either of them," Halders said. "Records don't show who they worked for. They're both independently operating hatchetmen."

"Worthless scum," Echo spat.

The words bounced around my skull. "The judge."

I stood, towering over the big man. "It was the judge. The

judge who set Anya Fortner free had the same symbol. It was on the band of his watch, but I swear it was the same stylized crescent and stars."

"What are you talking about, Demarco?" said Halders.

"Their rings," I said. "They had the same symbol that the judge had. I'm sure of it. Let me talk to that guy you picked up and I'll confirm the connection."

Halders stared at me. "You can talk all you want, but he's not talking back."

"Why not?"

"He's dead," Echo said. "Shot in the back on that busy square in the Sinless."

"Lead bullet," said Halders. "Straight through the heart."

And just like that, I knew exactly what I needed to do.

Chapter 31

I'VE BEEN ACCUSED of many things. Shoplifting. Fraud. Murder.

I have never been accused of being too friendly. All my life, I've made enemies of allies.

To be fair, though, I've made enemies of assholes too.

Kaegan Fortner had told me how to make an enemy of him. It wasn't through his family, and it wasn't through his shop. Fortner cared about the guns. They were everything, according to the old oligarch, and when I thought he was a good steward of them, I had grudgingly acknowledged that throwing the entire contents of his vault into the recycler wasn't going to happen.

There was more than one way to render a weapon useless. In Customs, they drilled holes in the barrels. A tiny cosmetic change destroyed the integrity of the weapon, making it dangerous to operate. It could still be bought and sold. I didn't have time to drill all those holes. They removed the firing pins, but pins could be easily replaced. That would never do.

I wished that I could recycle the guns. The component materials could be processed and fed into the ever-present need for metal in the fiber production process. It would be like the last good deed, but for guns. Unfortunately, I couldn't see myself transporting all those guns across Haven Nicodemia to get them into a recycler big enough to handle them. What if someone stole them in transit? What if not all of them were invisible to Trinity's systems? There were too many complicating factors.

Then I remembered what Anya had told me in the antique shop.

"Fluid," I said to the foreman. "Or foam. They use it to make reinforced windows."

The construction worker stared at me. Behind him, a crew assembled the fibersteel framework for a new row of tenements in the upper reaches of Haven Nicodemia. The old buildings had been knocked down as part of a neighborhood renewal project, and now it was time to build modern, new homes. Every building in Nicodemia had a lifecycle, and these crews were always building something new and something better.

I thought of Kaegan Fortner in his luxurious Hallow home. If the man suspected what I was doing, he'd have his hitmen waiting for me. He might even take it out on these construction workers.

The foreman said, "I might have something that'll work."

I tried not to think about the enemies I was making. Fortner, of course. But there would be repercussions for others. Smalley would catch flack. He was the one who had sent me after Fortner's family on a supposed contract. Their agreement involved me not causing trouble.

Blaize could get in trouble. That didn't bother me much either. I was certain he'd taken the Model 41 from the vault.

If that was the case, then all the more reason these guns needed to be destroyed.

Then there were the incidental contacts. The foreman might have trouble getting good construction jobs. My sister's diner might have an uptick in inspections. Any number of my allies and acquaintances might have trouble due to a crime I was about to commit.

But I couldn't allow those guns to exist. Not one moment more.

The canvas bag was heavy. I lugged it across Haven Nicodemia to the sealed door where Blaize had taken me. It wasn't hard to get through the physical lock. A Trinity-controlled system would have been more secure against me, but the paranoia that led the family to fear the computer actually made things easier for me. A pair of lockpicks in my clumsy fingers was enough to get through the hidden door. I used my lighter to illuminate the empty hallway.

The vast open blackness of the shooting range stretched into the void. The air still smelled of gunpowder and oil. Blaize had long since moved on, but I didn't know how much time I would have.

The safe was my next challenge. I could do this without getting into the safe, simply by sealing the whole thing. That didn't seem like enough, though. Someone could always crack it open.

The keypad blinked on the vault's main panel. The numbers stared up at me, blank and inviting. The pale blue shone through the smudges of Blaize's fingerprints. It would have been more helpful if the code hadn't used almost every number on the pad.

I should have asked for a cutting torch too, but would that even cut through this vault? How long would it take me to brute-force my way into the display? Too long. Guaranteed. I needed the code and cursed myself for not thinking far enough ahead.

Closing my eyes, I tried to remember the sound when Blaize opened the vault. It was a tune that played in my memory. I punched in the code that I thought would match that tune.

The lock buzzed failure. Something was wrong in my pattern. I hummed the notes again. No, that wasn't it. Higher at the end. I tried again.

Failed.

A digital display indicated that it would lock me out if I failed one more time.

Deep breaths. Steady. What was the tune?

I punched it in, this time adjusting a note in the middle. The safe flashed green and its door swung open. The tray folded out and expanded before me.

There they were. Dozens of implements of death spread out before me. Colt, Glock, Smith & Wesson. The flame of my lighter flickered across their dangerous black surfaces.

The Walther PPK was still missing. My search for the murder weapon wasn't going to get any easy solutions.

Swiping my light across the display, I noted that the Colt Python and Model 41 spots were both empty as well. Three guns missing. Blaize must have taken his favorite weapon with him, which didn't bode well. If what Fortner had said was true, the Python had been missing for ages. It was likely still out in the city somewhere, but until someone tried to use it, there was little chance of finding it.

Had Blaize been responsible for the missing PPK?

Opening the bag, I removed the device the foreman had given me. It was a backpack-mounted injection rig. Two thick tubes ran from the enormous pack, converging on a heated steel point. I donned it and flipped the switch near the trigger.

The tip heated until it glowed. Taking a cigarette from my pocket, I lit it on the red-hot unit.

Then I got to work.

It took time. More time than I would have liked, but it was important to me that the job be done well. Reactive material from the two tubes converged on the hot point, mixing to form a fiber-based epoxy. Slowly, making sure to fully engulf each of the guns, I encased the whole display. I filled each barrel, ensuring no bubbles were around the grips or triggers. I packed the glowing epoxy into the molded spaces for each weapon, even going so far as to fill the three empty spaces—the PPK, the Python and the Model 41. Once each weapon had been encased, I filled the rest of the tray until it was full to the top.

Then I shut the injector down and waited.

The fiber epoxy was the stuff used in bulletproof windows. An eighth of an inch would stop a ceramic slug. It bonded to metal materials and was perfectly clear once fully cured. It was used to protect the most valuable assets in Nicodemia, and a fortune's worth of it now encased Fortner's guns.

Full curing would take days, but even now, the guns were useless. I'd made an enemy of Kaegan Fortner. He had only to discover it. Hopefully Blaize wouldn't come back for a while. When he did, he would find that I'd turned his armory into a rather pleasant display case.

Once it cooled, I closed the vault and packed the injector back into its canvas bag. I would drop it off with the construction crew before returning to the Hallows. I made a mental note of it. That foreman was just one more person in a long list of people that I owed something to. It was worth it. With those guns destroyed, I could finally breathe.

Now if only I could find those last three weapons.

Chapter 32

JUDGE PINKER ARRIVED home long after the last rays of the Hallow twilight drained from the shrouded sky. The false stars of the night shone through the open window of his expansive condominium, and the shapes in the shadows were like sentinels awaiting animation.

I waited for him in a high-backed chair with lumpy padding covered in crisp new upholstery. The renovated chair was one of a dozen identifiable antiques. He owned everything from a solid wood desk to pewter candlesticks. His window overlooked the ornate gardens of the Gravity Lounge. It had been a long walk after my visit to Fortner's vault in Haven, but if I was going to make an enemy of Kaegan Fortner, then I needed answers, and the judge had them.

The first sign of Pinker's arrival was the glow under the door to the hallway. The splash of warm light spread across a woven rug, making it glow blood red against the black of the unlit room. He opened the door, whistling to himself, and the room's lights flared to life.

I waited until he had crossed the room and hung his coat and briefcase on a rack by the kitchenette. The one-shot holdout pistol I'd picked up from Anya was pointed at his chest. I had unloaded it, but he didn't need to know that. "Long night, Judge?"

He froze.

"I just want to have a chat."

The judge finished putting away his things and turned to me, his cold eyes fixating on the pistol. "You'll regret this."

"It's about one of your recent cases."

He sneered. "If I sentenced your friend, then their best option is to work their way through Reform. Most people come out better for it." He moved to a small table in his kitchenette and poured two glasses from a fancy-looking bottle. He placed one on the desk in front of me.

Outside, a series of flying transports lit up the Hallow night. I set the pistol on the desk and picked up the drink. It smelled like scorched leather and elderberries. "You wore a watch with a symbol on it. A crescent shape with some stars. Looked old."

The man's hard eyes twinkled. "A lot of what I have is old."

"Sure, sure." I sipped the whiskey. The smokey flavors were more complex than anything I'd ever tasted. Good? Maybe. Expensive? Definitely. I decided to play a bluff. "Fortner tells me he wants it back."

Judge Pinker's expression went grim. "Tell him he has no right."

That was one answer, anyway. Not a surprise. It must have been a bribe to set Anya free, but that still didn't tell me who wanted Anya out of the picture. "Come on, Judge. It's just a watch."

His eyes flicked to the gun sitting between us. The light of another flying vehicle flashed across his hardened features. "You're not one of Fortner's usual goons."

"Two guys I ran into today had that same symbol on a couple of rings."

"Matching sets are common in such things."

"Those men are both dead," I said, watching his reaction carefully.

He sipped his whiskey. "Are you comparing me to a couple of street thugs?"

"You're better dressed."

"Leave," he said. "I know what case you're talking about. I would have let the woman go free regardless. You can tell Fortner that. She had perfect Karma, and her crimes were justified."

Justified? "She murdered someone."

In the next flash of light from the flyers outside, the judge snatched up the weapon, pointed it at my chest, and pulled the trigger.

Nothing.

Peering at the weapon, the judge opened his mouth to say something.

Gunshots roared like the vicious yelps of a demon. The window exploded inward.

Bullets punched into Judge Pinker's chest and arms. The holdout pistol skittered across the floor, and the judge collapsed into the kitchenette, smearing blood across the cabinets.

I dropped away from the window. Bullets pounded into the countertop, shattering the whiskey bottle and glasses. I'd been out of view from the flyer. Did the shooter even know I was there?

The holdout pistol was close, and I still had the single bullet in my pocket. If I reached over to grab it, the movement might be spotted by the shooter. I swallowed my hesitation, reached out, and snatched the weapon.

The flyer hovered outside the window. The only sound was the dull hum of the flyer's rotors.

Boots crunched on broken glass. The shooter moved to the kitchenette, where the judge had fallen. I ducked low behind the high-backed chair and loaded the single bullet into the pistol. It felt like a toy in my hand. My heart hammered.

Outside, the flyer whirred in the night. The lower gravity of the Hallows allowed a wide variety of flying machines, but this was an impressive model if it could stay steady outside of the window on its own. If someone was piloting it, then that meant an accomplice. As if I didn't have enough to worry about. I only had one bullet.

The shooter—Blaize Fortner—stepped around the corner of the counter and raised his weapon. With one hand, he took the judge's briefcase from its hook. He dumped its contents onto the counter. "It's nothing personal," he said to the judge, plucking something from the pile. "I hope you realize that."

Judge Pinker mumbled something I couldn't hear. He was still alive. I had to do something.

I stepped out from behind the chair. "Your sister played her part well, Blaize."

He slowly turned to me. "Demarco," he said. "Wasn't expecting to see you here."

"The only thing Anya wanted was for me to make Trinity excommunicate her," I said. "Was everything else a lie? The arrest, the sentencing, the threat to her children?"

"Oh, the threat was real. This doesn't work unless the threat is real." As he glanced at the pistol in my hand, a flash of amusement pulled at the corners of his mouth. He held the Model 41 in his hand, pointed at the floor.

"You already tried to get me to excommunicate you," I said.

He twitched as if an ant had crawled up his leg. "You coulda saved us all this trouble."

"I get why you killed the thug, but why have Anya's wife shot?"

"It's always me cleaning up the mess," said Blaize. A ring on his right pointer finger flashed in the flyer's headlights. "It should be me making gold for the family."

Behind the counter, the judge moaned. Blaize glanced at him nervously.

"Your father won't clean up his own messes?" If I could buy enough time, he'd make a mistake, but I didn't know how much time the judge had left.

"Father would never dirty his hands," Blaize spat. "Anyway, he's too busy with that *Benevolent* crap."

I shuddered under a drastic uptick in my heart rate. "What does Kaegan want with the *Benevolent*?"

Blaize's hand started to gesture with his black pistol, but he stopped when I steadied my gun. A slow smile slipped across his face. "You wouldn't shoot me, Demarco."

"You think I'm too good a guy for that?"

"From what I hear, you're too smart," he said. "You try to run, and Mia's going to gun you down from the flyer."

"You brought your little sister?" She was a kid. Late teens at best.

"We all contain hidden depths," said Blaize. "Most of them are dark."

He was right. I didn't know if I could shoot Blaize. I'd been around plenty of death, and I'd even caused some of it, but there was something visceral about shooting a man.

Something about pulling that trigger and feeling the explosion of violence recoiling back through the hand, through the arm, and deep into the soul that made me doubt my own willingness. I didn't face repercussions from Trinity's Karma system. Pulling that trigger wouldn't affect my excommunicated life in the slightest, but it would leave a dark stain on my soul that I doubted would ever scrub off.

The thought made something click for me. "That ring you're wearing. The judge's watch. They make you excommunicated, don't they?"

His smile showed a row of white teeth. "A gift from my mother." He nodded to the judge. "Something this asshole didn't deserve."

"Why bother with full excommunication if you have something that fixes Karma like that?"

He gestured with his gun again, but I allowed it this time. "You know, I almost thought Anya's plan was going to work. She wasn't supposed to let you find the kids so quick."

"She could hardly have known I'd have Cain with me."

That got an actual chuckle out of him. "Hell of a dog you got there."

"He doesn't like to give up."

The corners of Blaize's lips turned slightly down. "I guess we both know what that's like." He leveled his gun at the judge again.

"Put the weapon away, Blaize."

"You know I can't do that, Demarco. Father doesn't like failures."

"You shoot him, and I'll shoot you," I said. "I won't hesitate." I would. I *knew* I would. I was already hesitating, and any savvy killer would know that the time to kill Blaize had arrived. He was a danger to everyone around him, especially with the Model 41 in his hand.

Long ago, before the tragedy that had destroyed my family, I had been trained as a medic. It was all I thought I'd ever be. The very first day of training, they made us swear to always help, never harm. In the competing goals of Trinity—the body, soul, community—we were dedicated to the body. Even the worst of souls deserved sound health. Even those most poisonous to their communities deserved to benefit from the best medical care technology could offer. If not that, then the lack of care would be the wedge driven between humanity and its transcendence. *That* was what they taught us on the first day of medical training, the second day, and every single day after.

It was the core fundamental belief of those dedicated to the noble cause of fixing that which was most broken in us all.

At least that's what I thought back then. After the *Benevolent*, I realized that the thing most broken in us was never a function of our physical bodies. It was the tumor of despair rooted deeply in our souls. If we fed that tumor, it grew. If we starved it, we could ignore it. For a while.

But it never went away.

Without taking his eyes from the judge, Blaize whispered, "You don't know what it means to be desperate."

I saw what he was about to do long before he moved. The muscles of his neck tensed. His jaw hardened.

His eyes turned to me, and I saw not hate but raw determination, devoid of compassion. Gone was the lively, fun caricature of a man I'd met days ago. Gone was the devoted son and enthusiastic entrepreneur. This Blaize was a killer, cold and simple.

So, I fed the tumor.

My gun didn't have stopping power. It fit in my palm like a bad joke. I aimed for his chest. The light, frangible bullet would make a hash of the man's organs, but maybe he could be saved. It would never stop him from pulling the trigger, but it was the best I could do.

Blaize swung the long-barreled pistol toward me.

I pulled the trigger. My toy gun barked. The sliver of plasti-ceramic plunged into his left eye. It shattered on impact, spreading to scramble the insides of his skull with a single shredding impact.

Light from the flyer played across his upright form. The gun fell. His arm dropped. His legs gave way, and he toppled backward.

"I shoot plastic well enough," I muttered.

Outside, a young woman screamed over the hum of the flyer. Mia. She'd watched me kill her brother.

The judge lay where he had fallen, in a pool of his own slick blood. He had died as I'd dealt with Blaize, and Blaize had known it. He had watched the man bleed out, even as he'd had a conversation with me.

When I turned, I saw Mia staring at me from the pilot's seat of the flyer. Her eyes were wide, and her nostrils flared. I knew that look. She was stunned, unable to move after having witnessed the horror of her brother's death.

I scooped up Blaize's gun, wrenched the ring from his finger, and after a little probing, took the judge's watch. Then, without another glance at Mia in her flyer, I crossed the room and walked out the door into the night.

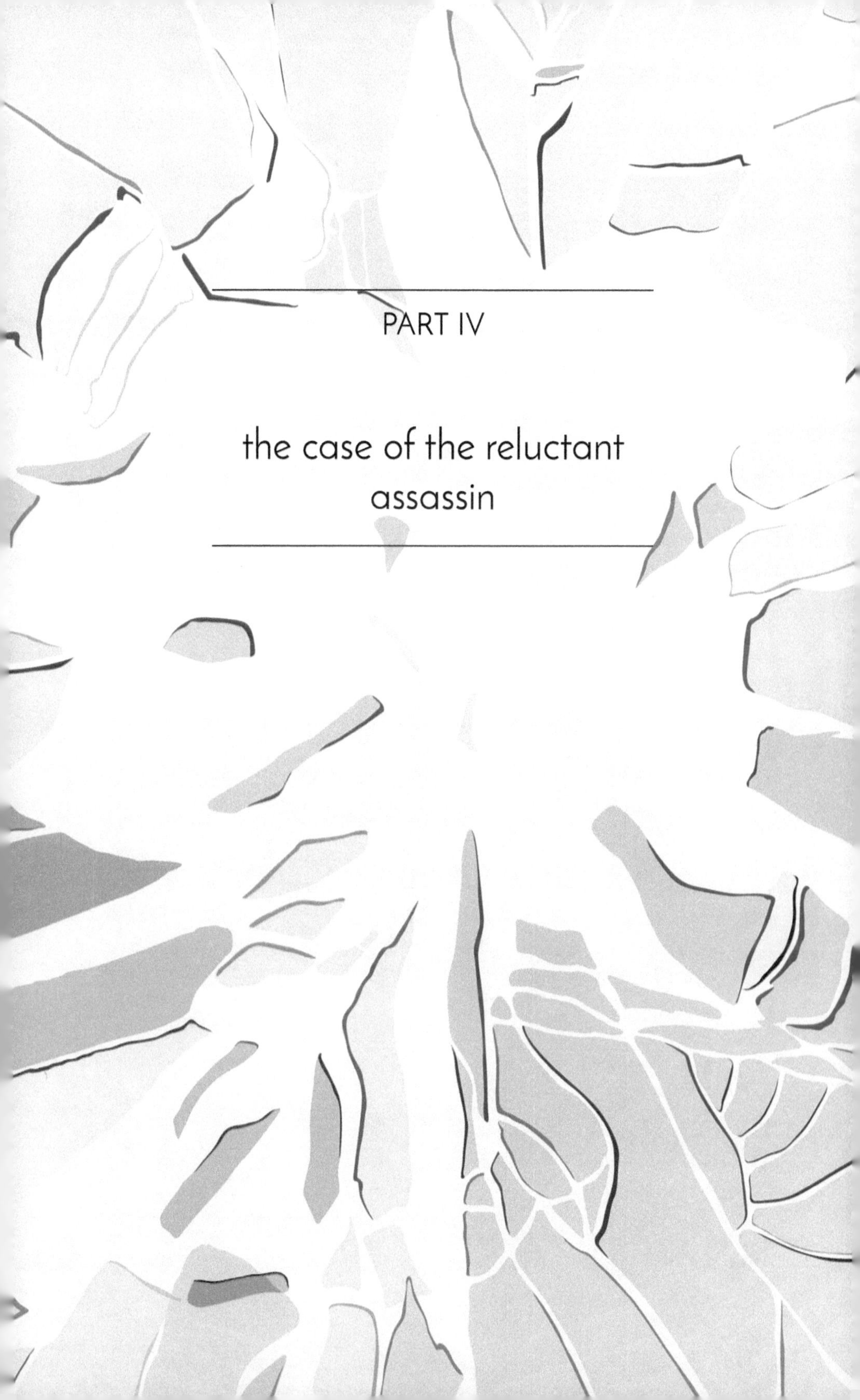
PART IV

the case of the reluctant
assassin

Chapter 33

AS I MADE my way through the eaves of the Cathedral of Saint Benedict in Haven Nicodemia, the monks watched me closely. Light didn't follow me. False candles didn't flicker as I passed. I was a ghost. I had adjusted the bandage on my face so that it wouldn't draw as much attention, and I had even exchanged a few smooth words with a laundromat to get my clothes reasonably clean. This should have made me at least marginally presentable, but the monks didn't care.

The cathedral's high arching pillars and thundering bell tower never felt like home to me, but it had all the hallmark Catholic flourishes one expected. The Stations of the Cross decorated the interior of the chapel, both grisly in their detail and beautiful in their design. The cross above the central altar bore a bloody Jesus, and the true gold of the tabernacle shone like the noonday sun. Saint Benedict had the same funeral chapel as Saint Francis, but with an extra carved swirl on every pew and several bonus icons depicting the glory of Mary, mother of God.

Somber funeral tones sounded throughout the chapel, so

I approached the front, where a coffin stood open. The deceased was an elderly man with a bushy mustache and a pinched expression, even in death.

"He was a good man," said the tall priest.

"A rich one too," I said.

"All we can take with is our good deeds."

I touched the dead man's cold hands. "Maybe that's why there are so few good deeds left for the living."

"Did you know the deceased?"

"Not particularly."

The service was about to start, so I sat in the rear of the chapel. The pews were just as uncomfortable as I remembered, and the priest took his place in the front of the church so that he could drone on about forgiveness.

I hardly took notice when someone sat next to me. Then she reached for a hymnal, and I saw the ring with the crescent symbol on her slender finger.

"Mia Fortner," I said.

"Garret," she whispered. "Mia Garret. I have my mother's name."

"Your brother would have killed me."

"Blaize was the only one in my family who treated me with respect."

"Then why are you still working for them?"

She chewed her lip as the priest droned on about redemption.

"You're looking to inherit," I postulated.

"Can you blame me?"

"Let me guess. Killing me will earn their respect?"

"I'd settle for taking back that gun you stole from Blaize."

"I don't have it." If she knew where it was, she'd be a lot more upset.

"Where is it?"

"Gone."

"That's not good."

"I've seen worse." I glanced to the coffin in front of the altar. The dark wood shone in the flickering candlelight. "Kaegan Fortner's not a good man, Mia. He won't deal fairly with you."

"I can convince him to back off if you give me the gun."

"That weapon's too dangerous, and you know it."

"Too dangerous for who? For me? What makes you think it's better in your hands?"

I showed her my empty hands.

"That collection means everything to my father." She ran her black fingernails through black hair. "God, it's like he's obsessed."

"You're in a church," I said, channeling my mother. "Don't blaspheme."

"I hate it here," she said, her lip twisting up in bitter disgust.

"Then leave."

There was something she wasn't telling me. A secret pain lingered at the edge of her brittle voice. "He wants you dead."

"Why?"

"Because when you're dead, Trinity will have a slot open for a replacement. You can make this a whole lot easier by—"

"I'm not going to ask Trinity to excommunicate you."

"Trinity's *done* with you. That's what my father says."

The priest droned on, then lit the incense. Despite my best efforts, the heady smoke dug into my heart and wrestled out a shred of peace by way of distant memories. My mother took us to church every Sunday for a large part of my life. My father might have gone only to maintain his professional image, but Mom bought into it. It was her faith that kept our family strong right up till the end.

Maybe what happened on the *Benevolent* wouldn't have been so bad if I hadn't cared for her so damn much.

"I know what it's like to have a criminal for a father," I said. "You love him, but you don't have to love everything he does." Maybe that was wisdom, but I didn't believe it. When I learned what my father had done, all my love turned bitter. He was a cancer in our peaceful family. When he died aboard the *Benevolent*, the world had come out better for it. "Sometimes, stepping away is the only way to find peace."

Something hard pressed painfully into my ribs. I looked down to see the Walther PPK in the shadows between us. She said, "What makes you think I'm looking for peace?"

"Sometimes you get a choice between peace and a last good deed."

"Fortners don't believe in last good deeds," she said.

"Die as you live?"

She eyed the coffin in the front of the chapel with an expression of mild disgust. "Father trained me for this, Mr. Demarco. I've worked for him my whole life. I'm not sloppy like Blaize. I'm not careless like Lorrel."

"What about Anya?"

"She didn't want anything to do with this. It's no surprise she screwed up her part."

"I'm not going to contribute to your lost cause, Garret."

Just like that, the PPK disappeared under the folds of her coat. "You know where to take the gun," she said. "Bring it by midnight, and I can convince my father not to have you killed." The offer at least told me that Fortner hadn't discovered what I'd done to his collection.

Mia stepped from the pew, genuflected, and left the chapel. I sat a long time, stewing in the mix of holy aromas.

What did it mean that she had the PPK? My exhausted brain struggled to put the pieces together. Finally, the priest concluded the service, and the funeral entered its final stages.

Behind the altar, a screen crawling with religious iconography slid to one side as the wall opened. Six men and women stood from the front pews and lifted the coffin to their shoulders. Music played on a small organ, and a choir of five women sang something in its original Latin. It was beautiful, and it made me wish I had known the deceased.

I hadn't, though, which made me almost feel a little guilty for what would happen next. Maybe the deceased couldn't take anything with but his good deeds. Maybe by the grace of God, he would find himself walking in heaven that day. He'd leave behind his wealth, his family, his friends. He'd step onto the shore of that great ocean with nothing but the suit on his back—

And Blaize Fortner's Model 41 pistol tucked in neatly by his side. I hoped it served him well.

The pallbearers brought the coffin into the funeral recycler and set it on the central platform. I caught a whiff of the acidic chemical slurry that would soon break down everything in that chamber. It would be the man's last good deed, the good deed that helped feed the city of Nicodemia as it continued to spin relentlessly into the future.

The gun that I'd hidden in his coffin wouldn't dissolve immediately. The slurry wasn't designed to take apart non-organic materials. Eventually the surviving steel would be filtered out and fed into a furnace. Its materials would spread throughout the system. That gun would strengthen the fiber-steel construction of the next bridge or building or tools or clothes. Maybe all of the above.

What it *wouldn't* do is defend me against whatever Fortner had planned.

The pallbearers exited the recycler and stood at attention as the door slid shut. Mass finished, the mourners shuffled out of the chapel. I sat quietly as they disappeared.

I closed my eyes and observed a moment of silence not unlike a prayer. Why did things keep coming back to the *Benevolent*? Smalley had agreed to take me on his ship if I managed my goal soon enough, and I was finally making progress. One gun was destroyed. Was it enough for now?

Maybe.

First, I needed to lose Mia. I drew a deep breath and exhaled slowly. There was something peaceful about the funeral chapel. This was a place where everyone knew where they were going. The only differences were how we got there and how fast.

Chapter 34

I SLIPPED through a maze of dark alleys, and she was there. I walked invisibly through a complex security checkpoint, and she was on the other side. I ran as fast as a person could reasonably run, and she followed. Effortlessly. In the black of the Haven night, Mia Garret was my shadow, and the worst thing about shadows in the night is that it's impossible to know they're there.

She expected me to go to wherever I'd stashed the gun. How long before her frustration led her to violence?

The Ever Upward smelled of stale cigar smoke and sickeningly sweet mixed drinks. The place was packed from its fiber-mahogany booths up to its shining fibersteel bar. At first, the bartender, Aiken, locked in conversation with a couple of middle-aged women in tight-fitting blouses, didn't see me enter. By the way his dimples kept appearing over his beard, I could tell he was enjoying the topic. It was too late for the supper rush and too early for a proper post-curfew speakeasy.

I shouldered into a spot at the bar and waited.

Aiken spotted me and the dimples disappeared. He

excused himself from the ladies and came over to me. "Demarco."

"Whiskey." I slid a dime across the bar. "Rocks."

His eyes narrowed. "That's how it's going to be? You're just going to pretend like nothing's happening?"

"Too many ears," I said.

"Always too many around here." He poured two fingers of whiskey in a glass and slid it over to me. No rocks. My dime disappeared. "Heard a rumor you were in some kind of trouble."

I glanced at the women he'd been talking to. "Heard any other good rumors lately?"

"A priest got in trouble last week. There was an immigration ship from Earth a few months ago, and people aren't adjusting very well. Word is there's a new bakery down in the Blue Rock neighborhood. Good rumors are a trade, Demarco. You got anything to offer?"

"I hear the *Benevolent*'s orbit is passing close."

"It's not much of a rumor if everyone knows it," said Aiken. He worked his way down the bar, refilling drinks. When he returned, he said, "What really brings you in?"

"I need to know about Kaegan Fortner's kids."

"They're trouble."

"One of them's dead."

He shot a nervous glance at the people flanking me at the bar. "Too many ears, Demarco."

"Tell me about Mia."

His frown softened a bit. "Decent kid from what I hear."

"Ask me about that again after midnight."

Aiken's eyebrow shot up. "Trouble?"

"A misunderstanding."

"I bet."

"What's her relationship to dear old dad?"

"Sour," said Aiken. "Are you planning on getting to the *Benevolent*, then?"

"The blue is sending a team in the morning."

"That so?"

"I plan on joining."

Aiken's dimples returned. "Thought for a moment there you were going to try to wedge yourself in with the Fortners."

Were the Fortners planning a trip as well? I didn't want to show my ignorance. "How does an antiques dealer get to the top of the food chain around here?"

"The Fortner family has been playing the long game for as long as there's been a long game to play."

"In antiques."

"There's a lot of power in history, Demarco."

I sipped my whiskey and winced. It tasted like kerosene. After that, we burned the hours talking about soccer matches past and future. It wasn't the worst way to spend one's final hours, but as midnight approached, I felt the pressure of Mia's deadline. The crowd thinned as the late hours approached. Aiken's lady friends disappeared into the night with raucous laughter and glittering jewelry.

When it was only me left in the bar, Aiken leaned forward. "Closing time, detective."

I slid my last few dimes to him. "I appreciated the company, Aiken."

He stared at me for several long breaths. "You're really worried, aren't you?"

A headache pulsed in the back of my skull, so I closed my eyes. "Worried is too strong a word. More like resigned."

He pushed a folded triangle of paper across the bar to me. "Hang in there, buddy. Mia and her girlfriend aren't such bad kids."

I opened the paper and glanced at it. Scrawled in Aiken's messy handwriting was one word: *Upstairs.*

Aiken indicated a nondescript door behind the bar. I tucked the paper in one pocket and, without another word, proceeded upward. The stairs led to a short hallway, at the end of which was a closed door.

I stared at it a long time before I figured out what I was looking at. The door was built into the side of the building. This was an external door, but the adjacent building didn't look like it was attached.

Opening the door a crack, I peered through. Sure enough, it opened above a dark alley. I held my breath until one of the shadows below shifted slightly. It might have been Mia, or it could have been anyone out after curfew. It could also have been one of the many goons helping Mia track me.

A mesh bridge connected to the building across the alley, and I stepped across as quietly as I could. I found a bundle of Aiken's things, which I left alone. There wasn't anything there that I needed. All I needed was a way out.

This was a dingy hotel, and its hallway stretched all the way across, ending in another door. Opening that, I found a connection to yet another building. Secrets upon secrets, I thought. This time, it didn't make me step across an alley. It was a simple doorway and a shift in wallpaper, and then I was in an apartment building.

Like this, I moved from building to building without ever touching the street. Sometimes the way was obvious. A doorway on the outer wall of the building or a window looking out into a fiberoak panel. Other times, it took me precious minutes to find my way through. Some doors were completely hidden. Others were half-sized utility crawlspaces built into the backs of closets. Each one took me farther from the Ever Upward, where Mia and her goons awaited me.

They must have known I left, though. The place was closed, and Aiken might have helped me, but he wouldn't have spent much time defending me if she confronted him directly. It was about as much as someone could expect, I figured.

Midnight passed. A deadline in the strictest sense of the word. Mia had offered me an olive branch. Promised not to kill me if I handed over the gun. It had been a lie, but a mind slipping under the waves of stress will often cling to the flotation of a flimsy lie.

Was it a lie? She may have been mistaken about her ability to convince Kaegan, but instinct told me she really believed she could save me. She *wanted* to believe that she could save me. Something niggled at the back of my mind. A mystery, just like any other I'd tried to solve. Why was Mia threatening to kill me if she didn't actually want to kill me?

Then, I thought of Anya. Anya had tried to convince me that she was being forced to act because her children were being threatened. It was a low and pretty basic tactic. That had been because she wanted me to excommunicate her, something I wouldn't do even if I knew how.

Mia *did* have a girlfriend. If I was going to solve this mystery, I needed to know more about the significant other. I needed Mia's girl.

I could leave. Now that I was free of my tail, I could make my way through Customs to the port where Smalley would soon leave for the *Benevolent*. I pressed my forehead against the cool wall and closed my eyes to the all-encompassing darkness.

Was I sabotaging my own chances of reaching the *Benevolent*? Maybe it *was* best if I stayed away. I'd lived this long not knowing my parents' final moments. Couldn't I continue like this?

Midnight had come and gone, but Smalley wouldn't leave until noon. That gave me plenty of time, and the late hour meant my greatest assets could come to bear.

I pushed the back wall of the closet and the invisible door opened before me. I stepped out into the starlit streets of Haven Nicodemia.

Chapter 35

THE HAVEN NIGHTLIFE simmered under the still surface of the curfew night. Nightclubs and gambling halls dotted the neighborhoods like pinpricks of light in the false night sky. Some were open secrets among the silent populace. Others were hidden in earnest—private clubs open by invite only.

"I'm on the list," I said to the bouncer as I approached from the shadows. He was a wiry guy with a pencil mustache and a cheap circuit board tattoo on his neck. His fedora shaded the dark features of his face.

The bouncer leaned against a wall at the entrance to a dark alley under the yellow glow of a dim street lamp. "Nothing going on tonight," he said.

Bullshit. "That so?" I said, wishing I'd kept a few dimes to bribe the guy. "Then you won't mind if I pass through this alley?"

He held up a hand to stop me without losing a beat. "This is a restricted area."

"Maybe I have an invite."

"There's a curfew."

I stepped forward into the light so the yellow glow washed across my face. I couldn't see his eyes under the shadow of his fedora, but I'd have bet a stack of dimes that they widened. "My invite is implied by the darkness. My pass comes in the form of a thousand steps in the darkest shadows of Nicodemia. When your last good deed goes to feeding the fish of the Heavies or the crops of the Hallow, I'll be the one to see you on your way. In this world of measurements, I'm the one unmeasured."

His thin lips split into a wide smile. "Jude Demarco," he said. "They said you might come."

"Is Polly around?"

He waved me forward through the alley. "She's not in a good mood."

Halfway through the dark alley, a red door sat in the side of a fiberbrick building. Using my lighter as a torch, I made my way to it and passed through. A short set of dingy stairs led down into a fiberstone-walled basement where the air hung thick with smoke and the dim lights shone from the low ceiling.

Four men sat across from a heavyset woman in a green visor. The men wore the rugged remains of business suits, their ties loosened and their cuffs open. All four looked like they'd been run over by a trolley.

When I walked in the door, the woman, Polly, didn't even glance at me. Flipping her cards, she flashed a sneer of a smile. "Twenty-one, gentlemen."

Her words were met by a series of groans.

"Take a break," Polly said.

The four men didn't move. I knew that feeling. Being told to stop could be jarring for someone deep in the throes of a gambling addiction. They weren't winning. That much was apparent by their small stacks of chips and the destitute horror lingering under their furrowed brows.

"Taking another group for all they're worth?" I asked as Polly approached.

"They'll win it back," Polly said. Her quick fingers flipped a blue chip that caught the light in a hypnotic rhythm. "You're a little late to join us tonight, Demarco."

"I'm not here for pleasure."

"You never were."

"Says who?"

Polly shot a sideways glance at the four men still sitting at the blackjack table. "I know when someone's here to blow off a little steam," she said. "Those guys? They're not here to win. They're here because their lives are shit and they can't imagine anything better than losing their last few dimes to the house."

"Winning might be nice."

"Men like you don't win," said Polly.

"Men like me don't *play*. I gave up gambling."

"Then you won't mind sitting in for a few hands."

I'd wasted too much of my life slinging cards in the dark underground of Haven Nicodemia. The promise I made to my sister rattled around in the back of my skull. No more gambling. Not even a little.

"I haven't got a dime to my name," I said.

"I'll spot you." A sliver of a smile crossed her lips. "For old time's sake."

"All I need is information."

"If I'm talking, I'm playing." Polly returned to her table and motioned for the men to make room for me, which they reluctantly did.

I shuffled my big body onto the end of the table and watched as Polly slid five red chips across the felt table to me.

Touching each with my ring finger, I slid them around until I was happy with their arrangement. Five chips, five chances. All I had to do was keep her talking.

Polly's hands were quicksilver as she shuffled the cards. Nothing fancy, nothing showy, but efficient and complete. She opened four new decks and combined them, shuffling each into one greater whole. Then she divided them again and shuffled each. Finally, she set the stack in front of the man closest to me and waited for him to cut it. After a few seconds of consideration, the man complied with a fifty-fifty cut.

Everyone wagered, and Polly dealt.

"What do you know about Mia Garret?" I asked, earning an ugly look from the guy next to me.

"Suicide queen," said Polly, flicking a Queen of Hearts into my square. "There are some families we don't mess with around here." She dealt me a two of hearts.

Blackjack was a numbers game. Pure and simple. The odds were direct and knowable. Play it straight, and your odds were only slightly worse than the house. Counting cards, a person could walk away with better odds, but that wasn't easy with a four-deck shuffle. My mouth went dry and my palms started to sweat. I glanced at my fellow players' cards.

I could win. My heart hammered, and my teeth ached. I *knew* that I could win. How much would a pocketful of dimes help as I tried to avoid Mia and her goons?

"What's her connection to the Fortner clan?" I asked.

"Better off if you stay out of that trouble." One of the players busted on a bad hit.

"You know trouble likes to follow me."

"I hope it didn't follow you here."

"Me too." I met her eyes. "Hit me."

An eight of spades. Twenty. My odds were excellent. Thrilling. My heart pounded in my chest. Out in the city, I never won. In life, I'd pulled up nothing but twos. Here, in a smoky basement game, I had as good a chance as any to walk away with something.

"Hit me again," I said.

"Demarco." Her voice was flat. A warning. The irritable guy next to me muttered something like a curse under his breath.

"I said what I meant," I said. "I'm not here to gamble."

"You're here to lose?"

"If that's what it takes."

"You used to be one of my best guys," Polly said. "Came every Wednesday. Won more often than you lost."

"But when I lost, I lost big."

She placed a ten of diamonds in front of me. Bust. It hit me like a punch in the gut. Worse, even, when Polly pulled up a Jack and a seven. "Dealer stays on a seventeen," she said. Three of the four other players picked up a win. The surly guy next to me crossed himself. I hadn't pegged him as the religious sort. Polly's hands were a blur as she dealt the next hand.

"There was some bad blood a while back," Polly said. A ten of diamonds and six of clubs landed in my box. She revealed a ten of clubs. "Those rich families always draw in the biggest drama, you know?"

"Money's gravity," I said.

"That it is."

The guy who had previously lost now ended up with an ace and a king of hearts. He took the win without so much as a flicker of an expression.

"It wasn't Mia's fault," Polly said as she worked her way down the line. A couple of busts and an eighteen fouled up the table. "She would have been a kid at the time."

"It's tough being a kid with all that attention."

"Don't feel too sorry for her." She looked meaningfully at my lousy hand.

I gave the cards a tap and she busted me with a six of spades. Again, I felt a lump of coal in my gut. She flipped her hidden card to reveal a ten of diamonds. The guy with the eighteen didn't twitch. It amazed me how little emotion these gamblers showed in their late-night game of choice.

"It was her grandfather who started it all when he died." Polly dealt the next hand when the wager was in. "Bastard had the audacity to give each of the kids an equal share in his will."

"That asshole," I said.

"You can imagine the outrage. Mia was the offspring of some two-bit hustler from the Heavies. Giving her an equal share was like a slap in the face."

A hard eleven looked up at me from the felt table. Six of hearts, five of spades. A clear chance to double down, but I wasn't gambling. Dealer revealed a jack of clubs.

When it was my turn, I tapped the cards.

"Really?" said the guy next to me. By the scattered trio of eights in front of him I saw that he'd busted.

"It's a long game," I said.

Polly dropped a card on my stack. A king of spades. Twenty-one. Despite my best effort to squash it down, a thrill of the hunt made my heart stutter. I met Polly's eyes and knew that she knew. I was hooked.

Then she revealed her second card. An ace of hearts. "Dealer blackjack," she said. "Push."

Push. I slid my bet back over to my side of the table and stared at it. It wasn't as if winning was the barbed hook in my soul. If I'd collected on my blackjack, that wouldn't have sealed my addicted fate. I was stronger than that, wasn't I?

The sour realism at the bottom of my soul told me to back away. Get out now.

"So, Mia made out pretty well in the deal. She feels like she owes the family?" I slid another chip in for a wager.

Polly offered the deck to the loser next to me. He dismissed it with a tap. "Imagine being the rebellious daughter of a single mother. You're in school. A kid doing kid things. You have friends. Maybe a whole group of friends. Imagine one day some old shit dies and makes you the focus of a whole crime family's worth of ire for the rest of your childhood."

"Sounds unpleasant."

"Extremely." Polly dealt the next hand. She pulled up a six of clubs, and my hand showed two black twos.

I winced despite myself. It was a shit hand. I could split it, but only if I wanted a double kick to the teeth. I glanced at my fellow players. Not a good hand among them. "If she's got such a gripe with the family, why's she working for them?"

Polly bit her lower lip. "Lack of options?"

"Hers or theirs?"

"Good question."

The asshole next to me said, "How about you just play?"

"How about you wait your turn," said Polly. To me, she said, "What's your business with the family, anyway?"

"Antiques."

When the guy next to me busted out by hitting on a twelve, he pushed away from the table and growled in frustration. The other players didn't even bother looking at him. I split my twos and, after a long string of bad cards, busted on both. The dealer hit on a twelve and stood on a seventeen.

"Come on," said the asshole. "Can we get this guy out of here?"

"Can't leave till I have my answers," I said.

"You're welcome to cash out, Orin," said Polly.

He pushed a handful of chips in for a wager and swore under his breath.

I had two chips sitting in front of me, but I was close to the end of what Polly was going to give me, so I wagered them both on the next hand. "When did Grandpa Fortner knock off?"

Polly held the remains of her deck in her hands and watched me with narrow eyes. "Must have been a little over a decade ago."

"Around the time of the *Benevolent*?"

Her eyes narrowed even further. "Maybe."

"It was," said the asshole.

"Shut up," said Polly.

"How do you know?" I asked.

"It was right around the time that Huff fellow started working for Kaegan," said Orin.

"That the truth?" I asked.

Polly started dealing the cards.

"If you want to know anything about the Fortner business, Harley Huff's the guy to talk to." Orin watched his first card land. A ten of clubs. "He's been on board since before Kaegan took over."

A king of diamonds landed in my box. "He's in charge?"

"Not a chance," said Orin. "But every good org needs an accountant." A jack of clubs landed in his box. "Now will you get the hell out of our game?"

I put a hand forward to surrender but froze when I saw the card landing on top of my king. An ace of spades. Blackjack. My heart stuttered.

"Dealer stands on eighteen," Polly said. She slid two chips to join my wager. "Let it ride?"

Still frozen, I stared at the minuscule fortune. It didn't

even matter what the value of the chips was. In a fraction of a second, it had doubled its value. What could I accomplish with enough coins rattling around in my pocket? Only a few more hours of playing, and everything would go so much easier for me.

"You leaving or what?" Orin asked.

"Yeah," I said, pushing the chips toward Polly. The words were ash in my mouth. "I need to cash out, Polly." I shot a glance at Orin. She'd set the man up. Tugged his strings like the expert gambler she was. "Keep one of those for a tip."

Her lightning-fast hands swapped three red coins for three rolls of dimes. "You're tipping me with my own money, you know."

I pocketed the dimes. "That's why I'm so generous." With my best crooked smile, I bid her a good night and disappeared into the darkness.

Chapter 36

HARLEY HUFF WAS A BLANK SPACE. It was as if the man cultivated an aura of forgettableness with his pasty skin and formless body and bland fashion. He cultivated his nondescript image with a plain bowtie and flat brown combover. This was the man Kaegan Fortner had hired to manage his finances. He was the legal face of the entire Fortner organization.

Then why was he riding the Haven trolley in the middle of Haven's long dark curfew?

When I stepped onto the trolley, I didn't think he saw me. The dim running lights followed him, illuminating the floorboards so he wouldn't trip. They ignored me. I moved as a shadow in a pool of ink, and my silence hung heavy like a wool blanket.

The trolley started to move up the long spiral. Not bothering to face me, Huff said, "I'm armed."

So that was how it was going to be. "I'm looking for answers, Mr. Huff."

"Aren't we all?"

"What does Fortner want with the *Benevolent?*"

"My employer requires a certain amount of confidentiality." He turned to me, clutching his briefcase in front of him so hard his knuckles whitened.

I stepped close enough that the light warmed my face. "Mia doesn't think the rules apply to her."

Huff took a step back, and the light followed him, plunging me back into darkness. The trolley rumbled along its track. I looked into his wide, terrified eyes and for the first time I felt sorry for him.

I said, "I can help you disappear, Huff."

He scoffed. "There's no hiding from the Fortners."

"I'm still here."

"You might as well be dead already."

"It's a big city," I said. "Lots of people out there to help you blend in."

"Trust me," spat Huff, "when they want you found, you're found."

The trolley jolted as it switched to a faster track. "You'd be surprised at how easy it is to not be found."

His lips sharpened into a fine line, and his cheeks flushed. "You'd have me what? Hide in the Heavies? Scrub floors in the Hallows? I can't disappear any more than you can survive after killing my boss's son."

"It was self-defense," I said. "Allegedly."

"Motive doesn't matter to a bullet."

"What makes you think they're so great at finding people?"

He threw a hand up in exasperation. "Mia got everything those other morons never got, but for some reason it stuck. She was tiny when her grandfather died, but old Drake Forner had all the pieces in place for her training. Kaegan got that too, but it never really landed in the same way. That's why he's so set on seizing control up in the Hallows."

"You say that like it's a mistake."

"People always want what they don't have."

"It's hard to want anything else."

Huff clutched his briefcase.

I stared out into the rushing night, where the city buzzed by at breakneck speeds. Air rushed in through the open windows. "Drake must not have liked Kaegan's wife."

At that, Huff's expression grew dour. "No. I guess he didn't." The words gave me no information, but they dripped with history. The man crumpled into himself. "I've worked for the Fortners for a long time. You could say I'm complicit with everything they've done for the past twenty years."

I should have despised him as much I despised the rest of the family. There was a twisted kind of helplessness to the man that dug itself into me, and I had to make my offer again. "I can keep you safe."

He wasn't having it. "There was a time I might have taken you up on that, Mr. Demarco." Maybe before we turned Mia against her mother. Maybe before Kaegan hooked his claws into the Haven underground. Maybe before I ordered the transactions that would plunge a hundred innocent families into poverty just so that we could claim our own district. There might have been a time when I was worth saving, but that time's long gone. You want to know who's the worst of the Fortners? It's not Kaegan. He's a good man turned bad by the corrupting influence of his own power. It wasn't Blaize. That man had a kind streak like you wouldn't believe. Anya has a family that loves her very much. *Had* a family. I hear that's gone bad too. And Lorrel? Well, Lorrel was a piece of work, but he had his moments.

"No, Demarco. If you're looking for the worst of the

worst, then guess what? You've found me. Right here on this train. You want me to escape the monsters of a broken crime family? Well, I'm worse than every single one of them. You know why?"

"Because you're not family."

He raised his briefcase in front of his chest. "I did this all willingly. It was a job for me, and every single one of those awful things was a choice *I* made."

I stepped forward. "The Church says nobody's beyond redemption, Huff."

"The Church says a lot of things."

"How do I get to Mia."

"You're going to kill her?" His eyes were wide again.

"I need to stop her."

He stepped back again, but he was smashed against the back of the moving trolley. I realized that I had been slowly advancing on him. The persistent pressure of acceleration had nudged me forward, pursuing the little man all the way to the end of the line. The trolley's wheels rumbled along the track and my feet shook under me. It felt like the whole world was unstable.

His briefcase came up even higher, blocking my view of his fabulous bowtie. "Drake used to always say that there was only one thing that could turn a good person bad or a bad person good."

"So *he* believed in redemption."

Outside, the Cathedral of Saint Benedict glowed in the first embers of the morning light. Amber played across the simple spires that reached almost up to the ceiling above. Stained glass glinted like a million candles. I wondered if God watched what happened below, and if he even cared what sins we brought upon ourselves.

I stepped back so that I wasn't quite so intimidating. Huff lowered his briefcase a few inches.

He said, "A good antiques dealer knows the value of something. No matter what it is or no matter when it's from, he'll be able to quickly assess its value and name his price. If the price is good, he'll make the deal. If the price is bad..."

"Then no deal."

"You get the picture. Kaegan Fotner, like his father, is an excellent antiques dealer."

The implication was clear as a Haven afternoon. Kaegan didn't just understand the value of objects. He knew how to get the value of a person, and a value of a person was the leverage it would take to own them.

"What's Mia's price?" I asked.

"It's never as simple as that," said Huff. The trolley started to slow. Our ride together was almost finished.

"Love," I said.

Huff shrugged, but I could see the truth in his eyes. "Her motivation isn't what you should be worrying about."

"What value *should* I worry about?"

"Ask yourself," he said, "what's *your* value?"

The trolley slowed quickly. When it was still rumbling along the track, Huff pulled the emergency release. The brakes squealed, and I had to grasp the railing to keep from stumbling backward. Before the trolley had fully stopped, Huff peeled open the back gate and stepped out into the rising dawn. By the time I recovered, he was half a block away, watching me through dark hooded eyes.

<hr>

Chapter 37

<hr>

COFFEE AND A GOOD BAGEL.

If the love of anything would turn me bad, it would be the love for the Haven breakfast. For some reason, probably having to do with the boiling point of water, the best bagels and coffee existed only in Haven. As soon as the first shops opened, I pounced on one and spent the first of my gambling wins on a luxurious feast. It was fabulous. Cream cheese melted against the heat of the toasted bagel. Black coffee swelled with nutty hints of almond.

This was corruption's influence if ever I tasted it.

It was also a delay I couldn't afford. As more people flooded the Haven streets, I grew paranoid about Mia's followers. They could easily work their way into the flowing crowds, picking up my trail again and pouncing whenever they felt appropriate.

I didn't know what to do about Mia, but I knew that I couldn't wait for her to make the first move. By the time that happened, I'd be done.

What Huff had said had bothered me, but there was

something else sparked by the sharp blade of coffee as it sliced into my brain. There was something Mia had said back when I first met her in Fortner's antique shop. She had spoken with her half-brother Blaize. What had she said?

"It smells like Grandpa."

Drake Fortner. I had assumed that the old man had smelled like gunpowder and oil, but how young would she have been when he was alive? Would she have even remembered what he smelled like? Maybe. Some memories lingered.

More likely that the shooting range reminded her of a more recent memory of Drake Fortner. Mia had mentioned that Fortners were above the simple rites of a Last Good Deed.

Then it hit me. The Last Winter Orchard. It was more than a cold orchard on the lower level of Haven. The place was a cemetery for those rare few who decided to refrain from having their bodies recycled after their deaths. A fluke of the climate control system allowed for seasons of variable temperatures. The pungent, peppery odor from the factories that surrounded the place made it smell a bit like gunpowder.

That had to be where Drake Fortner was buried.

Smalley's launch was happening too soon. It would take time to move through Customs, but I figured I had another hour or two to work with. I suspected the orchard was *where* something important was happening, but I still didn't know *what* the problem was. Was this like Anya, where Fortner had someone hostage? Was the threat something to do with Drake's body?

Mia would have the place watched. If she didn't already have my tail again, then going anywhere near the orchard would reveal my location.

Something else bothered me that I hardly wanted to justify with the full examination of thought. If Fortner had kidnapped Anya's kids to get her to comply, and Fortner held some leverage over Mia to get at her, then what would he do to take me? Huff's question still haunted me. What was my price?

The only person who came to mind was my sister. I'd do anything to keep her safe, and Fortner knew it.

Mia knew it.

As soon as that thought came to me, my sense of urgency rose. I'd ditched Mia, but I'd be a fool to think she'd sat around doing nothing all night. What if she sent people down to Haven to harass my sister? What if she went down there herself?

I couldn't wait any longer. If there was something to find at the Last Winter Orchard, then I'd find it. If Mia was there, then so be it. There had to be something we could work out.

The morning crowd moved like cold molasses through the narrow side streets. I passed under the spires of Saint Benedict, choosing to circle back into the outer reaches of the district rather than brave the open spaces of the central spire.

It occurred to me that I could visit the cathedral. Maybe a priest would have solace to offer, or maybe I could gain some insight into the workings of Fortner's criminal enterprise. I'd always found answers in the Church, but a cathedral isn't exactly the same thing. The Cathedral of Saint Benedict was a mausoleum of lost faith. Those tall spires and golden statues paid tribute to a belief system long absent. I didn't know if it had been lost before Nicodemia set out to the stars, or if something had happened along the way, but it seemed to me at that moment that any church that dedicated itself to gold and marble couldn't also dedicate itself to the souls of its followers. A man can't have two masters, the saying went.

I'd find no solace there.

As the spires disappeared behind the tumble of squat

offices, I found myself truly and utterly alone. I picked up the pace, despite my aching muscles, each step pinging my knee with a shock of pain.

It wasn't long before I reached a fiberwood sign that read Last Winter Orchard. It stood on the side of a long expanse of a hedge row flanked by red fiberbrick buildings. Even outside of the orchard, I could feel the cool breeze blowing up from the long slope. Trees arched above the narrow road. These were the only fruit-bearing apple trees in all of Nicodemia, but they weren't in season right then. Their small leaves varied from dark green to dull maroon, and not a flower or fruit was in sight.

Instead of following the path, I made my way through one of the nearest buildings. Sometimes the division between districts was a solid wall or a fence. Sometimes it was a painted border along a courtyard or road.

Other times, the division between districts was as natural a border as a space station could manage. The trees didn't thrive at the edges of the orchard, even though someone had intentionally planted them there. The final brick buildings along the border were surrounded by stunted, feral-looking trees populated by actual black squirrels. Closer to the center, where the seasonal fluctuation of temperatures was the greatest, the apple trees thrived.

It seemed strange that the plants would do better in the varied, harsh environment, but in a way, it made sense. They grew strong through the adversity. Once winter couldn't touch them, nothing could.

A gentle breeze rolled through the forest carrying the murmur of quiet voices from somewhere deep within. I closed my eyes and concentrated on the rush of air and the click of branches against branches. The ground was soft in the orchard. It was a simulation of true soil from Earth, and the undergrowth of soft grass made for a whisper-quiet footfalls.

There *were* footfalls. I heard them in the distance.

Leaving the building, I made my way quietly through the edges of the forest. The dark leaves blocked the daylight glow from above, making a network of cool shadows for me to move through. Listening, I paused under one of the larger trees. Still, the voices lingered on the edge of hearing. Leaves rustled in the wind.

I crouched low and made my way forward. A cobblestone path wove its way through the orchard, but I kept far away from it. The orchard wasn't a popular destination, but if anyone was around, they would be on that path.

"All clear, boss." The voice came from above and several trees away. It was followed by a crackle of static through some kind of analog comm. "Yes, sir."

Sir. Then the boss probably wasn't Mia. Unless they were using a gender-neutral form of the word. That could be. The blue tended to use neutral forms, as did old military. I doubted these were the police speaking from a hiding place in the trees. They might be military, but military by nature didn't have a presence in civilian areas. They didn't have much of a presence at all in Nicodemia, actually, since the whole city was occupied by civilians.

Most of it, anyway. I remembered the abandoned district where Anya's family had been held. But what would the point be? A military establishment in the middle of an occupied city didn't make any sense. Not when the blue and Trinity kept things pretty well under control.

Three trees away from where I was hiding, heavy boots clumped into the soil. I ducked behind the trunk of the ancient apple tree as well as I could. Its low branches must have hidden me well enough. After looking around, the man started walking away.

I followed.

Slowly, quietly, we made our way through the forest. Every time I moved, I risked him looking back. Every time he looked back, I was behind the dubious cover of the scraggly branches of the overgrown trees.

He was dressed in black fatigues, with a holster strapped across his chest. He wore dark glasses, the kind that people use to hide where their eyes are wandering. Maybe those glasses were the reason he didn't spot me.

There were others around. There had to be. When I had a chance, I paused and listened for more of them. Nothing. Either they weren't close or they were being perfectly still in their watch positions. Whoever this guy was, he *had* to be part of it. I drew in a long slow breath. The cool air evoked a shooting range—cool and pungent and a little stale.

The trees were larger in the center of the orchard. The leaves were a lush green, and branches stretched high above our heads. The cool breeze smelled of crisp greenery and sour apples. It was a paradise right there in the farthest reaches of Haven Nicodemia. I crept slowly forward , having lost my direct line of sight to the man in the fatigues. He was still there. I could hear him.

He stopped.

Carefully, deliberately, I edged forward until I could locate him. To my surprise, a small building stood nestled among the grasping trees. It was a copper brown, much like the bark of many of the trees, and a little space of fiberstone marked a patio in front with a small table and two chairs. On one of the chairs sat a woman swimming in baggy clothing. She held a book in her lap and a sour expression on her lips.

This had to be it. The woman was who they were using to

control Mia. Mia could visit, but with all the guards around, she'd never break her free. I didn't know how I could possibly do the same, but something had to be done.

And fast.

I drew a calming breath. Things were about to get ugly. I clenched my fists and drew myself up. I'd crash out and take the man down before he could react. Then it was a matter of getting her out before they closed the perimeter.

"Don't even think about it," hissed a voice behind me. Sharp pain blossomed in my lower back. I tried to turn, but the blade dug deeper. "Step out there and you're dead."

"Dead's just a matter of time," I whispered.

The knife disappeared.

Mia gestured for me to follow her away from the small building. Our eyes met, and I saw a grim, fierce determination in her. She could have killed me. A flick of her blade and I'd have been bleeding out in this exquisite soil.

She crept back into the orchard, and I followed.

———

Chapter 38

———

"I SHOULD KILL YOU RIGHT NOW," Mia said once we were in the small building at the edge of the forest.

"Maybe."

"It would be a lot easier."

"Who's the hostage?"

"Where's the gun?"

Mia must have read something in my expression because she threw her hands up in disgust. Dust-covered decorations filled the tiny space. Statues of mythological creatures leered at me in the dimly lit room. "You are a fucking idiot," she said.

"Those weapons have no place in this city," I said.

"Tell that to my father."

"I'm looking for the final two weapons. You have the PPK. Where is the Python?"

With a quick turn, she disappeared through the door. Like a fool, I followed.

"Tell me what's happening, Mia," As I stepped into the short hallway, the door slid closed behind me. Too close—it wouldn't respond to me and didn't acknowledge that I was there. "Why haven't you killed me?"

"Is that a complaint?"

"Call it a curiosity."

She spun on me. Instead of a knife, she held the Walther PPK. The snub-nosed little pistol fit perfectly in her hand like it was meant to be there. "You're making me reconsider, Demarco."

"You ought to be careful with that thing. Someone could get hurt." My knees shook with adrenaline.

"That'd be a shame."

"Your father kidnapped Anya's kids and killed her wife. He had that lady back there holed up so that you'd behave." I could see by her expression that I'd hit on something. "I thought family was supposed to mean something around here."

Her lip curled up in disgust. "Family is what you call someone when you want them to work for free."

"That's some family you got."

"How's your sister?" Mia said. "Still feeding you every day?"

Dammit. "Not lately."

Mia took a step back. "Stay away, Demarco. There are things going on here that are way above your pay grade."

"I'm an independent contractor. It's all above my pay grade."

"What if I told you those guys back there aren't keeping that woman hostage? They're keeping her safe."

"Until they don't."

There was a sigh of resignation behind her voice. "It's been a long damn night."

"Aren't they all?" I dared a step forward, and she didn't

bother to stop me. I was still too far away to manage anything. "I'll leave," I said.

"If I was going to shoot you, your heart would already be Swiss cheese." The gun didn't move. "What happened with Anya?"

"Don't your people tell you anything?"

"My people are his people," she said, a note of bitterness in her tone. "I don't trust you, but I trust them even less."

"Is that why I'm still alive?"

"It's a complex situation."

"I've never lied to you."

"You've never exactly told me the truth, have you?"

"Put the gun away, and maybe I'll find it easier to chat."

She stepped back and the door at the end of the short hallway opened. Behind her, I could see the cluttered entryway to the small storefront. Shelves were packed with the dusty remains of a once-thriving clothing store. She stowed her weapon. "Tell me what happened."

"There were two goons. Both dead now. They picked up Anya's girl and her kids. Not sure if the wife was in on it. It didn't seem to help her. When we arrived, one of the goons shot the wife. Anya didn't take too kindly to it."

"How'd the other guy die?"

"Shot in the back. Lead bullet."

"Is that why you killed my brother?"

The question brought me up short. If she liked her brother, she'd be mad if I admitted to killing him. If she hated him, she'd be lost if I told her how much I regretted pulling that trigger.

Mia let out a huff of frustration and turned to leave. I followed her through the maze of a building, the door slamming shut on my heels as we passed through one room to the next. Each new door opened for her and closed when she was through, so I stayed closer than was necessarily comfortable, given how well armed she was.

Finally, she spun on me in the dim recesses of a cluttered office. She jabbed a finger at my chest. "You were supposed to bring the gun."

"Guns are dangerous."

"*He's* dangerous. Just give him his stupid weapon and this will all be over."

"For you, maybe. What about all those people who might die if one of those guns is turned on Trinity's core systems? What if they're used to crack containment on the recyclers?"

"He wouldn't do that."

"Then why have the guns?"

She turned on her heel and was off again, furiously marching from the room into a long wide hallway. I followed and the door slammed behind me. She didn't look back for the whole length of the hallway, and as we approached the door to the outside, she veered left into a small room with a front desk and a large window. She started tossing through papers like she was searching for something in the ancient documents.

As I stepped inside, the glass door slid shut behind me. "Talk to your sister," I said. "She knows what it's like to have a hostage lorded over her by your father, and she knows what it's like to try to keep them safe."

"She knows what it costs to go against him."

"Anya was nothing but loyal."

"She led you to them."

"My keen investigative skills led me to them. Anya couldn't have stopped me if she'd tried."

She stopped what she was doing to stare at me through narrowed eyes. "You mean your dog led you to them."

"What's the abandoned district going to be used for, Mia?"

Mia returned to the papers, rifling through a stack of manila envelopes. When she got to the bottom of the stack, she grabbed one and scattered the rest. Then, abruptly, she left the room. I followed on her heels, again leaving before the door closed behind me. She stalked back through the dusty building, her footsteps echoing against the high vaulted ceiling of a large foyer. She walked like she knew where she was going, as if she had a purpose being in what must have been a defunct government building or some kind of accounting office. She left the main corridors through a large metal doorway and we wove through narrow hallways the color of unbrushed teeth. The lights were dim, but they followed her wherever she went, illuminating the space in front of her and a short distance behind.

"Stop following me," she growled.

"I need answers."

"I still have a gun."

"There are things more dangerous than guns."

"Even if those guns can crack recycler containment?" She rounded a corner.

"Maybe."

She spun and gestured at me with the envelope. "Make up your mind, Demarco. What's more dangerous? A few guns or some information that could sink this whole ship?"

I tried to snatch the envelope from her hand, but she was too quick. She was gone again, moving fast through the narrow corridors.

"Talk to your sister," I called out to her as I caught up.

"*Half*-sister!"

"You can't do what he wants," I growled. "Every time someone gives in to his pressure, they end up regretting it."

"I haven't killed you, have I?"

"Not yet."

"Keep bothering me, then. See what happens."

"We can get her out of there," I said.

She stopped and stared at me. Her whole body was tense, like she'd been fighting her whole life for just one more inch, and I was there to stop her. "You think I care about that woman out in the orchard?"

"Isn't that why you're doing this?"

"The only one in that family who was ever decent to me was Lorrel," she spat like venom. "And *he* died ages ago."

"On the *Benevolent.*"

She blinked. "So you know."

"I know Lorrel died on the same crash that took my parents."

The hard line of her lips softened. A sliver of that tension disappeared from the hunch of her shoulders and her death grip on the manila envelope eased by a hair. "I didn't know."

"It was a long time ago."

"But you've never stopped caring."

"Not once."

She gave a little shake of her head. "I don't want to kill you, Demarco."

"Why does your father want to control someone who's excommunicated?"

"He told you about that?"

I thought of the pressure from both Blaize and Anya. "In as many words."

Mia stared up at the ceiling as if she were praying to God. "She's a honey trap."

"The woman in the orchard?"

"If he doesn't have his claws in you, he tries to get you to fall for someone he controls. Love is the only thing that can turn a good man bad."

"Or a bad man good," I said.

"We don't do much of that around here." Mia turned and dashed through the narrow hall again.

I followed, quietly this time. She found a room in the middle of a long section of hall, and the heavy door slid open at her touch. Inside was a utility closet stocked with chemicals, cleaning equipment, and a wall full of poorly organized tools.

It was also a dead end. She reached the far side of the tiny room and faced me, the envelope clutched in her two hands. Above, a dim light flickered to life, casting her face in an ominous shadow.

"Do you want to know the truth, Mr. Demarco?" she said.

"I can't imagine wanting anything else."

"I've always known that the woman in the orchard was there to manipulate me. My father has always owned her, and I've always kept up the act. It's not like I was going to fall for anyone else, right?"

"It still seems like—"

"Yeah, she's still a person. A decent one, even." There was a hitch in her voice that I didn't think she intended to be there. "But if there's one thing I hate, it's being manipulated. By my father, by my half-sister, by you."

"I'm not—"

"He wants you out of the way."

"Of what?"

"He never ordered anyone to kill you."

"Blaize sure had other ideas."

"The judge was planning to betray the family."

"*Your* family."

"That's right." Mia pressed the envelope onto the wall and stabbed a screwdriver through it, pinning it to the wall. "And do you want to know what my family is planning?"

I glanced at the envelope. Mia stepped to the side and watched me with cold eyes.

"Go ahead," she said. "Take it."

As soon as my hand touched the envelope, I knew my mistake. She slipped past me and through the door. I tried to grab her, my hand closing on something cold. A flash of steel bit the back of my hand, and we pulled apart.

Then she was through, and the door slid shut.

And my shoulder slammed into the closed fibersteel door. The light dimmed slowly to nothing.

I was left in the black, in pain, wallowing in regret. She'd been playing me all along, and she'd won. I was trapped.

She had gotten me out of the way.

I flicked my lighter, illuminating the room in a faint candlelight glow. In that flickering light, I looked at the thing I had grabbed while grappling with Mia.

The Walther PPK. Its matte black surface sucked in the light of my flame, but it sat in my hand like it carried all the weight in the world.

Chapter 39

ONCE, in the early days of my excommunication, I found myself in the processing centers for pigs in a secluded Haven district. I'd ventured there because I needed food, and where better to find it than the source? There was a room where they processed meats into various cured forms, and the workers there had a little side operation selling meat on sticks.

They were kind people, and when a scruffy, scrawny giant emerged from the shadows, they did as any good Christian would do. They fed me, clothed me, and showed me kindness. In return, I helped them untangle a tricky problem in their automated equipment and acquired medications that Trinity hadn't seen fit to send. It was my first mutually beneficial encounter with anyone after the wreck of the *Benevolent*. The memory still sits bittersweet on the tip of my tongue.

Before the workers left for the weekend, they told me I could stay in their facilities as long as I liked, and I was considering it. I wandered the whole processing plant from where the pigs were slaughtered to the final packing line where bundles of meat were wrapped in a clear fiber to be shipped up to the Hallows.

It struck me as unfair that the bulk of the best meats went north, but at that point my life had benefitted from this injustice. I'd been breathing the spoils of inequality so long it felt like suffocation to leave.

Lost in thought, I had wandered into cold storage just as the last workers had left. As soon as the lights went full black, I knew my mistake. The doors were all automatic, run by a Trinity that absolutely would not acknowledge me, not even, I thought, in times of dire danger. It was cold in that room, and I felt my way around the hanging corpses of slaughtered pigs until I reached the door.

It wouldn't open.

I spent three full days in the room of hanging corpses, blind to everything but a single red light above the door—a lone pinprick telling me that the door would not open. By the time the workers returned, I was a shivering, ragged mess. Thirsty, hungry, and barely able to lift myself from the cold floor. They told me it was lucky that I had found a long trench coat to keep me warm and a cheap, manual music rig to keep me sane.

Luck was not what I would have called it, but it taught me fear.

I flicked my lighter so that I could assess my situation. There were chemicals, tools, and a manila folder stabbed to the wall with a screwdriver. What had her plan been there? Was she expecting me to want whatever was in that envelope? It had distracted me enough for her to escape. Was there anything more to it than that?

The air in the utility closet was stuffy. Stifling, even. It pressed on me like a heavy blanket, forcing the air from my lungs until I sat gasping on the floor. There were no vents in the closet. No normal circulation of air through the tightly controlled space. Eventually I really would suffocate in the tiny space. How long did I have? I didn't know. It felt like no time at all.

Time. I had no time. If I wanted to visit the *Benevolent* with Smalley, I needed to move. The thought sent me into a rage again and I kicked at the door. My knee blazed with pain and I collapsed again.

Hands trembling, I retrieved the music rig from my pocket and set it to play a random selection of blues. A thousand hours had passed since Mia locked me in the closet. Days and days and days. But I wasn't hungry or thirsty. I ached. My lighter flickered and shadows danced.

Salvation started with Ma Rainey's scratchy recording of "Bo-Weevil Blues"—the blues distilled into its purest form, with long-held vocals and a clarinet clinging to powerful notes. By the time the song finished, my sense of time had returned, and my body returned to my control.

It was too late to join Smalley. My goal was already a lost cause. I'd squandered my chance to ever lay my parents to rest or pay them any kind of respect. There would be no bringing them back for their last rites, and there would be no discovering the events leading up to their deaths. I might never know who was truly responsible for the wreck of the *Benevolent*. As Robert Johnson's "Hellhound on My Trail" settled my soul with the clean strum of a guitar, I considered my options.

Trinity had sensors in the room. They weren't detecting me, but they *had* to exist. They were everywhere, after all. If I could trigger something in those sensors, I might be able to get it to open the door. I looked at the cleaning chemicals in their bottles and the papers pinned to the wall.

Fire?

What would Trinity do in a fire? I didn't think it would open the door. Not if it were a chemical leak of some sort. It would seal off the area.

So, that was probably not a great idea.

Then, of course, there was the gun. Even a small-caliber weapon like the PPK could smash through fiber-made material. It would be a miracle if I could smash the right stuff to make the sliding door open, but it might be worth a shot.

Then again, it might also solidify Trinity's resolve to have me killed. If that was even a thing anymore. For now, the gun stayed in my pocket. I wasn't desperate enough for that. Yet.

I pulled the envelope from the wall. It had been an obvious decoy. She'd used it to distract me, and that was it. After all, she had pulled it at random from the strewn remains of some defunct business. I uncoiled the string sealing the envelope and peered inside.

The first thing I saw was the black-and-white photograph. A woman with long dark hair wore sunglasses in a bright Haven afternoon. Behind her, a vendor sold the kebabs I'd eaten a hundred times. Above, on the side of the building, was a mural depicting the triumph of the Green Ridge soccer team over a rival. That same mural was there today, but in much worse condition. She was beautiful. Her expression was a steadied neutral, but there was something morose about the set of her lips. Something terribly tragic.

I knew the location. I had visited it too many times over the years. It sat outside the docking port where the *Benevolent* failed to dock nearly fifteen years ago. I don't know what I'd ever wanted from those visits, but an ache deep in my chest always brought me back there.

It took me a moment to remember where I recognized the woman. As Bessie Smith's "Nobody Knows You When You're Down and Out" steadied my nerves, I stared at the photograph. This would have been taken years ago. A decade, maybe, based on the age of the mural.

This was Carrie Fortner. Her formal portrait still hung in Kaegan Fortner's home in the hallows. What was she doing in these records? On the back of the photograph, someone had written a date. It was the day of the wreck of the *Benevolent*.

The only other thing in the envelope was a sheaf of papers, stapled together and marked up with a black marker. The pages had been printed using the kind of cheap printer used only for government work and keeping the records for low-end gambling halls. The origin of the records was unclear, but as I peered at them in the dim glow of the flickering lighter, something became very clear.

Someone had been tracking Carrie Fortner. Dates and times were recorded in plain text across from quick notes regarding her location. "Ate at the stand across from Green Ridge." "Spent the afternoon atop the Trowbridge apartment complex." "Slept in the Halifax Coffins."

They were tracking her the way they now tracked me.

I scrolled through the printout. Statement after statement pinpointed the location of Carrie Fortner as she moved throughout the city. The tracking became less precise when she moved through the Heavies or the Hallows, but in Haven, every moment of her time was accounted for. Paging through, I quickly moved to the end.

"Body found in the aftermath of the *Benevolent* disaster."

My heart pounded so fast it felt like it had stopped. *I* had been there at the wreck of the *Benevolent*. The catastrophic aftermath of the ship tearing away from the docking port had injured my sister and knocked me flat. Had someone else been there in that lock? I tried to shake the memories loose in my head, but all I could remember was the video of the event, which I had watched so many times.

But Carrie Fortner had been excommunicated. She wouldn't have appeared on the video of the event. The implication shattered me. Papers fluttered to the floor. I had thought for so long that Trinity was punishing me for my actions. I'd killed all those people, so excommunication was my penance. Then, when I learned the utility of my condition—that I was one of the few who could update Trinity's parameters and speak to it directly—I thought it might be a reward because I had prioritized the city over my own family. That hadn't made penance any easier, but it made a kind of sense.

This, though. If an excommunicated person died in that same event, had she somehow transferred her status to me? Did Trinity select the nearest citizen? Or did Fortner select me because she knew she was on her way out? It could have played out a dozen ways, and the papers left me with nothing but questions.

Lightnin' Hopkins played his "Katie Mae Blues," singing goodbye and wailing on his guitar. A great pit opened under my stomach, and I started to doubt my own memories. My own *self*.

When the door behind me slid open, I didn't even twitch. The shadows of two women darkened the far wall.

"All right, Demarco. We believe you," said Anya. "We need to talk."

Chapter 40

I TOSSED the Walther PPK onto the Cathedral of Saint Francis of Assisi's funeral recycler platform. Priest Cano had been reluctant to open the chamber on special request, but when I explained the purpose, she understood. Sometimes one's confessor is the only person who will really listen.

"The last time I was in here, Trinity tried to recycle me," I said.

Priest Cano folded her hands in front of her. "That's one way to get something useful out of you."

"It won't try anything as long as you're here."

"Let's call that a metaphor for walking with Jesus."

"Are you Jesus in this situation?" The heavy door closed behind us with a hiss.

"I'm the best stand-in we have around these parts," she said. "Unless you can think of someone better."

"There's never anyone better than you, Cano."

Her sigh captured the bone-deep weariness that I felt. The air took on a bright acidic smell as the central pit opened. The gun tumbled inside.

"Will it be able to handle that?" Cano said.

"Recyclers normally work with organic materials or fiber compounds, but they'll handle steel and lead just as well. It takes time, but I feel bad for anyone trying to reach in to pluck that weapon out of the system."

"Good as it's going to get, I guess." Her fists clenched.

"What is it?"

"Those two women waiting outside. I don't think you should trust them."

She wasn't saying anything I didn't already know. "Any particular reason?"

Cano chewed her lip. I knew that look. There was something she needed to tell me, but the confidentiality of her position kept her from saying it outright. Finally, she said, "The younger one was in the church the night that man was killed."

Mia. She'd been there the night that man had died. "Not the older sister?"

"It was definitely the younger. She prayed in the main chapel for hours after the evening's Mass. I remember because I didn't recognize her."

"But the guy was killed immediately after Mass."

"She could have disappeared for a bit and come back. Or not. I don't exactly track all my parishioners' movements."

"That's not what I'd call damning evidence." The pit closed with a resounding thump. "But it's helpful," I said. "Thanks."

She took my hand in both of hers and looked up at me. "Jude, I want you to be careful with them. That's all I'm saying. There's something dangerous happening, and I don't like it."

"Angel paid you a visit, didn't she?"

"The words are mine," she said. "I wouldn't speak them if they weren't."

The pit in the center of the recycler chamber closed. I waited, half-expecting Trinity to attempt to digest me now that I'd willingly stepped into its gullet.

"Are we good now, Trinity?" I didn't expect an answer with Cano standing there. "That's the gun. I've destroyed every other gun that I can locate. You're safe. No need to take it out on me."

The walls flashed blue, and Trinity's smooth voice said, "Affirmative."

The recycler chamber opened. Mia and Anya sat in the front pew. Mia's hands were clenched together in front of her in something like a prayer, but Anya rested her hands in her lap like she was as calm as a monk.

I wanted to confront them about what Cano had told me, but that would mean revealing where I had gotten the information. It would have to wait until later. After Cano left through the back exit, I said, "It's done. We can talk." I had made the destruction of the weapon my price, and they'd both surprised me by agreeing to it.

Mia said, "That thing might have been useful." She hadn't been happy that I had taken it from her. The only reason she didn't take it back was… well, I didn't know why. It didn't matter anymore. It was gone.

"I'd sure like to get my hands on that Colt Python," I said.

"Father wouldn't go unarmed," said Anya.

"He could carry a more conventional sidearm," I said.

Mia snorted. "Sling ceramics like a common criminal? That's not the Fortner way, Demarco."

Anya glanced at her little sister. "He'll either bring that

weapon if he has it or he'll pick up another one from the vault."

Heat rose under my collar. It was time for a confession. "Your father's not going to like what he finds in his vault."

They both stared at me with wide eyes.

"Clear fiber resin," I said. "It's still a nice display, but those guns will never fire again."

"We're talking to a dead man," said Mia to her sister.

I tried to change the subject. "Are your kids safe?" I said to Anya.

"As safe as they can be until our monster of a father is out of the picture."

"You always knew what kind of man he was," spat Mia.

"And you didn't?" Anya snapped. "You went along with everything he did, same as Blaize."

Mia said, "At least I didn't have access to his whole finances for years."

"The books are clean," Anya snapped. "Whatever he did didn't show up on the store's books."

"The store wasn't a front?" I asked.

"If it was, I wasn't in on the secret," Anya said.

I said, "He always said family was everything."

"Well, there's family, and then there's *family*," said Mia.

Anya stood without genuflecting. She faced her half-sister, her face growing red with fury. "You were lucky to get let out of his inner circle."

"Sounds like you were too," Mia retorted.

The older sister's jaw clenched.

"Ladies," I said, "you can resolve your differences later."

They both turned to me, and I might have preferred stepping into the line of fire.

Anya said, "Fine. We need to figure out what we're going to do."

"Tell me about your mother," I asked Anya.

Her expression softened, but she said, "We're not supposed to talk about her."

"Your father's rules?"

Anya paced the length of the funeral chapel. "She was like you. Excommunicated."

"How?"

"I don't know. It's a family thing. Or at least it used to be. Father always said he hoped I could get the blessing, as he called it. I never could, and I guess I always thought that meant there was something wrong with me."

"Your mother had it," I said. "Your grandmother too?"

Mia retreated to the farthest corner of the chapel, slinking into the candlelit recesses where the Stations of the Cross hung in obscurity.

"Yeah," Anya said finally. "Grandmother. I don't know the history before that. When Father got married, grandmother left and passed the gift down to his wife. When they were divorced, mother took it with her."

"By then, she'd given birth to you, Blaize, and Lorrel. One of you was supposed to get the gift. What happened?"

"The *Benevolent*," came Mia's voice from the corner. "I was just a kid, but it was the big event that fucked up my whole life, so I kinda remember it."

"It wasn't exactly a parade for the rest of us," snapped Anya. "Our *mom* died."

Mia crossed her arms and leaned against the wall.

"She died in the port airlock," I said. "Same place my sister was injured during the wreck. Why was she there?"

Mia scowled but didn't answer. My gut told me she was hiding something.

"You got her gift," Anya told me. "Father said it passed to you when she died. That's why he's so obsessed with you."

"Obsessed is a strong word," I said.

Anya barked a bitter laugh. "You've made a hell of an enemy, Demarco."

"And I wasn't even trying."

"Father tried everything else," said Mia. "Told Blaize to be your friend. Told Anya to act like transferring the gift would be the only way to save her family."

"Sent you to kill me," I said. "Hoping that my death would somehow transfer it to you by proximity."

"Good thing I'm so nice." Mia stepped from the corner. Her ring still flashed on her finger.

"Tell me about the symbol," I said.

"It's good luck," said Anya.

"It's a hack," I said.

Mia slipped the ring from her finger and stowed it in a pocket.

Anya said, "Father's planning something."

"He's going to go to the *Benevolent*," said Mia.

"We finally spoke to each other," Anya said, gesturing to her sister. "And you were right. Father's been playing us against each other our whole lives to get what he wants. He's manipulated us into hating each other so that we might compete for his attention. When Grandpapa died and left a portion of the business to Mia, that wasn't some fluke counter to Father's grand plans."

"It was a way to drive the wedge," I said. I tried to resolve the Machiavellian maneuvering with the charming but practical man I'd met in the Hallows. "He's really planning to visit the *Benevolent*?"

"What do you know about that?" asked Anya.

I thought of the way Kaegan Fortner had talked about his eldest son. There was something unresolved in it. "He's going after your brother."

Mia retreated to the dark corner again.

Anya shook her head, pacing around the chapel. "He wouldn't go personally to retrieve a body. He doesn't even believe in last good deeds."

"Not even for his son?" I asked.

Mia said, "Not even his *favorite* son."

"Blaize was right up there," said Anya.

"Second place isn't 'right up there' if there are only two contestants," said Mia.

Anya jumped like she'd been prodded by a hot poker. "Listen, you little shit—"

"Ladies," I said, interposing myself like the idiot I was.

Both sets of furious eyes focused on me.

"The Python," Mia said.

"What about it?"

Anya gasped, "Lorrel."

I said, "Blaize told me Lorrel hated guns."

"People hate a lot of things," said Mia in a mockery of her Father's voice, "but that doesn't mean we get to choose our place in life."

Anya sneered at her half-sister. "He isn't that bad."

"Maybe not to you."

Anya clenched her fists. "He treated all of us with respect. You were just too self-centered to see it."

"He didn't expect much of his eldest," said Mia.

I stepped between them again before they could escalate any further. "It feels like you two have a lot to work out, but I need to be on that ship."

They both stared at me.

"The blue has already sent an investigative group to the wreck of the *Benevolent*," I explained. "Guy by the name of Smalley is leading it. He's probably docking with the ship as we speak. There are secrets Kaegan Fortner won't allow out, and he's planning to visit the wreck. I figure he's leaving from the Heavies, where his shipping operation just finished emptying a cargo vessel." Now it was my turn to pace around the chapel. "I want aboard that ship, and I don't want your father to know about it."

Mia's eyes twinkled. "You're planning to catch him in the act."

"I'm planning to get my hands on that gun before he does and try to resolve everything else peacefully." I was also planning to learn the truth about my parents' death, but the sisters didn't need to know all the details on that. "It's going to go a lot smoother if I'm not raising flags on my way in."

Anya stared at me for a long time before responding. "Father's ship is the *Lost Saint*, but there's a problem."

Mia picked up on it immediately. "It's not a Trinity-linked vessel. It's an Earth voyager. It won't ignore you."

"Great." I had grown so used to invisibility that it hadn't occurred to me that a disconnected system would easily detect me.

Anya said, "It's also an *Earth* voyager. Father is likely sending it on its way to Earth. He'll use a smaller pod to return to Nicodemia."

"So if I go, I might not be coming back?" I asked.

Mia said, "Why pack an extra pod for a passenger who doesn't exist?"

"I can come back with the cops," I said.

"Planning on getting arrested?" said Mia.

"If that's what it takes."

"There are ways to get around the ship's systems." Anya started toward the big fiberoak doors.

"Where are you going?" Mia asked, following.

"If we're going to make this work," said Anya, "then we're going to need to hurry."

"We?" said Mia.

"Might as well work together."

Mia's lips pressed tight, like she didn't know how to process this.

To me, Anya said, "We'll be in touch. Just find the *Lost Saint.*"

With that, the half-sisters were gone. Instead of following, I genuflected in the front row and sat as still as death on the pew for a long time. After a while, I became aware of a presence beside me.

"You don't need to go," said Priest Cano.

"You were listening?"

"A priest needs to know what troubles her flock."

"Then you know I need to go."

She stared at the side of my face for a long time. "There's a good chance you won't be able to return."

"I've always wanted to go to Earth."

"You know those ships aren't manned."

"Then I'll fit right in." I rose from the pew, genuflected, wincing at the pop of my knee, and gave the sanctuary one last look. "I've seen too many people sent to the great beyond in this chapel. I guess I always thought this would be me someday."

"Then you have two choices," said Cano. "Don't go or promise to come back."

I let out a long sigh. It would have been nice to make that promise, but right there in the funeral chapel, I couldn't bring myself to lie.

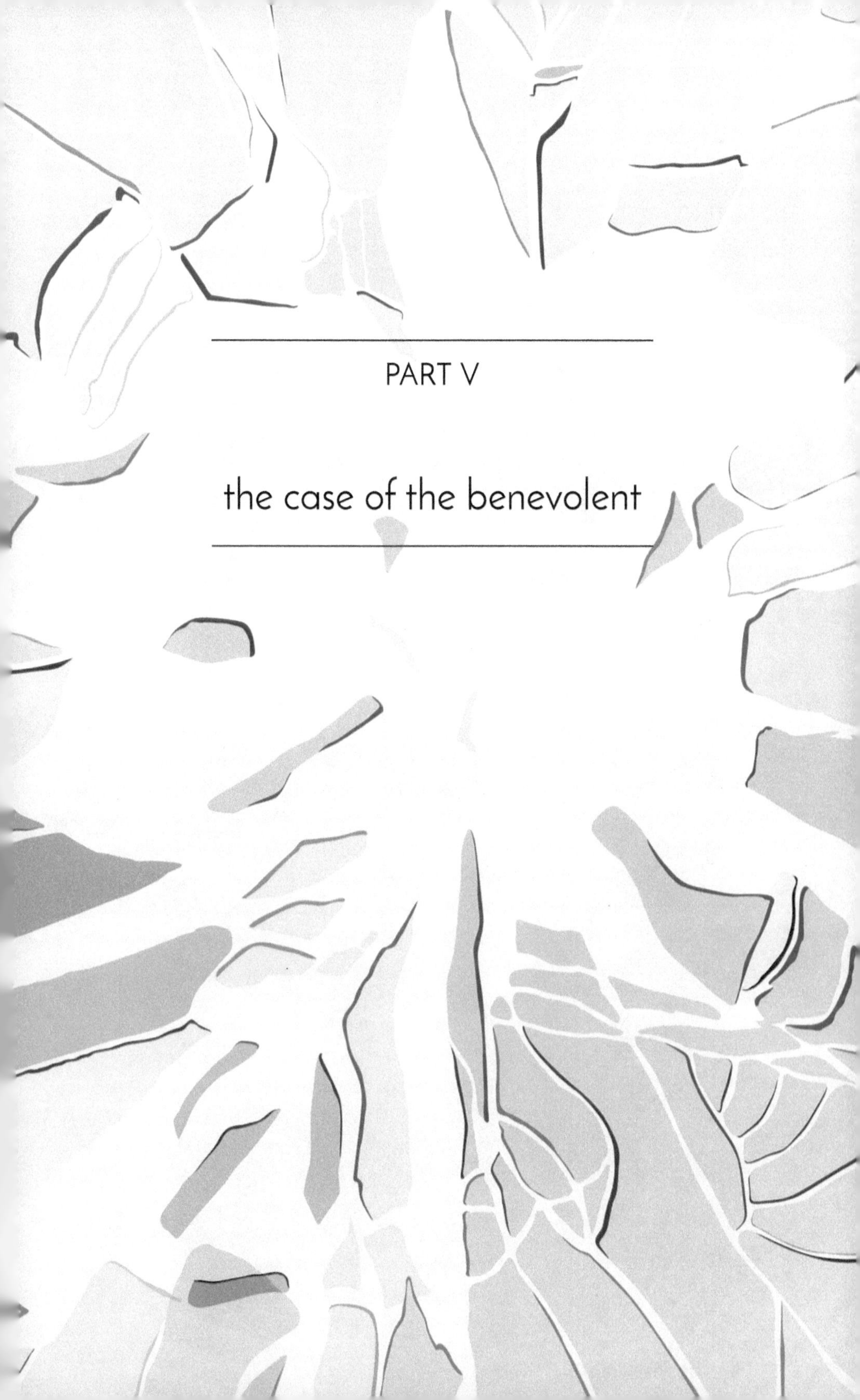

PART V

the case of the benevolent

Chapter 41

"YOU GOTTA BRING A WEAPON." Retch sat on the counter at Angel's Diner.

"I don't feel good about guns," I said.

"Yeah? Well, guns don't care about your feelings," Retch said. "Bring brass knuckles or a decent stunstick if you have to, but bring something." He touched the stunstick on his belt and it crackled. "So that they take you seriously."

"He's right," said Angel. She sat with me at the corner table. "You can't go unarmed."

"I'm not going there to pick a fight," I said.

"You never are." She gestured at my whole body as if it were proof of her point.

It was. "Hey, Retch, can I borrow that stunstick?"

He narrowed his eyes. "I need this."

"We both know that your control over the Screaming Jesus gang is entirely psychological." I took a bite of apple pie, wondering if those apples had come from the orchard up in Haven.

"Will you bring it back?"

"I might not be coming back."

Angel stared at me as if I'd cursed our parents.

After another bite of pie—it was too sugary for my taste, but the tartness of the apples made the whole thing worth it —I said, "There's a chance the ship I'll be on is only making a stop on the *Benevolent* on its way to Earth."

"That's a five-year trip," said Retch. "You'll be ancient by the time you get back."

I elected not to mention that the ship likely wouldn't be stocked for passengers, in which case I'd be both ancient and dead.

"There are cryopods," said Angel. "*If* he comes back, he'll probably be the same insufferable age."

"Let's face it, sis," I said, "I'll be insufferable at any age."

The others agreed to that a little too easily. Retch hopped down from the counter and thumped the stunstick down onto the table next to my pie. "I want this back, old man."

"Is it charged up?"

"Have you ever known me not to be prepared?"

I took his hand before he could pull it away and looked into his eyes. "I appreciate this, Retch."

"Hey, I'd go with you if it wasn't an obvious suicide mission," Retch said.

"Excuse me?" said Angel.

"Nothing," said Retch. "Just don't let him leave without paying you for that pie."

I put the last of my winnings on the table, hooked the stunstick to my belt, and left out the back door. Cain was there, lying in the shade of the adjacent buildings. He raised his big head as I approached, but didn't bother to stand. His chest was bandaged, but otherwise his eyes were bright and his nose wet.

"You did good, buddy," I said, scratching him under his jowls.

He leaned into my hand. When I started to pull away, he scooted his whole body forward to keep me going. Defeated, I sat next to him and, for a few precious minutes, just existed.

"He's on painkillers," said Helen, stepping into the yard.

"I shouldn't have put him in danger."

"You're a magnet for trouble, Jude, and he cares about you."

I took Cain's head in both hands and gave him a good wobble. "Should I go?" I don't know if I was asking about the trip to the *Benevolent* or leaving on a more permanent basis. She was right, though. I was danger, and whenever I was close, Angel, Helen, and even Cain were also threatened.

Helen placed a warm hand on my shoulder. "You're always asking the wrong questions, aren't you?"

"What's the right question?"

"Maybe one that you don't know the answer to." Helen crossed the yard and peered through the alley into the street in front of the diner. The foot traffic had been light all day, and there was nobody there that I could see. "We would all live our lives differently if risk was the only factor." She gestured at Angel's Diner. "We wouldn't have all this. Angel wouldn't be out advocating for neighborhood improvements. She wouldn't be with me, that's for sure. We'd have taken our default lives and coasted through with the best Karma we could manage."

"Cain was shot."

"Who among us wouldn't take a bullet for the one we love?"

"He's never really liked me."

"But he *loves* you."

"Fair."

She fixed me with a hard gaze. "Your parents would have made that same choice that day."

She was saying that they would have sacrificed themselves to save their children. I wasn't so sure. "They were art thieves. Criminals. Everything I ever knew as a kid was a result of their corruption."

"People are more complicated," Helen said. "Especially parents."

"There's nothing complicated about it," I said. "My father helped move stolen art from the people down below to the people above. For a long time, he was one of the biggest reasons that people in the Heavies struggled. They say Karma's not a zero-sum game, but it is. When it comes right down to it, without the art to build museums around, communities failed to thrive."

"Yet the Heavies now has its own thriving art scene," said Helen. "Have you looked at the walls in the diner lately? We've started posting paintings done by people around the district. We're selling them, Jude. Selling them and making people's lives better in the process. Up in the Hallows, they worship the art of long-dead cultures. They listen to music recorded before mankind set foot on Earth's moon."

I thought of the blues music I listened to as often as I could. I loved how it plucked at the strings of my heart, but Helen was right. It was the worship of a people long gone.

"We don't need museums for culture," continued Helen. "There's plenty right here. Our community is strong and it's growing stronger. Remember Willie Fleck?"

It was only days ago, but the ache in my bones had flushed the experience with the up-and-coming crime boss out of my brain. My conflict with Fleck was another danger I'd placed on my sister's family. I buried my face in my big dog's short fur. "Don't tell me he's giving you trouble."

"Not exactly," she said. She was standing above me, and I don't remember her crossing the room. "He's decided that taking over all the crime in the lower districts isn't a great long-term strategy for survival. Rumor is, someone talked to him and convinced him to back down."

I looked up to Helen to see if she was joking. When I'd last left Fleck, he'd just seen his best friend killed, and he'd been determined to continue along the same path. "If it's not Fleck, then it'll be someone else."

A broad grin spread across Helen's face.

"It's Retch, isn't it?"

"Close."

"My sister? She doesn't have what it takes to be a crime boss."

"She isn't a crime boss. She's a community leader. Her project is to make her district safe again, and the people support her."

"So, she's a politician? A politician with a target painted on her back for any aspiring criminal."

"Community leader." Helen scratched Cain on the top of his head, and the traitor of a dog leaned away from me to get more of her lovin'. "Angel is a powerful advocate with a bulletproof dog the size of a small horse."

"My sister's going to be fine, isn't she?"

"I'm not sure that the stress of leadership is good for her."

"She thrives on it," I said. "Guaranteed."

"The point is that your sister causes her own trouble. If you're worried about endangering the people around you, then you should take into account the fact that we're doing a great job endangering ourselves."

"That's not comforting at all."

"It doesn't need to be."

I stood and stretched. "I might not come back, Helen."

She sighed. "We'll be fine if you don't come back, but also we won't."

"Hey, bro!" Angel called through the back door of the diner. "You got a visitor."

Inside the diner, Anders waited with a slab of apple pie in front of him. He sat in the booth in the back next to a painting I hadn't noticed before. It incorporated fibersteel textures and depicted an endless upward spiral. It reminded me of the view from the very bottom of Heavy Nicodemia, at the docks.

Anders looked up as I approached. "I always like it when I have business here, you know."

"My sister's too nice to you."

"I'm good for the Karma."

I sat across from him in the booth. "Smalley wasn't too disappointed?"

"He thought you'd be there," said Anders. "But he was hoping you wouldn't be."

"I had a scheduling conflict."

"Understandable."

"What's the word from the ship?"

"They're still on approach. Should be there soon enough. Smalley's looking forward to getting back already. You can hear it in his voice."

"So there's direct communication?"

"We've dedicated a channel to it. This is a big deal, Demarco. Not often we have a chance to run a mission outside the city."

"Who's on the team?"

"Small group," said Anders. "Smalley. Couple of forensic engineers."

"Not you?"

"It was decided that I should probably take care of some things down here." He didn't look terribly disappointed. "They need to take some readings to try to discover why the failure happened in the first place. Their pilot happens to also be a priest."

"For the bodies."

"They want to make sure the souls are put to rest, even if they can't haul all the bodies back."

"Fair enough." I took a sip of my water, expecting him to continue. When he didn't, I said, "Who else?"

"That's it."

"That's it? The biggest shipwreck in the last century, and they're sending four people?"

"It's a preliminary scouting mission," said Anders. "If they find anything that needs further investigation, then the *Benevolent* will swing back around in ten years."

"Maybe you'll be in charge of the investigation by then," I said.

He blew some air through his lips. "Not likely."

"Career trouble?"

Anders leaned forward and whispered, "You're not exactly Karma fuel over there, Demarco."

Anders had always been a decent cop in a swarm of belligerent assholes. Nobody else on the force ever wanted to work with me, and what he said clicked in place. Of course, they didn't want to work with me. I was a giant blank spot in the positive Karma that would determine their career progression. Anything they did to help me as a citizen would give them exactly zero progress toward their goals.

But I helped Anders help people. That had to count for something.

"It doesn't count," Anders said. "Whenever you help, it…

doesn't. I don't know how it works. *Nobody* knows how Karma works. You know that."

I knew how it worked. At least I thought I did. Was I like the odd symbol the Fortners wore to keep their Karma from adjusting? Was I the black hole in the middle of a crowded starfield? The void in the swarm of pluses and minuses?

"I hate to do this…" I said.

"You need a favor."

"While I'm gone, look after my sister. And Retch."

"Of course," he said, because he was that kind of guy. "I was going to."

I stared at the glass surface of my water for a long time. Eventually, Anders finished his pie and took his leave. Angel cleared his plate and tapped the table in front of me to get my attention.

"You're coming back," she said, as if she knew the thoughts racing through my head. "You're going to go. You're going to figure things out. Then you're going to come back. We need you."

"The only one of those I know for sure," I said, "is that I'm going to go."

Chapter 42

NICODEMIA HAD NEVER BEEN DESIGNED for resupply. It was a generation ship, with the only goal being a complete separation from Earth. Once the ship became a station, things changed. Trips to the local planets became common. Faster travel allowed resupply from Earth and other colonies. It became a hub of activity.

Every kilo of mass added to the city needed to be properly counterbalanced in the giant rotating chain or it threatened to throw the whole spinning thing out of balance. The workers in charge of port Customs were some of the best-trained dockworkers in the history of the human race.

That mass exchange was the first challenge to sneaking aboard the *Lost Saint*. I ditched a load of aluminum ballast in the staging area so that measurements wouldn't be off by enough to be noticed.

Nobody stopped me. I wore the coveralls and badge of a port worker, thanks to the access codes Anya had supplied. The uniform served as a much-appreciated safety precaution.

In an emergency depressurization, the coveralls would encapsulate me and pressurize. It wouldn't be comfortable, but it might save my life.

The second challenge to sneaking aboard the *Lost Saint* was simply getting through the door. I grabbed a dolly and loaded a stack of boxes. These were marked with a filing code and labeled as artwork. An odd thing to ship to Earth, but the residents of Nicodemia were obsessed with Earth art. Why couldn't the citizens of Earth be obsessed right back?

In most of Heavy Nicodemia, I stood out like a cigar in a box of cigarettes, but here among the dockworkers I was one big guy out of dozens. They all went about their business and ignored me completely.

Except for the foreman. "Hold up," he said, stepping in front of me on the walkway to the ship. "What's this all about?"

"Special shipment for the boss," I said.

"Fortner sent you?"

"Look, I got work to do."

He narrowed his eyes and sized me up. "I don't recognize you."

Trying to sound put out, I said, "This is a special task."

He glanced at the badge clipped to my breast pocket. "We do things by the book here, Mr. Whistles."

The guy didn't look like he was going to back down, and he was nearly as big as me. It wasn't going to be easy to slip past, and if I started a fight I could all but kiss my ride goodbye.

The light over the door to the last airlock flashed a brilliant blue.

"Hey boss," called one of the workers near the gate. "Fortner's requesting passage through."

The foreman glared at me. "Do the weigh-in," he said. "I don't want our numbers coming out wrong."

"Believe me," I said, "I don't either."

The foreman rushed off to attend to the airlock, and I shuffled my cargo to the weighing station. Once the mass was recorded, I continued onto the ship.

"Welcome to the *Lost Saint*." The voice was a smooth baritone, with clear crisp diction and one of many Earth accents I'd never been able to quite place. By the time I figured out that it was the ship talking to me, I had my hand on the stunstick, and the boxes I'd been hauling were scattered across the staging room floor.

"Thanks," I said tentatively. It had been so long since an automated system had tracked me when I wasn't specifically seeking a liminal space. I felt the weight of the thing's attention on me. "I'm here for the voyage."

"Cargo personnel must be evacuated before takeoff."

"Ah, um, hold on." I wasn't expecting this interaction yet. I cleared my throat and flipped my identification badge around. "My name is Jude Demarco. I'm a traveler, and I'm on my way to Earth."

The system took a moment to process that. "All passengers must proceed to cryochambers."

"Right," I said. "I'll get right on that." I couldn't tell if I was relieved that there were cryochambers or terrified that there was a possibility that I might end up traveling to Earth.

Also, the thought of being frozen for half a decade didn't settle well.

I gathered the boxes onto the dolly and carted them into the ship. The *Lost Saint* was a cargo hauler in every aspect of the term. The design was spartan, with a grid maze of long passages interspersed between the huge docking bay and minuscule bridge. According to the filing instructions printed on the boxes I'd taken, they needed to go deep into the maze of narrow passages. I followed the stenciled column and row markings at each corner until I found the appropriate enclosure.

It took some time to understand the locking mechanism, but I secured the boxes in the appropriate place. In another life, this might have been an acceptable job for someone like me. Big, strong, reasonably smart. I could get used to this.

The next voices I heard were distinctly human. They were the hushed curses of an irritated man, but the echo of the ship's solid walls jumbled the words into an undecipherable mess.

I wanted to get closer, but when I stepped into the hall, the light followed me. *Lost Saint* illuminated my passage, making it extremely difficult to sneak anywhere.

Hiding in plain sight was my only option, but I didn't like it. I moved quickly through the hall, listening to the hushed voices in a parallel track. Kaegan Fortner's Haven-influenced Hallows accent rattled through the ship. He was upset. Irritable. There were at least three other people with him. Still, I moved quickly down the hall until I was ahead of them. They were on their way to the bridge, if my guess was right. I took a perpendicular path toward them, crouched down, and faced away so that they would see my uniformed body but not my face.

"It's inefficient that they load everything at heavy gravity," said Fortner. "Why in the name of Mary don't we move this operation to the Hallows."

"It's protocol," said Huff. I recognized his reedy voice. "Everything needs to go through Haven and Hallows Customs."

"They need to reduce the gravity, then."

"It's not something we can really—"

"This is unacceptable, Huff." At this point, Fortner passed the intersection closest to me. "Get back to work, Customs," he snapped in my direction. "We're taking off in ten minutes."

I waved my acknowledgment and stood up. By the time I was up, they had moved past the intersection. I heard their footsteps retreat through the long hall. I turned.

Huff stood in the intersection, poking at a tablet.

Huff was exactly the kind of person I wanted to hide from. With a swipe and a press, he could call security down on me. He could delay the entire flight or have the blue arrest me. Huff could initiate a purge and flush me into space.

But I knew the little weasel better than that.

"Huff," I growled, looming over him.

He let out a little yelp and his tablet flew from his grasp. I caught it. The display flashed red. The little man glanced down the hall where Fortner had gone.

"You're not going to do anything." I stowed the tablet in one of my coverall's biggest pockets. "And you're not going to say anything about me being here."

He furrowed his brow. "You're in big trouble, Demarco."

"I'm in big trouble no matter where I go. This place just has the potential to be a little better ventilated, and I happen to notice that you're not wearing a safety suit."

He glanced down at his frazzled tweed.

"What's Fortner looking for, Huff?"

"I don't know what you mean."

"Sure you do." I stepped closer, looming over the little man. "He's not here for his son. A few dimes in the hands of the blue would return Lorrel's body to Nicodemia."

Huff wrung his hands. "People aren't as corrupt as you

seem to think, Mr. Demarco. Maybe it's your own motivations you ought to be looking at."

"Maybe." I stared at Huff right in the eyes until he flinched.

"What he's doing isn't illegal," sputtered Huff. "It's unregulated space. He can visit the wreck if he wants."

"Is the Colt Python on that ship?"

The whites of Huff's eyes flashed for a fraction of a second. "My boss is a collector. It makes sense that he would be looking for rare items in a place where he is legally allowed to take them." This last part he nearly shouted.

"Go," I said. "And we'll see how things turn out."

Huff turned to leave, then stopped. His shoulders were hunched with tension that he might have been carrying for years. "I don't know what he has planned," he said, almost too quiet for me to hear.

Fortner was there to cover something up. He had to be. There was no other reason for him to personally visit the *Benevolent*. Maybe his cover story was that he was there for salvage. Maybe only his educated eye could find the value left behind on the wreck of the transport.

That wasn't reason enough to visit in person. He could send his best-trained people and a couple of mooks. He could even have sent one of his daughters, since they'd trained under him their whole lives. No, this was something more valuable than the junk left behind on the ship, even if the final gun from his collection was somewhere on the ship.

Huff's fear made sense. If Fortner was so afraid to let anyone else handle the cover-up for him, then he was not likely to let anyone else survive the trip. An arranged catastrophe might wipe out Huff and his two goons. A small disaster might even kill the police mission if needed. Fortner, that cold bastard, must have had something planned, and Huff knew it.

But *what* did Fortner have planned?

"Stay close to your boss," I said. "I'm your ace, Huff."

"It feels like betrayal."

"Find out his plans," I said, "then tell me if betrayal's the worst thing happening here."

With that, I disappeared into the maze of the *Lost Saint.*

Chapter 43

THE LAST TIME I saw the *Benevolent* was the day my parents had died. I remember viewing it from the port in the Hallows, marveling at the sheer size of the thing as it docked with the city. It grew larger and larger as it approached, blotting out the night sky. There had been a point when I could see every perfect detail on its sleek gray hull, from the external access ports to the bristling sensor arrays.

It didn't loom, seeing it on Huff's tiny tablet display, but the detail was much the same. It had taken me some time to get the little screen to do what I wanted. So many years away from the technology of daily life left me unpracticed in the art of navigating menus and sifting data. When I found the external camera arrays, however, I was stunned.

The *Benevolent* hadn't changed. As catastrophic as the wreck was, there was little external damage visible. The problem had been entirely internal—something with the automated systems had failed to seal the inhabited portions of the ship when the airlock blew. Everyone on the ship should have been safe, but only the captain, copilot, and a few others from the bridge ever walked away from the wreck. Even they struggled to return to the city after the ship was flung free of its moorings.

At the time, I had thought the ship was gone forever. Docking with a rapidly spinning city was dangerous, and breaking loose had flung it so hard it had taken months for the few surviving crew to return to Nicodemia.

Gravity, apparently, did what gravity did. The *Benevolent* was in an orbit, and it was finally close enough to intercept. I mapped the ship's journey on the little screen. It wouldn't be close again for another decade, and even then, it wasn't going to pass as close.

This would be my only chance to discover my parents' fate.

If it weren't for the debilitating nausea of zero-g, the ache in my chest probably would have crippled me. As it was, I curled up in a ball, floating where I wouldn't bump too hard against the surrounding cargo crates when the *Lost Saint* engaged its approach maneuvers.

It would have been smarter and a whole lot more comfortable to find a crash seat and strap in, but all the seating was closely monitored, and I wasn't quite ready yet to give away my position. Instead, I found some spare straps in a drawer and tied myself to a side of the zero-g room that had once been the floor.

And I waited. The first hours passed in an aching eternity. The dark shape of the *Benevolent* didn't move on my screen. It would take ages to reach the ship, and there I was without even a deck of cards for company.

It was the pain in my knee that I noticed first once the nausea subsided. I'd lived so many years in the Heavies that the aches and pains of life were an absolute constant, but the knee pain was new. When it disappeared, I noticed.

Then, I started to notice the other pains. The sharp stabbing in my back disappeared. The muscle pain in my calves became a dull static. The headache that had plagued me for years didn't exactly leave, but it subsided into a hazy memory in the back of my skull. The sensation—or lack of sensation—was so startling that my heart raced. It felt wrong at first. Undeserved.

That didn't last, because it occurred to me that I was finally doing what I was meant to do. I was investigating my parents' deaths. I might not ever bring the truth back to Nicodemia, but I would leave knowing that I had finally done everything in my power to discover the circumstances of their death.

I *knew* that it was my fault they had died, but that wasn't enough. When I had finally talked to the copilot, he told me that there was something else behind the failure aboard the *Benevolent*, and all the research I did told me that my actions should never have killed everyone aboard. The ship was put in a maintenance mode that shouldn't have been available. It prevented a proper lockdown.

If this was the right path for me, then the easing of my pain was like a message from God. I drew a deep slow breath. By the time I let it all the way out, I was asleep.

When I woke, the *Benevolent* was much closer. My eyes were crusted, and a globe of saliva hovered in front of my bleary face. I swatted it away and then tried to wipe it on my non-permeable coveralls. The tablet rattled against the floor, and it took me a moment of sleep-addled thought to understand that this meant that a maneuvering sequence had begun. I stretched, still feeling great. The headache was completely gone now, though my nausea had been replaced with a hint of hunger. I ate a protein bar as I cycled through the tablet's menus to get a better view of the approaching ship.

The *Benevolent* was dark, except for one segment of the long sleek body. Outside of that section sat a small vessel. That would be the ship Smalley and the engineers took. It looked like they had docked on one of many hatches along the body of the ship rather than the main port connection.

Shredded metal bristled all along the rear of the ship. This was where the docking mechanisms would have been, but when I had released the clamps all those years ago, I'd caused the partially sealed lock to tear free. It had been the *Benevolent* that had suffered in that exchange. That had been the goal. Better the *Benevolent* suffer damage than the city itself.

The sight brought back every painful emotion from that day in full force. Rage, sorrow, guilt. Mostly rage. How could I have done that? Why did I pull that trigger?

The *Lost Saint*'s maneuvering thrusters fired, this time pushing me against the wall to my left. The strap held me in place well enough but dug into my hip. What followed was hours of intermittent adjustments to speed and trajectory. Sometimes the world rotated around me. Sometimes I was strapped to the ceiling or the floor. Thrust never approached anything like the simulated gravity of the Hallows, but it was, at times, enough to be uncomfortable.

It always returned to neutral. The main thrust of the journey had been achieved by the angle at which the *Lost Saint* released from port. It was angled to hit a tangent of the *Benevolent*'s long orbit, and the only adjustments needed were those to fine-tune its attempt at docking.

When the *Benevolent* was the size of my thumbprint on the screen, I navigated the external cameras to get a view of the city. Nicodemia rotated around a man-made star, a false sun that served as a brilliant power source to the ship as it crossed the heavens. A single chain rotated around that central flame. Some nodes on that chain were three deep like Nicodemia, making it appear as a gigantic rosary. I could not tell which was my home. From the outside, the half-dozen cities looked largely the same, save for a few.

Several had fallen in the long years since the ship left Earth. Some cities that failed had been evacuated, but many had moved past a need for evacuation almost immediately. Catastrophic failure from an outer breach was a sudden, terrible way to kill an entire city.

This might have been what I avoided when I detached the *Benevolent,* but knowing that did nothing to assuage my guilt. I switched the feedback to our approach and waited.

Thrusters fired, and the strap pressed so hard on my chest that I couldn't breathe. I was on the perceived ceiling, and the crushing force was enough to turn my face blue and make my hands go numb. A minute passed and I couldn't draw a breath. Black lightning crackled at the edges of my vision.

Weightless.

I gasped, desperate to breathe as much as possible in case the thrusters fired again. They didn't. The rest of the approach was a series of subtle nudges followed by a resounding clunk that shook the bones of the ship.

We were there.

Chapter 44

FORTNER AND COMPANY would enter the *Benevolent* via a secured airlock. It would take time to negotiate. Instead of waiting for them, I decided to brave the hard vacuum, putting all my faith in the cheap suit I was wearing.

As soon as the airlock opened, alarms fired in the suit's sealed helmet. The tiny oxygen pack wouldn't last more than ten minutes, but I wouldn't need it. I sighted the lit portion of the *Benevolent* and made my way to it. Magnetic boots let me shuffle awkwardly across the surface of the ship. My breath came hard, and the tiny oxygen meter dropped fast, but I found an airlock not terribly far away and took it, hoping that Smalley's engineers had figured out how to pressurize the ship.

"Shoulda known it was you," said Smalley. He wore a bulky vacuum suit and his skin was pale and sweaty. He held a small blue service pistol in his right hand, and he floated upside down. Zero-g took some getting used to. "The team breathed a sigh of relief when you decided not to show."

I collapsed my helmet into its shoulder pouch. "Sorry I'm late."

He stowed his service pistol. "How'd you manage to commandeer a vessel?"

"You give me too much credit."

"Yet, here you are."

"The ship is one of Kaegan Fortner's cargo haulers," I said. "And I'm more of a stowaway than a contributing member of the staff."

Smalley's thick eyebrows shot up. "Is this a salvage operation?"

"Maybe."

He clicked a comm unit on his shoulder. "Hey, Jurgens, can you get a message up to the aft airlock? It'd be great if their landing party could steer clear of our crime scene."

I stared at Smalley.

"It's been a hell of a trip," he said.

"Trouble?"

He tilted his chin to the door at his left. "Come have a look."

I pushed off from the doorway to spin after him through the door. From there, I could see that the lighting in this section of the ship was the dull, flickering emergency lighting of a ship in dire straits.

The first sign of trouble was a jagged gouge in one of the bulkheads. A long line ran along the shining metal surface, followed by the telltale hole of a small-but-solid impact.

I poked at the hole with a gloved finger. "Lead?"

"Got it in one."

"How come I'm not surprised?"

"Well, you're one up on me. Records show there wasn't a gun anywhere near the *Benevolent* when it went down."

My grip on the handrail went weak, and I had to take a moment to gather myself. "I've studied this ship," I finally said. "Every tiny detail of the diagram is burned into my memory from the hours of staring at the designs and wondering what could have possibly happened. I know where the recyclers and the power cores are. The ship is stuffed with critical equipment in a tiny space. Firing one of these would have been suicide." I ran a finger along the jagged edge of the rut.

"My thought exactly," said Smalley.

"This shouldn't have been possible. Nobody in their right mind would have taken the risk of bringing a gun aboard, let alone firing it."

"It gets worse," said Smalley. "You sure you're ready for this?"

Never. "Of course."

"You've built up a thousand preconceived notions of what you'll see in that room."

"My parents are in there." It was a statement, but every fiber of my being wanted it to be a question.

Smalley said, "I'm sorry."

Closure was a funny thing. Sure, there was no such thing as closure, but still…

I'd refused to help so many people over the years. They wanted to know. To know. That's all they wanted. I had refused because I knew they weren't going to like what they found. Their loved ones were dead. Gone to the fishes. Everything pointed to it.

"You're the guy who can find anything or anyone," said Smalley, reading my face as if my thoughts were broadcast all over it. "A real pain in the ass around the station."

"I only take the jobs that I think can succeed."

Smalley said, "That's a lie."

"People go missing all the time in Nicodemia."

Smalley narrowed his eyes. "You got something you want to say?"

I seethed. "Just that my job wouldn't exist if you did yours."

The detective stared at me. "You don't like what you're hearing, so you're going to try to pick a fight. Is this really your playbook?"

"I watched a man die in prison."

"Wen Cheng."

"They say its restorative justice," I said. "What you do there is nothing short of torture. That long cycle toward redemption is a slow spiral into hell."

"The budget—"

"To hell with your budgets!" I pushed from the wall and got right up into his space. "You're collecting people who don't need to be collected and putting them through a gauntlet until they agree to behave. That's not restorative justice. It's dangerous and manipulative, and it doesn't work."

"Then what works?" Smalley shoved me back, propelling both of us against opposite walls. "What, you think you can rework our whole justice system? The police don't manage the jail, you know. We just help provide security, because there isn't enough resource for anyone else to do it."

"And your people do the judging."

Smalley growled in frustration. "Look, Demarco, the system's not perfect. Your ideals are in the right place, but they take a back seat to reality. You're never going to get the perfect system in a place like Nicodemia. There are too many constraints. Too many people trying to get what they need to get through the day."

"The constraints of Nicodemia make it that much more important that we strive for a perfect system."

"What are you saying?"

"Cheng was afraid. He feared for his life in a world where there was nowhere else to run. One caring interview, one understanding judge. His life could have been saved. Cheng might have been a boon to his community, but all the blue did was throw him in a cell and walk him down the long spiral."

"He was a criminal."

"He was a *person*."

"It's not that easy." Smalley propelled himself down the hall.

I followed. More bullet holes streaked the fibersteel walls, shattering the crisp clean lines of the sleekly designed ship. I took the time to inspect each of them. They all appeared to be the same size, and they all wrought about the same amount of damage. A lot of damage. These bullets were larger than the Walther PPK or the Smith & Wesson Compact. The angle they'd hit the walls indicated a similar point of origin in the next room, but when Smalley pushed himself into that larger open space, I hesitated.

From the diagrams I'd studied so long ago, I knew this would be the lounge. It was the combination bar and sitting area where most passengers would have passed their time during the short journey down to the lower beads.

When I flew that fated journey, my sister and I had not been allowed in the lounge. There were no specific rules against children, but my parents had wanted some time to themselves, so they'd sent us to wander the public areas of the ship. That was why we had been near the lock when the docking sequence started. That was why we survived.

"Are they still in there?" I asked. Smalley floated between me and the closed bulkhead.

"It's a mess," he said.

I tried again, "Are my parents among the victims?"

"We haven't catalogued all the bodies." Smalley crossed his arms. "But probably."

"Then let me see them."

The grim detective said, "I need you to go in there with a clear mind."

My fists clenched at my sides. "You don't think I can be objective?"

"Not in this," he said. Still, he didn't move. "It's not what we thought we'd find, Demarco."

"The bullet holes tipped me off on that."

"That's not the worst of it, and we're still trying to untangle the story on this one. If I let you in here, I need to know you aren't going to contaminate my crime scene. From here on out, we're doing this one by the book or we're not doing it at all."

"Meaning you want me to be more than just an independent contractor."

"Paid consultant," Smalley said. "Officially deputized."

I didn't like the idea of working directly for the blue. Anders was fine. I knew him, and I believed that he wanted what was best. Smalley—I still didn't have a good handle on Smalley. The crusty old copper wasn't obviously corrupt, but he'd been steeped in the corrupt society long enough that there had to be something dark in his past. If he hired me, he'd own anything I found. Maybe it wouldn't matter to anyone else, but it would matter to me.

Then again, if I didn't agree to his terms, he wasn't going to let me through that door.

"I'll sign on," I said.

Smalley showed me the contracts on a small tablet, not even grumbling with impatience when I took the time to read them. It was standard stuff. A promise of secrecy. A loyalty pledge. An agreement not to break the law in the name of the blue. In the end, I signed it all. What choice did I have?

When it was finished, Smalley stowed the tablet and opened the door to reveal the scene of the murder.

Chapter 45

SOFIA SOOK FLOATED in her pale blue gown. Gable Storm was stuck to a chair with freeze-dried blood. His chest was open to the cool dry air, and the viscera that emerged was crusted with the crystallized fluids of a life long lost. A woman we knew as Countess Havenna was still curled near the floating inner bar. She hadn't been touched by the blood that spattered the rest of the room, but she'd died just the same.

There were others. Dozens. Their faces had haunted me all these many years since the wreck, and here they were, perfectly preserved in the haunting destruction of sudden decompression. Their ruined faces still bore the features that were burned into my mind, but now they were distorted with disfigured, puffy faces and skin that looked like it might shatter if touched.

A pair of technicians worked in the far end of the room. They wore coverall suits like my own, but in university colors. These were two of the scientists Smalley had brought with—

one man, one woman. They bore such a strong resemblance, I wondered if they might be brother and sister. As I watched, they packed a floating bullet into a small sample container.

"Soon as we saw this mess, I deputized them," said Smalley behind me. "Demarco, meet Tabby and Nico Polaris."

The duo looked up from their work long enough to nod acknowledgment.

"They'd rather be working on their research projects, but I needed help processing this scene."

There were bullet holes everywhere. In the walls, the furniture, and in people. Many of these people hadn't died from decompression. They'd been killed before my mistake could ever do them in. On a long shot, I hoped for the best. "You've already picked up the gun?"

"Haven't found it yet."

Hence the urgency. If there was no gun, then whoever took the weapon away might have been the killer. With this in mind, I took in the scene again. Based on the angles of the bullet holes, I could estimate the location of the shooter. It was near where the twins worked.

"How long have you been here?" I asked.

"Only long enough to restore the environment and do an initial assessment of the scene."

"Then the gun might be somewhere else in the ship?"

"It's a big ship."

Nico shot a look at Smalley, then returned to his work. The twins didn't like being pressed into service for the blue. We had that in common, at least.

Smalley's comm chirped. He touched two fingers to his ear to listen. "Keep me updated," he finally said.

"Problem?"

"Nothing we can't handle."

"You have a guy in the computers?"

Smalley grunted his assent.

I pointed to an almost-invisible nodule on the wall near the door. "Have him find the video feed from that camera."

"That's a camera?" Smalley almost sounded impressed.

"It's an addition to the original ship's design, so it won't be in the regular records. Someone thought it would be a good idea to spy on the conversations of the rich and powerful." There was power in knowledge. Willie Fleck knew it.

Smalley fixed me with a serious look. "There's something else you need to see."

He pushed off and floated across the room. I followed, a little inelegantly, but effectively enough. I was accustomed to heavy gravity and light gravity, but zero gravity twisted me around and kicked my ass.

Then, he was there.

He wore the same suit as he had the last time I saw him. It was a black four-button number that did everything it could to shape his large form. The cuff links shone in the frigid air, the gemstones encrusting each like mini tributes to the man's impressive wealth. His red silk tie drifted up around the ruined flesh of his puffy face. He was purple and limned with the ice crystals that had burst from his freezing face, but I still recognized my father.

Was this the same man I knew? He was frozen solid. Crystalized in the moment of his death and wrapped in the stasis of hard vacuum for all time, but there was something changed when I saw him there. A deep, sour anger burned deep in my chest. All I could see were those studded cuff links. The cut of his too-expensive suit. He wore his wealth like a peacock wears feathers, strutting around, showing it off.

The extra silk lining of his suit. The shine of his perfect shoes. Next to him floated the fedora I hadn't even remembered, but now that I saw it, I knew I could never picture him without it. It was a signature of his. I plucked it from the air and held it to my chest.

"Stay objective, Demarco."

"Objectivity is overrated."

I couldn't stop staring at my father's hands. Those soft, perfectly manicured hands. Those were the hands that had ruined the lives of thousands of people in the Heavies just to enrich a few in the Hallows. Those hands may not have stolen the art, but they had a part in the movement of illicit goods to collectors in the highest reaches of society. How many people had died because of my father's greed?

My breath fogged the frozen air. Smalley's people had returned air to this section of the ship, but they had wisely left the temperature cold. The dry air sucked the moisture and heat from my skin, but bubbling rage kept me warm from within.

Smalley watched me work. It was unclear if he was watching to keep me in line or to study my excellent technique. I had no technique.

My father's frozen flesh was rough where I touched it. Every cell in his body was ruined by the explosive decompression. The coarse, frozen skin sucked the heat from my hand as I held him. I felt a prayer for peace welling deep in my chest. Even though the man had failed me, didn't he deserve rest at the end of his life?

But I didn't say the words. I couldn't ask for his forgiveness when I knew I couldn't forgive him.

From where my father floated, I looked back at the rest of the room. When the decompression had hit, the sudden whoosh of air had evacuated the room, stirring everything up, including furniture, drinks, papers, and people. My father was no longer where he had been when he died, but I was getting a pretty good idea of where things were when it went down.

I held his unmoving hand and closed my eyes. The memory came back to me of my time with Blaize. That bastard had done his best to charm, even if he wasn't very good at it. My father had been so much better. I remembered the ache of my muscles after my time at the shooting range. The ache, and the numb sensation on my hand. And the smell. Like metal and sulfur.

"Check his right hand for gunshot residue," I said to the twins. The angle wasn't good, but I could see the pattern of rough skin on my father's palm. "This man was the shooter."

Nico stared at me.

"Do it," said Smalley.

The scientist floated over to my father's body and started working with his collection equipment.

Seeing my father hurt more than I had expected. The red-hot iron still burned in the space behind my chest. I'd carried so much anger for so long. I fought the urge to crush his hand. Instead, I placed his hat on my head. It surely looked ridiculous with my coveralls, but I wasn't going to let that hat go. I caught a look from Smalley, but one glare sent him back to his own work.

The detective was on the horn again with the other engineer. He whispered urgently into his comm and listened in turn. Something was happening, but I didn't care. I'd found my father and it had only spawned more questions.

Like, for instance, where was my mother?

She wasn't in the room. A quick inspection of every floating, frozen corpse eliminated that possibility. Even with the damage to the bodies, I would have recognized my own mother. Something like relief pulsed in my gut when I didn't see her, but I knew it wouldn't last. She had to be in one of the adjacent rooms.

"Are there more bodies nearby?" I asked.

Smalley held up a finger to silence me and hissed into his comm. He was floating upside down to my perspective, so the gesture was a little silly. I got the message anyway and waited for the exchange to finish.

Finally, Smalley said, "Brace yourself."

There was no time. The ship rattled around us. Every floating object in the room—including myself—slammed at an odd angle to what would have been designated the floor. The acceleration wasn't hard, but it was enough to hurt. The contents of the room all slid toward the corner where the siblings had been working.

I braced myself on a handhold. Smalley had had a much worse time of it, being upside down when he landed, but I caught him on the way past and kept him from piling into the corner with all the frozen bodies.

Acceleration settled at half a g. Maybe less. The force was inconveniently low, but better than nothing.

"Fortner's ship is pushing the *Benevolent*," Smalley said, fuming.

"Where to?" I asked.

"No idea." Smalley fished a tablet from his pocket and handed it to me. "Jurgens picked up that video you wanted."

My hands shook as I took the device. It was paused on a segment of a video feed, focused on the room we were in. There was no gravity in that room, so it must have been during the short voyage between beads. I tapped the screen and started the video, but stopped it again immediately.

My father was center frame. It could have been any

moment from any day of his life, but something about it felt wrong to me. I zoomed in on his features, and his expression came through crisp on the captured image. Around him were the other guests, oblivious to the stress on display. Not far from him floated Lorrel Fortner, locked in conversation with a woman in a green dress.

The man who had raised me was more upset than I had ever seen him. Furious. Maybe the heavy gravity made his face red or the low atmospheric pressure made his jowls puffy, but the man was mad. His hands were stuffed in his pockets, and he was pacing. Scrubbing forward on the video showed his eyes darting to each of his fellow passengers. His lips moved.

"Audio?" I asked.

"Gone," said Smalley. "Either it was erased or it never existed."

I scrubbed back. My heart pounded in my chest. This was my father, moments before his death. He paced. He fumed. He gestured. Who was he gesturing to? I took in the whole room. There.

My mother was in the doorway. He was gesturing for her to leave. His head turned, so I couldn't see his lips move, but something he said finally convinced her to turn and run. She disappeared through the far door toward the outer reaches of the ship.

The video cut out.

"What happened?" I asked.

"Jurgens, what's going on?" Smalley listened for a response. "What the hell." He tapped his comm and tried again, but there was no response.

I looked to the door where my mother had exited the room. That's where I needed to go next. If I was going to put everything to rest, then I needed to find my mother's body.

Kaegan Fortner stepped into the room through the same door I'd entered. He had a smug expression. Harley Huff and two goons entered at his heels.

"Inspector," Fortner said to Smalley. He drew a slim blue pistol and pointed it at my chest. "I would like to report a crime."

Chapter 46

FORTNER'S WEAPON looked like a toy, but it was the deadliest medium-range pistol available on Nicodemia's black market. It didn't sling lead, but it was the closest a man was likely to get.

He holstered the weapon. "I should thank you," he said to me.

I couldn't find the words to respond.

"I watched you open my vault. The whole time you worked, I knew exactly what you were doing."

My mouth went dry. He could have sounded the alarm. They might not have gotten to me in time, but they would have found me cornered.

"They were a safeguard, you see," said Fortner, pacing. "A counterbalance to the absolute power that Trinity holds over the population."

"Hell of a safeguard," I said, "if it's the one thing that could kill everyone in the city."

Fortner paced with long, loping steps. "Owning those weapons was always so much pressure," he said. "We were meant to be constantly vigilant. Ready to strike at the first sign of corruption in the machine."

"There's always something," I said. "The richer you get, the bigger the something."

"When I saw you destroying those weapons, all I could think of was how it meant I was no longer responsible for them."

"What's with the acceleration?" I asked, bouncing gently on the balls of my feet.

Fortner gestured with one finger, and one of his goons split off to take position against a far wall. "Makes walking a little more pleasant." He scanned the bodies with his beady eyes.

"Your son's not here," I said.

"Word is, I have you to blame for Blaize's death."

"Different son."

"Even so."

"Violent lives have violent ends," I said.

He drew his gun and leveled it at my chest. "Say that again."

"What was Lorrel doing here?"

"Business."

I took in the situation, acutely aware of the futility of my lone stunstick against a couple of well-armed thugs. Fortner controlled the room. I knew it, the twins knew it, and by the twitch of his bushy mustache, even Smalley was starting to figure it out. Locking gazes with Fortner, I said, "Sentimentality's a powerful force, isn't it? Even if we don't believe in a higher power, there's just something about the past that keeps digging away at the present. You lost Lorrel years ago, and despite your status, despite all that power you've pried from the social ladder, and despite all that wealth you've clawed from the people of Nicodemia, you still can't get over the fact that your son never returned.

"A man needs to care for his dead," I continued, pacing in long, floating steps around a room cluttered with corpses. "We can hold a ceremonial service, and we can pray our best prayers, but without a body, there's some part of our loved ones that never really dies. Something in us keeps them alive in our hearts, and we *long* for them. We *demand* that they return." I placed a hand on my father's stiff shoulder, and a memory returned to me of a time when he'd lifted me on those shoulders and carried me through the busy streets of the Hallows. "We can work something out here, Fortner. You and I are equals right now. Outside of Trinity's Karma and far from the social structures that make Nicodemia work, you and I are the same. We're men looking to bury our dead. All we need is for our loved ones to have their last good deed. It doesn't matter what came before."

Fortner lowered his weapon.

"Plus," I said, "there's one more gun that needs to be destroyed, and it's got to be around here somewhere."

To my surprise, it was Huff who responded. "That's the first smart thing you've said all week, Demarco." He drew the Colt Python and leveled it at Fortner's head. It was a ridiculous weapon, giant in the man's small hands. "Drop the peashooter, boss."

Fortner placed the gun in Huff's hand, a stunned look on his face.

Smalley's wasn't halfway to his weapon before one of the goons took it from him. After a brief scuffle, the gun flew across the room.

I winked at the other goon, knowing that if I went for my stunstick I'd be a raw, well-tenderized steak.

"What is the meaning of this, Huff?" asked Fortner.

"Lorrel made it back to Nicodemia." I said.

A grin split Huff's pasty face.

"You killed him and took the gun." I nodded to the weapon. "This is the missing Colt Python."

Fortner's face twisted in rage, but Huff kicked back and drifted in a long arc across the room. "How about we call it divine providence finally smiling on me. Isn't that what it was? God made everything just kinda work out for the Fortners?"

"You were behind it all," I said as the pieces clicked into place.

Huff's lips twisted into a smile. "You weren't even good at picking antiques, Kaegan." He braced himself against the wall. "Value is subjective, isn't it? As soon as you picked that garbage out of the junk pile, I got to work generating buzz."

"That's not true," Fortner said.

"Oh, the stuff made from pure metals or rare gems were worthwhile, all right. Anything made of wood is going to have value to someone."

"You ungrateful little shit." Spittle fluttered from Fortner's lips. "My father took you in when you were nothing. He taught you how to run the business because otherwise you had *nothing*."

"Nothing?" scoffed Huff. "You were the one with nothing. Do you know what he was going to leave you in the inheritance? A floundering business with debt from a dozen sharks." He gestured with the gun. "I built this business from less than nothing, and you're going to divide it among your gutless spawn as if *you* somehow hunted and killed it yourself."

Smalley twisted in the goon's grasp, but he couldn't get leverage in the low gravity. Cops from the Heavies rarely made it out of their home bead, and the old cop was no exception. The goon, on the other hand, knew exactly what he was doing. He got a knee in Smalley's back and wrenched his arms into a lock.

"You had Anya's family kidnapped," I said to Huff. "Was killing her wife your idea?"

"What?" Fortner's fists clenched.

I kept my hands up. "See, it never made sense to me that Fortner here would try that kind of leverage on his own kids. He knew how to get them to behave, but you, Huff, you never knew what you were doing."

"I know *exactly* what I'm doing," said Huff.

"Anya might have turned against her father if all you did was offer to help her find a decent job. In fact, I doubt any of Fortner's kids felt particularly loyal to their old man."

"That's not true," said Fortner, but something in his voice hinted that he didn't believe it.

"Blaize would have turned if you told him he'd have freer rein to do what he wanted. Mia doesn't want to have anything to do with the family. Tell her she can leave, and you'd never see her again. Instead, you made her kill Rawles and forced Anya to help cover it up."

"Lies!" shouted Fortner. He squared up against me now, ignoring Huff's gun. Even now the old man wasn't taking his assistant seriously. "They were *all* loyal."

"The only one loyal to you was Lorrel," I said, "and the rest of them saw what that got him. You turned on Lorrel, didn't you? In the end, it was *you* who sent him to the *Benevolent*."

Fortner's jaw worked, but no words came.

"The sins of Harley Huff go much deeper than recent events, don't they?" I flexed my calves and pushed myself taller. In the low gravity it took little effort, and the balls of my feet barely scraped the floor. "In fact, I think we might be standing in Huff's first big crime scene."

Huff swung the gun around to point at me now. I made sure my hands were up with my palms out. No threat here. Just the truth.

Behind me, Smalley said, "Say it, Demarco."

"You speak one more word and you're dead," said Huff.

"Dead?" When I didn't die, I continued, "It would be a big mistake for you to shoot anyone, Huff. The blue is scanning this crime scene as we speak. Anything anyone does here is going to be a matter of record as soon as Smalley uploads it."

"Lot of assumptions in those words," said Huff.

"Sure." I lowered my hands. "Whose idea was it to put Lorrel on the *Benevolent*?" When neither Huff nor Fortner answered, I said, "He was just the backup plan, wasn't he?"

Fortner's voice cracked. "Harley, I treated you like a brother."

"You treated me like a servant!" The gun pointed at Fortner again.

"That's enough, Huff," I said. "Whatever drama you have with your boss doesn't matter now. We both know you're not going to kill him."

"I'm not, huh?" Huff swung the gun around at me.

"You don't inherit a dime if he dies. In fact, I have a pretty good feeling that Fortner's death would be the end of you. Those debts still exist, don't they? The fortune will go to Anya and Mia, but the responsibility is going to stay with you."

"Debts?" asked Fortner.

"You're heavily leveraged," admitted Huff. "It takes leverage to grow. Even an asshole like you can understand that, right?"

Fortner shook his head, as if to clear it of cobwebs. "I thought we were successful."

"We are!" shouted Huff. He gestured with the gun like a madman. "Because of *me*! Because of the financial tricks and the back-office deals. *I* made this business what it is. All you've done is ride the wave. Then, I come to you and ask for a share of what I made, and what did you tell me?"

The words were met with silence.

"What did you tell me?" he repeated.

"I told you I would give you a bonus."

"A bonus!" shouted Huff.

"A generous one," said Fortner with a hint of resignation.

Huff unleashed something between a painful wail and a furious yowl. He leveled the gun at Fortner. The weapon shook with Huff's righteous fury.

But he still didn't fire.

"The *Lost Saint*," I said.

Huff's fury melted. A thin smile crossed his face. "It won't be so bad, boss. When you get to Earth, you'll still have plenty of junk to sell as you try to rebuild your empire."

Fortner's expression went from furrowed confusion to open understanding to rage. "You wouldn't."

"I would," said Huff. "But I'll give you a choice. Die now if you want. Raise one more hand against me and I'll shoot you down now. It'll be worth it. I'll take your place on the *Lost Saint* and *I'll* know what to do to turn that junk into a fortune once I get to Earth." He pushed off the wall and took several long steps toward Fortner until he was within arm's reach. "Or you can live, and I'll maintain control of your empire until such a time as you can afford a ride back to reclaim it."

Fortner stared at his assistant with wide eyes, but the fight had gone out of him. Life on Earth was preferable to death on the *Benevolent*, but just barely.

Huff's eyes were dark and calculating. As he considered his options, he came to the same conclusion I'd figured out a long time ago. There was no way he could let Smalley and me walk out of that ship. The single hibernation chamber on the *Lost Saint* would send Fortner to Earth, but there wasn't room for the two of us.

Huff gestured with his gun and the goon holding Smalley backed away. To Smalley, Huff said, "I've got nothing against the blue, and you haven't done anything but your job."

I bent my knees slightly so that I could move when needed. Things were going to get real dicey real fast.

"Kill him," Huff said, but he wasn't speaking to his goons. He spoke to Smalley. "Shoot Demarco in the head."

I didn't much like the sound of that.

One of the goons scooped up Smalley's gun and tossed it to him.

"Do that," said Huff, "and I'll let you and your crew go back home." He glanced for the first time at the twins, who were still hunkered back into the corner. "I know they'll be quiet." The way he said it made me think he'd already dealt with the scientists.

"This whole thing smelled like a setup from the start," I said.

"It was," agreed Huff. To Smalley, he said, "What'll it be, inspector?"

Smalley stared at me. His thick mustache twitched, and the line of his jaw hardened. It was life or death for him. Kill or be killed.

His weapon shook.

The goons retreated into the corners of the room. Smalley's eyes narrowed. From behind their cover, the twins spoke in harsh whispers. Smalley had me dead to rights, and there wasn't a damn thing I could do about it.

My knees were bent and my feet were flat on the ground, but it wouldn't be enough. There just wasn't enough traction to accelerate quickly enough. There was no point in trying.

But I tried anyway. It was suicide but I tried. My feet scraped. My body moved. It was like a slow-motion crash. Like the *Benevolent* ramming into a port not ready for her. The realization came to me in a flash a moment before I was gunned down. All the angles finally clicked into place, and the wreck of the *Benevolent* was as clear to me as a bright-lit Hallows afternoon. It came to me as I always knew it would: seconds before my death.

The funny thing about how I was gunned down, though, had nothing to do with who was doing the gunning, but everything to do with how the trigger was never pulled. As I approached, Smalley—veteran of the blue, longtime hero in the eyes of the law—looked me dead in the eyes. He didn't pull the trigger.

I chopped hard at his gun hand. The weapon didn't fly free, but the aim went wide. Grabbing his elbow and twisting, I flung him around behind me and kicked, launching myself beyond and toward the exit where my own mother had gone in the video. He let me win, and I couldn't help but think he was making it look good. The same kick sent Smalley hurtling toward the opposite door, but I couldn't think about his fate. His hesitation bought me a chance to get away.

I ran.

Chapter 47

AS I ENTERED the next room, lights flared to life. Would I ever get used to that? I knew the layout of the ship, but I didn't know where I was going. All I knew was that I needed to get away. As I moved, the gravity ebbed until it was nearly nonexistent.

The tall goon clawed his way into the room as I launched myself for the exit at the far side of the room. He fired once. A single snapping shot destroyed itself in an explosion against the bulkhead. Then I was gone.

I'd done my fair share of running in the last decade, and I knew exactly how it went. Beat feet for a few minutes to buy time to think. Find a shadow deep enough to die in and run to it. Worked every time.

Except now there were no shadows.

The room was a parlor of sorts. Another art-decked waiting room with viewing angles and video screens. There were shards of broken glass glistening on the frozen floor— the remains of the drinks once held by wealthy patrons of the paintings on the walls.

A Renoir sat as the centerpiece of the viewing area. Haystacks. One of many. A beautiful work of craftsmanship on a painting that, as far as I could tell, essentially meant nothing. It was the perfect representation of artistic beauty for the passengers of the *Benevolent*. It showed wealth and power and extravagance without really challenging anyone. Some people don't like to be challenged.

Others thrive on it.

I threw myself forward. The extra-light gravity was infuriating. I couldn't get traction and ran a serious risk of stranding myself in a slow arc as my pursuer aimed at me. When I reached the sealed stand with the haystacks, I grabbed it with both hands and pulled. My bulky form slipped past as the pedestal toppled.

Gunshots broke against the reinforced glass of the display case. My angle was bad, and I slammed against the wall several steps from the door. I spun.

The tall man drifted at an odd angle. The skewed gravity slowly pulled him back around. When he had leaped into the room, he must have misjudged his angle—or the gunshots were enough to throw him off. Either way, I had seconds to decide where to go. Out? Away?

I launched myself directly at the goon as he spun. He tried to fire at me behind him, but he failed to get the angle.

The stunstick crackled to life. I swung. The snap of power wasn't enough to drop him, but I hit his wrist hard enough that a sickening crack snapped louder than the electrical pulse. He screamed and the gun flew. He landed and scrambled back before I could lock him down.

The man cradled his broken wrist.

"Take a walk, buddy," I said. "This has nothing to do with you."

"A job's a job," he said.

A knife flashed in his good hand, but I contorted away before he could plant it in my gut. The move sent me off-balance, tumbling in a slow spiral downward. He came at me hard, slashing, but his foot slipped out from under him. I kicked, catching him under the chin as he fell forward. His head snapped back. I landed with a thump.

I scrambled back, but I didn't need to. The man's throat made a sickly gurgle. He gasped. Turned purple.

"Drop the knife," I said, rising into a crouch. "Buddy, drop the knife and I can help."

He stared at me with horror in his bulging eyes.

There was a ruckus elsewhere in the ship. The tinny echo of gunshots sounded through the door I'd come through. Each shot sent a spike through my chest. Was that Smalley getting his end? Was it Huff getting what was coming to him? A vein in my forehead pulsed. The goon made a sickening, choking sound, clutching at his throat with his one good hand. The knife clattered to the floor. I kicked it aside as I approached.

A thunderous boom—it could only be the Colt Python—rattled the walls. Huff was close. One shot. Two.

Looking into the man's eyes, I slowly peeled back his grip on his neck. His throat was crushed. I swore under my breath. All my medical training flashed before me. Trauma surgery was never my forte.

"I'm sorry," I said. "This doesn't look good."

The struggle in the ship rose to a fever pitch. The rattle of gunfire made my hands shake. Any second, the other goon was going to come in or Huff would show up with his—

Another boom. Closer this time.

"All right," I said. "I think we need a tracheotomy." Every room in the *Benevolent* had the requisite equipment for emergency surgery, but it was old. It had been sitting in stasis for a dozen years.

The man wasn't going to live without a tube in his throat. Once he was home, maybe they could fix what I'd done, but to get that far, he was going to need a tube for breathing. I swore under my breath. Red turned to purple. Purple deepened.

"I need a tracheotomy kit," I said to the machine. It wasn't Trinity-based, but the interface could understand basic orders well enough. "Come on."

Error.

I swore again. Mashing buttons on the device, I ordered up a sedative and it started printing.

Error.

It had stopped halfway through the print. Unable to fabricate the medicine. Now I was a fountain of profanity that any dockworker in the bottom of the Heavies would be proud of. This wasn't going to work. All my training, all my work, meant nothing if I didn't have access to the equipment I needed to help the man.

Help him. A minute ago, I'd been trying my best not to let him kill me. What messed up part of my brain wouldn't let me leave this guy behind when there were dogs at the gates and danger in the skies? Any second, Huff was going to come in with his giant gun blazing and fury melting his pasty face. Even with all that, I couldn't just leave the guy.

More gunshots. Two of them, farther away this time. The ship rattled. Alarms blared. Lights flickered.

The First Aid machine threw a dozen more errors. This was why I didn't mind living without the machines. They were always failing at the worst possible moment. In a minute, the sad sack of a goon would be dead, and the trauma package would still be throwing errors. Grabbing the knife from the floor, I pried open the front of the emergency medical unit.

A syringe lay in the delivery plate where it was supposed to be filled with the appropriate amount of sedative. There was no sedative—only a sticky, cold mess extruding from a broken nozzle. It didn't look like something I wanted to inject into anyone, whether or not they had just been trying to kill me. Next to the syringe sat a pair of half-formed sterile gloves.

"Damn it, I should run," I muttered to myself. "I *know* I should run, but here I am not running." There was a man in need, and I was the only one there who could possibly save him.

I marveled at the chances of my boot catching his throat in that way. It was a long shot, and never something I would have tried. I had been aiming at his chest to keep him off balance. It was only his odd bounce from the floor that had caused my kick to land on his throat. Now he was going to die, and I was going to add one more reason to feel guilty onto a growing pile.

God, I dreaded my next confession.

I grabbed the empty syringe and gloves from the medical station and approached the goon again. His eyes, bulging already, doubled when he saw the knife. The whites shone like the outer rings of the targets I'd shot at with Blaize.

"Now, listen." My voice almost choked me. "This isn't going to be pretty."

He lets out the most tortured gurgle I've ever heard. The air smelled of a sharp sour acid. The lights flickered again.

Using the knife, I cut the ends off the empty syringe. The process could have been faster, but I was doing my best to keep everything sterile. During my medic training, it was drilled into me a thousand times that it didn't make sense to save someone just to have them die from infection later on. Meds were good at fighting those infections, but a little incubator like Nicodemia brews some pretty nasty bugs. Not all of them can be treated.

Not that I could do anything about cleaning the knife. At least it hadn't recently cut anyone. Once the ends were cut off the syringe, I had a narrow tube long enough to use as a breathing apparatus. My chest clenched. Nothing mattered but the dying man in front of me. Not the flickering light or the ominous tinge to the atmosphere or the shouts in the nearby halls of the ship.

I drew in a shaky breath and exhaled smooth calm. The man met my gaze. He didn't want to die. As brave as he'd seemed, he wasn't willing to die for Huff. He wasn't ready to die for anything. A spark of cold determination flared in his eyes, and the gurgling stopped. He was still. Alive, but still. He was ready.

The surgery was fast. A cut with the knife deeper than any cut ought to go. An insertion with the tube into the bubbling innards of the man's neck. The placement was tricky, and the chance of infection was high, but it took only a few seconds.

With a sputtering wheeze, the man drew in his first cold air. Too fast. He coughed and I had to hold the tube still as he descended into a gagging fit.

Then, he was calm. I'd saved him.

"Good?" I asked the man.

He nodded, winced, and then blinked his assent.

I glanced over my shoulder at the door. The fighting had gone silent, which made me nervous. "I need to leave you here," I said to the man. "Lie still, and we'll get you some help as soon as we can."

This time, he stared at me, expressionless. He didn't want me to leave, but he couldn't afford to try to stop me.

But I couldn't stay. "Get back to the *Lost Saint* and use the hibernation chamber. That should get you to Earth, where you can find medical help." I took a step back. "Otherwise, your best bet is to make your way to Smalley's ship. Turn yourself in."

He stared at me and drew a long rasp. His long torso convulsed with the effort of each breath.

"It's a chance at redemption." I looked at the bloody knife in my hand. The stunstick was missing, having spun off into the clutter somewhere. "You don't mind if I borrow this, do you?"

I left him. The man was still in a dangerous state, but danger was different from certain death. Some broken part of my twisted ethos allowed me to leave a man at risk. It was only when death was a sure thing that I found I needed to help.

Which was good, because I had work to do.

Chapter 48

ENGINEERING CONTROL WAS A MASSACRE. *My* massacre. There were no bullet-riddled corpses or wounded travelers. The working men and women of the *Benevolent* had died in the catastrophic depressurization. Most bore the bulged bloodshot eyes and ruined flesh of the initial shock. Three of the dozen wore coveralls with automatic helmets. They had lived longer, desperately trying to regain control of their failing ship.

They had died just the same. They were huddled in the corner, where their bodies had landed after the return of low gravity. The other frozen corpses were scattered around the room, frosted from the return of moisture after years of empty cold.

The ship still ran on low power. Its engine hadn't returned to full function, but the electrical system continued to light the spaces as I entered. Control panels flared to life with readouts depicting a thousand ways the ship was failing.

Still, there was no sign of my mother's body.

Finding her felt more urgent than anything else

happening around me. More urgent than Huff and his plans. More urgent than Fortner and Smalley's fates.

Something scraped metal on metal from across the room. Without making a sound, I peered in that direction. The ship's lights followed me, but they also followed everyone else, and there was a faint glow across the sprawling control center that indicated someone else was there.

"Jurgens?" I guessed.

The man stood from his hiding place. He was a man made of sticks and bubble gum, and he held a red fire extinguisher above his head like a club. The collar of his coveralls bore the white markings of a priest.

I showed him my palms. "I work for Smalley," I said. "In an official capacity."

Jurgens nodded to the screens, which now sat blank. "I watched you fight that man."

"He was disagreeable."

"You killed him in cold blood."

I blinked, not understanding immediately what he was talking about. "The tall guy?" It clicked. He would have seen me leaning over the struggling man with a bloody knife. "I saved his life."

Jurgens shook his head. The whites of his eyes shone in the harsh glare of the emergency lights. "I think you better go."

I said, "I'm looking for Grace Demarco. She was a passenger."

He stared at me.

"Check the computers. There's got to be a trace of where she died."

The extinguisher slowly sank until Jurgens held it in front of his chest. "You do it."

"I'm not much of a computer guy." But I capitulated.

When I sat in front of the screen, it flared to life. It showed a flickering display of the various ship support systems. It was a lot of yellow and orange, with the brightest red reserved only for the ship's engine core. "The engine's not on?"

Jurgens took a brave step closer to me. "The *Lost Saint* is providing the thrust."

"Why?"

He shrugged his bony shoulders, which made his white coveralls billow like a tarp. "Firing up the fusion core on a ship like this takes a lot of energy."

"All right." It must have been frustrating for the engineer to watch me struggle with the ship's interface, but I navigated it and found the ship's roster. "Now what?"

"Touch her name and find her tracking key."

My hands shook, but I selected her name and waited as the sluggish display brought up her data.

The engineer hissed and raised his extinguisher. When I looked behind me, I saw what provoked his response. The lights were coming to life in the adjacent room. As soon as I saw that, I heard Huff's high, nasal voice.

I pushed away from the desk and motioned Jurgens back into hiding. The guy didn't need any convincing. The space wasn't large enough for the both of us. Instead, I ducked low into another corner of the room and pulled a couple of corpses up around me. It was a grisly move, and I had to grasp my own hands to keep myself from shuddering enough to reveal my location.

"Get a move on," said Huff as he shoved Smalley into the room.

The detective's police suit was darkened by a growing stain on his left shoulder, and he favored one leg, even in the low gravity. "What do you want from me, Huff?"

"You killed one of my best, and Demarco made a bloody

mess of my other guy. That means you get to volunteer for the next phase of this operation."

"Operation. What operation?" Smalley cast a glance in my direction and for a fraction of a second, our eyes met. He knew I was there, but Huff hadn't seen me.

"Maybe if you hadn't let Fortner get away, this next part would be easier."

"There's nowhere for him to run," said Smalley. The two men passed the screen where I had been working, and its glow illuminated his face from below. The shadows that played across his face made him look devilish. "Unless he's planning on hunkering down in the *Lost Saint*, which is what you wanted anyway."

Huff glanced at the screen and his eyes widened in surprise. He scanned the room, no doubt looking for me. When his gaze brushed over the pile of corpses where I hid, I did my best not to jump up and challenge him. He still held the big black gun, and I wasn't looking forward to being on the receiving end of it.

Seemingly satisfied, he gestured for Smalley to keep walking. Before leaving, he punched a few controls on the screen. "His only smart move is the *Lost Saint*," said Huff, "but you'd be surprised what a lifetime of greed can do to a man's intelligence."

With that, the two disappeared through the far door. As soon as they were gone, I whispered, "Jurgens, where does that go?"

He emerged from his safe place behind the control console and pointed to the label next to the door. In plain silver block print, the label said: ENGINE ROOM.

"What does Huff want in there?"

"Ships like these are tough. Even after what happened to the *Benevolent*, it would probably be safe for an interstellar voyage."

"But there are no cryochambers."

Jurgens stared at me.

I returned to the screen to find that the record I had been looking at—the record with my mother's information—was gone, and in its place sat a diagram of the Engine Room's inner chamber.

"What is he doing?" I asked.

Jurgens peered over my shoulder. "He's going to start it up."

"Can he do that?"

"No," said Jurgens. "He can't."

I drew a long breath and let it out slowly. It fogged in the cold air of the derelict spaceship. If Huff couldn't start the ship, then what was he doing in the core? I took a moment to think about the pieces as I understood them. Huff had worked for the elder Fortner for years, then for Kaegan Fortner. Fortner loved those guns of his, the ones I'd destroyed except for the one Huff carried.

They needed to be destroyed because they were dangerous. *Very* dangerous. If they were fired aboard a ship, they could puncture the recycling fluid. I remembered the acid in the air. It reminded me of Trinity's recyclers when they had tried to recycle me. Huff had already punctured the recyclers.

He could do the same to the core. Could he be planning to spin up the core just to puncture it and destroy the ship?

Absolutely.

The detective thought there was still a chance of getting out of there alive, and all the fight had gone out of him. He'd comply just to get back to Nicodemia for another chance to see his family.

But he wasn't going to make it that far.

"Get back to the ship," I said. "It should be safe now that Huff's in the Engine Room."

Jurgens clutched his extinguisher close. "What about Fortner?"

"Harmless," I said. "Probably."

Jurgens didn't look convinced. "Can I trust the twins?"

The twins. Were they really working with Huff? If they were on the take, then there was no telling what they'd do to keep the secret. Then again, they didn't look like the overtly violent type. I tossed the knife to Jurgens. "This'll work better than the fire extinguisher."

He backed up to the door, hazarded one last glance at the Engine Room door, and then fled away through the ship.

"You could have left me the extinguisher," I said to an empty room.

The screen blinked in front of me. I knew the commands to get the information I wanted. It would tell me all about Grace Demarco, and finally I'd be able to put her memory to rest.

But Smalley was in danger. Huff wasn't going to let him live, and whatever they were doing in the engine room wasn't going to take very long. Cursing, I fixed my father's hat on my head and followed.

Chapter 49

"HUFF!" I hollered as I entered the central chamber. "That's enough!"

The engine room was a perfect sphere of shining metal. It was only a dozen paces across, but line of sight was obscured by the orb of the reaction chamber at its center. A metal walkway led the whole circumference of the room, but hand-holds that dotted the exterior walls indicated that this room was meant to be experienced without the inconvenience of gravity.

On the far end of the small engine room, the walkway branched, giving access to the central chamber. Huff stood at the outer end of the walkway with his gun at his side. Smalley worked on an open panel on the chamber.

"Stay where you are, Demarco," said Huff.

"I've never been good at that."

"You'll learn." He aimed the gun at Smalley.

I strolled forward.

"I said *back*, Demarco." Huff held the gun in two hands, apparently having learned his lesson about the thing's kick.

I stopped. "You know, for the longest time I thought the wreck of the *Benevolent* was an accident. I was afraid to look into it because I thought that everything I found would be more evidence of my own failure." I took another step. "You never had that problem, did you, Huff?" When he didn't answer, I continued, "I've been wondering why Fortner wanted to visit this old wreck, but that wasn't really the right question. The answer is obvious. You convinced him that he needed to find that gun."

This got a response from Huff. "He thought it was to save his son's reputation. Could you imagine if the police discovered that Lorrel Fortner had shot someone?"

"Kaegan Fortner is the greediest man I've ever known, and I've known a few." I kept my hands raised. "He didn't care about his son's reputation. He cared about his own."

Huff pressed his lips together. There was something he wanted to say, but he wasn't going to spill quite yet. To Smalley, he said, "Keep working on that, inspector. You don't want us to be late."

Smalley's brow furrowed with anxiety. His breath came out in billowing plumes.

"Who does he have, Smalley?" I asked. "Wife? Kids?" They should have been protected. I'd made sure of it.

"Niece," Smalley spat. "The bastard found my niece."

"It really simplifies things, don't you think?" said Huff. "My people in the Heavies were finally able to contact me with some good news." He turned to point the gun at me. "You, on the other hand, don't have anyone, do you?" His face twisted into a sneer. "Well, there's your sister, but I doubt you'd prioritize her over anything. You might even be relieved when she dies. She's such a reminder of your failures."

My tongue tasted like acid. "Leave my sister out of this."

"Oh, she won't be touched. If she learns of your death,

she'll have the choice to skip your funeral. Do you think she'd take a day off of work for you, Demarco? It's a sad thing when a funeral is completely unattended." He cocked his head. "Then again, if you die out here, what are the chances that *you'll* even be there to attend your funeral. No last good deed for you, I guess."

"You like to think of yourself as clever, but you never really change strategies, do you? All you do is threaten families to get what you want. Anya's. Smalley's." My eyes bore a hole through him. "My father's."

A satisfied smirk crossed Huff's face. "How much have you figured out?"

"How long was Carrie Fortner under your thumb?"

Now his smirk turned into a full grin. "Under my thumb? She was a full-fledged accomplice, Demarco. Until you fucked everything up, she was going to be my partner in crime once Kaegan fell victim to his own misery."

"Carrie was there to threaten my sister and me. That's why she was there at the airlock. She'd followed us off the ship just to make sure my father did what he was supposed to do. But my father sent my mother away, and I know he fired the gun, but he didn't shoot Lorrel, did he?"

"Defiance runs in your family."

"That defiance was enough that you decided to put the ship in maintenance mode, opening all the airlock doors so that one message to Carrie Fortner would kill everyone aboard. The perfect hostage situation."

The gun shook in Huff's hands, but it couldn't have been heavy. Not in that low gravity. "Your father figured out who my people were in the *Benevolent*. He turned on them. And your mother? Well, let's just leave that as a little bit of knowledge as leverage."

The core hummed to life and Smalley pulled his hands back as if burned. The low vibration buzzed through my bones and rattled the handrails.

Huff wasn't going to tell me what happened to my mother, but I couldn't help but ask. "What happened to her?"

A choking sound deep in his throat might have been a laugh. "That's the look of a man who will do anything to learn the truth."

Waves of heat flowed from the reaction chamber. It curled my eyebrows. Smalley staggered back from the engine, holding his arms up to block the intense heat.

I ignored it all. "You've got one bullet, Huff."

"That's the thing, Demarco," he said. "If we're living our lives right, we don't need bullets, do we?" He lowered his gun. "Come along quietly, and I'll tell you everything you want to know."

I said, "You make a pretty strong argument."

Smalley stared at his burned hands, his brow furrowed in deep concentration. "I forgot what it was for."

Huff stared at him, his lip curled in disgust.

Smalley clenched his fists. "When I was young"—he looked at me—"when I was the same age as Anders, I was just as idealistic. Maybe more so."

"Hard to imagine," I said.

He stared at Huff. "I'd chase down every bent nail. Arrest every crook. It was black and white back then." His throat clicked when he swallowed. "Now everything's so damn gray."

Huff glanced at me. Then at Smalley. The muscles in his neck twitched. "All you need to do is what you're told, Smalley."

"Because you have my niece," Smalley said.

"Because I'll give you plenty of crooks to take down. Together we can make Nicodemia better. Safer. Isn't that what it's about, copper?"

"Safer?" Smalley growled. "You threatened my niece."

"For the greater good—"

"You threatened my *niece*!" The big cop slammed a fist into the side of Huff's head, spinning him backwards over the rail. "*You* are the problem here, Huff. I never should have given you an inch."

The engine kicked in and gravity pulsed upward almost to Earth norm. Huff tumbled, grabbed a railing, and prevented himself from falling down to the new bottom of the sphere.

Huff's feet landed on the walkway, and the gun rose again. It wasn't pointed at Smalley or me, this time, though. He was aiming it straight for the core.

"Things are going to get real interesting real fast if you don't let me walk out of here," Huff said.

Smalley shifted, putting himself between the gun and the core. "Harley Huff, you are interfering with a legitimate police investigation, putting you in violation of the law. You have the right to remain silent—"

"Silent!" cried Huff. "Silent? I'm the only one here who knows *how* to be silent. I've kept secrets for *years*, and I'll take them to the grave if you don't let me walk from here." He took a step around the walkway, moving away from me and starting to circle around the back side to the exit.

Smalley stepped closer to the scorching core, keeping his back to it. On the inner walkway, he was able to block at least part of the line of fire. "This is a legitimate police investi—" He caught a fresh wave of heat in his back, and it staggered him. "Legitimate—"

"I'm leaving," said Huff. "Now. You two can fight over

your legitimate police investigation until the remains of it burn in the sun."

I started moving the other way around the circle. The ship rumbled around us, and gravity increased another notch.

"You need to ask yourself what's important, Demarco," said Huff. He was nearly to the exit. "Save the old cop or learn what happened to your dear mother? Which would you like?"

"Both," I said.

Huff gave a little shake of his head. "You know how I feel about greed."

Huff shot Smalley in the chest. The gunshot rang in my ears. Huff ran for the exit.

I had to choose: chase Huff or help Smalley?

In a handful of strides, I was there at Smalley's side. His wound pulsed blood like the reactor pulsed heat. It scalded the side of my face, and I could feel it through the fiber-reinforced insulation of my coveralls.

"Smalley," I said, tearing back the cloth around the wound.

A weak smile crossed his pale lips. Even his mustache looked like it had lost a third of its liveliness. "My niece."

"We'll get to her." Clearing the blood away with my sleeve showed a clean entry wound. It could be stitched if it didn't hit any organs. How could it have missed his lungs and heart? My anatomy knowledge wasn't good enough to understand the odds, but maybe—

The heat intensified. We needed to move. I got a hand under Smalley. Gravity increased, and my back pinged with the effort of lifting him. He wasn't helping at all.

"No," he rasped. "Demarco."

"We gotta move you, Smalley." My hand on his back slipped. Blood. Lots of it. There was another wound on his back. This wasn't anything like the bullet wounds I was trained to treat. This was a lead bullet—a much larger caliber than the Walther PPK.

Understanding hit me like a trolley at rush hour. I looked up from the inspector at the reactor. The spot where he had been standing there was a crack. More than a crack. A single pinpoint hole leaked the brightest light I'd ever seen. This was the light of redemption times ten, and the searing beam was inches away from my face. It was light so intense it ignited the very air it struck. Its diffused glow was bright enough to burn holes in my retinas.

Containment was broken. The bullet had passed through Smalley and gone straight into the core—the worst possible place for a lead bullet.

"Help me," I said, heaving Smalley forward.

He made his best effort. The man heaved, pushing against the harsh authority of gravity. With my help, he moved along the walkway, gritting against what must have been inconceivable pain. Red slick blood poured from his wounds, pulsing as we circled the crashing reactor. The wall where the beam of light had struck grew red hot. Metal and fiber walls flared under the energy discharge and the thin veneer peeled away like burning paper.

Smalley collapsed just outside the engine room. I heaved him to the side and pushed the door closed.

"Leave me," gasped Smalley. "I'm done and you know it."

"You're not done, cop." He was done. Nothing would get him the medical help he needed. Not even if the local medical station were fully functional could I stitch up what that bullet had done to his chest. "Anders is going to kill me if I don't bring you home."

The old detective coughed a laugh. "That fool could use a better role model."

"But all he has is you."

"The kid…" Smalley wheezed until his face turned blue. "The kid has a good head on his shoulders."

With that, Smalley fixed his stare up at the ceiling. I held him. Sometimes, there's nothing a medic can do but be with a person. Smalley had played his part. He'd done his best. At the end of the day, he earned everything he got, no matter what that was. Maybe he had made some bad choices along the way, but he went out on the right side. His eyes drifted shut.

I was surprised to hear him speak again. It was barely a whisper. "He'll have to go around."

"Around what?"

His eyes snapped open. He stared me right in the face. "Huff will need to go around."

Around. I remembered the long arc of the ship. To get to Smalley's craft, Huff could go straight back the way we came. Unless—

"Hit." Smalley took several rattling breaths. "Recycler."

My heart pounded. Huff hadn't just shot the core. That alone would destroy the ship. He'd already fired the Colt five times, and one of those had breached the recycler fluid containment. There might be whole sections of the ship that were now impassable. He needed to go the long way around if he wanted to be safe.

Which meant I could still catch him.

The wall near the engine room door burst, searing light melting everything within reach. Despite myself, I staggered back from where Smalley lay.

"Go," he said, his voice suddenly strong again. "There's another way."

There wasn't. I remembered the ship's diagram. I had studied it for years. The only possible way to catch Huff was to follow him along the long outer arc or through the center where the recycler fluid will have dissolved the very walls. "What other way?"

He gripped me on the arm, his strength fading as he pulled me closer. "Down," he said. "Through the cryopods."

I ran.

Chapter 50

THE SHIP BURNED. The ship dissolved.

Down, Smalley had said. It didn't take long to find the bulkhead that wasn't on the map. It was an addition to the long viewing arc. The air smelled of acid and fear. The walls were slick with the dissolving death of the cracked-open recyclers unleashed on the fibersteel structure of the ship. As I moved through the halls, I recognized the rooms nearing where I had fought the goon. Frozen corpses lined the tunnel. Most hadn't dissolved much, but a fresh body sat in one corner. It was the second goon. The lower half of his head was missing in a great blister of ooze. The recycling fluid was dissolving him, starting with the exposed flesh of his wound.

Gravity intensified. It was heavier than the Heavies, and my legs ached from just walking. My bad knee threatened to buckle under the pressure, but I strode forward and searched for the exit. When I found it, I discovered that the recycling fluid had corroded the locking mechanism. I kicked the door open and descended into the lower bay.

Lights activated as I entered. It was a utilitarian space, not decorated for luxury like the other sections of the ship. This added section—no doubt welded into place shortly after the ship's creation—had the stripped-down functionality of a cargo vessel. It hadn't been on the diagrams I'd studied. A dozen cryopods lined the walls, each emitting an eerie glow.

The ship shuddered under my feet, and I grasped a handrail to keep from toppling.

"Detach complete," droned an empty voice above.

"Detach?" I asked the ship. My heart pounded. Was that my last chance at escape? "What detach?"

A screen next to the door flared to life as I approached. It was filled with the technical details of the bank of cryopods. These same devices were used for long-distance space travel. They could keep humans in a state of enhanced hibernation for years. Sometimes decades.

Decades. The implication hammered in my chest.

A diagram of the ship appeared on the screen, depicting the vessel detachment. Based on the map, it was the *Lost Saint*. There was no way to know if Fortner had made it back to the ship or if Huff had taken it, but that wasn't my most urgent problem. The only ship that now remained connected to the *Benevolent* was Smalley's police cruiser. They could detach at any moment, and they were sure to go once they knew that Smalley was dead.

They might not even wait that long.

I walked through the pod bay. The first few cryopods were empty. My footsteps thundered against the fibersteel floor. Cracking the core hadn't yet decreased energy production. It must have ruined the core's ability to regulate. Above, the ship shook as the engines reached their overload capacity. The basic mitigation strategies of this model of ship involved venting extra power production into the thrusters. If it bled off enough, it could shut down the core. That wasn't going to happen, but the automated systems tried anyway. The alternative was an earlier death. It even channeled power into everything it could, and the lights above intensified.

The recycler breach meant that whole sections of the ship could no longer consume power. The remaining power did as power does. It corrupted. Overwhelmed. Destroyed.

"Of course, you've figured out who's in one of these, haven't you?" came a voice behind me.

Without turning to face him, I said, "I figured you'd be on the long arc back to the ship, Huff."

"Ruined," Huff said. The screen controls near him beeped as he cycled through the menus. "This place is falling apart faster than you might think. And the *Lost Saint*? Well, she's not a subtle ship."

"Subtlety's overrated." I turned to face him. He still held that massive gun, but in the increased gravity his muscles shook trying to keep it raised at my chest. "You might as well put that away. We both know there are no more bullets."

He opened his hand. As if pulled by a string, the heavy gun dropped, slamming into the floor with a solid clang. "It wasn't supposed to go down the way it did, you know." Huff pressed a button, and the first two pod doors hissed open. "She was supposed to cancel the maintenance override before anyone could get killed."

"Who?"

"I think you know."

"I like to hear you talk."

"Is this what you wanted? The truth, at long last? Your mother back from the dead?" He pushed another button, and two more pods opened.

The one on my left had a body. Dead. Its sunken eyes sat in a desiccated skull. Not my mother.

"Carrie screwed the whole thing up, but it was your father

who really caused the problem. He waited so long before acting, how was she supposed to cancel the commands?"

A pulse of acceleration shook the ship. Huff dropped to one knee, and I barely stood on my two feet. He reached up to the controls and two more pods opened. Empty. He hauled himself back to his feet.

I said, "My father found the tails you'd set to follow him and shot them both. That's why they failed to signal Carrie Fortner." I stepped back. He couldn't get past me, so I didn't have any reason to move closer to him. "You were having an affair with her."

"She was always mine. Not Kaegan's. If she'd just been willing to give up her cushy life with him, we could have been happy."

"A cushy life that you built for him. Ironic, isn't it?"

"The best fates always are." He punched the screen, and two more pods opened.

Both were occupied. The one on my left was a member of the crew in full gear. He'd run for the pods after the ship depressurized. It hadn't saved him. The cryopod might have kept him alive for a while, but it must have lost functionality long ago.

The pod to my left held my mother.

And the readout indicated that she was still alive.

Huff stepped forward. "You could save her."

Impossible. I took my mother's hands in my own. They were ice cold but soft. She was much smaller than I had remembered. We Demarcos were a large lot, but my mother in particular had always dominated every space she entered. She was tall and large and beautiful. Now, after over a decade in enhanced hibernation, she'd burned through all of her fat and most of her muscle.

Those muscles twitched, and she flinched away from my touch. It must have burned on her too-cold skin.

Huff was within reach. "Let me pass, Demarco."

The passage was narrow, but not so narrow that he couldn't walk by if I let him. I shot a glance at him and knew that I was going to let him go. This was my mother on her deathbed. To abandon her now would be—

"She's too far gone," I said.

"She's your mother." Another labored step. His movements were sluggish, like a puppet with tangled strings.

The ship roared around us. The door we'd entered from showed a glisten of sweat as the corrosive recycling fluid ate through its bulk. Not long now before that or the core breach punctured the outer hull.

"Go," I said. "Just go."

He pounded past me, each step tearing a whimper from deep in his chest.

I checked the readout on the cryopod to verify what I knew to be true. She was dying. Left alone, she was near the very end. Her organs were a slow train wreck. Her nervous system was irreparably damaged. Despite the twitch of her wrists, I took her hands in my own and drew them close.

Fluid pumped from the cryopod into my mother's veins, and a pulse of power hummed under her body. It was engaging the wakeup protocol, but to my mother, waking meant death.

My mother was never the easiest to get along with. She was severe in sharp and stubborn ways. She liked her children to behave in a certain way, and impropriety grated on her like a statue bracing against a cold wind.

But she was my mother, and mothers, no matter how cold, can melt the stoniest heart.

"I'm sorry, Mom," I whispered, holding her close. "I screwed up so bad."

All the days since the wreck of the *Benevolent* crashed over me. Gambling our fortune, failing to protect my sister, ending drunk and destroyed in the alleys of the worst neighborhoods. It wasn't the failure on the day of the wreck that trampled me with accumulated guilt. It was everything I had done every day since.

Every. Single. Day.

The ship rumbled, its acceleration increasing. My knees finally gave out, slamming me to the ground. My mother let out a hiss. She couldn't survive this. Then again, neither could I. It was only a matter of time.

"I thought about you every day," I said. Hearing is the last thing to go, and I hung my hat on the last hope that she could hear my words. "Every time I stepped into a church, I thought of all those times you taught us to look up for the truth. Every time I listened to the words of someone wronged by life, I remembered that time you helped our landscaper reunite with the woman he loved. Every time I helped someone who needed it, I remembered what you—" I choked on my words, ragged as they were in my throat, each one a razor blade.

Tears seared my burned skin. The air was warm in the cryochamber. Above, the ceiling started to sweat, and the door where we had entered was tumbling forward in a mess. We'd be gone soon.

Only then did I realize that Huff hadn't made it up the slope. He was on his knees crawling in the crushing gravity. As I watched, his limbs gave in and he collapsed.

My mother's eyes opened. She focused on me with yellow, bloodshot eyes. It was like looking into the ruined orbs of a corpse, but when I shifted slightly, she managed to track my movements.

Her dry lips parted.

"I'm sorry," I repeated. "I'm so sorry."

I don't know what she saw in her last moments. She might have seen me. I'd like to think that if she ever truly saw me, it would have been in that moment. She never really knew me as a child, but who knows their own children? Certainly not those who love them. They see only what they want their children to become.

I certainly wasn't that.

She might have seen my father. After all, I was still wearing his battered fedora. Grown as I now was, I resembled my old man more than I cared to admit. Physically and emotionally, I'd somehow managed to become him. The path I'd taken was different, but the result was the same.

Close enough, anyway.

My mother drew a single long breath through her parted lips, pulling in the now-scorching, dry air. It smelled of the self-replicating acids of the recycling fluid.

I couldn't see through the tears, but I heard her final breath as it escaped her lips. She might have spoken my name, or maybe it was the last spasms of her death.

Then she was gone.

Time passed. It could have been seconds. It certainly wasn't more than minutes. My mother was dead. After years of sleep, she was finally gone, and I had touched the bodies of both of my parents. It was finally real.

The air whooshed around me, sucking back through the ship and somewhere emptying into the void. I didn't put my helmet on. It wasn't worth it. If death came for me, then let it come. The helmet would only prolong the inevitable.

But I wasn't ready to give in quite yet. Dumping all my rage, all my fury, into muscles given to me by a lifetime in the Heavies, I stood and took my first step. Then another. Then another.

Soon, I stood over Harley Huff. He looked up at me with panic in his bloodshot eyes. He mouthed the word, "Please," as I watched him suffer.

"My father once told me that we don't get to pick what's right or wrong," I said. "All we can do is our best to stay as close as we can to right."

Huff pushed himself forward. He moved by inches, and he'd never outrun the seething destruction behind us.

"He was never very good at that second part," I said. "Traded in illegal goods. Placated people more powerful and less savory than anybody ought to have been placating. It's common, of course. When people have power, it's easiest to just go along with it. Feed it."

I took a step past Huff, and he made a weak gurgle. The ship rumbled like it was about to fall apart.

"Maybe that's why I always hated people like you," I said. "People who had a chance at a happy life but chose to instead trample others on their way to the top. You were never the unfortunate assistant of a powerful man, Huff. You were the guy in charge. Can't you see that? You had everything, and all you needed to do was turn your gaze outward and start to lift others up."

A crash. Automated voices echoed through the ship, but it was impossible to discern any information from them. My gut told me it was announcing that the police ship was about to separate. It should have already left, but the twins must have been loyal to Smalley after all. They were giving him until the very last second to reach the ship.

"You have to help me," said Huff.

I looked down my nose at him. He was pathetic. A blob

of a man like the wasted remnants of loose phlegm. I detested him on every level. Nothing would have felt better than leaving him to burn in the chaos of his own making.

"You're right," I said finally. "I do."

Taking a handful of his collar, I dragged him up the ramp. He helped as best he could, but as the acceleration grew, he became more and more worthless. His weight dragged me down. It risked my life.

In the hall, the lights were a stuttering mess. The ship lurched sideways, and the ruins of the luxury lounge slammed against one wall. Red flashes intermingled the harsh white emergency lights. The air that had been rushing past my face intensified. Holes in the rear of the ship were increasing. Huff closed his helmet. I did not.

Gritting my teeth, I powered ahead. My legs burned as if from squatting a thousand pounds. My arms ached from hauling Huff. The ship was going somewhere fast. Burning hard toward a destination out in the great beyond. At this point, I didn't know how the cruiser could ever reunite with Nicodemia.

But that was a concern for another time. An imaginary time. A time that might not even happen, based on the terrible outlook.

Not once did I consider dropping Huff and running. It would have been the smart move. It would have destroyed me.

Because I wasn't my father.

The airlock slammed shut behind us and cycled quickly. We stumbled through, and one of the twins caught me.

"Smalley?" she asked.

"Gone," I breathed. "I'm sorry."

"Go!" she shouted to Jurgens. The ship wasn't large. A single room, with sections for limited privacy.

The cruiser detached from the *Benevolent* as I crashed into one of the open seats. The harness clicked into place around me. Huff probably found his own place. At that point, I didn't care whether he did or not. The intense gravity of acceleration disappeared, and all the blood rushed back into my skull.

I watched as the *Benevolent* sped into the distance. A plume blossomed from its side, and the lance of light made me think of the laser-light concerts I'd attended as a youth.

Then the *Benevolent* exploded. The core finally fully breached, and the energy split the whole thing into a supernova that lit up the whole screen.

Chapter 51

"A MAN like Tobin Smalley doesn't need one last good deed." Anders stood in front of a crowd of hundreds, mostly cops. "He's accumulated enough Karma over the years to last all of us until the next millennium."

It wasn't exactly a funeral. Funerals involve bodies and the big recycler. Funerals involved the Church. This was something else, and it was being held in an auditorium that the blue normally used for lectures on the proper ways to throttle criminals or the best way to cause fear without cracking a smile. Call it a wake or a celebration of life. It didn't matter. Smalley's niece was there, cute as can be in her pigtails and olive-green overalls. The rest of his family was in attendance too. Anders had done his part to keep them safe.

I wore my father's hat and a black trench coat made specifically for my larger frame. There was a kind of comfort back in the shadows. It felt like home, no matter where I was. I might not ever reconcile with Trinity, but not because my guilt stopped me. My choices were my own. I could deal with that.

But excommunication put me right where I wanted to be. Outside.

The view from outside gave me a perspective nobody else had. It let me pull apart persistent problems and tweak the system in ways that were impossible from the inside. It's what made me special, even if it sometimes made life difficult.

The celebration of Smalley's life was set to go for hours. There would be dinner served, but I'd already taken what I wanted to eat and I could do with a little less conversation. Anyway, there were some chores that needed attending. I slipped out the back through the shadows of an unkempt alley and made my way over to the Reform building.

"How did you get in here?" demanded Huff as I stepped into his tiny cell. His world had shrunk to half a dozen paces in each direction, and he was the master of it. Behind his bars were the trappings of a pleasant office done up in warm tones. His bed was soft. His walls were covered in locally crafted art.

"Haven't you heard? I'm now an independent contractor for the blue. Fully deputized."

His lips turned up in a sneer. "My access to the latest rumors is a little restricted in here."

"Sounds like paradise."

Huff ground his teeth. "How do you deal with all this gravity?"

"You get used to it." I scratched my chin. "Or your heart gives out."

Looking up at me, he said in a quiet voice, "I never wanted things to happen like this, you know."

"From our first steps to our last breaths, nothing ever goes according to our plans. That's the problem with life, isn't it? It isn't about the curve God throws us. It's about how we swing."

"My Karma's good," he said. "My intentions are good. I'll be out of here in no time. Once I'm out, you know I'll rebuild. I'm clever. Resourceful. I have connections—"

"You're not getting out, Huff." I had meant to break it to him earlier. In the weeks since our return from the *Benevolent*, we'd never had a chance to actually talk.

His expression grew hard.

"Nothing personal," I said. "It's the nature of restorative justice. As long as you intend to game the system, and as long as you plan on rebuilding your empire, you'll be prevented from returning to society." I looked around his little room. "Learn to appreciate what you have, Huff. It's not a bad life."

"It's hell," he spat.

"Purgatory is how I like to think of it. As long as you believe it's hell, though, hell is the only life you'll know."

His legs went weak and he flopped onto his fibersteel chair. "Then why are you here, Demarco? Coming to gloat?"

"Kaegan Fortner is dead."

Huff scowled. "I don't understand."

"Murdered in hibernation by the goons that I nearly killed. We received a data dump as the *Lost Saint* left the system on its way to Earth. If the guy survives, he'll have a little legal trouble when he gets where he's going."

Huff stared into the distance, as if he could see the ship flying away.

"I needed to ask you one last thing," I said.

He looked up at me. "Shoot."

"It was your plan to force my father to kill those people aboard the *Benevolent*. Your contingency plan to wreck the ship and kill everyone. Your plan to have Carrie Fortner help you in your most ambitious project to date. It was all you."

"What's your point?"

"How do you feel?"

"Is that your question, Demarco? Look, I appreciate the company, but—"

"Did you ever get over the guilt?"

He stared at me as if my words were a jumble of nothing.

"You killed her. You, the guy pulling the strings behind everything that happened that day. You got the woman you loved killed, and you've had to live with it all these years. All I want to know is how did you deal with the guilt?"

"She was supposed to—"

"It was you, Huff." I loomed over him. "You did it all."

"She—" he choked. His eyes went puffy, and snot started to flow. Finally, like a dam finally bursting, he dissolved in a torrent of tears.

Maybe one day he'd get out of there after all.

On my way out, I checked the registers. Harley Huff was marked as a manipulative, unrepentant prisoner. Trinity didn't trust anything he said, anything he did, or anything anyone else said about him. It would keep him there until something truly changed.

Maybe he had a chance, but it wasn't a good one, and it wouldn't happen anytime soon.

"I want a replacement for that stunstick," said Retch when I met him at Angel's Diner. He had a new butch haircut with shockingly violet tips.

"You knew better than to lend it to me," I said.

Angel rolled up to the table. "You made a promise, bro."

"I'm not sure that I did."

"It was implied." She slid a slice of peach pie in front of me. I wasn't hungry after the wake, but the pie was the kind of perfection that transcends hunger.

I put an arm around my sister and gave her a hug. We spent the rest of the afternoon reminiscing about our lost parents. I told her everything I knew—all that I remembered and all that I'd discovered about Huff and Fortner and their parts in the wreck.

"And you still let him live?" she asked when I was finished.

"It seemed like a good idea at the time."

"I will never understand you."

When the pie was gone, and I'd drunk a whole pot of bad coffee, I went around back and picked up Cain for a walk. We meandered upspiral, until it became apparent that the dog had healed enough that he could outwalk even me. The dog was as happy and dumb as always, and I spent an hour feeding him treats and training him. In the end, he mostly just paid attention to the treats, but that was close enough to respect for me.

I tied him up in front of the Cathedral of Saint Francis of Assisi and made my way inside. It was early before the Saturday evening Mass, and only a few parishioners mingled about the narthex. When I saw the confessionals, I drew up short. My breath caught in my chest, and the air felt ten degrees colder.

"I don't know if I believe in God," I said once inside.

Priest Cano spoke from the other side of the screen. "It's only natural to doubt."

"The Church has caused more problems than good," I said.

"Fair."

I pushed the barrier aside so I could look Cano in the eyes. "I can't possibly confess it all."

"Nobody expects that of you, Jude."

Burying my face in my hands, I drew a long breath. It felt like a thousand years of sin and suffering drawing deep into my chest. When I let a fraction of that pain out, it came in the form of ritual. "Forgive me, Priest, for I have sinned."

Also by Anthony W. Eichenlaub

Short Stories

Not Done Yet: Sci-fi Stories of Wisdom and Fury

All Things Found

The Man Who Walked in the Dark

Devil in the Gravity Lounge

Nicodemia Station Blues

Old Code Series

Grandfather Anonymous

Grandfather Ghost

Grandfather Guardian

Grandfather Zero

Grandfather Crypto

Cascade Crash

Colony of Edge

Of a Strange World Made

Upon Another Edge Broken

On a Forsaken Land Found

From a Barren Seed Grown

Above a Distant Sky Seen

Metal and Men

Justice in an Age of Metal and Men

Peace in an Age of Metal and Men

Honor in an Age of Metal and Men